'Bath has always spawned ch[ ]
This novel captures both marvellously'
William Bertram

'Impossible to put down – compelled to
discover what happens next'
Malcolm Austwick

'Fascinating insight into the history of Bath
interwoven with a great story'
Peter White, Resident Manager Lucknam Park Hotel

'A hugely enjoyable book, entertaining,
informative and poignant – I loved it'
Jane Shayegan

'A young man's struggle against the odds in
post-war Bath – a romping good read'
Alan Buxton

'A finely drawn narrative creating a constant
delightful tension between plot, place and
relationships'
Anna Jacka-Thomas

'A compelling and enjoyable story'
Kathryn Anthony

'A vivid and moving account of growing up in
war-torn Bath'
Sandie Whitcroft

'An absolutely
enthralling read'
James Beer

Go swift and far

A novel of Bath

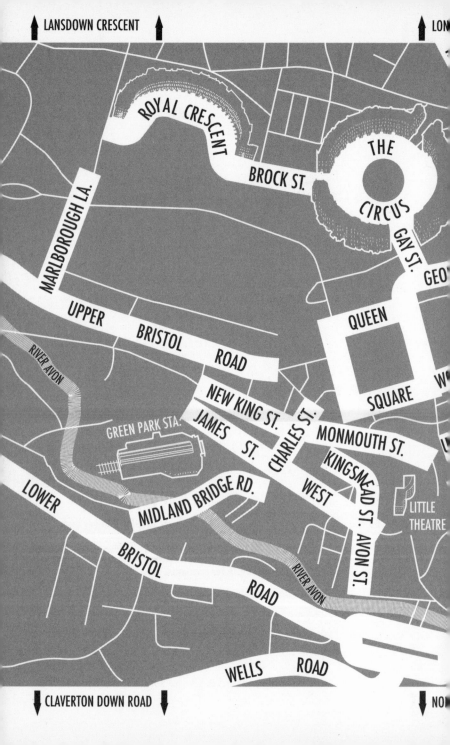

LANSDOWN CRESCENT

LON

ROYAL CRESCENT

BROCK ST.

THE CIRCUS

GAY ST.

GEO

MARLBOROUGH LA.

UPPER

BRISTOL

ROAD

QUEEN

SQUARE

W

RIVER AVON

NEW KING ST.

CHARLES ST.

MONMOUTH ST.

GREEN PARK STA.

JAMES

ST.

KINGSMEAD ST.

AVON ST.

L

LOWER

MIDLAND BRIDGE RD.

WEST

LITTLE THEATRE

BRISTOL

ROAD

RIVER AVON

WELLS

ROAD

CLAVERTON DOWN ROAD

NO

ACKNOWLEDGEMENTS

The author gratefully acknowledges the contribution, often very substantial, of Judith Cameron, Carol Easton, Alastair Giles of Agile Ideas, Steven Williams of Midas Publications, The Arvon Foundation, the Staff of the Bath Central Library, Colin Johnston of the Bath Record Office and the Editors of the Bath Chronicle. The support and stoicism of Liz and the encouragement of the 40 or so Bath citizens in the story,

Go swift and far

A *novel of Bath*

douglas westcott

VALLEY
SPRING
PRESS

Valley Spring Press
P O Box 2765, Bath, BA2 7XS
goswiftandfar@outlook.com

1st edition (hardback) published 7 November 2013
2nd edition (hardback) published 28 November 2013
3rd edition (paperback) published 11 April 2014

ISBN: 978-0-9926397-3-0

A CIP catalogue record for this book is available from the British Library.

Printed in the UK by CPI Group (UK) Croydon CR0 4YY

'For my late Mother and the wonder of one's own family.'

"Your children are not your children.

They are the sons and daughters of Life's longing for itself.

They come through you but not from you,

And though they are with you yet they belong not to you.

You may give them your love but not your thoughts.

For they have their own thoughts.

You may house their bodies but not their souls,

For their souls dwell in the house of tomorrow, which you cannot visit, not even in your dreams.

You may strive to be like them, but seek not to make them like you.

For life goes not backward nor tarries with yesterday.

You are the bows from which your children as living arrows are sent forth.

The archer sees the mark upon the path of the infinite, and He bends you with His might that His arrows may go swift and far.

Let your bending in the Archer's hand be for gladness;

For even as He loves the arrow that flies, so He loves also the bow that is stable."

"The Prophet" by Kahlil Gibrain

PROLOGUE

Ernst Richter sensed the other nine Luftwaffe planes bank and turn as he led them between the hills of the Limpley Stoke valley. Flying in formation two thousand metres above the meandering River Avon, the squadron of Junkers Ju 88s followed the silver ribbon sparkling in the moonlight, guiding them to the centre of Bath – Hitler's immediate retaliation to the Royal Air Force bombing Lubeck.

They were the first wave of a hundred and sixty German bombers from France, loaded with more than three quarters of a million kilograms of high explosives and incendiaries destined for the city in the next six hours. The note written below the two perforated aerial photographs of Bath, torn from Richter's target book, simply stated: 'Aim to the south of the largest crescent shape housing block.'

CHAPTER ONE

'Smashing film,' Fred said as he unhooked his white helmet and greatcoat from the stand in the hallway of the ground floor flat. Although exempt from conscription because of his reserved occupation as an engineer, Fred Miller still had to spend his nights as an Air Raid Warden.

'It was OK, I suppose,' Doreen replied. She put his usual thermos of Bovril and a sandwich wrapped in greaseproof paper on the side table before folding her arms across her ample bosom as she watched him get ready to leave.

Stagecoach, like all Westerns with the likes of John Wayne, offered little attraction for her, but the trailer for *Mrs Miniver* with Greer Garson and Walter Pidgeon, was much more her cup of tea.

Due at the air-raid shelter at 11 pm, Fred put the food and hot drink into his canvas bag and bent to kiss Doreen goodnight.

'Sleep tight, love.' After sixteen years of marriage, he still enjoyed the touch of her puckered lips and knew he was a lucky man.

As Fred stepped into the communal hallway of the house, his downstairs neighbour, Ruth Morris, arrived from the opposite direction, closing the street door behind her. Heavily pregnant, she stood with her legs apart and splayed outwards, but despite this duck-like pose she was still a beauty with dark brown eyes, a velvet olive complexion and thick black hair falling to her shoulders.

'Good evening, Mr Miller.' The Polish accent only added to her attractiveness as did the hesitant smile that showed small even teeth. She moved towards the stairway down to her basement flat and Fred had to turn sideways to let her pass.

'How are things, Mrs Morris?' He manoeuvred awkwardly around her. 'Not long now, I imagine.'

'Maybe one week, if the baby is on time.' She patted the floral print of her dress that protruded through the opening of her coat.

'All four of ours were, so chin up, not much longer,' he reassured. 'And don't forget that Mrs Miller is just upstairs if you need her.'

Fred shut the front door behind him and, stepping onto the pavement, adjusted his helmet strap. She needs a man to protect her, he thought as he strolled along the blacked-out New King Street towards Kingsmead Square. She rarely mentioned the husband, and Fred wondered if he'd been posted abroad. Even when around he was a sullen type drinking alone in the Griffin, and not much support for his pretty wife; not a real man, not like John Wayne. Fred's gait almost grew into a swagger as his mind went back to *Stagecoach*.

Colonel John Bradshaw checked his watch as he signed in at Apsley House; it was a few minutes before 11 pm. Best yet. The tour of the wardens' posts and back to Newbridge had taken only ninety-three minutes. He looked in the mirror. Not bad for fifty, he thought and instinctively flexed his stomach. He knew there wasn't an ounce of fat on his wiry six-foot frame. Fingering the perfect knot in his regimental tie, he turned smartly, stiffened his back and strode into his office. Still feeling like a professional soldier, he wished he had never retired from the regiment back in 1936. But the lure of the inheritance including the Georgian house at the top of Bathwick Hill had proved irresistible. A Bradshaw had lived there since the Battle of Waterloo, but he still wondered if it wouldn't prove to be his own downfall.

He picked up that morning's edition of the *Bath Weekly Chronicle and Herald* but, as usual, there was no real news. It was a city of 'old crocks' with many who had fled the London Blitz occupying the best hotel rooms, because Bath was of no strategic importance, only a place for rest and recreation. Apart from an influx of evacuees back at the very beginning, part of the programme that removed three and a half million children from vulnerable cities, the war had barely touched Bath. The first bomb to land near the city was in late 1940 – and it killed a rook. A month later, another two bombs from a straying German plane hit the football ground and killed a pony. Bathonians felt immune. They were unaffected by modern warfare, especially after the article in the *Chronicle* suggesting that it was protected from enemy bombing, because the valleys around it were too narrow for the German planes to navigate.

The red telephone with a direct line from the Regional Commissioner rang and roused Bradshaw from his musings.

That's strange, he thought as he picked the receiver up, there hadn't been a raid on Bristol in months. It was 10.58 pm.

'John, Red Raider Imminent Warning for Bath. No doubt it's Bristol, but better sound your sirens to be on the safe side.'

'Yes, sir.'

He pushed down the switch on the console. Instantly a wail arose. Then another starting fractionally later, and another and another, each one fainter than the last. It was as if echoes answered the call from every part of the city.

Action at last, he thought, but he didn't expect anything to come of it. Still, he tingled with the pleasure of having power. To instigate, to control, to command, even if it was only the push of a switch with just one finger for a fraction of a moment.

The black switchboard telephone rang.

'Marlborough Lane ARP on the line, sir,' the operator said.

'Put them through.'

There was a roaring sound with distant shouting and for a moment Bradshaw wasn't sure if the commotion he could hear was around Apsley House or if it was from the receiver. Whichever it was, he knew that the action he had sought for the last three years was upon him.

'Hello? Hello?' There was no answer, just a mangle of deafening noise and crackling before the line went dead.

It was 11.03 pm and it took a few seconds for Bradshaw to realise that he had lost his entire means of communication. He was unaware of the high explosive bomb that had landed in the Lower Bristol Road and detonated causing a twenty-foot deep crater. Amongst the shattered and twisted gas and water sewerage pipes lay the severed eleven communication cables linking Apsley House to every rescue service centre in Bath.

In less than ten seconds, another six bombs containing ten thousand pounds of high explosive fell in the three hundred yards between Kingsmead Square and New King Street. The first blew off the front of the oldest building in Bath, Abbey Church House. Soon after, the roof and floors of the nearby St Lloyd Church caved in, exhuming fourteen long-buried corpses.

The next bombs straddled Kingsmead Street, exploding

twenty yards apart; the local primary school folded like a pack of cards, and the seven houses on either side of the road instantly imploded, with the Holy Trinity Church collapsing into its crypt. One bomb ploughed into the centre of Kingsmead Square, twenty yards from the deep warden shelter, where Fred Miller was re-enacting John Wayne in *Stagecoach* for the benefit of his fellow Wardens. The roof collapsed, burying everyone.

The last bomb dropped directly in front of 37 New King Street; it crashed into the vaults under the pavement and exploded. The detonation wave from the blast expanded at a speed of over 20,000 feet per second, pulverising the bottom of the front wall. Unsupported, it tumbled into the crater in the street, setting fire to the severed gas main. The wave climbed vertically up the middle wall, slicing through each of the four floors as it went. In less than a second the blast overpressure in the house reached four tons per square inch, and the temperature had risen to 1,500 degrees Fahrenheit. Roof, walls and severed floors crashed down. The 200-year-old Georgian house had been reduced to sixty tons of rubble in less than three seconds.

Mrs Miller would never see *Mrs Miniver*, and her husband, trapped under a ton of Bath stone, would never see her or their four children again.

Ruth Morris was not instantly killed by the bomb. Her electric meter had clicked off a minute or so before it struck, and she was in the vault at the back of her basement flat, away from the destruction at the front, feeding it a shilling.

The wave of tightness, as the muscles around her swollen belly contracted, was unlike anything she had felt before.

CHAPTER TWO

'Here's the score sheet, Dr Abrahams.' David Medlock, the junior houseman, passed him the admissions book. 'When stumps were drawn the Germans were 248 without loss, the follow-on was slightly better at 106 for 1.'

Even now, some forty years after his arrival from Poland, Isaac Abrahams never ceased to be surprised by the manner and attitude of the English middle class. He wondered if it was worth a paper for *The Lancet*; 'Cricket – The public schoolboy's ability to cope with death and trauma.'

Isaac opened the heavy leather book with the list of every patient admitted to St Peter's hospital over the previous twenty-four hours. The afternoon and early evening had been unusually quiet for a Saturday – just a chap with a fractured wrist from a football match, and a couple of drunks who had collided with something in the blackout.

The first entry following the bombing raid was timed at 12.31 am on Sunday morning: Samuel Mendelssohn, a fifty-year-old hit in the face by flying glass. Despite a heavy dose of morphine, the man had screamed as they removed the last layer of field dressing, glued to the skin with blood. His face had become a swollen sponge, red and pitted with glass shards.

Isaac looked across at the prognosis column: 'One hundred and seven glass fragments removed, sent to opthalmics at 2.06

am'; and in a different hand and ink: 'Irreparable damage to both corneas. Sedated. Condition stable.'

After that, casualties had poured in from dressing stations. The pattern was much the same as he had read about in the London Blitz. First had come the glass wounds, then the burns, followed by the shrapnel. Finally, there were the crush victims with serious multiple fractures. The whole scenario repeated itself twice more as the bombers returned.

Some cases remained clear in his mind. There was the unconscious woman with the bandaged head where the skin and hair had simply come away with the dressing. Scalped by the blast, she had died within the hour. Then there were those from the shelter outside the Scala Cinema in Oldfield Park. Most had died when they were blasted into the two-foot gap between the outside wall of the shelter and its inner row of sandbags. Unable to breathe, their chests and lungs crushed, they suffocated.

Against the twenty-four wickets, as the houseman called them, the movement officer had printed in capitals in red ink 'DEAD – MORTUARY' and the time the bodies had arrived.

Rapid footsteps interrupted his reading and he looked up from the ledger to see the dispatch rider from Apsley House standing in front of him.

'Colonel Bradshaw has asked that I wait, sir,' the Civil Defence motorcyclist handed over a black pouch.

Isaac opened it and, pinned to a sheaf of flimsy pink sheets of paper, he found a hand written note.

Apsley House - Sunday 26th April – 17.30 hours

Isaac,
I have divided the bundles between those that include fatalities and serious injury and those that are less

urgent. The Ministry is pressing for information on estimated casualties. Just two figures needed from you for the time being: Serious (unlikely to survive), and Others.

Do you have any immediate requirements? Whitehall has promised assistance.

John

Isaac went back to the admissions ledger. He rummaged in his pocket for paper, found only a small yellow prescription pad and wrote:

Sunday 26th April – 18.00 hours

John,
Serious - 49
Others - 281
We have an acute bed shortage and cannot admit more patients. Transport and alternative accommodation is urgently needed for 100 non-critical injuries in case of a repeat attack.

Isaac

After the messenger had left, Isaac started to look through the first bundle of 'urgent' pink flimsies – copies of records that were sent to the Civil Defence by the rescue services digging out victims from collapsed or burnt out houses and shelters. They described the human misery that had resulted from the previous night's bombing.

One detailed the discovery of five bodies – a woman and four children – from a house in New King Street. A man's entire family had been wiped out in a provincial city like Bath while he was probably away fighting the Germans; so many London children had been removed from their parents and evacuated. As he went to put the bundle of papers down, he looked again at the address. New King Street, wasn't that the address of one of the ARP wardens brought in earlier with a suspected concussion? He hoped not and left the pile of pink slips next to the admissions ledger. Someone would have to make a comparison of the two records to see how many patients could be accounted for and let Bradshaw know, but for the moment there were other priorities.

The bombers left behind 19,000 damaged buildings and 411 dead bodies, which were later to be buried in Haycombe Cemetery. Many people were never found or accounted for, they simply disappeared, while other bodies, and parts of bodies, remained unidentified.

CHAPTER THREE

Under the rubble of what had been 37 New King Street, Ruth Morris was trapped in the vaulted basement. Her body was protected in a sarcophagus-shaped hollow formed by a massive beam that had settled just inches above her. For two days she lay on her back barely aware that she was still alive; she drifted in and out of consciousness as if waking from a deep slumber on each occasion until she gradually became mindful of her surroundings. She bent her head backwards as far as it would go, seeking the source of the light. It came from a small hole behind her, the same direction as the occasional draught of fresh air. Tilting her head forwards, she looked down. Her arms were held firm by heavy slabs of brickwork and her body appeared to stop at her protruding stomach, pinned down by bits of wood and stone. The child in her womb was dead, and this was how she would die. Why not? Why should she be different, the only one to survive?

Aged eight, back in Poland, she had stood alongside her mother and all the other Jews in the square in Lodz. The soldiers came at dawn. A rabble in dirty uniforms, carrying rifles with long bayonets, they had rounded up entire families from the outlying villages and marched them into the town. The officer on the platform was shouting. Mutti's hand clenched hers. She understood what was to happen, how it would end.

Grandfather was in a line of men standing next to the officer. He looked old and frail, wearing that shabby brown coat with the fur collar which Mutti hated so much.

Mutti pulled Ruth's head hard into her stomach, but she had squirmed and looked.

She saw a row of limp puppets hung on tight strings, no necks, just heads resting on their chests, her grandfather's legs kicking.

The contractions had stopped. The child within her was dead; another in a long line of deaths.

She felt no pain, shock had too tight a hold. Night came and went. Shock subsided and was replaced by resignation.

My whole family will have been destroyed, she thought, every single one of us, even my unborn child. Why always Jews? She had so wanted this baby, it would make everything better with Janeck, especially if it was a boy. She cried but no tears came.

On the dawn of the second day she discovered that she could move her right hand, and stretching out her fingers, she touched a smoothly rounded metal object. It was a spoon.

Looking into the huge hole that had been Kingsmead School and its adjoining cottage, Miller wondered what had become of Mrs Hunt. His children thought she was a wonderful teacher.

Bill Mitchell, the Home Guard posted at the end of the street to deter looters, came up to him.

'Fred, you look bloody awful. I thought you were still in hospital.'

'I discharged myself. Had to come. Doreen. The kids. You know… I wanted to see if I could find anything. A photograph, jewellery, something. Anything.'

Bill propped his rifle up against the remnants of the front

wall. 'Just terrible about your Missus and the youngsters.'

Fred nodded, unseeing.

'Couldn't believe it, we're all so sorry, mate.' Bill made to put his arm around his friend's shoulders, but Fred stepped back. He didn't want to be touched. 'Will you let me look?'

'Not meant to let anybody past, except bomb squad – possible unexploded outside number 42.' He hesitated. 'But here, take my torch, just be careful, the whole lot could come crashing down.'

He stopped in front of his home. Nothing. You could see right through into the back garden. A gap like a missing front tooth in the row of houses still standing on each side. The large 'Dig For Victory' hoarding, with smiling farm girls holding a wicker basket of fresh vegetables, hung untouched.

He climbed up and over the pile of fallen masonry and charred timbers, scanning the ground. Although he knew that all of their bodies had been recovered and that what he hoped for wasn't possible, he still prayed there had been some mistake and Doreen or one of the children would suddenly appear from the ruins. But there was nothing to show that his family had lived here, only a few pieces of broken crockery displaying a familiar blue pattern among the burnt out shell evidenced that this had been his home. Nothing to show for sixteen years of married life. No Doreen and no kids. Beautiful Sophie, their first, his favourite, and bright as a button, gone at thirteen. What would she have grown up into? Then sunny little Katy and the twins, Sam and Grace. All gone, everything and everyone he lived for. His legs crumpled and he sank onto the rubble.

Then he heard it. A faint regular metallic tapping sound coming from the brickwork below. He bent down, ear just above the ground, and listened. It was coming from a small hole by his feet. He switched the torch on and shone it into the small opening.

Jesus Christ, he thought, it's the Morris girl. How had they missed her? She was nodding her head; he could see the whites of her eyes and could barely believe it. After nearly three days!

'All right, I see you.' He clawed his way frantically back over the ruins of his home and shouted at the Home Guard. 'Bill! Get some help! My neighbour, the Morris girl –she's still alive!'

'You sure?'

'Of course I'm bloody sure. She's trapped. We need lifting gear and a doctor. She's nine months gone, you know, pregnant.' He scrambled back and put his mouth to the hole. 'It's OK, Mrs Morris, we'll get you out.' He listened for a response but could only hear the tapping of the spoon get faster.

He straightened up and studied the ground as Mitchell arrived. 'Help's on its way,' he said, but Fred was already trying to work out how they were going to free the woman.

'We can't get in from up here,' he said and pointed to the remains of a wall with the beam hanging down from it, 'if we try to move that, everything is bound to collapse down on top of her, so the only alternative is to burrow in from over there.' He indicated to the far side of the mound of rubble and clambered over. 'I'll pass the stuff to you, Bill.'

Where to start? If lying straight, her feet must be a good eight feet below him. He knelt down and gingerly pulled out some loose bits of brick and stone, and passing them to the Home Guard and others who soon arrived.

Slowly, very slowly he untangled the collapsed ruins of the house on top of the trapped young woman. He stopped every so often to listen for her, but often strained to discern a response.

After an hour Fred was standing up to his knees in a six-foot wide hole. He was determined to save Mrs Morris. One more survivor meant one less dead. Now there was room for Bill Mitchell to work alongside him and it went quicker. The hole was up to his waist, then his shoulders, all the time passing bits up from hand to hand along the chain of men.

The end of the large beam was exposed and he started to clear the rubble below it, very carefully, piece by piece. Fred's head was at least two feet below the top of the hole that was now a crater in the rubble, but there was still no sign of the woman. He began to worry in case he had chosen the wrong place to dig.

He lifted up a piece of broken floorboard, and the black pointed toe of a woman's shoe appeared. Gently he scraped away the muck until the top of the foot was visible. It did not react to his touch.

Having cleared the area around the foot until the whole leg was visible, it was obvious that Mrs Morris was lying on her back and, working sideways, it wasn't long before another motionless leg appeared. Although her lisle stockings were torn and very dirty, with the exception of some superficial grazes both limbs appeared undamaged. The timber beam lay diagonally six inches above her and it had stopped the woman from being crushed. Fred knew that if it was moved everything could come crashing down. Desperately he stretched out his arm, probing the area beneath the beam with his fingers, and a piece of white crumbled stone came away.

'I wondered where you went, we missed you,' said a voice behind him. He looked around to see that the doctor who had treated him at St Peter's had clambered down into the hole and joined him. With a stethoscope around his neck and wearing a pristine white coat, he looked incongruous in the dust and filth of the bomb site.

'Give me a minute, Doc. I've just got to clear a little more.'
But suddenly an avalanche of rubble cascaded into the hole.
Thick stone dust engulfed him, filling his eyes and mouth and
billowing upwards. The beam groaned, but did not move.

Abrahams opened his eyes. Both of the woman's legs had
disappeared under a blanket of stone dust, which reached up
to his knees.

'She's pretty far gone, about nine months.' Fred Miller was
still there but leant back to give the doctor some space. 'Baby
was due next week, I think.'

Carefully, they removed the dust and within a few
moments the doctor had checked for the dorsalis pedis pulse
on the top of her foot; it was fast, but that was only to be
expected. Slowly the legs were re-exposed and feeling up,
towards her torso, he found the woman's stomach. He cleared
the debris until the belly was in full view. Her back was arched
over a piece of rubble, blocking any sight of her head or chest.

'Please don't worry,' he spoke into the darkness. There was
no response. 'I am Doctor Isaac Abrahams and need to
examine you. Try to keep as calm as you can.' Again nothing.
With both hands on top of her stomach, he felt intuitively for
the baby's position and his spirits rose as his fingers found the
rapid pace of the unborn child's heart. But its head was fully
engaged. He started to feel further down, towards her pelvis
and as his fingers searched through the tangle of damp
clothing she stirred, and he felt the tightening of a contraction.
He looked over his shoulder at Miller.

'Do you know her name?'

'Mrs Morris, Ruth Morris, a Jewish girl from Poland.'

Abrahams turned back. Without thinking he spoke in
Yiddish into the rubble.

'Be still Ruth, just keep perfectly still.'

15

There was no reply, but the tension in her belly eased as the contraction softened. They were of the same tribe and spoke the same language.

'You're being very brave.' His hands felt the warm wetness. The waters had broken.

'It's all right Ruth,' his soothing voice continued, as his fingers found the cervix. Fully dilated.

He turned to both men. 'She's in the second stage of labour. I need a stretcher, blankets and water down here, now. We've got to get her out immediately. I can't deliver the baby while she's under this lot, and I have no idea what condition the rest of her is in.'

'But, Doc-'

'We have no choice.' There was no time for discussion. After being trapped for three days, the mother would obviously be in shock. If there was the slightest complication not only would the baby not survive the birth, but the mother could haemorrhage and bleed to death.

He spun back again to the prone body and this time reached for the femoral pulse in the mother's groin to check for any change in the tachycardia. There was none and when he brought his gaze back to the men, saw that only Miller remained. He was holding a stretcher with a green drinking canteen and a Civil Defence jacket on it. 'It's all they could find.' He shrugged his shoulders in apology.

They put the stretcher on the ground between them.

'Be brave, Ruth, we are going to get you out,' Abrahams told her, even though he did not believe it. 'Mr Miller is here with me and we will be as gentle as we can.'

'Take it really slowly,' Abrahams instructed the warden, 'move your hands up and under her body, as she comes out. Ready?'

The body violently pushed down, as they took hold of the

16

woman's thighs but gradually it came towards them. Six inches, a foot, then there was another contraction and Fred stopped pulling.

'Don't stop, damn you,' Abraham whispered angrily.

Her chest, streaked with soot and white dust was exposed and then her neck before, at last, her head.

Fred gasped as they lay her onto the stretcher. The woman's face was as white as chalk with cracked dry lips, her mouth full of stone dust.

No wonder she hadn't been able to speak. Abrahams reached for the canteen, and carefully poured the water on to her face, very gently prising the dust out of her mouth with his fingers. She groaned and muttered 'Thank God' in Yiddish.

Swiftly the doctor moved between her legs to deliver the child. The crown appeared.

'Push, good, again, push,' he paused. 'Well done, good girl, no more pushing now, just pant, nearly there.' Another groan, another contraction.

'Push, not too hard, don't force things. The top of baby's head.' She groaned again as the head and then the baby emerged, a bluish grey colour. Abrahams placed a hand under the little body, shielding the face with the other.

The baby was not breathing.

He reached into his case found the two clamps and surgical scissors, attached the clamps and cut the cord.

With one hand he picked the baby up by its feet so it hung upside down and slapped its bottom. Nothing happened. He did it again. There was a sharp intake of breath. The porcelain blue colour was rapidly replaced by a pink hue that spread through from the top of the child's head to its toes. Satisfied, he wrapped the baby in the jacket. The mother's eyes were closed and her breathing very shallow. He placed the baby in Fred's outstretched hands.

'To the hospital as quick as you can and two strong men down here, ready to lift her out.'

Now to try and save the mother. Would she have enough strength left to expel the placenta? He smiled when he heard the cheer from the men above him as Miller appeared with the baby. He looked down at the fine features, still smeared with dirt and dust and spoke, again in Yiddish.

'Young lady, congratulations. You have a healthy baby boy, but now we need to attend to you.'

She was barely conscious and he didn't know how much longer she could survive. He also knew the perineum must be badly torn from such a violent delivery.

He turned to the stretcher-bearers. 'Out now, quick as you can,' he ordered. He would try to deal with any hemorrhaging in the ambulance.

As he looked up at the men lifting the stretcher, the woman's right arm hung over the side; it was only then that he noticed the metal pudding spoon clasped in her hand.

Isaac finished his ward round and leafed through a copy of *The Bath Chronicle and Herald*. The baby's arrival and his mother's rescue were described in melodramatic terms with the front page headline:

PREGNANT WOMAN SURVIVES UNDER RUBBLE
FOR THREE DAYS
MIRACULOUS BIRTH OF SON

Doctor Isaac Abrahams delivered…

He knew the birth had been a very close call. The bleeding had stopped eventually and the child was finally put to the breast for the first time. As with most new mothers, Ruth Morris had winced as the child's mouth clamped around the nipple and the uterus contracted like a vice but the bonding between mother and son was intense. Her dark brown eyes never left those of her son.

The telephone rang.

'Isaac, how are you?' John Bradshaw asked. 'How's the Morris woman and her child doing?'

'Both well. Why do you ask?'

'I've had a message from the husband's regiment, they've given him compassionate leave. Should be with you within the next twenty-four hours. Also, I've had the mayor on the telephone. The story about her and the baby hit the national press this morning and has caused quite a stir. Human spirit triumphs in adversity, new life in the midst of death, great morale booster and all that. His Worship wondered if she was up to a VIP visit? It would involve the newsreel cameras.'

'That very much depends on Mrs Morris, doesn't it? How VIP, and when?'

'The highest in the land, in three days.'

CHAPTER FOUR

The regiment had arrived at the Liverpool barracks two days previously and were awaiting embarkation orders when Jancek Morris was summoned to the adjutant's office.

'Stand at ease, Sergeant,' the adjutant ordered from behind his desk. 'The Colonel had a call in the mess late last night from a Civil Defence chap called Colonel Bradshaw in Bath. Your home town, I believe?'

'Yes, sir.'

'Took a bit of a pasting three nights ago from German bombers. You're married aren't you?'

'Yes, sir.'

'Well, the good news is that you are now a father, and mother and son had a remarkable escape, and the Colonel has agreed we give you seventy-two hours compassionate leave before we sail. Take this to the Movements Office.' He held out the travel warrant.

Morris hesitated for a moment, but then took the note.

'Thank you. Is that all, sir?' The soldier's face remained expressionless.

'Yes, Sergeant. Dismissed.'

Morris came to attention, turned and left the office.

Cold fish, the adjutant thought, quite unusual for the Polish lot; it was as if Morris didn't want to go.

Jancek stood on the platform at Lime Street Station in Liverpool waiting for the London train. It was all so different from when he had stood here eleven years ago.

In 1929 he and his second cousin, Ruth, had fled Lodz to join family in New York.

His father had come to him the night before he left with the necessary papers. Whilst only sixteen, Jancek was big for his age. The papers were fixed to show eighteen so he could enter the United States with Ruth, who was only thirteen.

'Be strong, Jancek. Ruth is still a girl and has a weak chest; I have made a solemn promise to her mother that you will look after her.'

He had placed Jancek's hand on the *Torah*, and made him swear on his life not to leave his little cousin until he had handed her safely over to her uncle in New York.

The man from the Jewish Agency had collected them at dawn, going from house to house, gathering up others; there were twenty by the time they reached the railway station. Ruth had sat in the corner of the train compartment, clutching her brown cardboard suitcase. She had a persistent cough but said nothing. At every station, more fleeing Jews joined the train. By the time they boarded the steamer at Danzig, there were over fifty family groups. None had ever seen the sea before.

The winter crossing was rough. Locked in steerage below the water line, they retched and vomited as the old ship battled its way over the North Sea. Amid the exhausted, frightened and praying families, Jancek comforted Ruth as they sat in the stench for twenty-eight hours, until they landed at Hull on the east coast of England.

The Jews had been the first to board and last to leave the ship, kept out of sight, until all other passengers from the decks above had gone. Ruth was slow in getting herself together and up onto the bleak dockside.

'Good riddance, little Yid whore,' the Polish sailors had shouted at her, 'Poland doesn't want you, Jewish scum.' They were manhandled off the ship and into the grim warehouse, last used to welcome soldiers back from the Great War. Jancek guided his frail little cousin, her eyes glazed, to the row of wooden benches.

The immigration officer inspected the papers Jancek produced from the special pouch tied round his belly. It was perfunctory and no one questioned his age. The Jewish Agency people then arrived, accompanied by others from the Red Cross. Everyone was very kind. The strange sweet tea with milk in it. Jancek marvelled at the never-ending supply of hot water, soap and towels, as they showed them how to work the showers, sinks, and flushing toilets.

The Agency people then matched each refugee to their shipping line ticket from Liverpool to New York. They waited that first night and all of the following day in one vast dormitory until they finally joined the train to Liverpool at about midnight. The last to board, he and Ruth had been allocated the end compartment of the corridor-less train. Ruth's normally pale cheeks were highly flushed and her cough worse. Jancek watched her in the dim light of the unheated carriage as the train pulled out of Hull station; she seemed to be only half awake and having difficulty breathing.

An elderly round woman filled the seat opposite. She had a gentle smile but the worry in her voice frightened him.

'What's wrong with the girl?' she asked.

'I don't know, she was all right when we left.'

The woman stretched her hand forward and felt Ruth's forehead.

'She's very hot, too hot. It's a fever.'

At that moment, Ruth started shivering violently. The woman looked across at her son, who was sitting next to

Jancek. 'Stand up both of you, we need to lie her flat, and give me your coats, I need to cover her.'

There was little space in the crowded compartment, so the two boys stood awkwardly between the seats, manoeuvring their arms out of their jackets. The woman laid Ruth flat and covered her with the extra clothing.

'Here,' she said, handing a rag to Jancek, 'lower the window and hold this outside until it's ice cold, then place it on the girl's forehead. We have to get her fever down.'

Jancek lost count of how many times he held the rag outside the window and applied it to his cousin's forehead. As the hours passed the woman clucked with increasing worry. There were many stops and starts as the train crossed the country and Ruth was barely conscious when the train drew into Liverpool Station. It was just getting light.

People from the Jewish Agency were waiting on the platform with clipboards in their hands and went down the length of the train, opening the carriage doors and ushering everyone into the station with their luggage. The door of their compartment opened and when the man looked in, his eyes immediately focused on Ruth.

'Who's with her?' he asked in Yiddish.

Jancek raised his arm.

'You stay. The rest of you out as quickly as possible.' He ducked back out of the carriage and shouted something in English, which Jancek didn't understand, and then started checking the names of the people spilling out of the train with those on a list on his clipboard.

'*Mazel tov*, Jancek. Please God we will meet again in New York,' the kindly woman called out before leaving.

Jancek waited.

After a few minutes the Agency man ushered another man onto the train, who carried a small black bag. He waved Jancek to one side and drew down all the blinds so no one could see into the carriage.

The doctor put his hand on Ruth's forehead. Nodding, he opened the bag, took out a strange silver and black instrument, and plugged its two ends into his ears. He lifted Jancek's jacket off the girl, opened her coat and lifted up the blouse, so that he could place the other end on her chest.

'How long has she been like this?' he asked.

'Since we got on the train. She has got worse during the journey.'

Suddenly Ruth's head jerked forward, her mouth opened and she coughed up a stream of blood-speckled phlegm over the doctor's overcoat.

'You. Out now.' He gesticulated for Jancek to leave and started to unbutton his coat. Over the departing boy's shoulder, he addressed the Agency man who was still waiting on the platform in English. He sounded anxious and while he spoke, he removed his coat, rolled it up so the blood did not show, and handed it to the man. 'Make sure that you burn it.'

Jancek did not understand what the doctor was saying and stood bemused as he watched the stretcher arrive and Ruth lifted on to it and covered with a blanket. With the Agency man beside him, he followed her down the platform and would have continued until the man put his hand out to stop him. He looked down at the checklist on which he had been ticking off the other passengers.

'Morrishowl, and the girl's name is Lohrowski, right?' he asked.

'Yes, sir. Are they taking her to the ship?'

'No, she is very ill. They are taking her to hospital. She won't be going anywhere. You can kiss New York goodbye. Pick up your luggage and come with me. You need somewhere to sleep tonight while I sort this mess out.'

Jancek's memories were interrupted by the arrival of the London train. Not for the first time he wondered why he was bothering with such a *schlep* for such a short period of time. The buses had long stopped running by the time he arrived at Marylebone, so he walked to Paddington from where Great Western operated trains to Bath. Dawn was breaking as he crossed the station forecourt and asked about the next train to Bath.

'It'll have to be Bristol, mate,' came the reply, 'nothing in or out of Bath since the bombing.'

CHAPTER FIVE

They had closed the curtains and the ward had quietened for the night. Ruth was feeding the baby when Isaac Abrahams walked in. She smiled as he approached her bed. They spoke in Yiddish

'Great news for you, Ruth. Your husband is on his way and should be here tomorrow. He's been given compassionate leave.'

The smile faded.

'Is there something the matter?'

'My husband can be difficult and won't be happy away from his regiment.'

'Surely he'll be pleased about the baby? How long have you been married?' Sensing her anxiety, he drew a chair over and sat down beside the bed.

'Nineteen thirty-seven, when Jancek finally abandoned the idea of going to America, after I got out of the sanatorium.'

Isaac was surprised, it was the first time she had mentioned she had been ill.

'Which sanatorium was that?'

'First the Liverpool Isolation Hospital, then I was transferred to the Winsley Chest Hospital, and the charity bed maintained by the Bristol Synagogue.'

Isaac knew the large isolation hospital, about five miles south of Bath. He had referred a number of tubercular patients to it, although few had survived. It was solely for the treatment of tuberculosis with long open verandas overlooking the Limpley Stoke valley, onto which the patients were wheeled every day, summer and winter alike. The pure air of Limpley Stoke had a reputation of longevity stretching back two hundred years.

'You had tuberculosis?' he asked.

Ruth nodded.

Slowly Isaac coaxed the story out of her about her near death in Liverpool followed by the long, slow recovery at Winsley.

'Is that where you learned to speak English?'

'Yes. I had to if I wanted to eat; no one there spoke Polish, let alone Yiddish,' she laughed, 'but I still make very many mistakes. It feels good to talk to you in the old way.'

'Where did you go after they discharged you from Winsley?'

'Jancek had followed me down to Bath and was working as a night cleaner for Jolly's in Milsom Street. We lived in a small room in Westgate. I had nowhere else to go so I moved in with him. There was no furniture, just a table and two chairs, and I slept on a mattress on the floor while he slept on his coat on the bare floorboards. We were very poor, but we were so happy. Later when I got the job at the Regina Hotel Jancek suggested we get married, something about it being easier to emigrate as a couple.'

'And now, where do you work?'

'Same place. I started as a chambermaid at the hotel. Now I'm in charge of all the rooms – assistant housekeeper,' she said with pride. 'Many lords and ladies. It's very hard work and some of the residents, especially those who ran away from the London bombing, are awful and rude. But it's not far from home and my neighbour, Mrs Miller, has offered to look after the baby once I'm ready to go back. I am hoping to become housekeeper.' Her voice trailed off as the reality of the baby occurred to her.

She was a strikingly attractive woman but even at her young age, Isaac could see the pain and sadness endured over the years etched into the fine features of her face. He was reminded of what his own mother had suffered when escaping prejudice and violence a generation earlier. It was too soon to tell her that the Regina Hotel was flattened, and Mrs Miller dead. Hopefully the miraculous gift of a child would change things.

'I'm sure that your husband will be very proud of his son,' he said, 'once the war is over, you can build a good life for yourselves here.'

'Perhaps.' She didn't sound sure. The baby had fallen asleep and she took him from her breast and gently laid him in the cot beside her bed. 'Jancek is a good man but very ambitious. All the time I was ill and nearly died, he stayed with me although he burned to go to New York. While he says that he has given up the dream, I know this isn't true. A child makes it even more difficult.' She sighed and lay back onto the pillow.

'When he sees this perfect little boy,' Isaac smiled down into the crib at the contented child, 'I'm sure he will be a happy man.' He looked back to Ruth. 'But now, you must get some rest. I will come back in the morning.'

'Goodnight Dr Abrahams, and thank you for everything,' she replied before adding, 'but I think you should be the first to know something.'

'Know what?'

'I'm going to call him Yann, after my father, and I want you to do the *bris*.'

'Yann Morris. Yann Morris,' he smiled again, 'a good choice Ruth – it has a nice ring to it. I haven't carried out a circumcision since I was a junior doctor, but I would be proud to do it. Thank you, Ruth.'

Jancek asked himself why he had married Ruth. Yes, she was pretty and he was fond of her, but the question kept coming back over and over again, during the endless journey from his regiment to Bristol.

For years the sacred oath to his father, sworn on the *Torah*, had kept him close to Ruth, so that they could go on to New York after she had recovered. Then had come the rumours from the Jewish Agency about what was happening after the German invasion and the news that everyone, his father and both their families, all the Jews in Lodz, had gone, disappeared without a trace. Now what? he wondered. He still felt obligated but wanted to get out of England. Even after changing their name to Morris to sound English, everyone knew they were Jews, and only the lowliest jobs were open to them. There was more, so much more in America.

There had been the night of the terrible row, when she had told him that she refused to go; England had been good to them and she wanted to stay. They had argued for hours. In the end he had become angry, lost his temper and hit her so hard that he broke her nose. There was blood everywhere. He left her sobbing and went down to the Saracens Arms and got drunk.

The next day he walked into the army recruiting barracks on the Lower Bristol Road and signed up. It offered the chance of an escape and who knows, maybe a way to get on in life.

Now there was a baby.

The train drew into Bristol, but Jancek didn't get off. He just sat. In due course it started its journey back to London.

CHAPTER SIX

'Well, Mrs Morris, they tell me you have been a very brave young woman, buried for three days, and now you have a beautiful little boy.'

Ruth could not believe her eyes; Queen Elizabeth of England was standing by her bedside talking to her. Only in Great Britain could it happen that someone so important could be interested in talking to Ruth Morris, a nobody, a peasant from a tiny village in Poland that didn't even have a proper name. She couldn't understand why Jancek hadn't come to be part of this.

There was a bright light shining on her with the Pathé newsreel camera whirling and the photographer from *The Bath Chronicle* hovering.

'Yes, ma'am,' pronounced as ham, not farm, and she bowed her head as they had told her. She remained silent – don't speak until spoken to, they had warned.

There was a smell of spring roses about Her Majesty and for a moment Ruth thought it was because she was a queen, but then guessed it was her perfume. She was beautiful, very dignified, but natural; the black hat with a small rosette, the simple but perfectly fitted black coat with the grey lapels that matched the grey dress underneath, all set off with three rows of pearls and soft leather gloves. Just how someone royal should look.

'What was your work before this terrible raid?'

'I worked at the Regina Hotel, ma'am.'

'You must hurry up and get better so that you can go home. When will that be Doctor?' the Queen asked, turning to Dr Abrahams, who was flanked by John Bradshaw and the mayor of Bath.

'Very soon, ma'am. She has made a remarkable recovery, and the child is thriving.'

'Ah, yes, the little boy. What's his name?' the Queen asked, bending over the cot next to the bed.

'Yann, ma'am.' Ruth hoped that the question had been adddressed to her.

'He's very handsome, you and Mr Morris should be very proud. He's probably destined for great things, given the very unusual start to his life. Good luck to you both. Goodbye.'

'Goodbye, and thank you ma'am.'

The Queen moved away, paused for a moment and spoke quietly to the mayor and Dr Abrahams.

'What awaits her on the outside world?'

'Utterly destitute, her flat gone, and the Regina Hotel was totally destroyed ma'am, and,' the mayor paused for a moment, glanced at Abrahams, but then went on, 'her husband has just been posted overseas.'

'I should be obliged if you would ensure that she and the child are cared for.'

'Yes ma'am,' the mayor and Abrahams answered in unison.

The Queen moved on down the ward, followed by the entourage and the whirling camera. Dr Abrahams smiled and winked at Ruth, before following them.

Not for the first time, Ruth looked down at the cheap dented tin spoon, still lying on the bedside locker where Isaac had placed it the first morning.

CHAPTER SEVEN

Ruth emerged from the warmth and security of the hospital into the weak sunlight of a cold Friday morning. She shivered in her Salvation Army coat. She daren't even stop to think about Jancek or where he could be. She held Yann close.

What if Mrs Abrahams doesn't like me? The doctor opened the Riley's door and helped her into the car. The smell and feel of the old leather was comforting. Sensing her anxiety, Isaac tried to put Ruth at ease as he drove onto Bradford Road and headed west.

'Don't fret, *bubala*, it's going to work out.'

'Thank you, Doctor.'

'No, no Ruth, not Doctor. Now we are out of the hospital, please call me Isaac and my wife's name is Naomi.'

'Yes Doc- I mean, Isaac.' Ruth clutched her child.

This was not an area that Ruth knew, but as the car turned left they passed Rainbow Wood with its abundance of new green leaves, but to those whose families were conceived there, it was known as 'Pudding Club Wood'. She remembered the wonderful warm summer evening when she and Jancek had walked across town and through Widcombe before climbing up the hill to this beautiful spot.

The car turned into North Road. Halfway down the steep hill it slowed, turned through two large stone pillars on which 'Lundy House' was carved in faded lettering, and stopped.

Ruth peeked out at the grand-looking house with its beautiful proportions and large blue front door. A moment later it opened, and a slim, elegant, middle-aged woman with black hair walked down the front steps. Smiling, as Isaac helped Ruth and the baby out of the car, she approached with her arms outstretched to draw them to her.

'Welcome Ruth, and welcome little Yann. I am so pleased that you are here. Do come out of the cold and into the warm.'

Ruth's eyes filled with tears.

'Come, come, child. The time for weeping is over.' She held Ruth and Yann even tighter and Ruth knew everything was going to be all right. Naomi ushered her into the house.

'I want to show you to your room. I have found a lovely cot for Yann, and Isaac and I have tried to make it rather special with…'

Ruth gazed out of her bedroom window at the spectacular view of Bath and beyond to Bristol. It was a crystal clear day and the city centre lay peacefully bathed in sunlight hundreds of feet below her. It looked deceptively undamaged by the recent air raids with the abbey dominating the city, completely unscathed.

Nearby was the Empire Building, and perched on the hills opposite was the mirrored beauty of the Royal Crescent and Lansdown Crescent, all untouched by the bombs. Her eye was caught by the blackened shell of the rugby stand at the Recreation Ground, and the collapsed end of St John's Church. The mayhem of Kingsmead and New King Street were hidden.

Yann was asleep in the lovely little wooden cot after his feed. All apprehension gone, she wrapped her arms around herself and hugged her body.

'Yann, we are so, so very lucky. Thank you dear God for Isaac and Naomi, thank you.' She sank down onto the soft bed and glanced around the room.

Naomi had chatted on about how she had run up the blue and white curtains on her sewing machine, while Isaac had cut out and pasted the jolly nursery rhyme figures on the wall around the cot. She handed Ruth one of two pink clothing ration books, which had been left on the small dressing table. Not one of the dozen or so blue, orange, magenta or crimson pages of coupons had been cut out.

'I am afraid the little wardrobe is bare. I didn't dare buy you or Yann any clothes,' she said, 'but with our unused coupons and the clothing being sent into the city by the relief organisations, we should be able to sort you both out with the essentials in the next few days. Yesterday, I had a look around some of the shops in Milsom Street, and they have put aside a few things. We'll go down tomorrow morning, Isaac can drop us off on his way to the hospital. Now you just settle in, and come down to lunch when you're ready; it's not much but it will certainly be better than hospital food!'

Naomi kissed Ruth lightly on the cheek before leaving.

With the door ajar in case Yann woke, Ruth walked down the wrought-iron staircase with its grand sweep into the hall below. Gliding her fingers along the polished mahogany handrail, she felt like a film star on the newsreels making an important entrance into the popping flashbulbs. She smiled at her silliness but was almost giddy with apprehension and excitement. If only Jancek could see her now!

Isaac was waiting in the flag-stoned hallway and led her past a gilt-framed oil painting of an unsmiling gentleman in a morning suit with a stern-faced woman at his side. The sheen on the blue silk of her dress looked so real that Ruth wanted to reach up and touch its folds. It so suited the sheer elegance of the house.

'It's all so beautiful, all so beautiful,' she said wistfully.

'Yes, it is,' he glanced up at the painting before adding, 'but none of this belongs to us; Naomi and I are only the caretakers. We rent the house, with all of its wonderful contents, through an agent of the Lundy family. Although they live out at Rowas Grange, this is the family town house, and when we moved down from London at the outbreak of the war we needed somewhere to live. I can show you around, if you would like to see the rest of the house after lunch?'

'Yes, please. How old is it?' she asked as he led her into the dining room.

'It was built at the beginning of the nineteenth century, and apart from the addition of modern plumbing along with the installation of gas and then electricity, little has been altered. Like most houses in the city, it's built with the so-called Bath stone that is still quarried nearby. This place came as a dowry when Michael Symons, now Lundy, took a bride – that was him and his wife in the hallway. Hopefully she was kinder than she looks.

'But enough history, sit yourself down. Naomi and I need to talk to you about something. No, don't look so worried.'

Naomi had entered, pushing a wooden trolley of food, and took up the conversation.

'Isaac has told me everything Ruth, about Lodz, the tuberculosis in the Liverpool isolation hospital, then the Winsley Sanitorium, and we wondered,' she started to serve the food, 'are you going to bring Yann up in the Jewish faith?'

The question hung there for a moment, Ruth fearful of the effect her answer would have. Firstly, she couldn't remember ever having been driven in a car, and by an important doctor who had invited her to come and stay in his home. His wife was lovely and brought her into this beautiful house with a bedroom that, instead of being in a dark basement in New King Street, had marvelous views over the whole city. Then there was the history lesson that reminded her of how little education she had received, and now she had to answer a question that she was surprised to be asked. Bring Yann up as a Jew? How could she do otherwise? She had not stepped inside a synagogue since Liverpool, because Jancek was so violently against it, but she was a Jewess and Yann was a Jew.

Fortunately, Naomi decided to fill the silence before Ruth had got around to answering.

'Isaac was brought up as an Orthodox Jew, real *frumer*, but lapsed to Reform many years ago and I don't keep a kosher home. As his father used to say, "Goodbye O'Lord, now we've come to England!" Isaac doesn't work on Saturdays, unless it is an emergency, and we belong to the Synagogue in Bristol; there isn't one in Bath. What with the petrol rationing, Isaac's work and everything, we rarely attend except on Rosh Hashanah and Yom Kippur, and we do have some friends over for Passover. I still love to light the candles every Friday night and see the Sabbath in with the usual meal, as far as this is possible with wartime shortages.'

'Fine, it's more than fine,' Ruth replied hurriedly, 'it will be great to have some religion back in my life. There has been none since I left Poland.'

Isaac sat back and observed the two women with pleasure. His gut instinct had served him well. A shared name and illness, the only difference was that their Ruth, their daughter, had died. She had been born after he got back from the First World War, and if she had survived would have been twenty-six now, much the same as this Ruth.

At last Naomi had found the daughter she had long lost and yearned for. And they had become instant grandparents!

CHAPTER EIGHT

The brief history lesson that Isaac had given Ruth upon her arrival at Lundy House became the first of many, and neither he nor Naomi ever made her feel conscious of her ignorance and lack of schooling. On the contrary, they encouraged Ruth not to hold back but to question everything she did not understand. No subject was taboo, and her self-confidence grew rapidly. On her first Friday at Marsh House Ruth helped Naomi prepare the Sabbath meal. She felt relaxed enough to ask about the couple's background.

Sephardic Jews of Portuguese origin, Naomi's family had settled in England during the seventeenth century. Despite adhering strictly to the religious teachings of the *Torah*, they had become assimilated into the British way of life and her father had followed his father into a successful medical practice in Harley Street. He was also a leading member of the substantial Jewish community in Hampstead, north London.

Isaac, on the other hand, was like Ruth, an Ashkenazi from Eastern Europe.

'He was a young child when his family arrived from Warsaw to escape the pogroms and they lived in a single room in London's East End.' Naomi kneaded the bread dough for the traditional *challah*. 'Like many others from his background, Isaac's father was poorly paid as a jobbing tailor for a smart Saville Row business. As a result, Isaac grew up with one ambition and that was to lift his parents out of poverty. Realising from an early age that a Jew's life is always precarious, he sought financial security. According to Isaac, nowhere is safe and no matter how many years Jews settle anywhere, as sure as night follows day, anti-Semitism bubbles below the surface. Even now he believes he must be ready to flee at a moment's notice, leaving everything behind.'

Hearing about Isaac's childhood made Ruth think about her and Jancek's own flight from Poland; almost half of a century later and nothing had changed for Jews.

'Isaac's mother suffered a stroke two years after they arrived in England,' Naomi continued, 'too poor to go into hospital, she lay for months in bed, paralysed, unable to speak. Isaac watched the centre of his world suffer, night after night after he returned from school. She died two weeks before his *bar mitzvah*. It was then that he decided to become a doctor. He realised at a very young age that knowledge and skill travel, away from the East End slums, even out of England if needs must as a Jew.

'Nothing else mattered; he was driven and clever. Scholarship followed scholarship. The Jewish Board of Deputies was there for him every step of the way; medical books, equipment, fees, as he sailed through the exams and eventually got a distinction for his finals. My father was one of those deputies, forever on the look out for a nice Jewish boy, and that's how we met.

'Until that evening, my father had brought me up to believe that nothing less than a Rothschild or Montefiore husband would be good enough. Then I came home one Friday to find this very earnest young man sitting at our dinner table, wearing the most ill-fitting suit I had ever seen.' Naomi laughed before explaining that she discovered later that Isaac lived with three other impoverished student doctors and they

38

had clubbed together to buy a communal suit. They averaged out their various heights and sizes with the inevitable result that the suit didn't fit any one of them!

'But that first time we met,' Naomi bent down and put the loaf in the oven, 'it was really boring because all Papa and Isaac did was argue about Theodor Herzl.'

'Theodor who?' Ruth asked.

'Theodor Herzl. He had written a book about a permanent home for Jews in Palestine. Isaac even had it with him. Palestine, Palestine, nothing but Palestine the whole evening. In the end Papa just smiled, and mumbled something about the idealism of youth.' Naomi smiled too as she walked across to the larder. 'Well you can imagine the rest – though we still argue about Palestine. I guess Papa had in mind that Isaac would come into practice with him, but it wasn't to be, because Isaac wanted to be a surgeon.' She handed Ruth a forlorn-looking cabbage. 'See what you can do with that,' she said, before putting a pan of water on the stove to boil.

'After we married we moved to Golders Green in north London and Isaac's father came with us – he was a lovely man. Isaac finally joined the surgical team at St Thomas's Hospital. At first Papa tried to help, but most surgeons were virulently anti-Semitic. Everything changed with the outbreak of the Great War in 1914, but that's another story.' Naomi reached back into the larder for a small blue package. 'My mother, God rest her soul, would turn in her grave if she could see what rationing and food shortages have reduced me to,' she said as she opened the Symington soup packet and crumbled one of the rock-hard chicken cubes into the boiling water.

They stood in the stillness of the dining room, as dusk fell on that first Friday. Yann was asleep in Ruth's arms.

Naomi lit the two candles in the silver candlesticks and

raised the fine lace shawl up from her shoulders to cover her head, bringing its two edges together over her eyes. She recited the Hebrew blessing quietly and dropped the shawl. Isaac, wearing a black skullcap, lifted the prayer book and started to sing the Kiddish welcoming in the Sabbath.

Finished, he raised the silver cup of wine and blessed it, and the two women intoned 'Amen'. He took a sip, passed it to Naomi, who drank and passed it to Ruth, who did the same. Ruth dipped her little finger into the deep red liquid, and then placed it on Yann's lips. It had been a very long time since Ruth had enjoyed such an evening, but it was a part of who she was.

'Welcome to your first Shabbos under our roof, *bubala*.' Isaac cut three pieces off the end of the *challah* and recited another Hebrew blessing. Again the two women said 'Amen' and each ate a small piece.

Isaac kissed Naomi.

'Good Shabbos, darling.'

'Good Shabbos, Isaac,' Naomi replied. They turned to Ruth, and in unison said 'Good Shabbos, Ruth.' Instinctively Ruth kissed each of them on the cheek.

'Good Shabbos, Naomi. Good Shabbos, Isaac. Thank you for everything.'

Isaac raised the silver cup of wine and looked at the sleeping baby. 'To Yann, the first of many Friday nights and the future.'

'Yann – and the future,' the women repeated, lifting their own glasses.

Ruth thought of Jancek and how good it would have been for him to also be here. Thinking back, she remembered the last family Friday night in the village outside Lodz.

'My last proper Shabbos,' she paused, trying to hold back her emotions, 'the last time was the night before we left. It wasn't grand,' she looked at the lace tablecloth, covered with

40

its solid silver cutlery and cut-crystal glasses, 'but it was beautiful and I loved them all so very much.' She swallowed hard but the tears fell. 'I'm so sorry, I'm ruining this wonderful evening.'

Naomi rose from her chair and came round the table and embraced the grieving young woman.

'Hush *kinder*. It's all right, we understand. Isaac and I can never replace your real family, but we are your *meshpokha* now, and we will make it better for you, I promise.'

Naomi stepped back, looked into Ruth's eyes and said softly, 'As the *Torah* says, Ruth, our house is your house, our home is your home.'

Ruth came to look forward to Friday evenings with her 'new' family and sometimes, after Naomi had gone to bed, she would sit and talk with Isaac late into the night. He would tell her stories that taught her so much about so many things. How little she knew, but she loved listening, absorbing everything, and always eager for more.

'Who was Theodor Herzl?' Ruth asked on one such night.

'Why do you ask?' Isaac appeared surprised by the question.

'It was just something Naomi said when she was telling me about the first time you met.'

Isaac laughed, stood up and went over to the nearby shelves from which he removed a book and walked back to her. 'Good old Theodor. The one thing Naomi and I have never agreed about.' He chuckled as he handed it to her.

Ruth looked down at the slim and battered book in its faded blue cloth cover: *The Jewish State* by T Herzl. She opened it and looked at the faded handwritten Yiddish: *'To my son, Isaac, a Doctor. Next year in Jerusalem?'*

'It was a gift from my father, one of his most treasured possessions,' Isaac said quietly, 'because of him I've always known that the only place us Jews will be safe is in our own country. If ever there is an Israel, I will go and live there.'

Ruth was in the garden enjoying the June sunshine and rocking Yann gently to sleep in his pram, when the letter arrived. Naomi had brought it out and handed it to her without a word before sitting down on a nearby garden chair. Although neither Naomi nor Isaac ever said very much about Jancek, it was more by what they hadn't said that Ruth knew they didn't think very highly of him. Isaac had not forgiven him for not visiting her at the hospital, and had made the odd remark afterwards, which she had chosen to ignore.

For a moment, Ruth peered down at her husband's childlike handwriting on the envelope. She wondered what had prompted him to write and felt oddly numb as she opened the envelope, and extracted the flimsy single sheet of white paper that had been stamped with the black circular endorsement of the Regimental Censor.

Ruth,

Can't tell you where I am, but it's a long way from Bath, and it's very hot. Tomorrow we move out, and so don't know when I'll next be able to write. I am sorry I could not make it to the hospital, but the trains weren't running because of the bombing. Look forward to meeting our son. Did you name him after your father, as you always said you would?

Jancek.

Warmth flooded through her and she smiled as she folded it and put it into her skirt pocket.

'You really love him, don't you, Ruth?' asked Naomi.

'It was a love that grew,' Ruth replied, 'he looked after me when I was very ill even though I stopped him going to America, which is all he wanted. Until he joined the army, he was always there for me.'

The letter from Jancek made everything so much better for Ruth. That awful night when he had hit her. Instinctively, her hand went to the scar under her nose, where his wedding ring had caused so much blood. She began to feel strong again, and recognised her need for some independence from Naomi and Isaac. She, not them, was responsible for Yann's welfare. She must find a job, some way of making sure that Yann had the opportunities she and Jancek would never have. Delighted that her husband still wanted to remain a part of her life, she had to find somewhere for him to return to after this awful war was over.

CHAPTER NINE

Isaac sat at the back of the inquest, listening to the Coroner's summing up. John Bradshaw came and sat next to him.

'Members of the jury,' Malcolm Austwick started, 'you have heard Dr Abrahams's post mortem report on Mr Frederick Miller, death by strangulation. I have explained to you what you have to consider, and the possible verdicts you may return. Mr Foreman, you may now retire.' The foreman quietly spoke to each jury member in turn and then stood up.

'We've reached our verdict, sir. His death was suicide.'

'Are you all agreed?'

'Yes, sir.'

'Have you got a moment Isaac?' John Bradshaw asked as they were leaving. After a mild autumn, the winter of 1942 had arrived in early December with a vengeance, and both men stopped before stepping out of the guildhall to button up their overcoats, pull on their gloves and adjust their hats.

'I'm already late, but we can talk as we walk. My car is just round the corner.'

Isaac sighed, still thinking about Fred Miller hanging himself over the loss of his entire family nine months earlier in the house off Kingsmead Square, where Ruth had miraculously survived.

'Dreadful business and the second suicide in a week,' Bradshaw said, 'what I'm seeing in the Bath Courts doesn't bear thinking about. And how is your young bomb victim coping?'

'Mother and baby thriving,' Isaac smiled as he thought of them both, 'Naomi and she have become very close, like the mother Ruth left in Poland, and the daughter we lost. Ruth wants to get back to work and although I can't see what the hurry is, I'm on my way to see if I can't arrange something suitable for her.'

'I wondered if you could be free next Thursday evening?'

'I'll check with Naomi, but I think so. Why?'

'I've been asked to invite you to a very special dinner. But it's men only and ten of us in all. Black tie, seven-thirty for eight at the County Club behind Queens Square.'

'It sounds rather mysterious.'

'Can't say any more, but I promise you an interesting evening.'

'As long as it is nothing to do with Freemasonry, you know how I feel about our Lodge friends, John.' They had reached the Riley and Isaac bent down to unlock it.

Bradshaw smiled, his breath crystalising as it escaped his lips. 'Don't worry, there'll be no secret handshakes or rolled up trouser legs on this occasion.'

Isaac drove out of the city along the London Road. After a few miles, he started to climb the long hill towards Box Village and halfway there turned into a little lane on the left that clambered on upwards until it reached Cassofiori House.

A nameplate topped two magnificent wrought iron gates, informing visitors that they had arrived at the Cassofiori Jewish Blind Home. He parked the car and crunched down the gravel drive to the double doors of the main entrance. It would be a good opportunity to see Sebastian after his meeting with Matron.

Cassofiori House was originally the country home of Sir Samuel Cassofiori, the founder of the prestigious London city bank in Leadenhall Street that bore his name. The Cassofiori

Bank specialised in discreetly serving the very wealthy and it was rumoured that a permanent deposit of at least £100,000 was a prerequisite for any potential client.

Sir Samuel had been blessed with three sons, and after Eton and Oxford, two had followed their father into the bank. By 1914, the eldest was heir apparent in the London office, and the middle brother was at the Paris branch. At the outbreak of the war, both had immediately volunteered and were commissioned into the Coldstream Guards.

Within months the eldest was slain after Antwerp fell, at the first Battle of Ypres, one of eighty thousand casualties in the British Expeditionary Force. The second died at the second Battle of Ypres, when chlorine gas, used for the first time by the Germans, felled 5,000 men in ten minutes. The life expectancy of an officer was just six weeks.

The youngest, Sebastian, barely seventeen and still at Eton, was all for quitting school and joining up as so many of his friends were doing. He had moved from 'second spare' to heir. Grief-stricken and desperate, his mother and father persuaded him otherwise. Reluctantly he stayed on, but instead of going up to Oxford in September 1915, he joined his father at the bank.

Everything changed a year later, when it became clear that conscription would be introduced in 1917 because of the massive slaughter on the Western Front. Even his father had to accept it was better to volunteer and choose your regiment while you still could, so in October 1916 at the age of nineteen, Sebastian was commissioned into his dead brothers' regiment.

Eleven months later Ypres reaped its harvest yet again. The Maschinengewehr 08, the new heavy machine gun, spat out forty-eight rounds every second, and scythed through Sebastian's platoon of thirty-five men in no man's land.

The stretcher bearers found him, blind and unable to move after thirty-six hours ensnared in the barbed wire.

'A hair's breadth from death,' was how the young medical officer from the Advanced Dressing Station described him. It was their first meeting and it took all of young Isaac Abrahams's skill, and much courage, to get him off the wire and back to safety. Most of the 310,000 other casualties from Passchendale were not so fortunate.

Completely broken in spirit, his ambition for a banking dynasty shattered, Sir Samuel sold the bank and retired to his country home outside Bath. There, he and his wife dedicated the rest of their lives to looking after their sole remaining son, and supporting charities for paraplegic and blind ex-servicemen. Lady Cassofiori died in 1936 and Samuel followed her to the grave within two years.

Under the terms of Sir Samuel's will, Cassofiori House, with its hundreds of acres, was bequeathed to a new foundation attached to the Blind Society and endowed with the bulk of his immense fortune. A single condition was attached to the bequest. The house was to become a home for the Jewish blind, in which Sebastian was to be cared for until his death.

Isaac pressed the large brass bell, and looked out at the magnificent view along the valley; a patchwork of wintry fields stretched as far as the eye could see towards the Quantocks and he thought about the home's sixty or so residents who would never be able to enjoy the visual beauty before him. The door was opened by the smartly uniformed matron, Amanda McKendrick.

'Dr Abrahams, how nice to see you, do come in. What brings you here this morning? It's not your usual day.'

It had been a long day by the time he arrived home and Isaac felt tired and ready to relax.

He put his key into the lock, opened the front door and, stepping into the hall, was immediately aware that something was wrong. There was no Naomi to greet him, take his coat and offer the customary embrace, a small but important ritual that he treasured.

The hall was in semi-darkness with the only light being that which filtered down the stairs from the first floor landing. Isaac slipped off his coat, hung it in the cupboard and switched on the light. As he turned, Naomi was descending the staircase towards him. She came into his arms; she had been crying.

'This arrived an hour ago,' she drew back and handed him an envelope, 'will it ever stop?'

Addressed to Mrs Morris in spidery writing, it was light brown and had been roughly torn open. Isaac extracted the flimsy matching brown telegram from inside onto which two strips of paper ribbon had been crudely glued.

THE WAR OFFICE REGRETS TO INFORM YOU THAT YOUR HUSBAND SGT. JANCEK MORRIS HAS BEEN REPORTED MISSING IN ACTION.

Although his meeting at Cassofiori House had been successful, Isaac decided not to tell Ruth for a few days, as he climbed the stairs to her bedroom.

CHAPTER TEN

Resplendent in full dress army uniform with polished medals displayed, Colonel John Bradshaw greeted Isaac as he stepped into the County Club.

'Welcome to the William Pitt Club annual dinner.'

'The what?'

'You will soon understand. The in-crowd that decides what's best for Bath. Come and meet our President and your fellow diners.' Isaac was guided towards a knot of people gathered around the splendid marble fireplace enjoying the warmth of the large fire in the club's Georgian drawing room.

'Earl Lundy, may I introduce you to this evening's guest, Dr Isaac Abrahams?' The elderly and grey haired peer already looked distinguished leaning heavily on his walking stick with its carved ivory handle, but straightened his back noticeably as he held out his hand.

'Glad to meet you, Abrahams. I've heard good things about you. Damned fine show you did up at St Peter's after the bombing. If only we had more like you.' He cleared his throat before adding, 'Well done.'

'Thank you, sir.' Isaac was pleasantly surprised by the compliment, without a hint of patronisation, and happily shook the proffered hand. Nonetheless, knowing the strength of anti-Semitic feeling among the British aristocracy, he couldn't help but wonder why his lordship was offering his hand so readily to a Jew.

Earl Lundy turned to one of the people with whom he had previously been in conversation. 'The Honourable Malcolm Austwick,' he said, 'Malcolm, this is Dr Isaac Abrahams.'

Isaac recognised the coroner and senior partner of Austwick & Company – fourth generation of Bath's most influential firm of solicitors, who acted for many of the old Bath moneyed families with their countless trusts and settlements. Through his work at the hospital, Isaac knew that Austwick advised the Bath City Council and sat on numerous government committees. It was rumoured that he was to be the next Lord Lieutenant of the county.

'Isaac and I have met before, but on more formal occasions.' As Austwick extended his hand, Isaac noticed the diamond set into the corner of the worn gold crested link securing the cuff of the dress shirt. This indiscreet gem emphasised the man's rather dapper appearance, and such flamboyance surprised him. Tall and slim, Austwick looked remarkably fit for someone in his late forties. His lightly oiled hair and pencil moustache reminded Isaac of Clark Gable. A decent man though, Isaac thought, and an excellent coroner.

'Nice to see you again, Mr Austwick.'

A waiter arrived holding a silver platter and Isaac took a flute of champagne as Bradshaw clasped his forearm and expertly guided him around the room.

'I think you know our superintendent of police, Commander Jack Jenkins, and Ken Kohut – our local industrialist.' Isaac knew the latter, a short balding man in his sixties. In his role as Councillor Kohut, he had twice been mayor of Bath and was the power and money behind the Bath Conservative Party, being the owner of the naval munitions factory on the Lower Bristol Road.

Next was Sir Peter Knee, a substantial shareholder in numerous regional newspapers, including *The Bath Chronicle and Herald*, whose society page constantly pictured his lovely younger wife, Lady Julie, and her royal progress around the city and its good causes. Through Knee Publications Sir Peter enjoyed a monopoly, and had an iron grip on the distribution of every newspaper and magazine supplied through the newsagents in the city and the surrounding countryside.

'I do hope you're going to join our centenary celebrations next year for the *News of the World*, Abrahams.' This hugely popular Sunday national with its weekly print run of over four million copies had one of, if not the largest circulation in the world. Isaac remembered the unanswered invitation, lying in his in-tray at the hospital, and smiled. As with most of the popular press, the *News of the World* had been very supportive of Mosley and his pro-Nazi Black Shirts before the looming war made such support untenable.

Of the last three guests, Isaac knew two in their capacity as trustees of the hospital. Peter Groves of Groves & Company, Bath's most prestigious firm of accountants, and Christopher Johnson, the general manager of the city's leading bank, the Bank of Bath. Still only in his mid-thirties, Christopher Johnson oversaw the bank's hundred or so branches that were spread across the southwest of England.

Bradshaw then introduced him to the third man.

'And last, but not least, David Lloyd.' Isaac recognised the name and knew he was the tough, no-nonsense proprietor of the Bath Building & Development Company. As he shook hands with the young man, Isaac wondered why he hadn't been called up to serve King and country. He decided that Lloyd must be involved in something important, just owning a business was not a reserved occupation.

The gong sounded, and the headwaiter announced that

dinner was served. Bradshaw turned to them both. 'David, Isaac is next to you, so why don't you take him in and make him feel at home.'

Isaac leant back in his chair and glanced round the table. It had been a fabulous dinner and a reminder that even during a war with shortages and rationing for the majority, there were always those who found a way around such difficulties.

From the moment Bradshaw had begun to make his introductions Isaac had realised that he was in the company of probably the most powerful group of men in Bath. They were the core of the Tory elite which had enabled the Conservative Party to control the city's political scene for so many years. Strange, only the clergy was missing, he thought. He was the only Jew present.

Seated between David Lloyd and Christopher Johnson, he had been quizzed about the planned improvement of St Peter's Hospital that had been postponed at the outbreak of war. Isaac was surprised by Lloyd's interest in the detail of this proposed modernisation where surgical capacity was to be tripled.

John Bradshaw tapped his spoon on his glass, and the chatter around the table ceased.

He rose from his chair and lifted his glass.

'The King.'

There was a shuffle of chairs as everyone stood for the toast.

'Gentlemen, you may now smoke.'

With a flurry of activity the club's servants cleared the plates and the port and brandy decanters were placed at opposite ends of the table. A pompous butler circulated with a large brown humidor of Havana cigars, cutting the end of each one selected and proffering a lighted match. He then shepherded his underlings through the double doors, closing them quietly behind him.

Beneath the sparkling chandeliers in the Georgian dining room, with the blue cigar smoke rising between the crystals, Isaac sensed an atmosphere of supreme confidence, control and quiet self-satisfaction. It was an air of complacency. These were the real rulers of rural England, where a quiet nod or word, not a council vote, decided what would or would not happen in town and city. He wondered why he had been invited to this powerhouse. Then the room stilled and John Bradshaw rose again.

'Well, gentlemen, now to business. First of all, it gives me great pleasure to welcome our guest, and hopefully after tonight, our newest member, Dr Isaac Abrahams. Since 1777, with the surgeon John Symons, some seventy years after the club's foundation, it has been our practice to have Bath's top medical man as a member, and the sad death of its last incumbent has created this vacancy. We are all aware of Isaac's outstanding service to the city through St. Peter's Hospital, but I would also like to mention something about Isaac that I only recently discovered.' Bradshaw paused and looked directly at Isaac. 'Forgive me, Isaac, but we always check before inviting someone to join, and your modesty will be safe with us.' His gaze returned to his audience.

'At the outbreak of the Great War, Isaac left St Thomas's Hospital in London and volunteered for the Royal Army Medical Corps. As battalion medical officer over the following four years, he was attached to the Coldstream Guards, serving in the Advance Dressing Stations, which as many of you know, were more often than not in the front line trenches. Now we come to the important bit, which I only discovered from his personnel file sent to me a few weeks ago by a friend in the War Office. Exactly twenty-five years ago, to this very day, on December 17th 1917, Dr Isaac Abrahams was awarded the Military Cross.'

Isaac was unnerved by Bradshaw's discovery; he had never discussed his personal horrors of the Great War and was shocked that Bradshaw had been able to obtain his military record. To his embarrassment, the entire gathering started to applaud by banging their free hands gently on the table. The room stilled again as Bradshaw continued, reading from a small slip of paper, which he had taken from his waistcoat pocket.

'I would like to quote the posting in the *Gazette* at that time. It reads as follows: "For conspicuous courage and devotion to duty in leading his stretcher bearers repeatedly into no-mans land. He displayed great gallantry and disregard of danger under the heavy shellfire, collecting and evacuating the wounded. He worked continuously for thirty-six hours, and because of his energy and determination in clearing of the battlefield, many wounded were rescued, and lives saved". A footnote from Isaac's medical records was attached to the file,' and again Bradshaw was reading from the piece of paper, '"subsequently, whilst Dr Abrahams operated on a gravely wounded officer, the Emergency Field Hospital became contaminated by gas. Unable to continue, because the eye pieces of his gas mask became fogged up, and aware of the consequences, he deliberately removed his gas mask in order to continue, and saved the life of Second Lieutenant Cassofiori". Dr Abrahams was himself blinded by the gas and remained sightless for five days. Mercifully his eyesight returned, and he survived to be with us tonight. Welcome, Isaac.'

More, even heavier hand banging. Bradshaw moved on.

'Now, gentlemen, to the main event. As always, Earl Lundy has agreed to brief us about the progress of the war. For this task he is in a unique position, being a member of the House of Lords Liaison Committee with the War Cabinet. I would remind you that, apart from the usual security considerations, the Chatham House Rules apply.'

Earl Lundy rose from his seat.

'Gentlemen, what a difference from our last dinner a year ago. God willing, I believe we will look back on 1942 as the turning point of the war.' He continued to speak with insight and without notes for twenty minutes about the previous twelve months' progress or otherwise of allied troops in Europe, North Africa and the Far East. He then brought his discourse to an end.

'I had a drink with the Prime Minister two nights ago, and asked him how he would describe 1942. As always, he summed it up succinctly, and I leave you with his words.' Earl Lundy took out a sheet of paper from his jacket pocket. 'Retreats have turned into advances; there will be setbacks, but this is the turning point; we will win this war.'

At the end of the evening David Lloyd walked with Isaac to the door. 'I look forward to working with you on the St Peter's modernisation.'

Isaac was puzzled. 'We don't even know if it will happen. First we have to win the war, and then it should go out to tender, and then someone will win that.'

'We will, it will and I will.' He reached his hand out to shake Isaac's. 'Have a safe journey home.'

As he drove back, Isaac pondered how many other deals had been schemed and struck with a handshake that night around the William Pitt Club dinner table.

Naomi was asleep when he got home and it wasn't until the following evening that he was able to tell her all about the William Pitt Club, while Ruth was upstairs putting Yann to bed.

'It's wrong,' he concluded, 'that a handful of men behind closed doors in a cigar smoked room decide what happens in this city. It makes a mockery of democracy – whatever happened to the people's voice?'

'Don't be so naïve, Isaac. Do you think it's different in any other provincial city? The Merchant Venturers have run Bristol since the slave trade. For goodness sake, it's been that way since time began; normally people like us are never invited to join the club, you should be flattered. Dragging up your old military records shows they want you.'

Laughing, she added, 'Goodness me, in 1777 Georgian Bath had barely got off the ground and yet the club dates back even further. It's no secret that the city was all carved up between a few notables of the time. I wager Ralph Allen, John Wood and Beau Nash were members, and agreed everything over the port.' She was obviously warming to her subject because she carried on as if she were Ralph Allen, in a haughty, upper-crust English accent. 'I say, Beau, you need to drum up a damned sight more visitors. Bath stone production is up twenty per cent this quarter and John is just itching to build more houses, his Palladian style is catching on in a big way. What about a couple of really big projects, say a dance hall and a meeting room? We'll need impressive sounding names, if we are to raise the cost by public subscription. How about the Water Room, no, better still the Pump Room – linked to the spa water, and the Assembly Hall, no again, Rooms.'

Isaac laughed. Although it saddened him to think that nothing had changed in two centuries, Naomi was probably right. After all, someone must have thought up the names of the city's most famous landmarks.

'But seriously, Isaac,' Naomi reached across the dining table to clasp his hand, 'it would make no difference to them if you don't accept the invitation because they will simply find someone else. And at least if you're on the inside, you'll know what's going on and might, just might, have some influence and achieve some good.'

Isaac sighed and nodded. For the sake of his beloved hospital, he would accept their invitation and join the William Pitt Club.

CHAPTER ELEVEN

It wasn't until after Easter 1943 that Isaac took Ruth to the interview. She had been hesitant about the job offer from Cassofiori because of the daily journey to and from Bath. However, Matron Amanda McKendrick's offer to provide a bed- sitting room for Ruth and Yann during the week overcame the problem. It was also agreed that Isaac would drive her to the home each Monday morning and collect her on the following Friday afternoon so that they could continue to enjoy weekends together as a family.

Matron McKendrick spoke in a very business-like manner and addressed Ruth's refusal to be parted from Yann. Smiling with reassurance, she pointed out that Cassofiori House had numerous 'want-to-be-grandparents' who would make excellent baby-sitters while Ruth went about her work.

'But aren't all the residents blind?' Ruth was surprised by the suggestion.

'But they are not deaf,' the matron's voice softened, 'and as you will quickly learn when you start working here, our residents have developed their other senses in an extraordinary way to compensate.' She then reverted to her usual formal tone. 'Well that's settled. You will address me as Matron and I look forward to seeing you and meeting your son next Monday morning at eight-thirty.'

'Yes, Matron,' Ruth had replied and before she knew it, she

and Isaac were out of the building and walking along the drive to the car.

'I do hope Matron McKendrick is happy with me Isaac, I don't want to let you and Naomi down.'

'I have no doubts, Ruth,' Isaac said, putting his arm protectively around her shoulder, 'you are a remarkable young woman and I feel sure that you will be an asset to the residents of Cassofiori.'

On the following Monday evening, Ruth smiled at the sleeping Yann and thankfully sank into the little armchair beside his cot. She thought back over the previous hours, with its constant activity and countless introductions. Was it only that morning that Isaac had dropped them off at the Home, with a reassuring hug?

Amanda McKendrick had wasted no time and immediately taken them up to this pretty little bed-sitting room on the second floor.

'Asking around the village, we managed to find a couple of cots for Yann,' she pointed to a carved wooden crib placed in the corner, 'we put one up here and the other downstairs so everyone can keep an eye on him while you work but you can still pop in to check from time to time. I'm afraid I've had no experience of young children, but you will see that I have created a little play area next to the cot downstairs.' She turned as if to leave but then looked back and smiled at Yann who rested his head on Ruth's shoulder and was clutching a small teddy bear.

'Bring Yann down to my office when you are ready. We'll get the lad settled. I must say, he seems very content. I can then introduce you to the housekeeper who will show you around and explain your duties.'

Once Matron had left, Ruth sat Yann gently on the pale green candlewick bedspread and reached for the purple gingham pinafore and starched white apron lying beside it. She decided to leave unpacking, but get changed into her uniform and quickly find out what was expected of her.

Yann sat silently, his big brown eyes following her every move. When ready, she hugged him to her.

'I love you, my beautiful boy,' she whispered, 'and I promise that you will never be someone else's servant, even in a grand place like this. I have no choice, but you, my son, with your father's help, and an education, can look forward to so much more.'

Ruth liked the slim dark haired housekeeper from the moment they met. Sandie Whitcroft greeted her with a huge smile and with such a broad Scottish accent that Ruth had difficulty in understanding her.

'Nice to meet you, lass, I've heard a great deal about you, even read about you and Yann in the *Chronicle*. I'm sure we'll get on just fine.' She bent down to Yann, who was grasping one of his mother's fingers, and tickled his chin, which made him giggle.

They sat down at a table in the staff sitting room, Yann on Ruth's lap, and although plenty was going on around them, before long he was asleep and she was able to put him in the downstairs cot. Sandie then proceeded to show her around the home. Ruth had been aware of the house's elegance during her initial interview. Now on walking around with Sandie, she was struck by the building's opulence, its sumptuous curtains, deep pile carpets and the numerous oil paintings that adorned most walls. Isaac and Naomi's home was modest by comparison.

As if reading her mind, Sandie explained. 'All the paintings and antique furniture were in the house, and came with the bequest from Sir Samuel; it is a condition of his will that nothing can be changed without his son Sebastian's consent. His father gave a great deal of thought as to how he wanted the house to look after he died. Nothing was left to chance. His will contained plans showing how the conversion to a blind home could be achieved with the minimum disruption for his son, and where every piece of furniture and each painting should be placed.'

Ruth gasped as they entered an enormous glazed orangery with delicate white wrought iron tracery and sweeping views across the verdant wooded valley below. The glass doors were open and a number of residents sat around the tables, involved in murmured conversations and basket making.

'As far as possible, the building has been kept exactly as it was when the family was alive,' Sandie continued and opened the door into a drawing room. Ruth saw a man sitting by the empty fireplace beside a table with a large glass sculpture resting on it. He was broad shouldered and wearing a tweed jacket with his back to them, but as they entered the room he turned around.

'Hello Sandie, who have you got with you? I don't recognise the step.' As he looked towards them, Ruth saw he lifted both of his hands from a portfolio resting on his lap. It took a moment for her to register that he had been reading, his fingers tracing a beige page of Braille.

'Good morning, Sebastian. I'd like to introduce you to our newest member of staff, Ruth Morris. She only started this morning, and you're not to be too rough with her.'

Ruth felt Sandie's hand clasp her arm and propel her further into the room. So this was the man Isaac had spoken about last night and their first encounter earlier in the First World War. Isaac had tried to prepare her. He was probably in his late forties, with thick brown hair above a large rather pitted face and prominent lower jaw. But it was the top of his face that drew her attention because she couldn't stop staring at its disfigurement. There was a great red angry weal crossing from temple to temple, through both closed eyes – as if he had been scalped. She dragged her eyes away from the scarred deformity to the perfection of the glass object catching the sunlight beside him; pale green with gold inlay, it was magnificent, a large animal with heavy front haunches, perhaps a bull or bison.

'Hello, Ruth Morris.' He paused at her silence and stretched out both of his hands. 'Oh don't let my stupid scar put you off because inside I have a heart of gold. Come closer so I can take a look at you.'

Gently, Sandie nudged Ruth forwards and downward, so that she was bowing over the wheelchair. She kept her eyes on the sculpted animal and concentrated on the beauty of how a shaft of sunlight cut through the mottled green glass to the gold within. Expertly, the extended hands lightly followed the features of her face, barely touching her skin with each of the fingers working separately.

Sebastian laughed. 'Goodness me, Sandie, she's almost as beautiful as you, and not a wrinkle. Ruth, welcome to Cassofiori House. Tell me, how old are you?' he said as his hand slid down her left arm to her hand. 'Damn,' he exclaimed, fingering the wedding ring, 'you are married!'

'Get away with you Sebastian. Be careful of this one, Ruth, he's a dreadful flirt,' Sandie snapped, laughing, 'see, you've turned her speechless, you shocker.'

Completely taken aback, it was all Ruth could do to mutter, 'I am very pleased to meet you, Sebastian,' before Sandie guided her out of the room and back to the staff sitting room.

'Let's pop in and see that young Yann is all right. That will give us a chance to have a quick cuppa, a ciggie and a wee chat. Then I'll take you upstairs to the bedrooms.'

Yann was lightly snoring in his cot, as the two women settled into the armchairs with their cups of tea.

'Help yourself, lass.' Sandie had lit a cigarette with a little chrome plated lighter, which she had taken out of her uniform pocket with a packet of Woodbine and laid them on the small table between the armchairs. 'There's few enough comforts for us women to enjoy in these times. It's my only vice.'

Jancek didn't like women smoking and so it had never occurred to Ruth to try although Naomi did so occasionally and the Abrahams always kept cigarettes in a silver case in the drinks cabinet. She hesitated for a moment, but then thought, why not? She could do with something to help her relax if she was going to get along in this enormous house full of people who can't see where they are going. Reaching for the untipped cigarette she held it to her lips between her index and forefinger as Sandie had done and looked down at the lighter. She suddenly realised that she didn't know how it worked but Sandie came to her rescue, picked it up, flicked it and held the flame to her. Ruth sucked in hard, inhaled and tried to control a reactive coughing fit but Sandie didn't seem to notice.

'Don't worry about Sebastian. I suppose I should have prepared you for his appearance,' Sandie puffed nonchalantly on her cigarette, unaware of Ruth's struggle to breathe. 'It's just that after a while one doesn't even notice the injuries or that they are sightless.'

She went on to explain that there were sixty-three residents, most of whom were elderly, although they had started to get some younger cases as a result of the war and more were expected. Ruth felt nauseous and decided not to inhale the smoke into her lungs but to hold the acrid tasting vapour in her mouth before exhaling it. She tried to concentrate as

Sandie explained how blind people usually developed their other senses far beyond the sighted. Touch, smell, memory and hearing were all enhanced. Had Ruth noticed how Sebastian instantly noticed her different step, but equally recognised that it was Sandie who had walked into the room with her? Another thing she needed to remember was that Sebastian, along with many of the residents, had learned to use other peoples' eyes, coupled with their silences and changes in tone of voice – hence his scar's impact.

Ruth was still feeling rather queasy by the time Sandie stubbed out her cigarette into the metal ashtray and proceeded to pick a piece of stray tobacco from her tongue.

'Wait till you meet old Mrs Mankovitz on the first floor,' she smiled, 'she can tell, just by the way I say good morning to her whether or not it is turning out to be so for me!'

At this point Ruth decided that it was all right to stub out her cigarette. Unaware of how she had been affected by her first smoke, Sandie had come to the conclusion that Ruth was worried by what other personal information a blind person could divine.

'Oh, don't look so worried,' she said, 'we've got some wonderful people here – one lovely man, Samuel Mendelssohn, was terribly injured from the Bath bombing, when wee Yann was born. Completely lost his sight and no spring chicken either. He's so cheerful, it's a lesson for the likes of us. It will all become like second nature after the first week or so.'

Over the next few hours, Ruth gradually became more familiar with the different areas of the home as well as the lessened effect of a second cigarette that Sandie insisted she enjoy at 'elevenses'. Just before lunchtime, Sandie took her into one of the two kitchens which led off either side of the dining room. They were mirror images of each other, superbly equipped with identical modern ovens, refrigerators, cooking utensils, sinks, plates, cutlery and drying up cloths.

'The home is strictly kosher; milk and meat and ne'er the twain shall meet! Red-rimmed crockery for meat dishes, blue for milk. Some of the residents are very orthodox, and you will see that the red crockery has slightly raised edges and the matching cutlery is embossed.' The aim was for all of the senior staff in the Home to be Jewish and thereby familiar with kosher rules, but the kitchen help and cleaners were gentiles, and mostly came from the nearby villages of Ashley and Box. Sandie explained that the *goyim* soon got the hang of it.

Breakfast was at eight-thirty with the main hot meal, lunch, at one, and high tea at six. One of Ruth's jobs would be to check that all was ready before she sounded the gong for meals. Sandie took her back to the dining room where she lifted the large felt hammer from its resting place, and gently hit the huge brass instrument that resonated with an ever-increasing crescendo of sound

Like ants, Ruth thought, residents immediately started to appear through various doors that led into the dining room. She was struck by the absence of white sticks, and the confidence with which, unaided, many felt their way to their seats at the ten or so round tables. About half a dozen, including Sebastian, expertly guided their wheelchairs to the table located in the large bow window. A moment later, a bevy of ladies bustled into the room, carrying steaming plates of meat and vegetables.

'Here you are, Mrs Mankovitz, all as usual, chicken at three o'clock, potatoes at six o'clock and carrots at nine o'clock,' one young girl said, as she placed a meal in front of an elderly grey haired lady who had her hands folded neatly on her lap.

'Thank you, Maureen.' The old woman raised one arm above the edge of the table and ran a bent and twisted finger gently checking the rim of the red plate and the embossed cutlery before lifting her other arm and starting to eat. Ruth smiled.

Isaac looked across the candlelit Sabbath table, caught Naomi's eye for a moment and winked; Naomi smiled back. As always seemed to happen on these Friday nights, Ruth was earnestly recounting the happenings at Cassofiori House over the previous week. No detail was spared, from Mrs Mankovitz's arthritis to Mr Mendelssohn's problems with his sightless eyes. Isaac's thoughts went back to that night of the Bath Blitz, and remembered the hundred or so glass fragments removed from the fifty-year-old's face; he had adapted remarkably well to his total blindness.

'I might as well give up my routine weekly appointment there, and just leave you to report to me about what's needed on a Friday night,' Isaac teased.

'Oh, I could deal with sorting out the medication,' Ruth replied, 'but how would all the ladies cope without the wonderful bedside manner of their beloved Dr Isaac?'

It was true that he never rushed through his visits to Cassofiori House and enjoyed spending time with the elderly men and women, some of whom had strong Eastern European accents and reminded him of his long dead parents. When he had first heard Ruth speak in English, he had been attracted by the familiar way in which she also clipped her vowels and trimmed her consonants. Now, hardly pausing for breath, she went back to describing the activities of the craft workshop to Naomi, dwelling on the intricacies of cane basket making, in readiness for the residents' forthcoming sale of Chanukah and Christmas gifts.

Isaac's thoughts ran on while the women chatted. Had six months really passed since he had delivered the nervous young woman to the Home for her first day? It seemed like only yesterday, when she had returned after the first week, and proudly shown them her first little brown weekly pay packet containing the two blue pound notes. On the following morning, he had taken her down to the little post office at the bottom of Bathwick Hill to open the savings account for her son.

He looked across at Yann, sitting half asleep on his mother's lap. Now eighteen months old, he was starting to talk and last night Naomi had proudly shown Isaac the little piece of paper pinned up in the kitchen on which she and Ruth religiously numbered and recorded every new word. It had reached twenty-five. The child had become the darling of Cassofiori, breathing energy and joy into the ageing atmosphere; knowing no different, Yann was at ease revelling in the residents' adoration.

Isaac had visited Cassofiori House earlier that afternoon, and it was over the customary cup of tea in the matron's office after his round, that Amanda McKendrick had suggested Ruth was ready to take on further responsibilities.

Sadly, Sandie Whitcroft's father had died earlier in the week and she had left to arrange his funeral in Glasgow. Her mother was in her eighties and also unwell, so Sandie was not returning to Cassofiori House and the post of housekeeper was vacant.

'Despite her short time here, Ruth has become invaluable and Yann has brought a real breath of fresh air to this place of the infirm and elderly,' the matron said as she poured him a cup of tea and passed him a plate of digestive biscuits, 'I have already had a word with the trustees, who are happy to leave the decision to me, but I wanted to talk to you about it before approaching Ruth. It would mean a great deal more responsibility, and although she would receive a higher wage, she would only have one day free a month.'

Isaac helped himself to another biscuit and pondered the question. In reality, it would mean that Ruth and Yann would have to make Cassofiori House their home and live there permanently. He didn't like the idea of not seeing Ruth and Yann each weekend and was sure that Naomi would miss them even more. At the same time, he knew that Ruth was keen to be independent and that her priority was to provide the best for her son. They all clung to the idea that Jancek was a prisoner of war and would be found alive, but, unlike Ruth, Isaac accepted that she may already be a widow, in which case the offer of a better position at the home was a good idea.

He finally replied. 'I am delighted it's worked out so well, and I know Ruth loves working here. I'm sure she would make an excellent housekeeper and am happy to discuss the idea with her over the weekend, so that she can give you her decision on Monday morning.'

'I'm most grateful and shall look forward to speaking to her.' Amanda McKendrick picked up her cup of tea and leaned back into her chair, looking much relieved.

'Now,' Isaac drained his own cup, 'I'd better go and find your potential housekeeper, and take them both home before the Shabbos comes in.'

Later that evening at the dinner table, Isaac waited for a break in the conversation between his wife and Ruth.

'Ruth and Naomi, I've got some interesting news for you.'

Ruth and Yann took up full-time residence at Cassofiori House a week later.

CHAPTER TWELVE

Professor Stanley Frith, an expert from the Urban Town Planning Faculty at a leading university and engaged at a cost of many guineas, was drawing his speech to an end. The late morning sunlight flooded through the tall windows of Austwick & Co's conference room, creating a halo behind his generous mop of unruly blonde hair, which was continually on the move as he attacked his subject with enthusiasm.

'The challenge of rebuilding Bath after the war will be immense. The 19,000 properties, together with those of its finest buildings, like the Assembly Rooms, destroyed or damaged by the bombing, has reduced the city to little more than a collection of bomb sites. It is these large derelict areas, which provide a golden opportunity – probably the first in three hundred years.'

His small but attentive audience followed his sweeping gesture towards the city outside, reduced to a honeyed blur by the strong autumn sunshine.

'I anticipate costs in the region of many millions of pounds. That, gentlemen, is where you play a vital role.'

The ten men, seated in two rows facing the professor, had enjoyed listening to the man's vision but as always it came down to cost.

'The City Council has one invaluable tool – the ability to compulsorily purchase every single one of the buildings and the necessary land. But it will be private enterprise that will be required to provide the money and the development expertise. To put it succinctly, gentlemen, if the city can be persuaded to acquire the land, it will be for you to rebuild Bath.'

The professor sat down to applause. Greed drove his audience's interest.

Ken Kohut stood up, belly amply filling his waistcoat, fob watch chain almost at full stretch. 'Gentlemen, Professor Frith has kindly agreed to answer any questions before we break for lunch.'

Isaac nibbled at the fresh smoked salmon sandwich. He never ceased to marvel at the William Pitt Club's ability to provide food that had long disappeared from shop shelves; he gathered that on this occasion it was Sir Peter's gillie who had sent the fish down by train from his Scottish estate.

Jenkins approached, awkwardly holding a delicate china teacup between the thick finger and thumb of his policeman's right hand. Like Isaac, Jenkins was an outsider, yet both were here and, more surprisingly, made welcome.

'Well Isaac, what do you think?'

'The salmon? Marvellous. I'd forgotten the taste of the real thing, after those awful little pots of Shippam paste.'

'No, I mean about Professor Frith and his plans.'

'Impressive, the sheer size of it all and the money involved. Bath will have to be rebuilt. Why not by these men?'

Jenkins nodded and must have thought the same as Isaac, that in this city these men, in their Saville Row suits and hand made Lobb shoes, were free to do what they wished. And, if he and Isaac wanted, they could be a part of it because they belonged to the club.

After lunch, Isaac followed the others back into the meeting room. Professor Frith had taken his cheque and departed. The room had been rearranged. Now there was a long mahogany table, behind which were eight chairs. Facing the table and chairs were five blackboards on easels, each covered with a green baize cloth, on either side of which were two large carver chairs, in which sat Earl Lundy and John Bradshaw.

Isaac found his allotted seat. A large brown envelope bearing his name was placed on the table in front of it. Named envelopes were in front of each of the remaining seven chairs.

Earl Lundy rose. 'Please leave opening the envelopes for the moment.' He looked across at Bradshaw. 'John, would you like to start the batting?' Isaac smiled – cricket again.

Bradshaw stood up, and removed the cloth from the first board. Pinned to it was the 1935 edition of the Ordnance Survey map, a large-scale street plan, showing every property inside the Bath city boundary.

CITY OF BATH

AIR RAID DAMAGE APRIL 25TH, 26TH & 27TH 1942

It was a mosaic of six different colours, with a key to these below; Red for totally destroyed, Pink for so badly damaged that demolition is necessary, Green for seriously damaged, but capable of repair, Yellow for evacuated pending repairs, Burnt Sienna for general damage, and Blue for glass damage only.

Bradshaw gazed appreciatively at it before he spoke.

'I must stress that this map is highly confidential, and because of the effect on morale, will not come into the public domain until next year. The effect of the air raids two years ago was massive, gentlemen.' He stepped back to the table, picked up a buff folder, and passed it to David for circulation among the listeners.

'Again, highly confidential – you will see it is marked "Secret", which I think is over the top – but of more, if not greater interest is the accompanying report by Mowbray Ashton Green and John Owens that lists every single property hit by enemy action, street by street and the local architects and builders appointed to deal with each.'

The room was silent as everyone studied the map, and the particular areas in which they owned property. Bradshaw moved to the second easel and removed the cloth. Identical to the first, black cross-hatching had been added to a third of the coloured areas. As if to make sure that he had the undivided attention of everyone in the room, again Bradshaw paused for effect.

'Every cross-hatched property is either owned or controlled by the people in this room: about forty per cent of the 19,000 buildings damaged in the air raids.'

The room rustled with anticipation.

His words hung in the air, and Isaac heard the slight intake of breath from David Lloyd next to him.

'Now for the first of our own maps.' Bradshaw moved to the third board and removed its cover. 'Mowbray Ashton Green is well known. The architect who, in the thirties produced the first, and only list of the buildings, which he thought were "worthy of preservation". These are coloured black. Notice how few. As you know, Sir Patrick Abercrombie has been appointed to prepare "The Plan of Bath" and this is due out next year. His approach will be very controversial, very radical. The city is to be split into nine or more neighbourhoods, with total emphasis on traffic and transport solutions. Significantly, only those properties on this board will be spared demolition.'

Next, the fourth board was uncovered. This plan was much simpler; colouring and cross-hatching had disappeared, instead dozens of properties were simply edged in gold, of different shapes and sizes.

'The second of our creations. This, gentlemen, shows what you don't own or control in the areas suggested by Abercrombie for development.'

Bradshaw returned to his seat and Earl Lundy rose slowly from his chair.

'So there you have it. The blueprint for the rebuilding of Bath when this war ends, as it now inevitably will, with an allied victory. Obviously, Winston Churchill will carry all before him, and the re-election of a Conservative Government, and in Bath, a Tory Council means,' he looked around at each of the men seated along the table, 'all of us are, and will be ready.'

The members banged their hands on the polished table. Not so much, sensed Isaac, for the victory at war, but for the re-election and the assured years of future Conservative national rule and local profit.

'A grateful nation's reward for Churchill,' Bradshaw added from his chair to more table thumping.

Earl Lundy waited for the room to settle. 'Winston reckons it will take another eighteen months to crush the Germans, and possibly a year longer for the Japanese. I'm sure I speak for you all, when I say that the William Pitt Club needs to be in on the ground floor in rebuilding Bath. Peter Groves will now tell us how best we can achieve this.'

Groves walked to the fifth board with a relaxed and self-assured stroll – very suave, a ladies' man in Isaac's opinion – and slipped the last green cover off. The large piece of white paper bore an oval blue logo depicting a line of three stone castellated towers, a large one in the centre, with identical slightly smaller towers on either side. A broad ribbon encircled the towers, elaborately tied at the bottom. Printed inside the ribbon were the words THE SECURITY OF LAND. Under this, spreading right across the page was printed BATH ESTATES LIMITED in large blue Roman capitals.

Groves spoke quietly, almost a whisper in a short series of abrupt phrases. The William Pitt Club had to lean forward to hear him.

'In accordance with Earl Lundy's instructions, Bath Estates Limited, a private limited company, was incorporated four days ago. It can, and will issue and sell only one hundred shares at one pound each. In this way the maximum liability of any director and shareholder, in the highly unlikely event of the company failing, will be no more than one hundred pounds. Whilst the company is registered as a property company, in essence, it can engage in almost any type of business activity.'

Groves returned to his seat. Austwick rose, holding a sheet of closely hand-written notes, and turned to face the others. He peered at his colleagues over a pair of wire-rimmed spectacles, perched on his long narrow nose. Now come the lawyers, thought Isaac.

'I have agreed to undertake the housekeeping. Don't open your brown envelope now, but take it away and read the contents when you are alone. We don't want any nasty leaks to the newspapers. No doubt I can leave you to watch over this aspect, Sir Peter?' He looked questioningly at Peter Knee, who nodded in response. 'In your envelopes, you will find a brief prospectus setting out how Bath Estates is to be run and financed, its proposed officers and professional advisors. The last sheet is an invitation for every one of the ten people in this room to subscribe for ten ordinary voting shares at a cost of one pound each. Every would-be shareholder must also simultaneously subscribe for 10,000 non-voting preference shares, again priced at one pound each. If everyone in this room takes up the offer, Bath Estates will have a total of 100 ordinary and 100,000 preference shares, owned equally by the ten of us.

'It is essential that you complete your application form and return it to me with a cheque for £10,010 by hand in the envelope provided, no later than midday on Thursday.

'I would draw your attention to two points: Firstly, to avoid paying tax I would suggest that you register the shares in the name of a favourite child, grandchild or some other person. Or perhaps even better, you can use an off-shore company and no one's name will then appear as the shareholder. Just tick the nominee box and this will be done when the war is won. Unfortunately, the Channel Islands are not available at the moment, but hopefully we will kick the Nazis out before too long!'

The William Pitt Club showed its appreciation with a burst of applause. Isaac clapped, even though he was only just following what it all meant. He knew that he could figure out later if he understood and wished to take part.

'Secondly, for reasons that will become only too obvious in a moment, the detailed aims of Bath Estates Ltd are not printed in the prospectus.'

Austwick sat down, and Earl Lundy slowly stood again and surveyed the men at the table, his eyes glistened with a look of slight mischief and his manner was of self-satisfaction, someone used to power.

'Quite simply, Bath Estates will, without fuss, quietly buy up available property at the knock down value of a bomb site. We then let on a short-term basis until development becomes feasible. Bath Estates will have just over £100,000 as its seedcorn capital.'

Ken Kohut raised his hand uncertainly. Lundy growled at this possible sign of dissent, but then sighed and yielded to the intervention.

'Wouldn't this be totally insufficient, given the scale of the property-buying and development programme envisaged by Professor Frith?'

Lundy's smile widened at the question, and at the questioner.

'I have followed the usual route and discreetly explored the possibility of Bath Estates raising the money required by issuing a debenture to various local trusts, and family settlements.'

Kohut smiled nervously, and as if to dispel any suggestion of doubt, eagerly nodded his agreement.

As if to be further reassured, Lundy turned and addressed Isaac.

'Our Jewish friend, I'm sure, will be familiar with the mechanics.'

Isaac, blushing, was now completely lost and prayed that Lundy wasn't going to ask him a question to which he would have no clue how to answer. He needn't have worried because Lundy barely paused before continuing.

'Some twenty-nine trusts have agreed to take up a £100,000 each. These debentures will be secured against the company's purchases, and they will pay a dividend of one and a half per cent a year. A widows and orphans fund, as we call it in investment circles. As many of you are probably aware, most of such trusts are completely discretionary, giving their trustees the freedom to invest as they see fit, as long as they abide within the Trustee Acts.'

Hopelessly out of his depth, Isaac nodded enthusiastically, eyes down, praying Lundy would look elsewhere.

'All being well, Bath Estates will have a war chest of shares, preference shares and debentures totaling £3 million, which will be deposited in the Bank of Bath by close of business next Thursday. Given the size of this deposit, the bank has agreed to pay a slightly higher than normal rate of interest on this deposit, namely two and three-quarters per cent.

'It will not have escaped your notice that the Bank of Bath will be paying us shareholders more than we, that is Bath Estates has to pay the debenture holders and the preference shareholders. So the ten of us in this room will enjoy an immediate profit of £37,000 per year until we need to draw the money down for property acquisitions.

'I am pleased to tell you that the Bank of Bath will provide Bath Estates with a loan facility of up to £7 million to be secured by way of mortgages against the properties to be bought, each loan to be no more than seventy-five per cent of the property's value. These will be interest only loans payable quarterly in arrears on the usual quarter days, at a rate of four per cent. The loan itself is to be repaid at the end of ten years, or earlier if the property is sold.

'Bearing in mind the number of individual properties to be bought, I have agreed that the paperwork can be kept to a minimum, with Austwick & Company handling all the legal work, and merely holding the title deeds to the bank's order.'

The murmur of approval that went round the room was the loudest yet. Earl Lundy spoke for the last time.

'So there you have it. I propose to hold Bath Estates's first meeting here in exactly seven days time on 30 September 1944 at ten o'clock. Hopefully by then the company will have cash and facilities of £10 million at the bank. This meeting is closed.'

Amazing, Isaac thought. That's how you turn £100 into £10 million in three days.

Isaac bade farewell to the others, and headed through the main offices clutching the still unopened brown envelope.

'Can you spare a moment?' It was Jenkins.

'Of course, Jack.' During their time with the William Pitt

Club, the policeman and the doctor had become natural allies because neither were businessmen.

They walked towards Orange Grove where Isaac had left his car by the guildhall.

'What do you think, Isaac? It's all very well for the others, they're involved in this sort of thing every day, but I can't understand why they've included us. What have we got to offer? And it sounds too good to be true. Can we be sure that it's all legal?'

Isaac laughed. 'Oh, I've no doubt they are operating within the law.'

'But why us two?'

'Why not us? For better or worse we are members of their little club, and we must have our uses.' Isaac paused for a moment, remembering David Lloyd and the award of the St Peter's Hospital contract. 'As I see it, the problem arises if we don't take up the shares. It probably hasn't even occurred to them that we might not have the £10,000!'

'Ah, that's where you are wrong Isaac.' They were rounding the corner into New Bond Street and Jack looked over his shoulder, and lowered his voice before continuing, as if he were concerned that he might be overheard. 'Christopher Johnson had a word with me as we were leaving and made it clear that "his door is open, if I were short of a few bob and the bank was always happy to lend." And I'll have to take him up on his offer if I do go ahead. What about you? Are you, you know, going ahead?'

'I don't personally have the ten thousand to spare, but Naomi's father left her a tidy sum. Christopher already knows that, since Naomi banks with him.' Isaac was starting to regret having been so candid about money that wasn't even his, before talking it over with Naomi. 'Look, Jack, go through the prospectus tonight and I will do the same. Call me tomorrow so we can talk again.'

Isaac left the hospital early the following afternoon and went home. He took the brown envelope into the library, opened it and withdrew the prospectus.

The front cover showed the blue logo with Bath Estates Limited printed in the now familiar large script. He studied it closely and then recognised the three castles. They were a replica of Sham Castle, the silent reminder of Ralph Allen's fortune made in the city in years past.

He turned to the first page, which listed the three directors and advisers. Earl Lundy was the Chairman, and Sir Peter Knee the Vice-Chairman, with David Lloyd described as the Property Director. The Company Secretary was John Bradshaw. Austwick & Company were appointed as the company's registrars and solicitors. Groves & Company were its auditors and accountants. It certainly was a cosy arrangement, very much jobs for the boys.

Clever, he thought, neither Malcolm Austwick nor Peter Groves were on the board, so no conflict of interest with their existing trusteeships, out of which the debentures costing millions of pounds were coming.

He spent the next two hours studying the twenty or so densely printed pages. Underlining and numbering the odd word or sentence, he compiled a list of various queries as he went. However, by the time he had worked through the whole document, he was able to cross out all of his noted queries as one by one they were dealt with in later pages. He was no expert but he felt it was a remarkably well-drawn document.

Over dinner Isaac summarised the meeting and mentioned the figure of £10,000. Naomi realised where the conversation was leading and promptly responded.

'Let's do it. I have more than that in my trust fund from

Papa. It's just languishing in the bank and earning a paltry one per cent interest. We are not getting any younger and it's not as though we can't afford it. You're earning a good salary and we shouldn't forget the additional consultancy fees that have been coming in since you joined the William Pitt Club.'

'What about Ruth?' They had discussed leaving something to Ruth as they had no other dependents.

'Surely Yann is a better idea. All being well, he will outlive all of us, and if this building project is as successful as they suggest, it will provide him with a nice little nest egg.'

Isaac didn't really approve of young people inheriting, but they finally agreed that Yann should only learn about his shares when he reached the age of twenty-five. Given her fervent desire for independence, they also decided to make no mention of the bequest to Ruth.

Isaac returned to the library and turned to the back page of the prospectus, which had to be filled in by any subscriber for the ordinary and preference shares. He detached the sheet along its perforated edge, ticked the nominee box, and, in the space labelled beneficial shareholder, wrote 'Yann Morris'.

CHAPTER THIRTEEN

'Good morning gentlemen, it being exactly ten o'clock, it gives me great pleasure to open this, the first meeting of Bath Estates Limited. You start John, as our company secretary.' Earl Lundy sat down.

The tables in the room had been arranged in a square, around which the nine men sat facing each other. John Bradshaw was sitting on one side of Earl Lundy, and David Lloyd on the other.

'Thank you, Mr Chairman. First of all, the issuance of the ordinary and preference shares. I am pleased to tell you that, with one exception, everyone has taken up their allotment.' Isaac had noticed Jack Jenkins's absence. Bradshaw went on. 'I recommend that we do not issue his unplaced ten per cent ordinary and preference shares for the time being. We don't require the money and they may come in useful at some time in the future.

'All the debenture stock has been taken up by the twenty-nine trusts and paid for, so that at close of business last night, Bath Estates's deposit account at the bank contained just under £3,000,000. The Board resolutions confirming the appointment of directors, the company solicitors, auditors and bankers are in place. The bank's facility letter for the £7 million has been received and accepted. The company's year-end for account purposes has been fixed at 31st December each year. I think that's everything I have to say, Mr Chairman.'

'Thank you John, all very satisfactory. Any questions?' Earl Lundy paused. 'Yes Ken?' The Bath city councillor had raised his hand. 'What is the problem with Superintendent Jenkins? Why didn't he come in?'

It was Malcolm Austwick who answered.

'He came to see me on Wednesday afternoon. He said the problem was money, but I don't believe that was the real reason, given Christopher's offer to arrange a bank loan. Both Isaac,' and he smiled across at Isaac, 'and I did our best to reassure him – but I think it comes down to, "once a copper, always a copper". I'm dining with his boss one day next week, and wouldn't be surprised if Jenkins is promoted away from Bath. In the meantime, you can rest assured that he will not disclose anything about Bath Estates; I have his word on this and have also taken the precaution of having him return the prospectus.'

'Can we be sure, Malcolm?' Ken persisted.

'Trust me, Ken,' Malcolm said quietly.

Earl Lundy interrupted. 'Let's move on. Our Property Director has more important things to tell us.'

He looked expectantly to David Lloyd, who unrolled a large plan and weighted its four corners down. It showed the rectangular area encompassing the whole of the Kingsmead area between Monmouth Street, James Street West and bounded by Avon Street and Charles Street.

'You will remember that this ten acre site was zoned for commercial use on the development plan. In my opinion, this area has the greatest potential of all the locations in the city. My staff have scanned the register of local ratepayers as well as the electoral register, in order to establish the ownership of every property. Half is already owned or controlled by us or our clients. As you will remember, Kingsmead Square bore the brunt of the first bombing raid and I request the board's authority to instigate the agreed buying programme immediately.'

'All those in favour?' Earl Lundy asked.

Isaac waited, took his cue from the others, and then raised his hand.

'Approved unanimously. Yes, Malcolm?' Earl Lundy continued, as Malcolm Austwick's hand remained in the air.

'Mr Chairman, I propose that each block purchase be completed in a different, and more importantly, a nominee company name. The acquisitions will then appear to be by different purchasers, and our interest and intentions can be concealed.'

'That would also be wise from a tax point of view,' Peter Groves said.

'Very clever,' added Ken Kohut, 'in the event of the council using compulsory powers, each purchase will have to be valued separately.'

'Agreed?' Earl Lundy asked. Again, all hands were in the air.

'Approved. Any other business? No? Good. I suggest that the date for the company's first Annual General Meeting be the 1st of August 1945 at ten o'clock, and for security reasons all future meetings will be here at Austwick's offices. Thank you, gentlemen. I declare the meeting closed.'

CHAPTER FOURTEEN

They have got it seriously wrong, Isaac thought, as he drove home from the hospital on a warm summer evening in 1945. His fellow members of the William Pitt Club thought electoral success for Winston Churchill was inevitable, but Isaac felt they were far too complacent. Cushioned against the hardships of everyday life, the cohort of the William Pitt Club was totally unaware of how ordinary people felt about the Conservatives. Although Isaac hoped and still thought that the Tories would win the General Election, he didn't think it would be the landslide predicted.

Parliament had ended on June 15th, but it had taken three weeks to gather in the votes of over three million service men and women scattered around the globe. Churchill was so confident of winning he had gone on holiday for the first time in six years on the day the election was announced. Of a similar view, the Bath Conservative Party Association was taking victory for granted.

In contrast, the Labour Party was well-organised and keen, with public meetings full to overflowing. Speaker after speaker hammered out the same simple message. Put Labour in, and the Beveridge Report, published in November 1942 and hated by most Tories, would be implemented in full. Nothing, the socialists claimed, had changed for the working classes since the thirties, and the war had merely been a necessary diversion.

A welfare state, with the whole of society cared for from cradle to grave, was appealing, but the implementation of the Beveridge Report would mean a vast increase in state spending, which could only be funded by a massive rise in taxation.

Unsurprisingly, the privileged membership and cartel of the British Medical Association, to which Isaac answered, were bitterly opposed to the nationalisation of hospitals. They recognised the need for change but preferred the measured approach suggested by the Tories. Nevertheless, many of Isaac's younger colleagues as well as other members of the hospital staff and patients didn't believe Churchill would keep his promise to instigate the long overdue welfare reforms.

But it wasn't just at work where people were talking about the need for change. Isaac had been surprised by Naomi's attitude to the general election. In the past it had always been him who had distrusted politicians and their platitudes about Jews. Now it was Naomi's turn to be appalled by the establishment's attitude to the displaced persons camps where, amongst many refugees, the pitifully few Jewish survivors of the Nazi concentration camps languished. Never a fan of Zionism, she was now talking about sending money to help the settlers in Palestine buy more land from the Arab farmers.

'I will vote Labour for the first time in my life.' She said it as if daring her husband to argue. He didn't.

Isaac parked the car and walked into the house. Naomi greeted him as usual, but the hug was cursory before hustling him into the library and the wireless.

'This is Alvar Liddell with the six o'clock news. The Labour Party has won the General Election.'

'Good God,' Isaac exclaimed, but Naomi put her finger to her lips, signaling him to keep quiet and listen.

The size of the Labour victory with a clear majority of 146

seats confounded the Conservatives. No more so than Winston Churchill, who had returned the previous night from the Potsdam Conference with Mr Stalin and Mr Truman fully expecting to return to Germany a day or two later in his role as Prime Minister. Instead, it was Mr Attlee who had gone to the Palace to see the King, and would be going in Churchill's place to meet the two world leaders.

Isaac turned the wireless off and walked across to the cabinet to pour himself a stiff whisky.

Two weeks later, the William Pitt Club assembled at Malcolm Austwick's offices for the first annual general meeting of Bath Estates Limited. It was a depressing affair. David Lloyd had already used the bank's loan facility to spend more than £2 million of the company's borrowed money. Isaac listened to the lengthy list of properties bought in the Kingsmead area and the prices paid.

Next had come Ken Kohut's summary – Abercrombie's proposals were becoming mired in local politics, because of the massive power swing to Labour.

Earl Lundy went on to confirm that the delay was severely hurting the company's cash flow. The need to pay interest on the bank loans used to buy these numerous properties, and the interest payments to the debenture holders left nothing for them.

'Regrettably gentlemen, we cannot afford to pay a dividend to ourselves, and I do not see this position changing in the foreseeable future,' the old man said.

Peter Groves's report had been even more gloomy, with most of the properties acquired being bomb-damaged sites and buildings that lay unwanted by tenants and incapable of producing rent. Bath Estates Limited was rapidly approaching a cash flow crisis. He recommended, and it had been accepted, that the buying programme should be suspended until further notice.

Isaac thought about Naomi's precious £10,000; it had yielded no return. How right Jenkins had been not to get involved. He hadn't heard from the Superintendent of Police since, as Malcolm Austwick had predicted, he had been 'promoted' out of the county.

Isaac should have felt content as he drove home. Whilst many of the buildings were blackened by centuries of chimney soot, the autumn sun glowed on patches of honey-coloured limestone and shone through the Abbey windows. He crossed Pulteney Bridge, and drove round Laura Place with its quirky little fountain, and along Great Pulteney Street. Normally his mood would be lifted by the handsome architecture and the pure symmetry of the Holburne Museum, but he had to prepare Naomi – would it all be lost?

More bad news followed when Earl Lundy suffered a stroke. He was at the Carlton Club in London when it happened, complaining about 'that bloody author George Orwell and his suggestions that the first Labour majority government should abolish Eton, Harrow and every Public School, together with all personal titles and the House of Lords'. He died ten days later. For the first time in living memory, the William Pitt Club's customary annual Christmas dinner was cancelled.

CHAPTER FIFTEEN

Isaac was chatting to David Medlock in the hospital staff room when the call came through from Amanda McKendrick at Cassofiori House. Such calls were usual if a resident was giving her cause for concern.

'Hello Amanda, what can I do for you?'

'It's Ruth, she's had a letter in the afternoon post from the War Office. Can you come over as soon as possible? She's very upset.'

Isaac feared he knew the reason. Unknown to Ruth, and using John Bradshaw's connections, Isaac had established who to contact, and had written over six months ago. He had received a curt acknowledgement early in the new year, but since then nothing.

Amanda came out to meet him in the fading daylight.

'She's in her room, Isaac, just sitting there. Yann is playing in the lounge with the residents. I have been up to see her two or three times, but nothing I say seems to get through to her.'

'Can you ring my wife, and let her know what has happened. Tell her that I will bring them both back with me, if you can manage without Ruth for a few days.' The matron nodded and Isaac made for the stairs leading to the small attic room.

He knocked but there was no answer. He opened the door.

Ruth sat motionless in the gloom, staring at the wall, her hands clasped in her lap. A single sheet of paper lay on the little table next to her.

Isaac switched on the table lamp and bent down in front of her, grasping her hands in his. 'Ruth, it's Isaac. What's happened?'

Her eyes were unseeing. He raised a hand and started stroking her face gently, all the time talking to her. 'Tell me, Ruth, talk to me, *bubala*.' His use of Yiddish seemed to register, the eyes flickered as if she had just seen him and she made a wailing sound. The words came, inaudible at first, but then in sobs. All the time he continued to stroke her face.

'Jancek is dead and it's all my fault. If I had agreed to go to America with him, he wouldn't have become a soldier and he would be alive. I was so sure he would come back to Yann and me; now we're completely alone.'

Isaac heard the note of fear, but this was not the time to reason with her. He just let her talk, all the time reassuring her, until the torrent of words slowed and then eventually stopped. Gently he pulled her to her feet and hugged her to him.

'Ruth, it's not your fault and you are not alone. Naomi and I love you and Yann; you are our family. You are both coming home with me.' He picked up the letter on the table, put it in his pocket and led her from the room.

Naomi took over as soon as they got back to the house. Later Isaac remembered the letter and took it out. Typed on a wafer thin yellow sheet, the full stops had holed the poor quality paper. Jancek had died while in a Japanese prisoner of war camp.

It was her first day back at Cassofiori House after the week spent with Naomi and Isaac. Ruth arranged the blanket over

Sebastian's legs, in turn he found and squeezed her hand.

'I was very sorry to hear about your husband. Everyone has missed you, and it's good you have returned.'

'Thank you,' she stammered.

Over time they had become friends. Most evenings, after she had put Yann to bed, she would read extracts from that morning's *Times* newspaper to him, often asking questions as they went along. When he had first asked her to read out loud, Ruth had been reluctant. She was ashamed about her difficulty in reading. She had been illiterate when she arrived in England, but Sebastian understood and gently corrected her pronounciation, so that her self-consciousness soon disappeared. Before long, her often bizarre mistakes became shared laughter. He was astonished by the depth and range of things that she found interesting.

Ruth approached with the newspaper in hand after supper, when the Home had settled for the night.

'Forget that for this evening,' he said, 'let's just talk.' Occasionally Ruth had alluded to her life before Cassofiori House, but only briefly, and to the happier moments. Sebastian had not pried, sensing her reluctance to talk about her past. He had gathered from Isaac that it had been a turbulent and often difficult time, but the doctor had never gone into any detail.

Sitting with her every evening, in the quiet serenity of Cassofiori House, they had often talked well into the night. He had grown fond of the woman and her young child, and in the loneliness of his blindness, her friendship was valued.

'Tell me about Jancek.'

'What do you want to know?'

'Oh, how you met, what sort of a man he was, you know, that sort of thing.'

Gradually, very gradually, she began. 'We grew up in the

same village in Poland,' and over the next two hours Ruth told him her story. He just let her talk. She reached the time when Yann was born, and Jancek's leave, then fell silent.

In an attempt to move her on, Sebastian said 'You must get great comfort, that Jancek did at least see his son before he died.'

In an instant she was on her feet, the unread newspaper fell to the floor as she walked away, without another word.

After that Sebastian studiously avoided discussing Ruth's personal life, but the subject of Yann came up by chance one evening. They were seated in their usual place in the orangery. Ruth had been reading aloud from that morning's *Times* about the American bombing of Hiroshima and Nagasaki.

Sebastian waited until he heard the rustle of the pages returning to her lap.

'Who could have believed that just one bomb could be so destructive? What a dangerous thing to have created,' he said. 'It will only need one power-crazy politician, and it could be the end. World War Three could be over in days, no winners, just utter destruction. I don't envy young people.'

'What do you mean?'

'Well, they will be growing up in such an uncertain and dangerous world. Attlee was right when he said on the radio last night that the A-bomb meant a naked choice between world co-operation and world destruction. Young couples must wonder what sort of world they will be bringing children into.'

'I disagree,' she said, 'I am very clear what Yann needs. Love and security, with faith as a coat hook, available to hang his coat on, if and when he chooses to. And then there's education. I still have to work out how he can get the best there is so that he's got a passport to freedom, for when life gets tough.'

Sebastian was fascinated by her analogy of the Jewish faith, and how she had it all worked out.

'Ruth, I have a personal question about Yann.' He sensed her apprehension, but went on. 'You don't have to answer, but trust me, I only have your and Yann's welfare at heart.'

Sebastian took her silence as a positive, and continued with care.

'I agree with what you say, and for now you are doing a fine job in providing Yann with love, security and faith, but with education,' he paused and took a breath, 'the best is in the private school system and that does not come cheaply. Hopefully, given the right start, Yann could turn out to be bright, and scholarships would follow, but it will still be very expensive; it isn't just the fees, but the uniform and all the little extras.' Sebastian paused again before asking the question he had been building up to. 'Is there anyone who can help financially?'

'If you mean would I ask Naomi and Isaac, the answer is no. I am sure they would help in any way they could, but they have done enough already. I am saving every penny, and one way or another, even if I have to work my fingers to the bone and go into debt for the rest of my life, Yann will get the start he needs. Thank you for your concern,' she said stiffly.

As good as telling me to mind my own business, thought Sebastian, and not the right moment to make any suggestions. He was annoyed with himself for having underestimated Ruth's independence. As far as the boy was concerned, he would have to wait for a more appropriate moment. 'That's fine, Ruth. Now let's see if you can find something more cheerful in the newspaper.'

Sebastian bided his time, and on a couple of occasions in the following months, after Ruth had read to him in the evenings, he thought the moment had arrived, but then changed his mind. She was obviously very able but also very proud; it was important that she didn't think he doubted her. Sebastian recognised that Ruth was innately intelligent but, lacking a formal education, had little choice in the type of employment available to her. He didn't want her son to suffer a similar misfortune due to lack of money. Finally, in November 1946 and quite unexpectedly, the ideal opportunity presented itself.

The conversation that evening, in front of the dying fire in the drawing room, had turned to the traditional Chanukah party to be held at the Home in December. Ruth was telling him about how thrilled she was with Amanda McKendrick's suggestion that Yann light the candles each night.

'How much does Yann know about Chanukah?' Sebastian asked.

'Not a lot, last year, he was too young to really understand.'

'And how about you?'

'Something about oil not running out in the Temple,' she said. 'As a child I remember Mutti making marvelous *latkes* and there was a strange game played by my father and the boys with a square top and matchsticks.'

'*Dreidel*,' Sebastian interjected, 'there are some lovely stories attached to the various festivals, which I would love to tell Yann, and it would help him understand about lighting the candles. Why don't you let him sit with me in the drawing room tomorrow morning, and I will explain the story of Chanukah?'

'What a lovely idea,' she said, 'thank you.'

Sebastian sensed that Ruth was smiling; he had taken the initial step in his plan for Yann's education and there was another first. Ruth gave him a kiss on the cheek before saying goodnight. Nevertheless, he did just check his Braille copy of *The History of Jewish Festivals*, and Chanukah in particular, before he went upstairs to bed.

Soon after breakfast the next morning, Ruth settled Yann by Sebastian's wheelchair, and left them.

'Good morning Yann, and how are you this morning?' He felt down and ruffled the boy's thick hair.

'Fine, Uncle Sebastian, Mummy says you want to tell me a Jewish story. What's it called?'

'Chanukah, the Jewish Christmas.' Sebastian went on to describe the victory of Judah Maccabee over Antiochus and how the oil in the Temple's lamp miraculously burned for eight days despite being nearly empty. With non-stop questions from Yann, he explained that the lamp was called a *menorah*, and the festival to celebrate the miracle, Chanukah.

'So every year, at about this time, and on each night for eight nights, we light our own *menorah* and bless its candles to remember the oil.' Sebastian then felt down to the other side of his wheelchair, out of Yann's sight, and with a flourish produced a beautiful silver candelabra, with its eight branches in a line, and one slightly lower in front. Yann's little hands eagerly reached to take it from him, struggling with its weight, but clearly fascinated. Sebastian was delighted with the child's curiosity.

'On the first night we light the *shammus*, or servant candle.' His hand found Yann's and guided it to the front candle. 'Then we say three blessings or short prayers. Each night we re-light the *shammus* candle and one more, so that by the eighth day all the candles are burning. Now shall I let you into a secret?'

'I love secrets.' Yann let go of the candelabra.

Sebastian lowered the menorah to the ground and his voice to a whisper so Yann had to lean forward to hear him. 'Matron would like you to light the candles each night, and there will be presents.'

'Presents?' Yann whispered in return.

'Mummy will give you a present, but you must give her something too. Something special.'

'But I haven't got anything.' His tone was such that Sebastian imagined the boy's eyes widening, his mouth dropping open and his hands lifting in an empty gesture. 'What can I get for her, Uncle Sebastian?' he asked forlornly.

'Let's see if we can think of something, it doesn't have to be a thing, a kind thought or action would be good. Although Chanukah is not a big holiday, not like Rosh Hashanah, Yom Kippur, Sukkot…' he got no further because Yann, no longer concerned about having nothing to give his mother, started to giggle.

'Kippers and sugar?'

'Those are Hebrew names for big Jewish festivals.'

Again Yann interrupted. 'What's Hebrew?'

'Hebrew is the Jewish language. Every boy has to learn it for his *bar mitzvah*,' and before Yann could interrupt again, he went on, 'a Jewish boy has his *bar mitzvah* when he is thirteen. He has to go to Synagogue and read from the *Torah*, which is the Bible written in Hebrew. When he has done this he becomes a man.'

Yann was silent for a moment as he thought through what had been said.

'Uncle Sebastian, will I be a man when I'm thirteen?'

'Of course.'

'Who will teach me?'

'Well, I suppose I could, would you like that?'

'Oh yes please. When can we start?'

'I have suddenly thought of the perfect Chanukah present for your mother.' Sebastian pretended to be excited as if he had only just had the idea. 'You remember that I told you about the three blessings, which are said as each candle is lit?'

'Yes.'

'Well, those prayers are in Hebrew and English. Why

don't I teach you one, and then you can say it for Mummy and all the residents every night of Chanukah.'

'Is it very hard?' Yann sounded unsure.

'No. I can start teaching it to you tomorrow and we can then practise it each day. But it will be our little secret, not a word to Mummy. All right?'

Yann nodded. Sebastian held out his right hand.

'Let's shake on it, that's what grown-ups do when they agree something.' He felt the child's soft hand in his; despite being very small, there was strength in its grip; he felt sure the child would be a good pupil.

He had been aware of Ruth looking into the drawing room at various odd moments during the morning, but each time Yann had been raptly listening and Sebastian was pleased that she had not disturbed them. Now, however, it was lunchtime, and she entered the drawing room just as they were shaking hands.

'What are you two plotting?' she asked. Neither answered.

Ruth broached the subject again with Yann, while drying him after his bath that evening.

'He told me about Chanukah and the oil,' and much to her delight, he recounted in every detail what Sebastian had told him that morning.

She certainly knew more about Chanukah after bath time than before it, and smiled in the realisation that she had been taught something by her young son.

'What were you shaking Uncle Sebastian's hand for?' she asked a little later, as she tucked him into bed.

'It's a secret,' he replied, 'but Mummy, when will you teach me to read from books?'

'Soon darling.' Given her regular practice with Sebastian and the newspaper readings every night, she was confident she could teach him, but finding time would be the problem. 'Would you like a bedtime story?'

'Yes please, the baby in the basket floating down the river.' Moses in the bullrushes was a favourite, and the child was asleep in a matter of minutes. Ruth kissed his forehead and went downstairs.

She sat down next to Sebastian in the drawing room, that morning's *Times* at the ready. 'Yann loved the Chanukah story.'

'It was a pleasure and I am happy to teach him other things Jewish. What do you say?'

'Are you sure? He can be very demanding and gets bored easily. Once you start, he will pester you for more and more.'

'I'm certain. In fact, I'll let you into my secret. Once upon a time I wanted to be a schoolteacher. That was until I got lured into my father's bank.'

His plan seemed to be working perfectly, but he didn't want to be overconfident. 'How about we try it for the next week or so and see how we get on? Until Chanukah?'

'All right. Talking of secrets, what are you two plotting?'

'Oh, all in good time. Now what's interesting in today's newspaper?' he said.

The next morning Yann was duly delivered by his mother after breakfast, and seated himself next to Sebastian's wheelchair – they had the drawing room to themselves. Sebastian started.

'Yann, do you know the alphabet?' Yann proudly reeled off his A to Z without hesitation.

'That's excellent.'

'Mummy taught me, and I have to say it aloud each night in the bath. She promised to buy a book and said she'd teach me to read, but I don't know when.'

'Well, today we are going to learn the Hebrew alphabet.'

'But what about the candle prayer?'

'Don't worry, Yann, I will keep my promise and we will learn a part of it each day. So, let's get started. You say the English letter first, starting at A, and after each, I will tell you the Hebrew letter.'

'A', said the child, and Sebastian spoke the Hebrew one, '*Aleph*'. And so they began.

As Yann could not yet read, he needed to learn by heart both the Hebrew and English blessings. It was taken one word at a time and one line a day. After four days Yann knew the first prayer perfectly in English, and could recite the Hebrew alphabet, up to '*Non*'.

'Now for the Hebrew prayer: I will say it all through once and then we will take a few words at a time. *Baruch atah adonai eloheinu melech ha'olam she'asah*. You try the first three words.'

Yann coped with the unfamiliar sounds well. As Sebastian had already recognised, the boy was not only bright, but keen and diligent too.

Thus Yann, not yet five years old, started to learn Hebrew from a blind man before he could read English.

CHAPTER SIXTEEN

It was customary for one of Cassofiori House's patrons to come down from London each year for the Chanukah party, and in 1946 the duty had fallen to one of its younger and newer members, Marcus Rose.

Amanda McKendrick had never met him before, but she had learnt that he was a businessman and important donor to the Blind Society. She gathered from colleagues at the Society's headquarters in London that he had brought some radical new thinking to the charity's somewhat conservative and aged management. Unlike previous patrons, who arrived at Cassofiori House in time for the evening festivities, Rose came through the entrance hall just after breakfast.

Over a welcoming cup of tea, it soon became apparent that his visit was not perfunctory. Marcus Rose lived at Widcombe House on the outskirts of Bath and wanted to understand how the home was run on a daily basis. As matron, Amanda was delighted by his interest and desire to meet and talk to as many of the residents and staff as possible. Given that her role was primarily managerial, and where necessary, medical, she decided to ask Ruth to be his guide.

They found Ruth in the drawing room handing Yann over to Sebastian for his morning lesson, and Matron made the introductions. In no way affected by Sebastian's disfigurement, she realised that Marcus Rose had done his homework.

'I've heard a great deal about you Mr Cassofiori, and your late parents.' He placed his hand in that extended by Sebastian and shook it. 'I am very pleased to meet you at last.'

'Do take a seat,' Sebastian replied, and within moments the two men were comfortably chatting about Cassofiori House and other related matters. They were of a similar age and it was apparent that they had taken an instant liking to each other.

Holding her son protectively in front of her, Ruth looked at the tall, elegant man; he had dark curly hair with just a hint of grey and a thick moustache. Wearing a dark blue suit and what she assumed was a regimental tie, she felt nervous about having to look after him for the morning. He had a bearing, as Naomi would say, and an air of distinction, and she wondered if it had something to do with the bushy moustache; he looked important.

'We should start on your tour, Mr Rose.' She had let go of Yann and gathered the courage to break in at a suitable pause in the conversation.

'Forgive me, Mr Cassofiori, but why don't we pick this up again later?' He stood up. 'I want to use my visit to meet as many residents as I can and see what I can learn.' He smiled at Ruth and although she knew he was trying to be friendly, she felt awkward and wished Amanda would show him around.

'That's fine. Ruth knows everything there is to know about Cassofiori House and us inmates – but don't let her boss you around.' Sebastian grinned as he reached out for Yann to climb onto his lap.

'That's not true Mr Rose,' she said, 'and, in any case, I'm not bossy.'

'Then why are you blushing?' Sebastian asked mischievously.

'I'm not,' she replied, reddening even deeper and, not for the first time, wondered how sightless Sebastian noticed such things. She moved towards the doorway and Mr Rose followed.

By later that afternoon, she was far more relaxed in his company and allowed Yann to join them for a cup of tea in the 'milk' kitchen. She proudly watched her small son nurse his cup between his hands, drink from it and then place it carefully back onto its saucer. His black hair, deep brown eyes and dark complexion complimented the olive green pullover that she had recently knitted. His skinny legs – the long grey socks had fallen half way down to his ankles – dangled out from his short grey trousers, swinging to and fro beneath the edge of the kitchen chair. Yann was recounting all that he had learned about Chanukah, barely stopping to breathe. Seemingly unused to small children, Marcus Rose just nodded and smiled. She saw Isaac arrive and stop to listen in the doorway.

'Well, young man, are you ready for a difficult question?' Marcus asked during a brief pause. Yann nodded.

'This year the fifth night of Chanukah will fall on Friday, when the Shabbos starts. Which do you light first, the Shabbos or the Chanukah candles?'

'The Chanukah candles,' the boy answered, slightly breathless with excitement. 'You are not allowed to work on Shabbos, and that includes lighting candles, so the Chanukah candles must be lit before Shabbos comes in on Friday.'

'Well done.' Marcus Rose reached into his waistcoat pocket and produced a bright new silver sixpenny piece.

'Oh, *gelt*! Thank you! Uncle Sebastian told me he used to be given some *gelt* by his father when he was a little boy and got questions right.'

Ruth was amazed at the detailed knowledge Sebastian had imparted to Yann in such a short time.

'Thank you Mr Rose, but it's quite unnecessary,' she said, but before she could say any more Isaac came into the kitchen.

'Hello Uncle Isaac, Mr Rose has just given me a Chanukah present.' Yann shot off his chair and went to give Isaac a hug. Ruth stood up too.

'May I introduce Dr Isaac Abrahams, a dear friend and Cassofiori House's medical adviser. Mr Marcus Rose, a Patron of the Blind Society.' The two men shook hands and Isaac drew out a chair.

'Now ,Yann, we must get you bathed and dressed for the party. That's quite enough showing-off.' She took her son's hand. 'I will tell Matron that you are here, Isaac.'

'Bright as a button, and his mother is delightful' she heard Marcus Rose remark as she closed the door behind them.

Scrubbed and brushed, Yann sat between Sebastian and Ruth who, because of the occasion, was wearing a red woollen dress instead of her usual uniform. The silver *menorah* was unlit on the table in front of them. Yann wore a small beautifully embroidered white *yarmulke*, a Chanukah present from Sebastian, the skull cap given many years ago to Sebastian by his mother for his first *Seder* night. Amanda McKendrick remained dressed in her sober work clothes and quietened the room.

'The youngest member of our little community, Yann Morris, is now going to light the Chanukah candles.'

Ruth struck the match and lit the taper in Yann's hand. The room was silent as Sebastian recited the first blessing. Then, to Ruth's amazement, and without a pause, Yann took up where Sebastian had finished.

> *'Baruch atah adonai eloheinu melech ha'olam she'asah*
> *Nisim la'avoteinu bayamim haheim baz'mahn hezeh*
> Blessed are you, our God, Creator of time and space,

Who performed miracles for our ancestors in the days
Of long ago. And in this time.'

As Sebastian recited the last of the three prayers, Ruth
guided Yann's young arm with the lighted taper to the
candles.

'That was the secret, Mummy. Happy Chanukah,' he said,
hugging her.

The tears came.

'What's wrong Mummy, why are you crying?'

'Nothing is wrong darling, it's the most wonderful present
I have ever received, and sometimes people cry because they
are happy.'

She kissed Sebastian's cheek. 'Thank you so very, very
much Sebastian.' She couldn't think what else to say, but
knew that Jancek too would have been overwhelmed by their
son's performance. She was more determined than ever for
Yann to achieve what his father would have wanted for him.

'It was a pleasure Ruth,' Sebastian replied, 'he is a wonderful little boy. This is only the beginning.'

Sebastian raised the subject immediately when Ruth sat with
him and *The Times* a few days later. The newspaper was
forgotten as he outlined his desire to continue his morning
sessions with Yann, coaching him much more, starting with
teaching her son to read.

It was a generous offer and she was delighted at the
prospect, but the suggestion of teaching Yann to read was
surely impracticable, and before she could stop herself
interrupted him.

'But that's impossible! How can a blind man teach someone
sighted to read? I mean...' Her voice trailed off as Sebastian
laughed.

'Believe me, with a little help from you, I've worked out how.'

He went on to explain that as long as Ruth was prepared to spend a quarter of an hour dictating a page or two from a reading primer, he could transcribe this on to his machine in Braille, ready for Yann's next lesson. It could be done before their *Times* get-together each evening. If she agreed, he would order the necessary books from *Mr B's Emporium of Reading Delights* in John Street or *Toppings* at the top of Broad Street, together with a children's dictionary. Enthusiastically he spelt it out and let it all sink in.

'Well, I know he is very keen to read,' Ruth said and wondered what harm it could do. 'All right, but how long do you think it will take?'

'Yann is bright, and already knows his alphabet, so I'll wager that he will be reading fluently before he is five.'

CHAPTER SEVENTEEN

Marmaduke, the third Earl Lundy tapped his wine glass lightly with his spoon and the room dutifully hushed.

'It now gives me great pleasure to introduce His Majesty's Loyal Opposition Spokesman for Foreign Affairs, the Conservative Member of Parliament for Bath, Mr Alan Buxton, MP.'

The third Earl Lundy was very different from his late father. Although pleasant enough, he was a timid and shy man who, it was said, was ruled with an iron fist by a harsh wife 'from a family in trade'. He had trained as an architect specialising in church restoration and as a result was reliant on the income from his late father's estate for a living. Isaac surmised that the family fortune was destined to last only for the proverbial 'clog to clog in three generations'.

It was the first William Pitt Club dinner for two years and a poor shadow of previous ones; lounge suits instead of dinner jackets, poor food and indifferent wine. But everyone was there; Austwick, Groves, Sir Peter, Kohut, Bradshaw along with David Lloyd and Christopher Johnson, between whom Isaac was seated.

The Annual General Meeting of Bath Estates Limited had preceded the dinner, and was a dismal affair. The company had gone backwards over the last twelve months, mired in the bickering of local politicians amidst an acute shortage of buildings materials, and a lack of cash reserves. The dividend on the preference shares was passed – so yet again, nothing for Naomi's £10,000. Worse, the company was even struggling to meet the half yearly dividend due on the outside investors' debentures, because of rising interest rates and increased mortgage payments to the bank.

Marmaduke Lundy had taken the chair, but was clearly out of his depth. The mood had been sombre with the fear of loss starting to surface in some hostile questions. The atmosphere was clouded by dissatisfaction and Isaac wondered where the whole affair would end. Their guest, Alan Buxton, the Conservative Member of Parliament for Bath and Shadow Foreign Secretary, had started his talk.

'And so, as 1946 draws to a close, the first eighteen months of a Labour Government have produced precious little but grief.'

He went on to summarise the austerity measures taken that his listeners were more than aware of. It was worse than it had been during the war, with the introduction of bread rationing a few months earlier, and other rations further reduced. The country was broke and waiting for Attlee to get his begging bowl out and crawl back to the Americans for more expensive loans. He also wondered at what price – more US military bases in the colonies? As for repayment, it would take generations before Britain could be free of the Yankee debt and become Great Britain once again.

Turning to the international scene, which was Buxton's portfolio in the House, things were an absolute mess.

'Just to mention a few,' he paused before continuing in single staccato sentences, counting them out on his fingers, and pausing between each:

'One, bread riots in Paris;

Two, civil war in China;

Three, famine in India;

Four, forced resignation of King Umberto II in Italy;

Five, King of Thailand assassinated;

Six, martial law in Vietnam, Ho Chi Min guerrilla campaign against the French;

Seven, riots in Bombay for independence;

Eight, violent demonstrations in Cairo, demanding unification with Sudan; and last, but not least,

Nine, Zionist bombings in Jerusalem.'

Whereas Isaac's chin fell lower onto his chest with chagrin as the list unfolded, the final item had quite the opposite effect. He smiled inwardly as he remembered Herzl and his father – 'Next year in Jerusalem?' Who knows? He wondered, at least something positive may result from the Second World War, and if so, at last he could get the chance to play his part, and that was a far more important legacy than Naomi's money.

Brought back to the present, Isaac listened to Buxton's assessment for world peace. The United Nations had been launched the previous February in London but the MP questioned its effectiveness given the failure of the League of Nations following the First World War. It did have both America and Russia on board, but how could you trust the Communists? Isaac tended to agree and Buxton went on to talk about the support that could be expected from the British Empire, or the Commonwealth as it was now called. He started to warm to this man with broadly similar opinions to his own, but his next utterance changed things.

'It is awful to witness, but our great empire is falling apart. The dominions that we have supported and nurtured over the centuries seem to think that they know better and are demanding self-governance. Nationalism is rampant, India is boiling over and its future independence is inevitable; the Indians want what Churchill promised them in desperation in 1942. God knows how this can be achieved without the Hindus and Muslims slaughtering each other. Palestine is awash with Zionist terrorists. We will be out of both within eighteen months, you'll see. Then the whole pack of cards will come tumbling down. I doubt if there will be a British colony left in ten years time: the catastrophe is unstoppable.'

With his strong Zionist principals, this desire for peoples and nations to be free from oppression seemed quite understandable to Isaac, and quite the reverse of catastrophic, but he kept his opinions to himself. As Buxton paused yet again, Isaac started to wonder if being a successful politician was something akin to being a successful actor. The MP certainly used both voice and timing to emphasise his opinion and this time the pause allowed the enormity of his unfolding prognosis to sink in before moving to its climax.

'As Tories you are facing your worst nightmare. Attlee may not strike you as dangerous, but he is surrounded by some of the cleverest people in politics. The hard left, such as Aneurin Bevan, is determined to bring about a social revolution within the next four years which will change this country forever. The National Health Bill, nationalising all hospitals, clinics, surgeries with their thousands of dedicated nurses, will get Royal Assent early next year. Every coalmine in the country will be publicly owned in three weeks' time. On 1st January 1947, 700,000 coalminers will become employees of the state. And that is only the beginning of Labour plans to bring everything under government control. Family concerns, which more often than not have been built up over generations of individual endeavour, including railways, shipyards, electricity, gas, and water companies; all will be confiscated for little or derisory compensation. With State control of the economy, coupled with massive bureaucracies and increased taxation, it means the death of free enterprise.' Again a long pause. 'And, gentlemen, there is nothing you can do, nor is there anything that can be done to stop it.'

Buxton sat down. No one applauded.

CHAPTER EIGHTEEN

Sebastian Cassofiori wanted a word, so Isaac went to the drawing room after his rounds on a freezing March morning in 1947. The newspapers had reported the coldest February for more than a century and the ban on all coal and gas fires was taking its toll on some of the more frail residents. Wood from the estate's own woodlands kept the fires going in the main rooms, but the bedrooms were bitterly cold. The members of staff were doing their best, but it was impossible to keep wood fires constantly burning in every grate all day. Extra blankets and constant vigilance was necessary. Nor had the added food rationing helped. Isaac found it bizarre to see residents and staff indoors in their overcoats with gloves and scarves on.

He slipped into the chair next to Sebastian's wheelchair. Yann was reading to him from the yellowed page of a thick book and when he stopped, Isaac could not refrain from gently applauding the child's flawless performance.

'Well done, Yann, let's stop now,' Sebastian said.

'Hello, Uncle Isaac,' Yann closed the book and put it onto a nearby table before coming across to give a customary hug. 'Can I tell Mummy that you will stay for lunch with us?'

'You do that,' Isaac replied and the child skipped out of the room. He turned to Sebastian. 'You've worked wonders.'

'It's mostly down to him. He loves books, and has an unquenchable thirst for knowledge.'

In just a few months, Yann was able to read as well as an average eight-year-old. The Cassofiori library still contained the books that had thrilled Sebastian and his brothers as youngsters and so Yann, with Sebastian nearby in his wheelchair, would crouch down, calling out the titles of the dozens of children's books, many untouched for decades. They had always occupied the bottom shelves for easy access by young hands, but it wouldn't be long before the boy explored the higher shelves and wouldn't seek Sebastian's advice in choosing a book. He, a blind man, had been able to gift the child a love of books.

'It's about Yann that I wanted to talk to you,' Sebastian started, 'he will be five in a month's time, and we must address his future education.'

'I agree, but when Naomi or I raise the matter with Ruth, she just says she will deal with it. A while ago,' Isaac said, 'I asked Ruth about her aspirations for Yann and her message was very clear, she wants him to have the best education available, and if possible, with Jewish boys of his own age. But when we tell her that such a school doesn't exist, she just changes the subject.'

'But it does,' Sebastian interrupted, 'my old school, Beaconsfield, near Tunbridge Wells in Kent would fit the bill.'

'Of course I know of it,' Isaac replied, 'but that's not practical; it is one of the most prestigious and expensive boarding schools in the country.'

He was quite right, and with good reason – the school was renowned not only in the United Kingdom, but worldwide. It was a by-word amongst the Jewish intelligentsia and the super rich, founded in the nineteenth century, and named after Benjamin Disraeli, the first and only Jewish Prime

Minister, later Earl Beaconsfield. Its existence came about as a result of the Jewish quota system, clandestinely operated by most English private schools. To counter this anti-Semitism, some influential and extremely wealthy Jews took matters into their own hands and opened a private preparatory school for Jewish boys, aged from five to thirteen.

Such was the wealth and influence of the individuals concerned, the school lacked for nothing. Housed in a massive mansion, three hundred acres of ground, and an academic fraternity in size and ability second to none. Jew or Gentile, only the best teachers were recruited, and coupled with classes of twelve or less, academic excellence was assured. Its prime agenda was no secret – its boys would bypass the Jewish quotas by winning open scholarships to the best public schools.

As its reputation grew, demand for places far outstripped the five hundred available. Resisting the temptation to simply enlarge the school, the Governors did two things: increase the difficulty of the entrance examinations and make it more expensive to attend. To have rich parents was not enough; a boy also had to be very intelligent. Conversely, academic excellence alone would not secure you a place. If parents could not afford the fees, regrettably they had to look elsewhere; that was what most people thought to be the case, including Isaac.

'It's an impossible pipe dream,' Isaac said. 'Even if Ruth could be persuaded, where's the money going to come from? We are comfortably off, but not in that league.'

But Sebastian knew differently and explained that over the decades vast sums had been donated and bequeathed anonymously, to the school by grateful parents. Never acknowledged nor publicised, these gifts accumulated in a separate scholarship trust, cloaked in secrecy and not referred to in the school's accounts.

After his two brothers were killed in the First World War,

Sebastian's father gifted the Scholarship Trust £100,000, and for many years acted as one of its three trustees. The availability of these scholarships was not advertised but the money was discreetly employed and sufficient to assist up to five boys at any one time. It covered not only the school fees but many additional costs, although the bursaries were not automatically awarded annually but only in exceptional circumstances.

Sebastian had contacted the present headmaster, Mr Corrigan, and learnt that all five grants were currently being used, but that one would become available in September. However, a meeting with the three present trustees at the school would be required before Sebastian's interest could be progressed.

'Well I never.' Isaac was no longer so dismissive. 'Do go on.'

Corrigan appreciated that it was impractical for Sebastian to go to the school in person and grudgingly agreed that Sebastian's London solicitor, John Jacobs, could attend in his place. Given that John was a friend as well as his legal advisor, and had also gone to Beaconsfield, Sebastian could think of no better person to put forward Yann's case. However, it was essential that Jacobs meet Ruth and Yann to understand the family circumstances. Hence a pretext had been arranged for him to visit the next day and it would be appreciated if Isaac could be there too.

'And there will still be the general entrance examination which every would-be applicant has to pass,' he concluded. 'It is very competitive and there are two areas where I need assistance from Naomi and you. Firstly, and probably the most difficult, is that we have to persuade Ruth to part with Yann. The opportunity of a free education at such a wonderful school, comes at a price – he will have to board. Secondly, someone has to teach him to write. His reading is superb, and his Hebrew is so good I reckon he could turn into a Rabbi in years to come, but I have no way of teaching him to write. Ruth does her best but English isn't her mother tongue and she received no formal education herself. I wondered if perhaps Naomi could help?'

'Leave both with me,' Isaac said, 'I am sure Naomi would love to be involved and we will think about how best to persuade Ruth to let Yann go away to school, when she comes home this Passover.'

The next morning, teacher and student were, as usual, working together in the library.

'And so, Yann, we get to the Festival of Passover itself. Have you got the Cassofiori *Haggadah*?' Sebastian asked, referring to the prayer book used on the first two *Seder* nights. Yann had stumbled across the beautifully illustrated volume on the library shelves. It had been printed in 1825, and a family tree had been drawn at different times by different hands and inks inside the front cover, showing the names and dates of the Cassofiori family for over a hundred years: the last one was Sebastian Tobias.

'Now, let's hear the *Mah Nishtanah*.'

It was a festival role reserved for the youngest male, and for the first time in the Home's history, a child, Yann, would ask the questions posed at every Passover for thousands of years. Previously the youngest blind resident, a man of over thirty had been allotted the task. Yann opened the *Haggadah*, and leafing the pages from right to left, found the appropriate page.

'*Mah Nishtanah…*' Yann recited and was nearing the end, when Isaac and John Jacobs slipped quietly into the drawing room, and stood silently behind the child's chair. Yann was word perfect.

'That was beautiful, Yann,' Isaac said. The boy had obviously not heard them come in and twisted around in his seat, smiling broadly.

'Hello, Uncle Isaac,' he said, getting up and planting a big kiss on his cheek.

'Yann, this is Mr Jacobs, a friend of Uncle Sebastian.'

'Bravo little chap, never heard it done better,' Jacobs said, holding out his hand.

'How do you do, Mr Jacobs?' Yann said, solemnly shaking the man's hand.

'Hello, John, and thanks for coming down,' Sebastian extended his own hand. He turned to Yann. 'Can you find Mummy and see if she can send some tea through to my study, with some of those wonderful homemade biscuits? Well done for this morning. We'll carry on tomorrow.'

'Thank you, Uncle Sebastian, see you later Uncle Isaac.' Yann, in contrast to the sedate shuffling pace of the home, dashed out of the drawing room on his mission.

'Now to business.' Sebastian began and over the next forty minutes the three men worked out how Yann could gain a place at Beaconsfield.

Following his visit to Beaconsfield and meeting with Corrigan, John Jacobs confirmed that Yann was now registered to sit the entry examination for a September admission. The boy would not have to travel to Kent to sit the test, as the school operated nationwide and worldwide reciprocal arrangements with other schools, once they were satisfied that the examination would be properly conducted. The reciprocal school for the West Country was fortunately in Bath – King Edward's, in Broad Street.

Beaconsfield differed from most English preparatory schools, because it had two types of entry examinations, most children were admitted when seven, but five special places were on offer each year for five-year-olds. Jacobs said that normally he was against sending a boy away to boarding school at such a young age, but explained that there were two advantages. If Yann could be parted from his mother, there was far less competition for the five-year-old places, but more importantly, there was a scholarship place available now but none would be available for the seven-year-olds' entry in two years time. Timing was critical because a scholarship could only be awarded after a pupil had gained a place at the school by passing both the entrance examination and a subsequent interview.

The separate scholarship examination involved written examination about an aspect of the Jewish way of life, and an oral test; the allocation of a scholarship was solely in the gift of its three trustees. It needed to be remembered that Yann might not be the only scholarship candidate, as other parents, guardians, or referees were free to make written submissions to the trustees. Whilst highly unusual, this could be done in person and given the Cassofiori connection to the school, and Sebastian's blindness, Jacobs thought this might just give Yann an edge. Lastly the bursar estimated that expenses over and above the scholarship were running at about £50 each term.

Sebastian digested all that his solicitor had said for a few moments before speaking. 'Academically, with the one exception of his handwriting, I believe Yann is up to it.'

'On that score,' Isaac added, 'Naomi is more than happy to spend time with Yann. I am taking them both home for a few days with us at Passover and we will tackle Ruth about the whole idea.'

'Should I move the paperwork forward?' Jacobs asked.

They both nodded and Isaac swallowed hard; he knew how difficult the task with Ruth would be.

Yann was asleep, stretched out under a blanket on the back seat of the Riley, his head resting in Ruth's lap, as they drove back from Cassofiori House to North Road. Three glorious days off, thought Ruth, as she gently stroked her son's forehead. *Seder*, the first night of Passover, had been wonderful with the starched white tablecloths, silver candlesticks, and everyone in their best clothes. Yann's *Mah Nishtana* had been so beautiful.

He had shown no nerves in the packed dining room with its audience of eighty or so residents, staff, guests and trustees. He just strode up and recited the whole thing from memory, he hadn't even needed the *Haggadah*. There was a murmur of approval and a ripple of applause as he sat down.

They reached the house and Ruth gently lifted the sleeping child out of the car and carried him through the front door.

'Come and join us for a nightcap when you have settled him,' Naomi whispered as she and Isaac made their way into the library.

When she joined them a few minutes later, she thought they both looked rather sombre, sitting apart in separate armchairs, rather than as usual, side by side on the sofa.

'What a wonderful party but it's so good to have this break.' Ruth took the sofa, kicked off her shoes, and tucked her feet beneath her.

'What can I get you?'

'Nothing thank you, I already feel slightly tipsy – all those glasses of Kosher red wine. Why so serious you two?' She was tempted to get up and reach for a cigarette from the silver box Naomi kept nearby, but daunted by the formality, stayed put. The hard work of the day and excitement of the evening had caught up with her. Suddenly she felt exhausted.

'Not serious, but important,' Isaac said. 'About Yann.'

'Why, what's wrong?'

'Relax, nothing is wrong. Yann will be five in a couple of weeks, and we need to think about the next stage of his education. Sebastian has done a marvelous job over the last year or so, but there's a limit to what more he can do.' He looked across at Naomi, as if waiting for her to say something, but she didn't.

'Why, has Sebastian said something?' Now alert and worried, Ruth felt her stomach tightening with alarm. 'Yann loves his morning sessions with him; I hoped they would continue until he started school.' Maybe she should have taken that cigarette after all.

'Sebastian is worried about Yann learning to write – it's the one thing he can't teach him. I know you are doing your best, but Yann really needs a whole morning each week.' Ruth immediately relaxed. For a moment she thought it was going to be something really important. Isaac then looked again to Naomi, as if there was more. 'Do you want to explain?'

'I could do a couple of Sunday afternoons after lunch,' Naomi sounded nervous, 'but you wouldn't get back to Cassofiori House until about six.'

'What a lovely idea, that's really kind. I have to admit that my handwriting isn't the best.' They all laughed at the understatement, and the atmosphere lightened. 'We've been struggling with trying to do it in the evenings, but Yann is usually so tired. I would have to ask Matron.'

'I have already talked to her and she's fine about it,' Isaac chipped in. 'You're sure you don't want a drink Ruth?' he asked, helping himself to a second, even larger whisky, but before she could decline, Naomi started speaking.

'You mentioned about Yann starting school. Tell me, Ruth what have you in mind? I know you and I have talked about schools.'

There was obviously more. This wasn't just about teaching Yann to write. Ruth felt her stomach tighten again before she replied.

'Of all the private day schools in Bath, the best is the Paragon. They could take Yann at seven, but-' Ruth hesitated.

'But?' Isaac prompted.

'I would never be able to pay for it, and was hoping you could lend me the money. I'll pay you back, I promise.' There, she had said what she had been thinking about for months.

'The other alternative is the local primary school Ruth,' Isaac said gently, 'and that's free.'

'In the end, I expect that's what I will have to do, but I did want to give him the best start possible. Sebastian is convinced that he would get a better education in the private system.' She wondered where this was all leading to. It had never occurred to her that Isaac and Naomi might not be able to afford a loan. As if reading her mind, Isaac ploughed on in a direction which she hadn't expected.

'You know that there is nothing Naomi and I wouldn't do for you and Yann, but once a parent chooses to take the private school route, it is very difficult to leave it, especially for the child. Financial security for ten or so years is a must.' He explained that whilst comfortably off, Naomi and he were by no means wealthy nor getting any younger. It would be unfair to Yann, if halfway through, he had to leave a private school and go into the state system because the money ran out. Although he would eventually be in receipt of a pension and had some savings, Isaac admitted to having made a foolish investment in a property venture just a few years ago and often regretted that he had not purchased a house rather than continuing to rent. He poured himself a third drink and sat down again, quiet for a moment.

Ruth looked across at this wonderful man and his wife who

had gathered her and Yann into their family, and listening to him making excuses about their financial situation only made her love them more. Her eyes moistened.

'Isaac, Naomi,' but before she could tell them this, Isaac pressed on.

'The more I have thought about it, the more I have had to agree that sending Yann to the Paragon, a lovely little school so near here, is not realistic. One would be faced with a decade or more of fees and costs and in today's economic climate there would be little or no leeway should even a term's fees fall in arrears. Ruth, you are a bright young woman but you earn little and that situation is unlikely to change, and even if a loan were possible, you would be in debt for the rest of your life.' Ruth stood up, walked across, bent down and in turn lightly kissed them both.

'Don't fret,' she said. 'I understand your concern and love you both for it. You have done so much for us and although it is a disappointment that he can't have the best, Yann will just have to go to the local primary school. Now I am going to take myself off to bed. Sleep well both of you.' She turned for the door.

'Stay a moment.' Isaac got up again and guided her back to her chair as the little French mantel clock chimed midnight.

'We think there may be a way, and I stress only may be – I don't want to get your hopes up.'

'Really? How?' It suddenly dawned on her that this was what the discussion had been leading to, but was puzzled by Isaac's apprehension. He knew how keen she was for Yann to get a good education.

'There's a possible scholarship available. It would mean that Yann would have to take two tests in June.'

'Tests?'

'First a quite straightforward written one, that's why

Naomi wants to start the handwriting. It would last around thirty minutes with a Religious Studies slant. Secondly, there would be an oral test, both at King Edward's, Bath.'

'King Edward's, that's one of the best schools in Bath, and I think many of the Paragon boys go on to its Senior School.' Puzzled she thought for a moment. 'But, Religious Studies? Yann knows nothing about Christianity.'

'The test would involve Jewish studies,' Isaac said. 'Whilst I said the test would be at King Edward's, the scholarship is for a Jewish school, the finest in England. It's called Beaconsfield at Tunbridge Wells in Kent, about thirty miles south of London.'

'Kent? But that would mean-' Surely he couldn't mean... surely Isaac knew her pain from leaving her own mother when so young. Yann was less than half that age, how could he even suggest such a thing?

'Yes Ruth, Yann would have to board if he got the scholarship.'

For a moment, she couldn't say anything, and when, with the greatest of effort she did manage to speak, her voice was a harsh whisper.

'Never, never, never, I'm not like the English. I will not send my son away to a boarding school unloved, out of my care, on the other side of the country. I love him too much. No Isaac, it's out of the question. How could you possibly think I would? I thought Naomi and you loved Yann.' Her heart was pounding and she knew that she had to get out of the room before she completely lost control of her emotions. She fled upstairs.

She looked down at the sleeping child. A filigree of light spread across his face through the fanlight above the bedroom door and accentuated his little nose. He purred softly, quite oblivious of the heart wrenching scene he had caused below.

She stroked his cheek and spoke quietly.

'My beautiful boy, no one is ever going to take you away from me.'

There was a knock at the door, and without waiting for an answer, Naomi entered and closed the door behind her.

'We need to talk.'

'It's no use Naomi. Nothing will make me change my mind.'

'I understand, but I need to talk about other things, just as important. Cassofiori House has been wonderful for you both, and Sebastian's interest in Yann has been marvelous, but sooner rather than later, you are going to have to make some other important decisions vital to Yann.'

'What do you mean?'

'Yann cannot go on living with you at Cassofiori House, surrounded by elderly blind people and no other children to play with. It's not natural. I don't say you have to give up working there, but-'

'That's why Isaac and you are suggesting a boarding school.'

Naomi nodded. 'If, and it's a big if, Yann could get a scholarship to Beaconsfield, it could answer all your hopes for him. At Beaconsfield he would be with other Jewish boys of his own age, receiving the best education money can buy.' She put down a small book she had been holding and reached out to clasp both Ruth's hands in her own. 'I have no children, although, as you know, I did once have a little girl and can imagine what you think of me, but sooner or later every parent has to let their children go. In your case the sacrifice has come early. You cannot deny Yann this chance, however painful it is for you.' She kissed her and left, quietly closing the door behind her.

As she was undressing, Ruth noticed the thin book where Naomi had left it lying open on her bedside table. She turned on the bedside lamp .

'And a woman who held a babe against her bosom
said,
Speak to us of Children.
And he said:
Your children are not your children.
They are the sons and daughters of Life's longing for
itself.
They come through you but not from you,
And though they are with you yet they belong not to
you.
You may give them your love but not your thoughts,
For they have their own thoughts.
You may house their bodies but not their souls
For their souls dwell in the house of tomorrow,
Which you cannot visit, not even in your dreams.
You may strive to be like them, but seek not to make
them like you.
For life goes not backward nor tarries with yesterday.
You are the bows from which your children
as living arrows are sent forth.
The archer sees the mark upon the path of the infinite,
And He bends you with His might that His
arrows may go swift and far.
Let your bending in the Archer's hand be for gladness;
For even as He loves the arrow that flies,
So He loves also the bow that is stable.'

Ruth turned to the cover – *The Prophet* by Khalil Gibrain.

Twice she read it before switching off the lamp. She didn't
sleep, with her mind turning over and over.

She couldn't bear the idea of Yann being taken away from
her; the whole reason for her existence gone. Waking up each

day without him. His lovely laughing face was even more treasured now that Jancek was dead. The tears came back when she thought of her difficult husband and the emptiness he had left behind, along with their wonderful son.

She turned the bedside lamp on again and reached for the book. This time she spoke the lines aloud, slowly. It said so much and she kept coming back to the one line that caused her to reconsider.

'...*And though they are with you, yet they belong not to you...*'
Yes, she loved him so much but...

'...*their souls dwell in the house of tomorrow,*
Which you cannot visit, not even in your dreams...'

She had to think of her little boy first. What was best for him, no matter the sorrow it would cause her, was most important. He came first, he was the reason for her life.

Exhausted when the dawn arrived, she put on her dressing gown and went down to the kitchen. Naomi was already there and they sat in silence sipping hot tea.

'You are right, Yann must go.'

Naomi rose and pulled the tearful Ruth to her.

CHAPTER NINETEEN

Yann held his mother's hand tightly, as they stood outside King Edward's School on that sunny morning in Broad Street, Bath. Maybe it was she who was gripping his. She wasn't sure who was more nervous.

'Now or never, Ruth,' Naomi said, and the three walked under the stone arch and across the courtyard, to the heavy wooden door. Naomi pulled the ornate wrought iron triangular handle of the bell chain downwards and Ruth was wondering if the bell worked, when suddenly the door was swung open by a stocky man with a ruddy face in his mid-fifties, wearing a black gown.

'Good morning ladies and young sir. Allan Brunton-Reed. How can I be of assistance?' His booming voice made Ruth shudder, but thankfully Naomi replied.

'Good morning Mr Brunton-Reed, I am Naomi Abrahams, this is Ruth Morris and her son, Yann, who has come to sit the Beaconsfield School Entrance Examination.'

'Ah yes, the legendary Beaconsfield,' he said wistfully. 'The other two candidates have already arrived. Please come with me. Our Senior English Master, Mr Andrew Robinson, is the examination adjudicator.'

Ruth wondered what an adjudicator was, as they followed the billowing black gown and heavy brown brogues echoing along the flagstones. The dimly lit corridor led to a door on which a faded white card had been pinned: *Beaconsfield School Examination In Progress – Do Not Enter*. The same printed notice had been used many times before as was evident by the numerous pinholes in each corner.

They entered a high-ceilinged classroom at the end of which stood a master's table and stool on a raised platform, faced by three small cast iron framed desks with wooden sloping writing tops and flip down bench seats attached. Two boys dressed in dark blue school blazers were already seated at two of them.

A kindly looking man with a shock of grey hair and thick horn-rimmed glasses, his gown faded and worn, stepped down from the platform as they walked in. 'Good morning Headmaster.'

'Ah Robinson, this is the Morris party. I will leave them in your capable hands.' With a flourish and nod to the women, the billowing gown turned and was gone.

'Welcome. I am Andrew Robinson. Morris, go and sit over there,' he said, motioning towards the vacant desk. Reluctantly, Ruth let go of Yann's hand and ushered him in the direction of the third desk. With the twill collar of his shirt showing beneath the v-neck of his hand-knitted, sleeveless jumper, Yann looked out of place next to the smart school uniforms. Although of a smaller stature than the two other boys, at least his haircut was regulation. Naomi had insisted that they go to Jenny's salon in Bridge Street for the traditional 'short back and sides' the previous afternoon.

'Now ladies, it's just before nine o'clock. Shall we say be back by eleven?'

The two women found themselves briskly shown back into the corridor and the door closed firmly behind them.

Robinson returned to his tall stool, took out a gold Hunter from his waistcoat pocket and carefully laid it on the high desk; it was three minutes before nine. Next to it was a large sealed brown envelope, on which was printed 'Beaconsfield Entrance Examination. Not to be opened before 9.00 am on Monday 21st June 1947'. In black handwriting was written 'Bath (3) – Morris (age 5), Diamond (age 7), Cohen (age 7)'.

At precisely nine o'clock he opened the envelope. He found no change from previous years – two sealed packs marked 'Adjudicator', one for the written exam and one for the oral, together with three sealed foolscap envelopes, each marked with an entrant's name.

Beaconsfield was so efficient, he mused, year after year and always well organised. In more than twenty years, never a single problem. Hardly surprising, given the school's superb academic achievement, relentlessly repeated. If only here at King Edward's, we had their talent and financial resources. Still, that's the Jews for you, looking after their own. Hardly surprising that they wanted a country of their own, after what came to light with all those awful concentration camps in Germany. And before that there had been all the pogroms in Russia…

He pondered if any of the three boys in front of him had relatives who had suffered and then, remembering the envelopes again, wondered if any of them would measure up to the standard required. Beaconsfield always informed him of the results, and he had grown accustomed to the 'Regrettably none'. When had the last boy got in? Strange little chap, parents fleeing Germany, 1931 or was it 1932? It was so long ago he couldn't remember. Still, something different this year; they had never had a candidate for a five-year-old place before.

He opened the envelope containing his instructions for the written exam procedures; the oral one could wait until the boys were writing. He looked up and addressed the boys.

'When I call your name, come up and collect your

envelope. Return immediately to your place. Do not open it until I tell you to.'

'Morris.' Robinson began. Yann went up, took the envelope and returned to his desk, laying it carefully in front of him. He was oblivious of the other two boys' names being called and concentrated solely on what was demanded of him by the Master facing him.

'Have you all got a pen?' Robinson asked. Yann nodded and took out the gift from Auntie Naomi from his trouser pocket, a mottled maroon Osmiroid fountain pen, and laid it carefully in the groove at the top of the desk.

'In a moment I shall ask you to open your envelopes. Inside you will find the examination paper and a quantity of writing paper. At the top of each sheet there is a place for you to put your name. If all else fails, hopefully you can remember that!' He smiled but none of the boys laughed. 'The examination will last exactly thirty minutes, and I shall call out the time every ten minutes. In the unlikely event that you have a question, please hold up your hand. You may not leave this room for any reason whatsoever once we start, is that clearly understood?' Again Yann nodded but became aware that he had a growing desire to pee.

'You may now open your envelopes and start.'

Yann pulled out the contents and looked down at the examination paper. It contained a single question:

Write an essay about your favourite Jewish festival in three parts:
a. *Why is it celebrated?*
b. *How is it celebrated?*
c. *Why is it your favourite festival?*

Yann picked up his pen, unscrewed the top and checked the

ink was flowing smoothly before starting to write. Instinctively he chose Passover.

As Uncle Sebastian had told him to do, Yann immediately finished off and moved to each new section when Mr Robinson called out the passing of ten minutes. Yann had covered a side of the unlined paper when the master announced the end of the examination.

Robinson collected the three envelopes and addressed them.

'Master Diamond and Master Cohen, you may now leave us. You will find some chairs in the corridor. Please wait there until I call you.'

Once the two boys had gone, the master left his high desk and came round and sat down on the top of the desk nearest to Yann. He smiled, trying to put the child at ease.

'Now Morris, what's your Christian name?' Yann looked at him blankly.

'What's the matter boy, cat got your tongue? What does your mother call you?' Robinson said, wondering what sort of an ordeal he was going to face over the next thirty minutes if the boy was even too shy to tell him his own name.

'Oh, you mean my first name, sir. Yann, my name is Yann Morris,' the boy answered brightly. Stupid me, thought Robinson, the last thing a Jewish child would have is a Christian name!

'Well, Yann, I want to talk to you about books and reading. Do you like reading?'

'Yes, sir. I love reading. Where I live has a marvelous library.'

Robinson moved on. 'Well I want you to tell me about something you have read recently, a favourite story – it has to be something you have read, do you think you can do that?'

he asked, looking down at the boy with what he hoped was an encouraging smile.

'Yes, sir – *The Emperor's Clothes*. I finished reading it yesterday. Can we talk about that?'

'That will be fine, Yann. Why don't you begin by just describing what the actual book looked like?'

'It was very old. It was one of a set of five given to Uncle Sebastian by his mother, when he was a child. They have green leather covers with gold lettering and the pages are really thick, much thicker than ordinary pages, with funny brown rough edges. The pictures are very colourful, and-'

Satisfied that the boy had actually read the book, rather than been told the story, Robinson interrupted him. 'That's fine, Yann. Now tell me the story in as much detail as you can remember.' Yann shut his eyes and started.

'*The Emperor's Clothes* by Hans Christian Andersen.'

Over the next fifteen minutes Yann related the entire story. He went into such minute detail, that Robinson began to think the boy had learnt the whole tale word perfect by heart, but then dismissed this as impossible. He wasn't to know, and Yann was too young to realise, that blessed with a photographic memory, he could instantly picture the actual printed page, although his recall usually faded after a few days; he was telling the story line by line, page by page.

Robinson stopped him every two or three minutes to ask a question, probing his comprehension. After half a dozen interruptions, one of which involved Yann spelling out a word and explaining its meaning, the master was satisfied and was struck by the boy's ability to pick up the story at exactly where he had left off before the interruption.

The boy finally came to an end, opened his eyes and sat quietly, waiting for the master to speak.

'Very good, Yann, in fact quite remarkable. Tell me what

do you know about the author? Have you read any of his other fairy stories?'

Eagerly, now with eyes wide open, Yann went on. 'He was born in Denmark about one hundred and fifty years ago. Uncle Sebastian says he wrote nearly two hundred stories, but I have only read four others so far. *The Ugly Duckling, The Fir Tree, The Tinder Box* and *The Red Shoes*. They are very clever, each one has a hidden meaning, which you usually only find out at the end, but I can't make up my mind whether *The Ugly Duckling* or *The Emperor's Clothes* is my favourite.'

'Why do you like those two particularly?' enquired Robinson.

'Well, The *Ugly Duckling* is about how cruel people can be, and teaches you not to judge people by how they look. The grown-ups in *The Emperor's Clothes* tell the stupid emperor what he wants to hear, just because he is rich and powerful and they are all afraid of him. Even though he might get his head chopped off, the little boy was right to tell the King the truth.'

Robinson glanced at his watch – the thirty minutes was up. 'Thank you very much Morris. I enjoyed listening to you. Now would you like to go and wait in the corridor until your mother comes to collect you, and send in Diamond.'

Robinson looked down at the oral examination paper. He quickly circled YES and EXCELLENT, awarded the maximum of ten marks to each of the five questions, and under ANY OTHER COMMENTS wrote, 'I think this child is outstanding and very gifted. I have no hesitation in recommending him for a place at Beaconsfield.'

It was the first time he had ever written such an unambiguous recommendation. He signed 'Andy' Robinson and dated the form, printed his name, qualifications and the school's name in the spaces provided, then put the completed form back in the return envelope marked MORRIS and sealed it.

CHAPTER TWENTY

The thick buff envelope, with its handwritten address, arrived by first post four weeks later. The school crest and BEACONSFIELD SCHOOL were printed in the left hand corner, causing Ruth's stomach to churn. Snatching it up, she left the staff room half running to the orangery. Sebastian recognised her hurried footsteps and turned his head away from the open sunlit French windows to face her.

'What is it Ruth?'

'The letter from Beaconsfield has come.'

'Well open it then, let's not hang around.'

She did and extracted a wad of papers. Unfolding the first, she read it out aloud at an ever-increasing speed.

BEACONSFIELD PREPARATORY SCHOOL
FRANT, NR TUNBRIDGE WELLS, KENT
From the Headmaster's Desk on 2nd July 1947

Dear Mrs Morris,

Your son, Yann Morris, achieved first place in the examination for the five-year-old entrant intake, achieving maximum marks. Therefore, I am prepared to offer him one of the five vacancies available for the next

Winter Term, commencing on 9th September 1947. This offer is conditional upon a satisfactory interview. If you wish to accept this conditional place, you must sign and return the enclosed Acceptance Form to my office by no later than noon on 16th July 1947.

Your son should be presented for his interview at twelve noon on Tuesday 30th July. This interview will be for about half an hour, after which he will be required to have lunch in the House to which your son will be allocated, if the interview is successful. If you are unfamiliar with the School and would like to be shown around by one of the boys, please tick the appropriate box on the Acceptance Form and attend at the Bursar's office by ten thirty.

The results of the interview will be communicated to you by telephone on or before 3rd August and confirmed by letter.

Given the demand for places, this offer of a conditional place for your son will be withdrawn and allocated to another boy if the Acceptance Form is not received by 16th July.

Yours

Alexander Corrigan
Headmaster

'Hallelujah,' exclaimed Sebastian. 'Now there's a great deal to be done,' he said, manoeuvering his wheelchair towards the door.

'I must telephone John Jacobs immediately. You find our

133

brilliant young scholar, and I suggest we break the good news to him together in the Library. I will also let Isaac and Naomi know, I am sure they will be delighted.' Then he was gone.

Somewhat dazed, Ruth tucked the letter and envelope into her apron pocket and went in search of her son. As usual she had to look no further than the Library.

'Hello Mummy,' the boy said looking up from the floor where he was lying, reading a book.

'*Bubala*,' she whispered, hugging him tightly. Alarmed at her tears, Yann looked up into her face, 'What's wrong Mummy? Have I done something wrong?'

'No. No darling, quite the opposite.' At that moment Sebastian propelled his wheelchair into the library. 'Here's Uncle Sebastian – he will explain.'

'Uncle Sebastian why is Mummy crying?'

'Those are happy tears, Yann, come, sit next to me.' Sebastian gently patted his usual chair and found the boy's shoulders with his hand. 'You remember the examination you took at King Edward's School? Well Mummy got a letter today, and you have passed. Not only you passed, you came top. Superb, very well done Yann.' Sebastian's voice sounded strange to Yann, and he was squeezing so hard it hurt. Everyone is behaving in a very strange way over such a simple test, he thought.

They took most of Tuesday driving across the country and reached Tunbridge Wells the evening before the interview. True to their promise on that March night, five months earlier, Naomi and Isaac brought Ruth and Yann to the White Hart, a sixteenth century coaching inn which suited them well.

Oblivious to the imposing surroundings and sheer size of the school, Yann sailed through the interview, reinforcing his examination performance, and was offered an unconditional place.

A week later John Jacobs sent a driver and car down to Cassofiori House, collected Sebastian and brought him up to London. After a pleasant night at his Hampstead home, they both left the next morning, and arrived at Beaconsfield in time for the early afternoon meeting of the Scholarship Trustees.

There were five candidates, and the Morris application was the last to be considered. Sebastian had never met Corrigan before, but sensed the antagonism in his voice. However, he and John were warmly greeted by the other two trustees, both of whom had been at the school with them and one had been in his regiment in France. Afterwards they returned to the White Hart. At six o'clock came the telephone call; Yann Morris had been awarded the scholarship by a majority of two to one.

John had not seen Sebastian so enthusiastic or excited for years. Clearly the boy meant a great deal to him.

It was a glorious August evening and John manoeuvred the wheelchair onto the terrace for dinner. Menu read aloud to Sebastian and choices made, the light-hearted celebratory mood suddenly changed.

'John, I haven't told anyone else yet, but when I get back to Bath, I am going to ask Ruth to marry me.' Sebastian waited for a reaction. None came, so he continued voicing what he knew his friend and solicitor was thinking. 'I know there is an age difference of nearly twenty years, but I have grown very fond of her and Yann, and I believe she and he of me.'

'Do you think she will accept?'

'I don't know. I think my proposal will come as a great surprise, maybe even a shock.'

'Normally Sebastian, you never ask a question unless you know the answer before the asking. I suspect she will accept. And it can't be bad to have a brand new family at your age. And that reminds me, do you know the story of the seventy-year-old widower, who took a bride of twenty-one?'

Sebastian shook his head.

'Well, he's walking down the street a week after marriage, and bumps into the Rabbi who married them. "How goes it?" the Rabbi enquired. "I so wish for a son," the newly wed replies. "Get in a young lodger," the Rabbi counsels. Three months go by, and they meet again. "How's your wife?" the Rabbi asks. "She's pregnant." "I see you took my advice about the lodger." "Yes," the man replies, "and she's pregnant too."'

Sebastian laughed. 'Seriously, if she does accept, I will need to change my will.'

John reverted, friend became solicitor. 'Remember, all previous wills become void upon marriage,' John said. 'We can look at it tomorrow when we get back to London, before you return to Bath and pop the question.'

Instead of staying the night as planned, Sebastian insisted that they set off for London, after dinner. They reached Hampstead at an early hour, unexpected and long after the Jacobs's household had retired for the night.

'Thanks for all your help,' Sebastian said as John opened the passenger door on their arrival in the north London suburb.

'I am truly delighted that all our efforts have succeeded,' Jacobs replied. He guided Sebastian's hand to the wheelchair arm that he had placed into position on the pavement. 'I'm sure that Yann is the perfect candidate for the scholarship, and will achieve great things in the years to come.'

'You sound tired, John. It's been a long day.' Sebastian grasped the arm of the wheelchair and confidently propelled himself into it. Too late they realised that the chair was moving and that the wheel lock had not been applied. The chair slid away across the pavement, and Sebastian fell head first onto the kerbstone.

Numb with grief and shock and in disbelief, Ruth attended the funeral with Isaac, Naomi and Amanda McKendrick in the little Synagogue just off London's Tottenham Court Road. It had been so sudden. Sebastian had never regained consciousness before the pneumonia, and within a week of the fall he was dead. No chance to thank him for all that he had done for making Yann's scholarship possible. She clutched Sebastian's exquisite small gold *Magen David*. John Jacobs had given it to her after the funeral. 'For Yann to remember Sebastian.'

'I suppose Sebastian's death will mean some changes at Cassofiori House, Amanda?' Isaac remarked, as he drove them back to Bath later than afternoon.

'Undoubtedly. As long as Sebastian was alive, the Society had the financial wherewithal and were bound to abide by the terms of his father's settlement. If there was a query or disagreement, everyone in London always deferred to Sebastian's wishes. In practice this meant that over the years Cassofiori House became autonomous, with very little interference from head office. I fear that now he is gone, all that will alter.'

'There will also be financial implications,' Isaac said, 'I can't remember the details but I seem to remember being told that Cassofiori House's endowment centered around providing Sebastian with a home until he died.'

Amanda, sitting in the front seat next to him, nodded. 'You're quite right. Because both his brothers were killed and there were no other children, the trust will have to be wound up and dispersed upon his death. Wall Street, the Depression, the Second World War, all took their toll, and Sebastian was forever making up the shortfall at Cassofiori House out of his inheritance.'

'I would be surprised if anything were to happen in the short-term but we are living in changing times and I don't suppose the Home will be immune to them.'

It had been a warm day and the evening sun shone directly into the car as it headed down the Great West Road. Ruth couldn't stop her teeth from chattering. For the first time she wept for Sebastian; he had become so much part of their lives. He had understood how painful the separation from Yann would be, and his constant reassurance over the past months had dulled this pain. Next to her in the back of the car, Naomi put her arm around the sobbing woman, and pulled Ruth to her. *'Bubula, Bubula.'*

For some time Ruth had known that she had loved Sebastian. She was not in love with him, but a deep comfortable affection had grown and she had taken for granted that he would always be there for her and Yann. Now that he was gone forever she felt lost and couldn't stop the tears. She was frightened. The doubts about Yann returned. Perhaps it would be better if he stayed, didn't go away to school. He was already very upset and angry – this was his first encounter with death, believing the accident had somehow been his fault, and he was being sent away because of it. She would talk with Naomi and Isaac. Surely they wouldn't want Yann to go off to Beaconsfield now?

CHAPTER TWENTY-ONE

The Beaconsfield Special, a steam train with four carriages and three guard's vans, was drawn up alongside Platform Twelve of Waterloo Station.

Wide eyed and holding tightly to his mother's hand, Yann followed the porter and the two-wheeled trolley carrying his school trunk into the mayhem; Naomi and Isaac were just behind them. The porter unloaded the large brown ribbed case, on which had been painted Y MORRIS in bold black letters onto the pile of other trunks stacked by the guard's vans, ready for loading.

Clutching his mother's hand tightly, Yann froze, suddenly frightened, and caused her to stop. Everyone he loved – his mother, Auntie Naomi and Uncle Isaac – had done their best. Told him how lucky he was, but he didn't want to go. He couldn't understand why they were sending him so far away, to be with people he had never met. What had he done wrong? Was it because of Uncle Sebastian's terrible accident on his way back from this new school? He didn't understand why his mother didn't love him any more, it made him feel very unhappy. He had promised no more tears, but his eyes started to prickle.

Ahead were dozens of boys and parents clustered around two schoolmasters clad in black gowns.

He had never seen so many boys, most of them much older

and bigger than him. Soon enough they reached the crowd and one of the schoolmasters pushed through towards them. He had a clipboard in his hand.

'Name?' He asked, looking at the adults.

'Morris.' Isaac answered.

'Ah yes, the little lad from Bath,' the master said pleasantly, finding the name and ticking it off. Then he looked down at Yann and held his hand out. 'My name is Martin Kohn, I shall be your housemaster in Galsworthy. Now let me see,' he looked down at his list again, 'just stand by me for a moment and I will find one of the deputy house prefects to look after you until we reach school.'

He looked up to the three adults again. 'Best to say your goodbyes here and now. Short and quick I think is always best don't you?' In a second he had turned to someone else.

Naomi bent down and kissed him on the forehead. Isaac just squeezed his arm.

'Good luck Yann and don't forget your promise to write to your mother each week.'

Ruth knelt down, so that her head was level with Yann's and hugged him so tightly that he was frightened she would crease his new blazer. 'Remember that Mummy loves you more than anything in the whole wide world and you make me so proud. Goodbye, my beautiful little brave boy.'

'I am sorry about making Uncle Sebastian die, Mummy.' He hoped she wouldn't start to cry, because it looked like she could and then that would make him want to cry too. But she breathed in heavily and quickly stood up.

He gave a small wave with a half raised arm, as he watched all three of them retreat down the platform. No one looked back.

The next thing he knew, Mr Kohn had grasped him by the shoulder. He turned round and saw a large boy hovering next to him.

'Morris, this is Freeman. He is in Galsworthy too and will settle you into the train.' He turned to the boy. 'Remember that you are responsible for delivering him to the Dame.'

Yann clambered into the carriage and Freeman motioned him to the corner seat by the door, with 'A new sprog, Morris' as an introduction to the other senior boys. None acknowledged him. Unnoticed, he sat stiffly erect and unblinking. He had never been on a train and was with complete strangers. He wished he was by a window so that he could catch one last glance of his mother, uncle and aunt.

With a final flurry and whistle blast, the train lurched, lurched again and jerkily moved off, gathering speed. Freeman stood back against the closed door to the corridor, preventing anyone from entering; all three corridor window blinds were down.

Throughout the journey, Yann sat on his hands and looked down at his neatly laced shoes as he listened to the group of boys swapping stories about their summer holiday. He felt very conscious of his new purple blazer, with its bright crest and gleaming yellow piping, unlike the other boys' dull and faded jackets.

Yann wept himself to sleep in the bleak dormitory that first night and for many that followed. To his shame and embarrassment, often he woke up in a wet bed the following morning. The Dame never said anything.

CHAPTER TWENTY-TWO

Old Earl Lundy would have sorted the sorry mess that Bath Estates had become, Isaac thought, as he sat in the small shabby room at Austwick & Company's offices on a bleak January morning in 1948. The company didn't even warrant a decent meeting room any more. Of the original nine founding share-holders, only five had turned up. Ken Kohut had sent his apologies due to illness.

The young Earl Lundy – he would always think of Mar-maduke as young – was ineffectively chairing the gathering – the perfect diplomat, agreeing and understanding everyone's point of view, however diametrically opposed they were to one another. He responded to each question or personal criticism with a nervous smile, perfect courtesy and bland indecisiveness.

John Bradshaw was doing his best to hold the meeting together but failing, as David Lloyd insisted that £90,000 must immediately be paid to cover an outstanding debt due to the Bath Building and Development Company. It was all quite pointless, as while he could shout as much and as long as he liked, the company did not have the money to pay him. Even Isaac understood that much.

Facing them were Christopher Johnson and Peter Groves. Malcolm Austwick was absent due to 'a conflict of interest', given the unpaid dividends owed to the various trusts he represented, the written apology said. Isaac was sorry Malcolm wasn't present because he was always rational, and a calming influence.

On the other hand, that Peter Knee wasn't there was no great surprise. He had fled that terrible winter for the West Indies, leaving his Bath newspaper empire in the hands of a competent manager. Word had it that his yacht was permanently moored at Montego Bay, Jamaica, where he was involved with a scheme to build a new luxury hotel at a place called Roundhill. Isaac envied him, far removed from the austerity and poverty of post-war England and its unrelenting icy rainfall.

He looked out of the window at the mackerel grey sky and the downpour. It had rained for days, the wettest January since records began according to the previous day's *Chronicle*. Unbelievably, there was a water shortage; the supply to every property in the city cut off for ten hours every night for the last three weeks.

Christopher Johnson was speaking slowly and more formally than usual. He looked very serious, and for once was referring to notes.

'And so, gentlemen, regrettably the bank has instructed me to present these two letters to this meeting,' he said, handing over two envelopes to Earl Lundy. 'In view of the unpaid interest on the existing loan, the first letter gives notice that the unused facility of £7 million, agreed three years ago, is now cancelled immediately. The second requires that the outstanding interest, calculated at close of business last night as £83,768 and 16 shillings, be paid within the next ninety days. Failure to do this and the bank will have no alternative but to call for immediate repayment of the whole of the existing loan, which presently stands at £2,462,387, again calculated as at last night.

'As I understand the position from the company's auditors,

Groves & Company, Bath Estates is unable to pay anything at all unless it either finds alternative finance or sells some, if not all, of the property on which this debt is secured. Given the present state of the property market, it therefore seems probable that by March the bank, as the largest creditor, will have no other option but to wind up Bath Estates and appoint a Receiver to sell everything.'

'Bloody hell!' David Lloyd exclaimed.

'I say, steady on, mind your language,' Earl Lundy said.

'Steady on?' Lloyd exploded. 'Steady on? Steady on? You bloody idiot! My company is about to kiss £90,000 goodbye, and all you can say is "Steady on"? You are a fool, Marmaduke, a bloody fool.'

'I protest! How dare you speak to me like that?'

'Oh shut up you pompous arse.' Lloyd turned to Johnson. 'That's going to fuck us up, Christopher. Is there no other way?'

'Sorry, but the bank is adamant – it's a big loan and they're worried – this Labour government has really rattled them. There is even talk of nationalising the banks.'

In the meantime Earl Lundy had stood up and walked to the door. He looked back at David Lloyd. 'My father was right about you, Lloyd, "just a jumped up foul mouthed jobbing builder on the make" is how he put it. I want nothing more to do with you or your grubby little company. I resign.'

'Good riddance.' Lloyd turned to Bradshaw. 'Well, John, what next?'

'Well, er… for a start someone has to take Marmaduke's place and chair the rest of the meeting. Any volunteers?' No one moved and Isaac sat looking down at his hands, gently folded in his lap. Silence prevailed. He could understand no one wanting to take the poisoned chalice offered.

'Under the Memorandum and Articles, in the event of the death or resignation of the Chairman, the Vice-Chairman is required to preside, unless or until someone else stands for election and is voted in. Unfortunately our Vice Chairman, Sir Peter Knee, is abroad at the moment, so all I can do, in my role as Company Secretary, is adjourn the meeting, until I have communicated with him and report back. Agreed?' Again, Bradshaw looked around the table.

'One moment, please.' This time it was Groves who spoke. 'John, I think I would be failing in my duty if I did not draw another matter to your and Sir Peter's attention, namely whether or not Bath Estates should continue to trade, and-'

Lloyd interrupted.

'Now hang on a moment, Peter, we still have the ninety days which the bank has given us to try and sort things out. Let's not go overboard.'

'Different point, David. It is illegal for any company to trade if its officers have reason to believe it to be insolvent.' Suddenly, Isaac sensed alarm bells ringing.

'But surely that cannot be the case here?' John Bradshaw asked. 'As I understand the position the bank loans are all well secured on the property bought. David,' he turned and stared at the man sitting next to him. 'You assured us that under no circumstances would we borrow more than three-quarters of value. You checked each valuation.'

'But,' Lloyd didn't raise his eyes to meet Bradshaw's, 'markets change, values are only opinions and they can alter. They can go up and sadly, from time to time they also go down,' he muttered.

Weasel words, thought Isaac, my God, we are going to lose the whole £10,000, every penny. He dreaded the thought of having to explain the loss to Naomi.

Peter Groves continued. 'I would like to return to my original point, Bath Estates must cease trading now if any of you think that the company's debts exceed its assets. If it is later discovered that a reasonable person would have come to the conclusion that Bath Estates is insolvent, the consequences for all shareholders could be horrendous.'

'Care to explain?' Bradshaw said quietly.

'For a start, it is a criminal offence and on occasions directors and shareholders have gone to prison. Secondly, even though Bath Estates Limited has limited liability, none of you, especially the directors and the advisers, can hide behind this. Trading when you are, or more to the point, think you are bust, is fraud. Should any creditor, not just the bank, demonstrate that this was the case, all of us, jointly and severally would be individually liable for any loss suffered by that creditor and all of the creditors – to the extent of everything we own.'

Isaac was stunned and, seeing Bradshaw wipe his brow, realised he was shocked. Lloyd on the other hand didn't react and Isaac guessed that, being in the building trade, he knew all about insolvency.

'John,' Groves went on, looking at the Company Secretary, 'I should be grateful if you would ensure that the minutes of this meeting fully reflect the caution I have given to all present, and your covering letter, circulating the minutes to those who are not here, should specifically refer to this.'

Bradshaw nodded.

The meeting broke up amid perfunctory farewells.

Isaac sat and found he was alone with Christopher Johnson, who was gathering up his papers.

'No doubt you've seen it all before Christopher,' he said, as he got up to leave, 'but I don't understand how it has all gone so wrong.'

In normal events, and as he had done many times before when loans had gone sour, the banker would have commiserated, shaken hands and gone on his way. But he looked at the troubled man facing him and softened. He had always liked this middle-aged Jewish doctor, and respected his wife who had banked with him for many years.

'Isaac, sit down.' Isaac returned to his chair. 'Unlike the rest of us, who knew what we were getting into, I think you got sucked into this without really understanding the risk. Bankers and most businessmen understand and provide for this, but rarely, about every four to five hundred years or so in England, a fundamental change occurs which irrevocably alters the game.' He went on. 'First came the Roman invasion, followed by the so-called Dark Ages and the Saxons, then William the Conqueror and the Norman occupation. Next Henry VIII and the end of the Catholic Church in everyday life. The Industrial Revolution with its flight from country to city followed. Now, last but by no means least, Clement Attlee and his Labour government.'

He explained that for hundreds of years prior to Attlee, power in provincial Britain had been held by a few local people. Every town, city and county had been run and controlled by an equivalent of Earl Lundy along with a group of local 'William Pitt Club' members. However, with universal suffrage followed by the Second World War, the first proper Labour government had been elected with a massive majority pledged to implement radical change. As a result, in less than three years, the old guard had been swept aside and replaced with central control from Westminster. In Johnson's opinion, there would never be another meeting of Bath's William Pitt Club because its members had been stripped of the power that had been taken for granted and as of right for over two centuries; Bath Estates was doomed.

Although he knew that it wasn't in the bank's interest, Johnson decided to give Isaac some advice 'off the record'.

'I have spent all my life in the bank and in the long term,

loans secured against property are probably the safest, and therefore one of the best forms of lending. There is an old adage "Property is just an excuse for a banking operation". But the caveat "in the long term" is the imperative condition. Sooner or later, the blitzed sites will be rebuilt but the delay has resulted in too little rental income at present.

'Again another old banking saying is "never, never do a deal where time is your enemy". Time, in the form of unpaid dividends and compounding bank interest has just piled up over the last two years, and made Bath Estates's position hopeless. And that, Isaac, is where we are right now.'

'But where does that leave Naomi and me? What should I do?'

'There are lots of different platitudes in such circumstances, like delay and pray, and pretend and extend; pretend that the loan is secure and extend it, often for years.' He stood up and patted Isaac on the shoulder before heading for the door.

'Never forget, if you owe a bank £100 it's your problem, £1 million, it's the bank's. My advice is to sit tight, as we say, have a square bum!'

CHAPTER TWENTY-THREE

Bath Estates unwound at a frightening pace. Sir Peter remained in warmer climes and quit as Vice Chairman. John Bradshaw soldiered on for a few months before his resignation as Company Secretary followed. Officerless, the bank placed Bath Estates into receivership without waiting out the ninety days. Isaac was initially surprised to read that Malcolm Austwick and Peter Groves had accepted appointments as liquidators and wondered why they wanted further involvement, until he saw the generous fees involved.

Isaac was confronted with a blizzard of paperwork and handwritten on the compliment slip attached to the last batch was written 'Square bum time!' It was unsigned but in Christopher Johnson's distinctive hand.

None of the £90,000 owed to David Lloyd's company could be paid and after one hundred years of trading, the Bath Building and Development Company collapsed. Lloyd fled to the anonymity of London.

Naomi was philosophical about the loss of her £10,000 and concentrated on her work for the newly created Bath Festival. Ian Hunter of Glyndebourne and Edinburgh Festival's fame had suggested a Bath equivalent and Naomi was the first to be co-opted onto his working party.

Much later in the year, towards the end of October, Christopher Johnson telephoned Isaac.

'Have you seen the front page of today's *Chronicle*?' the banker asked.

'Not yet, it's waiting for me at home, why do you ask?'

'It's all "square bums". Have a look and rather than talking now, let's meet for lunch and I'll explain what it means.'

Isaac went in search of the newspaper when he got home. The article was rather technical, mostly about road widening in and around the city centre. It was only when the Kingsmead subheading caught his eye that he became more interested. Six acres – virtually everything Bath Estates had painstakingly owned, and bought plot by plot over the past years – was to be compulsorily purchased by the City Council and developed for business purposes, whatever that might mean.

Christopher was sitting at the table in the window of the Circus Restaurant overlooking Brock Street, and welcomed Isaac.

'First things first; the food. Alison and her team work miracles,' Christopher said, handing him a menu. Isaac had never been to the restaurant before and was amazed at the choice; it was very imaginative, given the shortages available.

'Always a joy to come to, they change the whole menu every month, and I recommend the fish, it's all line caught by the day boats out of Lyme Bay in Dorset, and delivered overnight,' his host continued enthusiastically. Isaac chose the pollock, home-cured and marinated in sweet red onions.

Christopher raised his sherry glass. 'Here's to your first dividend on Naomi's £10,000!' Isaac reciprocated with a nod and Christopher got straight to the point.

'About your shares in Bath Estates Limited…'

After an excellent lunch, which Johnson insisted on paying for, Isaac headed away from the Circus, towards the Royal Crescent.

There was a great deal of commotion in the Crescent and he remembered the *Chronicle* headlines. Alexander Korda's *The Elusive Pimpernel* was being filmed there. He halted beside a stack of inappropriate street lamp posts, which had been temporarily removed from the roadside – no effort had been spared to turn the clock back to the eighteenth century. He saw David Niven and Margaret Leighton emerge in splendour from one of the houses into the fierce arc lights of the film company and board a horse-drawn carriage.

'Another land of make-believe,' he said aloud as he turned away and walked back to the city through the Botanical Gardens.

Later that night, in the dimmed lights of the Accident and Emergency Department of St Peter's Hospital, Isaac and David Medlock were using a lull in the nightly procession of injuries to discuss the 'welfare state'.

Medlock was sitting on one of the casualty beds, with Isaac in the chair next to it, drinking cups of hot chocolate, the curtains drawn around them.

'Reluctantly I have agreed to serve on the new BHGMC,' Isaac said wearily.

'The what?' asked the younger doctor.

'The Bath Hospital Group Management Committee. Not only is it responsible for St Peter's, but now I'm involved in nine other hospitals as well!'

'Did you hear Aneurin Bevan on the radio?' Medlock took another mouthful of chocolate before continuing. 'He is determined that nothing will prevent free health care for everyone. With penicillin and the new antibiotics he thinks costs will fall as the nation's health improves.'

'I'm not convinced,' Isaac said and remembered the William Pitt Club dinner at Christmas 1946. Everything Alan Buxton,

Bath's MP and the Shadow Foreign Secretary, had predicted was coming true.

'Socialist Armageddon. The wholesale slaughter of capitalism and the massacre of the middle classes,' was how Malcolm Austwick had dramatically described the position at the first meeting of the newly created Bath Group Hospital Management Committee. The William Pitt Club might be a spent force, but good old Malcolm still had plenty of legal work even if he was bemoaning 'the ultimate horror' of the latest Town and Country Planning Act.

Isaac had read something about it in the newspaper but found it hard to fathom, which, Malcolm explained, was totally understandable; such was its complexity that even the Lord Chancellor, the Chief Law Officer of England, found it totally incomprehensible.

'But don't be fooled, Isaac,' he said, 'its detail may be difficult to grasp, but its intention is very simple. This Labour government is stealing any future increase in value in every building and piece of land in the kingdom.' He then added that such complicated legislation was a gift for him and other professionals because it generated endless work and fees for years to come.

Suddenly, the curtains parted.

'Can you come quickly doctors, its Councillor Kohut, a heart attack,' the nurse said.

Yet another of the old guard, and member of the club, Isaac thought, nodding to Mrs Kohut as he went through the closed curtains. He liked this down-to-earth, bluff, no-nonsense man.

'Hello Ken, how are you doing?' As always with sudden emergencies, it took Isaac a moment to adapt to seeing powerful people, naked and vulnerable.

'Not so good Isaac.' The ashen but sweating face said it all.

'Can you feel anything in your chest, tightness, like a steel band?'

'Are you kidding, I've got a whole philharmonic orchestra playing in here!' Isaac laughed.

Kohut closed his eyes as the next wave of pain hit him. It proved too much, and Isaac declared him dead fifteen minutes later.

CHAPTER TWENTY-FOUR

Throughout his first months at school, acute homesickness motivated every letter Yann wrote to his mother. His surroundings, though beautiful, were harsh by comparison with the warmth and affection that he had received during his young life at the blind home. Instead of living among kindly elderly people who indulged him, Yann learned how to survive the cruel and often barbaric behaviour of a schoolboy herd. Be brave, Ruth wrote, this is a small price to pay to become a well-educated English gentleman.

Painfully he adapted and before long Yann was integrated into the English public school bear garden, hardened but never confident. His feelings and emotions figured less in letters during the spring term, and by the summer had vanished. His weekly epistles home, a compulsory part of Sunday evenings, spoke only of 'rugger', 'tuck', 'dorms', 'prep' and 'gatings', involving boys with 'Major' or 'Minor' after their names; it never occurred to him that his mother wouldn't understand.

He still missed her and like all boarders, looked forward to the holidays, but they proved an anti-climax. His mother's enthusiastic hugs embarrassed him and he was easily bored with the elderly patients and their basket-making. He deeply missed Uncle Sebastian, who he knew would have enjoyed hearing about what happened at school. He took to spending days alone in the library, undisturbed, with its books which he felt unable to share with his mother. He loved Uncle Isaac and Aunt Naomi, but missed the company of other boys, and his return to Beaconsfield could never come round quick enough.

Unspoken, another problem grew. He became conscious that his mother was different to other boys' parents, and, as a result he denied her any involvement with Beaconsfield. Yann's letters never mentioned the various parent occasions held during the school year. When occasionally she raised the subject he dismissed such events as unimportant. 'A waste of your precious pennies' he would say. Ruth believed him, relieved that she didn't have to ask for time off, and grateful that her hard-earned wages did not have to be spent travelling across country for a school function that would only last an hour or two. Yann separated home and school; this was easier for both mother and child. He could never admit to being ashamed of his mother. After all he loved her, but she was different from other boys' mothers, and this made him feel vulnerable.

CHAPTER TWENTY-FIVE

Amanda McKendrick's prediction about Cassofiori House proved accurate. In June 1949 she gathered the entire staff together in the drawing room and reluctantly informed them that the Blind Home would close by September.

It wasn't a surprise for many as over the previous twelve months, when some older residents died, their rooms had remained empty. The trust, they were told, was financially exhausted and the house and its contents were to be auctioned off. All the remaining patients would be dispersed to other homes and the staff were given notice.

Three months later, while Ruth waited for the taxi which would take her away from Cassofiori House forever, she took the opportunity to wander around the Home for one final time. On entering the drawing room, she spied Sebastian's magnificent glass bison, a foot long and nine inches high, resting as always on its plinth. An auctioneer's lot number ticket was tied round one of its horns in readiness for the sale of contents in a few days. She thought back to the first time she had seen the sculpture when introduced to Sebastian by Sandie Whitcroft. It had been one of his favourite possessions, and she remembered the story of how he had come by it. His father sent him to the islands of Murano at the behest of one of the bank's aristocratic

Venetian clients who owned a glass factory there dating back to the fifteenth century.

In 1915 Italy had accepted the British invitation to join the Allies and declared war on Germany. Desperate to get round wartime lira exchange controls, in 1916 Sir Samuel Cassofiori had created a highly convoluted method, employing letters of credit drawn on the Banca Di Venezia, and French bearer bonds, whereby much of the client's wealth could be transferred out of Italy to Paris and then on to the London Bank. It was Sebastian's first solo trip representing the House of Cassofiori. When all had been achieved at the bank in the Via San Marco and he was leaving Venice, the maestro had presented him with the magnificent bison as a gift and explained how it had been shaped out of a single block of pale green glass and then coated with gold leaf; the finished beast weighed over fifteen pounds.

Often, when she found Sebastian waiting for their customary newspaper readings, Ruth would come across him stroking the coarse glass finish and his fingertips continued to trace the bold contours as they talked.

Standing alone in the room now, she had an overwhelming desire to hold the beast, grasp it close to her, grieving the loss of Sebastian and the remembrance of all those glorious and countless hours spent together. She lifted the statue but it was far heavier than she realised. It slipped, and crashed to the floor. She stared at the dozen or so large pieces of green glass and the countless shards. It was shattered beyond repair.

'Sebastian, I am so sorry,' she sobbed, she broke down and wept, kneeling over the shattered beauty of the lost love and friendship.

CHAPTER TWENTY-SIX

Although she received an excellent reference from Amanda McKendrick, Ruth was anxious about finding another job after Cassofiori House closed. She moved back with Naomi and Isaac for Yann's summer holidays, but, despite their assurances that she could stay as long as it took to find the right job, she was desperate to become independent again.

Work was scarce and she soon realised that only menial work was an option. Panicking lest she found herself without income, and more importantly a home for Yann when he returned from Beaconsfield for the Christmas holiday, she was grateful for the offer of employment as housekeeper in a large house, in the nearby village of Limpley Stoke. It came with a tied cottage.

The house, Rowas Grange, was owned by the third Earl Lundy, Marmaduke, and although he was mild enough, his wife, Emily, had an awful reputation. Ruth soon realised that the title of housekeeper was a euphemism for a lowly paid general dogsbody in a large house with insufficient staff. She stayed because of the little cottage. She reasoned that this would provide a home for Yann, with the freedom to wander in the thousand or so acres of Earl Lundy's magnificent estate that stretched along the whole side of the Limpley Stoke valley. Yann might even make friends with the future fourth Earl Lundy, Alistair, who would return for Christmas from his Oxford boarding school. He was the same age as Yann and perhaps such a friendship could bring advantages to her son.

'As a matter of principle,' was Lady Lundy's excuse for refusing to let Ruth have a day off to meet Yann at Waterloo on his return from school. She thought it inappropriate for servants to send their children away to private schools. 'Isn't the local primary school good enough?' she asked. 'That would save you all the bother of going anywhere to fetch him and he might be usefully employed on the estate.'

The cottage was over a hundred years old, and included a very temperamental supply of cold water. In winter, Ruth discovered that it froze at the first hint of a frost and became a brown trickle if rain hadn't fallen in the previous week. When this happened, she had to resort to fetching water in a bucket from a standpipe in the courtyard at the rear of the main house.

Naomi collected Yann from Waterloo and Ruth was waiting on the platform as the train drew into Green Park Station. She wanted time to prepare him for their new home. During the bus journey she explained that although the cottage was 'in a beautiful setting', it was 'a little basic'. She told him of the Christmas service that they had been invited to at the main house and suggested this could give him a good opportunity to meet Earl Lundy's son, Alistair.

The bus dropped them off at the main gates and Yann was lulled into complacency by the imposing entranceway and long drive up to and past the main house. Then they reached the neglected cottage. An idyll in the summer when surrounded by wild flowers and roses rambling over the doorway, it looked drab and unwelcoming in the freezing drizzle of a dull December afternoon. Ruth leant her weight against the front door to coax the warped wood across the uneven threshold and Yann followed her into the gloomy front room.

Even to the child's inexperienced eyes in the dark interior, it was apparent that as little as possible had been spent on fitting out and furnishing the cottage. He started to wonder if there was even electricity until he saw his mother reach up to a metal box by the front door and push some coins into it. Then, a bare overhead bulb glowed yellow above a few shabby items of furniture. He rightly assumed that the brightly patterned curtains hanging at the window had been made by his mother because they were so incongruously cheery in the dingy setting. He swallowed hard and did his best to conceal the growing horror he felt, as his mother showed him around the hovel that was now their home.

They managed to maneouvre his school suitcase up the narrow staircase and into the cupboard-sized bedroom. There was just enough space for it to stand on its end and Yann wondered how they would manage in the summertime when his whole trunk would need to be accommodated.

Then there was the lavatory, or rather the lack of one. The tin Elson chemical bucket was in a small garden shed behind the cottage. Ruth quickly explained that it had to be emptied each week, but didn't dwell on what that meant.

Later, his mother had to return to the big house as it was the cook's night off and she had to prepare and serve the evening meal. By this time, Yann could no longer put off a trip to the privy. No matter how his mother had scrubbed and cleaned, the strong chemical could not mask the smell of decades of human excrement. Retching, he grabbed a handful of newspaper and fled into the woodland to the rear of the cottage.

A few days later it was Christmas Eve and all of the servants and their children were invited to a carol service around the big tree in the main house. The size and grandeur of the Grange reminded Yann of Cassofiori House, but it lacked the friendliness of the Blind Home and instead of being made to feel welcome within its walls, Yann felt very uncomfortable. He was struggling to deal with his mother's situation and attended the festive gathering under protest.

His love of historical novels had taught him about the class system, and though not yet eight, 'feudal' sprung to mind as he found his bearings in the geography both of the grounds and social structure of the Lundy's estate and Rowas Grange Estate. His face bore no emotion as he stood amongst the other estate workers and their children in their ill-fitting Sunday best, but bitterness grew behind the mask. His mother had insisted upon him wearing his school uniform, and clad in its purple blazer and yellow piping, he skulked behind the Christmas tree, silent during the Christmas carols, the words of which he did not know. Afterwards everyone filed out, shaking hands with Earl and Lady Lundy as well as their daughter, Fiona, and son, Alistair. Father and daughter were friendly with festive cheer, but Lady Lundy maintained her superior chill and her son wore a perpetual sneer.

'Oh yes, the housekeeper's son,' the pale boy said. Unlike Yann, he had obviously been allowed to wear mufti. 'Mater has told me about you.' He gave a half smile while looking Yann up and down.

'A very arrogant young man,' Ruth said as they walked back to the cottage. It was a clear cold night with a sharp frost, and a promise of snow.

'Don't let it upset you Mother,' Yann said, squeezing her hand. 'I've met the type before.' He pushed open the wooden gate to the cottage. 'I'm really looking forward to seeing Uncle Isaac and Auntie Naomi tomorrow – it will be just like old times.'

'I'm so sorry that I have to work but Uncle Isaac will come to collect you before I go on duty.' Ruth unlatched the front door.

Before leaving for the carol service, she had banked the little fire up and there was still a small welcoming glow. She bent to the coal bucket and reached in to put some more on the embers.

'I'm whacked and going to turn in,' he said and, kissing his mother, thankfully climbed the narrow staircase up to his bedroom. Conscious of the electricity meter's ferocious appetite for his mother's precious sixpences, once in bed he forwent his usual read and turned off the bedside light. He recognised the empty Chianti bottle with a straw base to which his mother had added a lampshade from Cassofiori House and thought of happier times before falling sleep.

For the next couple of hours Ruth ironed the clothes Yann would require over Christmas, alternatively using the two flat irons warming in front of the fire. Then she followed him up, and opened his bedroom door quietly to check all was well. She treasured these holiday nights together and lingered, watching him.

Unusually, the boy was restless. The sheet and blankets had fallen off him and hung down from the low cast iron bed. Lying on his stomach, his back was exposed where his pyjama top had ridden up. She moved towards the bed, and bending down, picked up the fallen bedclothes, before something on the boy's back caught her eye in the moonlight. She slowly raised the pyjama jacket and looked at Yann's lower back – it was covered with a latticework of bluish purple welts each yellow at the edges and about two inches wide. Numbed with horror, she very gently lowered the top of the pyjama trousers. He stirred but did not wake. The stripes extended all over his buttocks.

CHAPTER TWENTY-SEVEN

The beating from the headmaster, Mr Corrigan, came about as a result of the only real friendship Yann made at Beaconsfield. Lieberman was a year older and in the same House, Galsworthy. Unlike Yann, he never tried to hide his parents' humble beginnings, and the snobbishness of others made the two natural allies.

Lieberman's father, Max, was a Russian immigrant, who had found himself stranded and alone in the East End of London at the age of thirteen. Far taller and stronger than he should have been for his age, Max made a living among the tightly knit community of Irish Catholics who worked in the docks.

Thieving was a way of life among dockers as it was the only way they could often survive the corrupt and crushing casual daily hiring system. One day his gang boss had given Lieberman a small sack of peanuts, which had 'fallen off the back of a ship' and no one else wanted. Back at his digs, one of Widow Jablonsky's tiny attic rooms behind Hackney High Street, he opened the sack and shelled and ate one of the nuts. They were tasteless. He scrounged some brown paper bags from the downstairs greengrocer, and tried selling them to the chestnut vendors, who manned the roasting carts in Whitechapel. But there were no takers. So he spent a night shelling the whole sack. He was amazed at how small a yield of nuts such a large sack produced, but then he discovered one of the fundamental rules of marketing. Discarding the large brown bags, he switched to much smaller penny sweet bags, and the local music hall took the entire consignment on a sale or return basis. They sold them all at a single Saturday night's show.

On the following Monday morning he asked around about peanuts, and eventually found and followed the main consignment from the docks to Covent Garden market, and the importer. Trade was slack and the trader happily sold him another bag. Borrowing a docker's handcart, Max Lieberman was soon buying three, then four, then a dozen sacks of peanuts because of the growing demand from the East End music halls. When fifteen, he quit the docks, rented a small room and yard, bought his own handcart and paid his landlady's eighteen-year-old daughter, Zelda, to help him shell and put the nuts into bags. They were two of a kind; Lieberman saw his future in peanuts and Zelda in Lieberman.

Working up to twenty hours a day, seven days a week, the business flourished. Love never came into the equation because neither had the time nor energy to look for sex elsewhere. Soon they were hiring another girl, and then more and more came to work. Constantly moving, needing ever-larger premises, they finally settled for a warehouse fronting the very same dock from where Lieberman had obtained his first sack of stolen peanuts. His Irish dock gang were now on his permanent payroll and devoted to him. Although he was a yid, Max was a working class boy, one of them who had made good.

When, after four years of sharing his bed, Zelda announced that she was pregnant, Lieberman took her off to the local synagogue and married her. They only had the one son, Henry, and Zelda stopped working and stayed home. Within ten years Lieberman was the largest importer of nuts in

England. Not just peanuts, he branched out into other varieties, and his brand, with its cheeky little Miss Hazelnut logo became a household name.

The Lieberman home was a large modern house in Leytonstone that had been chosen by Zelda. She was clever enough to realise that her husband's only criterion was that it be in easy reach of his beloved warehouse.

Henry was proud that his father was a self-made man and sometimes he would deliberately mimic his father's bizarre way of speaking – English with a strong Russian accent, tinged with Irish and cockney. His father's attendance at school events in a pink Rolls Royce elicited snide comments from the other boys and earned him the nickname of Monkeynut Boy. But Henry had inherited his father's physique and, when necessary, his fists would silence vicious tongues into sullen respect.

Yann lacked Henry's confidence and size. All he wished was to conceal his poverty and his mother's Polish background. However, Mr Corrigan's sly and malicious hints about his background, along with his small size and naivety, immediately set him apart from the other pupils. His initial pride in his mother being housekeeper at Cassofiori House was met by sniggers, and by the time he had learned to keep his mouth shut, it was too late.

Every Saturday night a list would be pinned up outside the school tuck shop showing the boys for whom parcels had arrived from home. On the following afternoon, the eagerly awaited parcels were handed out in the respective houses by a prefect.

As often as she could, Ruth sent Yann a cake and on one particular Sunday afternoon some weeks prior to the Christmas holiday, Yann stood in line with the other boys looking forward to receiving his treat. The parcels were handed out in alphabetical order and so Lieberman stood directly in front of him. A boy called Weitzman was in charge. He was a bully and feared by the young boys, but as his father was one of the biggest benefactors to the school, he was a favourite of Mr Corrigan.

'Ackerman, Bloom!' he shouted, and the first two boys in line walked up for their parcels. More names were called and, two by two, the boys in front of Lieberman collected their parcels and departed.

'Lieberman, Morris!' Their turn came and they dutifully walked up to the older boy. 'Well, Monkeynut Boy,' said Weitzman, 'what do you think is in here? A sack of peanuts?' He started to shake the parcel violently until Lieberman stepped forward and grasped it, his large hands completely enveloping those of the older, but smaller boy. He stood there, staring at the prefect for a few seconds before taking the parcel. Weitzman blushed but turned to the package for Morris, and keen to make good his humiliation, held it at arm's length, slightly above Yann's head.

'Ah, Morris, you would think a housekeeper could do better than this – the one that works for my parents certainly can,' he said, holding the badly wrapped parcel at arm's length like a bad smell with the slack string between index finger and thumb. Yann stepped forward and reached out to take it, but before he could get to it, Weitzman deliberately dropped it. It fell to the floor with a thud, and the brown paper split, exposing the fruitcake.

'You did that on purpose!' Lieberman said.

'Who the hell do you think you are talking to, Monkeynut Boy?'

'Apologise to Morris.' He moved towards the prefect.

'You've got to be joking.'

'Leave it, Lieberman, it's not important,' Yann said, conscious of the boys still waiting for their parcels staring at them. But Lieberman ignored him and caught Weitzman's arm, forcing it up behind his back.

'I said, apologise.'

'Take your filthy monkey paws off me!' the older boy's voice quavered.

The arm was pushed higher. 'Apologise,' and then higher again.

The crack and Weitzman's scream were simultaneous.

Later that evening after prep, Yann was summoned to the headmaster's study. Lieberman was to follow him an hour later.   Such summonses always came at night, a boy being summoned from his bed into the utter darkness surrounding the headmaster's study. Corrigan glowered at him from across the large desk, lit by a sole table lamp. Yann had never seen anyone look so angry; he was terrified and started to shake violently.

'I always said it was a mistake letting someone from your background come into this school, but they wouldn't listen. Now I have an unholy alliance between the offspring of an Essex peanut seller, a bloody hooligan who goes around breaking other boys arms, and you, the son of a domestic servant. You have attacked and gravely injured one of our star pupils, the son of the school's most important patron and benefactor. We could be sued with unthinkable consequences. Well, I'll tell you what I am going to do in relation to you two louts. I am going to teach you to behave like gentlemen and give you a thrashing that you will never forget for the rest of your life.'

Corrigan reached into his drawer for one of the many means by which he could gain pleasure from beating boys. A two inch wide leather strap, originally designed for stropping cut-throat razors, was selected.

In the dormitory, long past lights out, and unable to sleep, Yann lay on his stomach, whimpering from the pain. Suddenly he was aware of a hand on his shoulder, and looked up to see Lieberman's face in the moonlight.

'How goes it?'

'Sore, very sore, and you?'

'I'm ok, but I'm sorry you got thrashed on my account. Anyway, just thought I would check that you were okay. Chin up, we'll survive.'

Over the next three years, the two boys became inseparable. Lieberman was Morris's first true friend.

Yann began spending many of his holidays with Lieberman at his Essex home. Ruth had to reluctantly accept this, but loved him the more when he did come home. During the Christmas holidays in 1950, Earl Lundy's son, Alistair, had come across Yann walking in the Rowas Grange Estate woodlands and questioned his right to do so. Balking at his patronising tone, Yann had simply walked away, leaving the boy fuming. Later that day Ruth was summoned by Lady Lundy and summarily dismissed with seven days to move out of the cottage.

Yann felt shame and anger at the gloating smile on Alistair's face, as he watched Earl Lundy's bailiff supervise the eviction of mother and son with their pitifully few personal possessions. He wasn't sorry to leave. He never forgot the stinking privy or the glistening slimy slug tracks criss-crossing the sitting room rug in that awful cottage.

CHAPTER TWENTY-EIGHT

The two sailors pulled the stern mooring hawser aboard, and the S.S. White Knight, a dry cargo ship of 5,000 tons, moved away from the derelict wharf buildings, and nosed her way out into the Thames. The heavy rain had eased to an unrelenting drizzle.

Naomi's hand grasped the wet handrail, the fingers of the other clasped Isaac's arm tightly; the feel of the smooth wood contrasting with the rough texture of his overcoat. Drips from his umbrella found their way between collar and neck, running down her back. The few other passengers on deck were mainly elderly and shabby, clad in the dull clothing of lingering wartime rationing. Everyone stared at the small knot of people standing on the Albert Dock; some of the women were quietly crying.

Watching Ruth and Yann on the dockside become smaller as the ship moved off brought tears to her eyes. Apart from Isaac, these were the two most important people in her life and she was abandoning them. The river's murky vapor, together with the drizzle, soon merged the two figures into one indistinct shape and then swallowed them.

The other passengers went below to flee the damp coldness but she and Isaac remained on deck. The dirty smell of water, diesel and London's smog had made Naomi feel queasy even before the ship had started moving but now she felt worse.

She was leaving England for the first and last time, never to return. She thought the decision was a terrible mistake but had no choice. Driven by his lifelong obsession, would Isaac have really gone without her? She had not been prepared to take that risk.

As the East End landscape slid by, Isaac's memories went back fifty or so years to his childhood; his mother's death and the Zionist meetings attended by his father. What if his father had never given him Herzl's book? Would he be here now, and if his father had never inscribed it 'Next year in Jerusalem?' Would he be on this rust bucket bound for the eastern Mediterranean? Had it only been two years since the phone call? He would never forget that day in 1947.

The persistent ringing had woken him and he fumbled for the light switch before lifting the black receiver from the cradle of the telephone. What emergency had arisen at the hospital to have prompted such an early call from the night staff?

'Isaac, it's Marcus Rose. I apologise for calling you so early but it's important that we meet this morning. I'm in London at the moment but have to pass through Bath to be in Bristol by noon. Can we arrange to meet at ten?' Isaac let the question hang for a moment – he had last seen him when they had sat *Shivah* after Sebastian's funeral; a dreadfully depressing affair amongst the blind of Cassofiori House. Mentally checking his day ahead, he replied, 'Yes of course, Marcus.'

'At your home would be best, and hopefully Naomi could then also be there, if that's possible?'

'I shouldn't think that will be a problem. What's wrong?'

'I'll explain everything when I see you.'

Mystified, Isaac replaced the receiver and saw that Naomi had awoken and was turned towards him.

'That was Marcus Rose.'

'From the Blind Society, what did he want at this early hour?'

'I've no idea but he's going to be here at ten o'clock and wants to see us both.' Isaac glanced at his watch; it was barely six o'clock. 'You go back to sleep and I'll bring you up a cup of tea in about an hour. Now I'm awake, I might as well get up.' Switching the light off again, he went through to the bathroom, pondering what Marcus might want.

After a bath, he stood before the washbasin, reached for his shaving mug and filled it with warm water. He dipped his brush into the water, vigorously applied soap to build a creamy foam and then brushed it onto his face with his right hand while wiping the condensation from the mirror in front of him with his left. Picking up his newly acquired Gillette safety razor, he started to shave. Left side from sideburn to chin and then the same sweep to the right. Why Naomi, he thought, as the razor moved from chin to neck and along each jowl.

By the time he returned to the bedroom, Naomi had fallen back to sleep. Leaving the door ajar, he quietly dressed in the light from the bathroom. He went down to the kitchen and put the kettle on.

A little later, he gently pushed the bedroom door open and placed the tray on the dressing table and poured two cups of tea. Placing one on her bedside table, he kissed his wife, and sat himself at the end of the bed sipping the other.

'What's the time?' she asked drowsily.

Without answering he went to the over mantel and the old Bakelite wireless. He switched it on and as the tuning dial glowed yellow, the set hummed and came alive. Permanently set to the Home Service, they listened to the general weather forecast followed by the shipping forecast before Isaac turned up the volume as the pips sounded.

'This is Alvar Liddell and here is the seven o'clock news for today, Friday the 14th of May. The Egyptian Government has announced that it will be moving troops across the Palestine frontier one minute after the British mandate ends at midnight tonight. The appointment of a neutral commissioner for Jerusalem has been made by the United Nations.'

There was other news but the only item of interest to Isaac was the news in Palestine. He listened avidly to the kitchen wireless for the eight o'clock bulletin and again at nine o'clock, while Naomi was baking. This time Lidell solemnly announced the news Isaac had been waiting for.

'At eleven o'clock local time the following statement was read out on the steps of the Tel Aviv Museum in Palestine: "On the 29th of November, 1947, the United Nations General Assembly passed a resolution calling for the establishment of a Jewish State in Eretz-Israel; the General Assembly required the inhabitants of Eretz-Israel to take such steps as were necessary on their part for the implementation of that resolution. This recognition by the United Nations of the right of the Jewish people to establish their State is irrevocable. This right is the natural right of the Jewish people to be masters of their own fate, like all other nations, in their own sovereign State."'

Liddell's voice became more serious as he continued to quote from his script:

'"Accordingly we, members of the people's council, representatives of the Jewish community of Eretz-Israel and of the Zionist movement, are here assembled on the day of the termination of the British mandate over Eretz-Israel and, by virtue of our natural and historic right and on the strength of the resolution of the United Nations General Assembly, hereby declare the establishment of a Jewish state in Eretz-Israel, to be known as the State of Israel".'

Liddell paused for a moment before continuing.

'This Declaration has been signed by David Ben-Gurion and thirty-six of some of the most eminent Jews in Palestine, or should I say Israel, acting as a Provisional Council of State. It will come into effect at midnight tonight, when the British Mandate over Palestine terminates.'

Isaac was shaking by the time Liddell had finished. He didn't know whether to laugh or cry or both. Naomi saved him the choice when she wiped her floury hands on her apron, walked around the kitchen table and took him into her arms.

An hour later, Naomi served the coffee and turned to leave the two men to talk in the library.

'Please stay, Naomi. What I have to say concerns both of you,' Marcus Rose said.

'Well, to what do we owe this pleasure?' Isaac had recovered from the news bulletin and Naomi sat down next to him on the sofa. Instinctively her hand found his, something she always did when anticipating bad news and he couldn't think why she should feel like this on a day like today.

'You heard the news?'

'Wonderful isn't it?' Isaac felt pretty sure that Marcus Rose would have been of the same opinion as him. Wouldn't every Jew?

'Although the next few days are critical if the State of Israel is to survive.' It was the first time Isaac had heard the name Israel instead of Palestine used in conversation and he felt a frisson of excitement pass through his body. Marcus then clarified something that had been alluded to on the BBC. All of Israel's Arab neighbours planned to invade simultaneously over the next twenty-four hours with the backing of the

Russian government. It was going to be down to just how much support America was willing to give the fledgling country. Marcus believed that if the State of Israel could survive its first two weeks, it would continue to exist.

'I'm assuming it can, otherwise my visit here will have been for nothing.' He looked at Naomi and then at Isaac. ' Look, I'm pushed for time, the aeroplane leaves Bristol in about three hours.'

'The aeroplane?' Isaac was trying to work out where the conversation was going.

'May I ask you to treat this meeting and what we discuss in confidence?' Without waiting for their affirmation, Marcus then posed another question. 'Do you know what I did in the Second World War?'

'Not really. I seem to remember that you were seconded to some obscure department.' Isaac couldn't even say where he had heard that from, but knew that Marcus Rose was known in Jewish circles to have had considerable clout behind the scenes during the last war.

'The obscure department as you call it, was Military Intelligence,' Marcus said. 'When the Brigade was formed in 1944 I was its Anglo-Jewish liaison officer, reporting directly to Churchill and the War Cabinet.' Isaac knew he was talking about the Jewish Brigade, but had no time to think about what this role entailed before Marcus added, 'And so I was pleased when you and I finally had the good fortune to actually meet – Isaac Abrahams, membership number 411.'

Isaac took a deep breath at hearing the number mentioned and felt Naomi's hand stiffen in his. 'How on earth?'

Marcus didn't give him the chance to continue.

'It was my job to know everything about the membership of the Zionist movement in England. And your very early membership along with your generosity over the years hasn't gone unnoticed.'

Naomi drew her hand away, and turned to her husband.

'All those years, when we had hardly two halfpennies to rub together, you were giving money to the Zionists?' She sounded incredulous more than angry, but disappointed too – probably because it was something he had kept from her.

'I will come straight to the point,' Marcus didn't react to Naomi's remark. 'We desperately need surgeons with war experience. I have been authorised to offer you the role of head of surgery in the largest hospital in Israel. If the pledges come through from America, you will want for nothing, it will be one of the finest hospitals in the world. Put simply, will you accept the position?'

Isaac wanted to jump up and hug the man but was too stunned to move.

'Next year in Jerusalem?' Oh yes! Oh yes! But instead he saw Naomi's slight figure rise from the sofa and loom in front of him.

'No, Isaac. Are you mad? England is our home. We are English, not Palestinian or Israeli.' Her voice rose with each word until she was shouting. 'Tell him. Isaac, tell him. No. Tell him we won't go. Never!'

Isaac gathered her to him, trying to calm the panic.

'Please let Marcus go on, Naomi. This is very important and the least we can do is hear him out.'

'You hear him out, I want nothing more to do with this madness. Yes, if you are crazy enough to give your hard-earned savings to a load of zealots, that's up to you. All these years and you never said anything. You didn't trust me, did you?' She didn't finish, sobbing, she fled the room.

The two men sat in silence.

'I'm sorry Isaac, I should never have come, but although there is no immediate urgency for you to depart, we have to put plans in place.'

'What does Susan make of all this?' Isaac had met Marcus's wife on a number of occasions at Cassofiori House, and there had been the odd invitation to Widcombe House. He knew that there was a very streetwise woman behind Susan's sophistication. Like himself, she had hauled herself out of the poverty of the East End.

'She's staying in England for the time being.' He did not elaborate and Isaac did not press him.

'I'm pleased you have come and rest assured, I will accept. I know I have to go, with or without Naomi. Although God help me if she refuses.'

But, as the good wife she had always been, and because she loved him, she eventually agreed to go with him. He wished he had told her about the money he had given to the Zionist movement. Initially there was sullenness and little conversation after Marcus's visit, but once she understood that Isaac was going, there could be only one outcome. It took much longer for the new country's plans to be acted on than Isaac had originally assumed, but finally the orders came through. The lease of the house was ended, and their lives in England finished. There was some talk of Ruth and Yann joining them in a year or two, but it came to nothing.

Isaac looked back along the grubby crest of wavelets that the SS White Knight left in her wake on the muddy waters of the Thames. Long out of sight of the quayside where he knew the mother and child would still be standing, Isaac wondered when or if he would ever see them again.

CHAPTER TWENTY-NINE

By the start of his fourth year at Beaconsfield, Yann had everything under control, with his two lives tuned to perfection and quite separate. Anything concerning Beaconsfield stayed inside school walls and to survive there, amongst the self-assured offspring of wealthy parents, he let nothing about home surface. One problem, however, that he couldn't overcome, was his mother's insistence on knitting his pullovers.

There were about thirty boys milling around in the main assembly hall at second break, when Hugh Jones, head of speech and drama, made his entrance. For that is what it was as he strode across the expanse of parquet flooring, black gown flowing behind him like a huge raven, and stopped centre-stage in front of the notice board. He located four brass drawing pins and slowly pinned up the cast list for *Quack* – his adaptation of the Hans Christian Andersen tale of *The Ugly Duckling* for which rehearsals would soon begin.

Excitedly, a dozen or so boys with theatrical aspirations closed in, jostling for first sight. Parts, no matter how small, were eagerly sought, because with rehearsals came staying up late, being excused choir practice, and best of all, extra helpings at late supper. The bigger the role the better, and enormous prestige went with the two lead parts, always allotted to boys in their last year.

'Well done, Morris,' Yann heard from someone as he walked

along the corridor towards the main assembly. On seeing the scramble of boys around the notice board, he assumed he had landed a small part in the forthcoming production and was pleased. He guessed that it would be a swan or something similar in a crowd scene. No lines but lots of rehearsals – the perfect role. He made his way through the dispersing throng amid groans of disappointment from the unselected. Some of the leavers slapped Yann on the back and others muttered, 'Congrats Morris,' or 'How did you pull that one off?' Confused, Yann looked up at Jones's large flowing handwriting:

QUACK
First lead:	*The Cat – Olsberg (Major)*
Second lead:	*The Ugly Duckling – Morris*
Swans:…	

Later he worked it out, it was the pullover. Why couldn't he go to Bentalls Department Store in Tunbridge Wells like the other boys? Money was short, but why couldn't she knit him socks or something that didn't show? He didn't care if handmade was better or warmer, he'd still rather freeze than be different.

He felt ashamed about the school photograph – row upon row of shop bought perfect machine made pullovers, and his awful baggy thing that hung down at the waist. And it was covered in bobbles, little mutating balls of fluff that he picked off continually but still multiplied daily.

He hated being different, really hated it, and Jones had no right making him play that part. Why couldn't his mother, just for once, listen to him? All he wanted to be was a swan in a Bentalls pullover.

His thoughts were interrupted.

'Morris!' shouted a prefect giving out letters. Yann had

completely forgotten why he had been making his way to main assembly in the first place.

'Morris!' again came the call, then the prefect spotted him. 'Wake up Morris, anyone would think you don't want a letter.'

He flicked the letter at him through the air like a cigarette card. Still pondering the implications of *Quack*, Yann wandered back to the junior study room where the letter could be read in the only private place a boy could find in the whole school – under the lid of his desk.

Bath 30th September 1951

My darling Yann,

Dreadful news. We must be very brave. There is no easy way to tell you this. Auntie Naomi and Uncle Isaac were killed five days ago. Their bus hit a land mine...

CHAPTER THIRTY

The bell for the first lesson was seconds away. Yann lifted the wooden lid of his desk and fumbled through books, papers, pens and pencils. He found his timetable and the relevant textbook, silently offering up a prayer that this Wednesday, always the crummiest day in the week, would be different. He sighed, it wasn't. 6th February 1952 was as crummy as the past four crummy Wednesdays, or for that matter, the past forty – worse still Wednesday crumminess stretched endlessly into the future. Latin, double maths, English Lit. All before lunch.

Why couldn't it be *Hornblower* instead of that soppy *Romeo and Juliet*? Then lunch with steamed white fish, smelling of sick and almost raw boiled potatoes with soggy cabbage, stewed to extinction. As always, Ackerman's protest that fish made him come out in spots would fall on deaf ears, and he would try to hide bits of it under the cabbage, but it didn't work. Still he'd got away without eating it all in the excitement of last Wednesday, when he had cut open a potato to reveal a live baby slug that had survived the boiling water. Fascinated, all including the table prefect had watched it uncurl and make a dash, albeit a very slow and unsuccessful one, for freedom. The table prefect hadn't made him eat the dissected bits, before the 'Dead Baby' arrived – dense grey suet pudding and lumpy custard, with its thick gelatinous skin from hours of overcooking.

His mood lightened when he thought about Games after

lunch, but instantly gloom returned. Wednesday was not a football day. Yann looked at the slate-grey sky promising yet more snow, and the dreaded cross country run, pounding across ploughed fields, the furrows hitting the soles of his feet through his plimsoles.

Then it would be back to the large concrete bath. If only he were a better runner – the first few got the water while it was still lukewarm, and free from the sweat and mud of the forty or so later finishers.

And after that it was crummy woodwork. An hour of misery in that ill-fitting brown overall with its missing buttons and chafing collar from years of fierce starching. Amid the oil and wood shavings of the unheated workshop, he was making a mortise and tenon joint, or at least had been trying to produce such a thing for the last six weeks. Why did his efforts never fit, or worse still, split when he resorted to hammering the two pieces of wood together? Now on his fourth attempt, his workshop master had put it succinctly in his last report: 'Morris is not a natural carpenter!'

The bell sounded and the classroom hushed, anticipating the imminent arrival of Mr North. The Latin master was strict, renowned for his punctuality, and like the subject he taught, demanded a slavish and meticulous adherence to the rules, be they for a verb conjugation or classroom behaviour. A minute late, or the slightest infringement, and the offender was put on report. But the master didn't arrive.

The lessons were boring because John North droned on with never a joke, or even a smile, the same old thing, lesson after lesson, day after day, week after week. Once he had caused a snigger. The usual sentences written on the blackboard for translation, involving Romans pursuing and killing Carthaginians in bizarre ways ceased, and were replaced by boys chasing maidens into the woods. A month later the Carthaginians were back killing everyone in sight and there was no more kissing. Lieberman, the worst Latin scholar in the class, worked out why the kissing had stopped – the newly married Mr North was back from his honeymoon.

Cohen at the next desk whispered loudly, 'I've never known Old North to be late. He's normally standing outside the door, waiting for the bell to ring. Perhaps he's dead and there'll be no Latin today.'

'Doubt it, nothing stops Latin, Corrigan will take over.'

Silence gradually deteriorated with rustles and evermore frequent whispers. After five minutes Cohen left his desk, walked slowly to the classroom door, pressed his ear against it, and then slowly opened it; no one! Yann got up and looked out of the first floor window at the other classrooms, arranged around the frost-covered triangle of lawn. Not a master in sight, all were unattended with other boys away from their desks staring out of the windows.

Suddenly a column of school prefects was marching in single file down the path, one peeling off to each classroom. 'Cave, prefects,' Yann hissed, and given the older boys' draconian powers to punish, instant order and silence returned.

Every classroom emptied and the boys were lined up on the freezing grass, and marched back to the main hall, as if for weekly assembly.

Hushed by such a momentous change in routine, the entire school stood six deep forming three sides of a rectangle. Facing them on the raised stage, the headmaster was on his dais, with all the staff arranged in a semi-circle behind him, everyone gowned and grim-faced. He crossed to the big wooden wireless and gramophone cabinet, usually used in Music Appreciation classes, and turned the knob. A minute or two of sombre music followed, then the announcer's voice boomed out around the hall.

'It is with the most profound grief that we announce the death of our beloved Sovereign, King George the Sixth. He died peacefully in his sleep early this morning, after retiring at Sandringham last night. In accordance with the constitution, Princess Elizabeth became Queen immediately upon the death of the King. This is the first time in British history that a Sovereign has acceded to the throne whilst abroad in the Commonwealth. The Queen is returning to London by aeroplane from Kenya today. She arrives at London Airport at six o'clock tonight.'

Yann had stopped listening. Good Old King George, he had stopped Latin. Who knows, this might be the best Wednesday yet. Double Maths, Shakespeare, the cross-country run, and woodwork, where would it all end?

After that it became rather boring, something about the Princess Royal convalescing from fibrositis and cancelling her trip to Switzerland, and Queen Mary becoming the Dowager Queen, now that her grand daughter is Queen. It went on and on. Yann had no idea what they were talking about and wasn't bothered about it. Forget the flags at half mast, he thought, is double Maths cancelled? Who cares about the Speaker of the House of Commons and the Privy Council, maybe the cross country and even woodwork could go. The headmaster switched off the wireless and walked back to the centre of the stage.

'This is a very sad day,' he said in a loud, slow and meticulously enunciated voice. 'I was born before 1901, and have known six reigns in the last fifty one years.' He ticked them off on his fingers. 'Queen Victoria, Edward the Seventh, George the Fifth, Edward the Eighth, George the Sixth and now Elizabeth the Second. As a mark of respect, all lessons and games are cancelled today.'

There really is a God, Yann thought, gratefully looking up at the ceiling.

CHAPTER THIRTY-ONE

Woken by his mother's rasping cough from her first cigarette of the day, Yann opened his eyes and looked for the colourful frieze that ran around the room at ceiling height with the Greek charioteer, reins in right hand and clinging on for life with his left, as he fled the blur of the pursuers with their spears. It wasn't there. Alarmed, he closed his eyes and opened them again before realising that it was the wrong ceiling, wrong picture, in fact no picture at all. Just yellow faded lining paper, peeling at the edges.

Then he remembered the week's holiday because of the Coronation.

Yann had crossed London with the Paddington Mob – the small contingent of boys who lived in the West Country – and was duly handed over to the guard on the Bath train. His mother had met him and they had walked from the station, up Southgate Street and into Paragon Buildings, where they had caught the bus that took them out to Snow Hill and their small terraced house in Mafeking Street.

In some ways, 36 Mafeking Street wasn't a lot better than the cottage at Rowas Grange Estate; it was gloomy with ill-fitting windows and no bathroom or hot water, but at least it had an inside WC. Also, Alistair Lundy wasn't lurking around to torment him. He was pleased that his mother had got a job as a hospital orderly at St Peter's and moved back into Bath.

The whole city seemed to be covered with Union Jacks, bunting, flags and banners. The formal and professionally made ones proclaimed: 'Greetings to her Majesty' and others, hand-painted: 'God Bless Our Bess.' All festooned the Georgian terraces. Some of the buildings damaged in the war added background colour; the Bath stone had gone pink from the severe heat generated by the bombs. In many cases trestle tables had been erected in readiness for street parties. Even in Mafeking Street, the majority of the modest houses had some sort of decoration hanging from windows or above front doors.

Yann didn't look forward to the day ahead but finally got up and dressed in the clothes laid out by his mother the night before. She had insisted that he wear his school blazer yet again, but at least that he would be able to cover it up with his raincoat before he left the house.

Ruth had secured two seats in the hospital lounge where Uncle Isaac used to work – she had actually won them in the hospital's Coronation sweepstake.

Later on, led by his mother, he crossed through the crowded canteen, full of people holding glasses, cigarettes or both and all talking very loudly, even shouting. They all seemed to have red cheeks and many had a sheen of perspiration on their palid foreheads. He was the only child present and felt trapped in the forest of white medical coats and nurses' uniforms towering over him.

Being on the domestic staff, Ruth didn't know anyone and so was greeted by no one as they threaded their way through the dense canopy of smoke and noise, into the staff lounge. All the sofas and armchairs had been removed, replaced by rows of canteen chairs with very little room between each. Those at the front were already occupied, so they took two at the back.

Facing them stood the television, placed on a pyramid of canteen tables stacked on top of each other. The first thing that struck Yann was how small the set was, it was tiny, much smaller than the one in the Lieberman house. He wondered how he would see anything, before realising that a large square magnifying lens had been fixed in front of its screen.

The room hushed as a man formally advanced from the front row and switched on the set as though it was the start of a magic show. The tiny screen lit up with a greenish light and the commentator's reverential tones overlaid the images.

'... and as I look at this vast throng of Her loyal subjects from the four corners of this United Kingdom, her Commonwealth, and indeed, the world who have flocked to pay homage to their beautiful young Queen. The whole might of British industry is here, short stocky coalminers from deep below the South Wales valleys, alongside burly ship builders from the great yards on the Tyne, used to hammering white-hot rivets into the steel plate of our mighty Navy. The tough men from Sheffield who made this steel. All standing shoulder to shoulder with our colonial cousins, spanning a third of the globe. Australia, New Zealand, India, Pakistan...'

Why did they always mention these countries in the same order? Perhaps it was because of the test matches and the cricket.

'Class and rank are forgotten on such great State occasions... All men are equal, master, servant, professional, shopkeeper, labourer...'

What nonsense, Yann thought, to suggest that anyone ever forgot their class in England. He looked at his mother, seated beside him, noting for the first time the few greying hairs and how lined her face had become. Her cheeks were sunken and he knew that not long ago her teeth had been replaced with a set of dentures. She told him it was due to gum disease, but he thought it was the cigarettes, and at least the false teeth weren't yellow. He examined the leathery texture of her skin that had developed, and the spidery wrinkles around her eyes, but she was intent on the tiny screen. He looked beyond her to the others in the audience and saw that everyone else appeared equally enraptured by the royal ceremony and wondered what all the fuss was about.

'…the King's Troop, the Royal Horse Artillery, and the mounted escorts from the Colonies…' the television presenter continued as if he was filling up time until something interesting would happen until-

'And now I believe, yes indeed, we see the Queen's State Coach coming through the Palace gates, drawn by its eight magnificent greys and riders, each one attended by a liveried groom on foot, flanked by a Beefeater and inside sits Her Majesty, our beautiful young Queen, Elizabeth II. Like her namesake over three hundred and fifty years ago, she heralds in a new Elizabethan Age, an age…'

The whole room erupted into spontaneous applause. Like everyone else, Yann stood up and joined in – what else could he do?

What an extraordinary day, Yann thought as he lay in bed later that night, looking up at the lining paper, still missing the chariot and spearmen. He didn't understand what his mother saw in it all. It wasn't for him, when he grew up. A life like hers stuck at the back of some awful hospital canteen watching the pageant on television – he would be there in the Abbey, one of the posh importants, with the likes of Earl Lundy. He wanted this so badly, it would happen no matter what it took. He switched off the chianti bottle bedside lamp, remembering with pleasure that in only five days he would be back at school.

Ruth woke early. She heard the rattle of the letterbox handle, just as the kettle came to the boil. She switched it off, filled the brown stoneware pot, covered it with the quilted teacosy and walked out into the hall. Lying on the doormat was a single buff envelope. It had the familiar Beaconsfield crest stamped on the back. It held no dread, given that the scholarship covered all of Yann's fees; such letters usually contained Yann's report, and she took it back to the kitchen, unopened. She enjoyed the anticipation of reading it over the first cup of tea and cigarette of the day. It never occurred to her that, being mid-term, no such report was due. Once settled, she slipped a knife under the brown flap.

When she opened the envelope a few minutes later a single sheet fell out.

ENTWHISTLES
Accountant and Authorised Bankruptcy Agents
340 Threadneedle Street, London EC

1st June 1953

Dear Sir/Madam

Beaconsfield School will not be re-opening after the Coronation break. Due to the lack of the financial resources required to support its continuing operation following the settlement of the Weitzman litigation, Beaconsfield is now permanently closed, and you will have to make alternative arrangements for the educa-

tion of your son. All your child's clothing and belongings will be returned to you via Carter Patterson as soon as possible. Whilst the time and location of the first Creditors' Meeting will be posted in the London Gazette and The Times in due course, it is my preliminary view that nothing will be available for distribution to either preferred or ordinary creditors.

Yours faithfully

T. O. Sylvester
(Trustee in Bankruptcy)

CHAPTER THIRTY-TWO

At the end of the summer term Yann Morris won a full scholarship to one of England's finest public schools, Pitt College, a magnificent Georgian mansion about twenty miles south of Bath.

First mooted by Pitt the Younger when he lived at the Circus in Bath, it had been founded by the William Pitt Club after his death in 1806 in response to demands by 'those engaged in prosperous trades' as an establishment for the education of the 'sons of gentlemen'.

Shocked, frightened and frantic for her son by Beacons-field's sudden closure, Ruth wondered what more could befall her and her adored son. Jancek, then Sebastian, Naomi and Isaac, all gone, who else could she turn to? A day or two passed in a daze before she remembered another letter. She went to the kitchen dresser and took out the old Peak Frean biscuit tin in which she kept her few precious and important papers. Here it was, Isaac's beautiful handwriting on the much handled envelope, from frequent reading two years earlier. Her eyes moistened as she read the words for the umpteenth time.

'*Bubala* Ruth, you will only be reading this if something has happened and Naomi and I are no longer...' She could have skipped, but she read on, the words so familiar, and was in tears by the time she reached the penultimate paragraph. 'In the event of disaster or a real problem, you should get in touch with Malcolm Austwick, my solicitor and more importantly, friend. He is a wise and kind man, and partner of Austwick and Company in Queen Square.' Then the final line. 'I am so sorry we were not able to enjoy you and Yann as we grow old, Goodbye our beautiful daughter. *Shalom.*'

She remembered the only meeting at his office to collect the small legacy, which had helped her to pay all those bills for extras at Beaconsfield that the scholarship did not cover.

Wearing her best shoes and coat, she went straight to Queen Square after work that afternoon. The secretary looked dismissively at her and muttered about needing an appointment, before disappearing to find Mr Austwick's diary. Suddenly Malcolm Austwick appeared in person and courteously shepherded her into his office. Ruth handed over the Entwistles letter.

'Pretty brutal.' He rang for his secretary. 'Take Mrs Morris back to the waiting room and find her a cup of tea and a biscuit will you? Now, Ruth, give me a few minutes, and I think we can solve the problem.'

Once the door had closed behind them, he picked up the phone and dialed the headmaster of Pitt College, Howard Edgington. They exchanged pleasantries.

'I think you said there were still spare scholarships in the Prep School when we met at the Governors' meeting. Are any still available?'

'Yes, we are desperate to fill them, but only with the right sort of deserving cases. Hopefully it will help to defuse the onslaught from the Labour lefties about the elitism of the English Public Schools – they are even threatening to remove our charity status. Why do you ask?'

'I think I have got just the right type of boy.'

'Go on.'

'Long story, but a victim of the Beaconsfield School bankruptcy, effectively the protégé of Doctor Isaac Abrahams, a late client and friend. The boy's name is Yann Morris. He's eleven and is sure to fly through the Common Entrance exam for the main school when the time comes.'

'Yes, we have already accepted half a dozen ex-Beaconsfield boys. They are very bright, which bodes well for university honours, and have parents, as rich as Croesus. Only one problem.'

'What's that?'

'I have already doubled the Jewish quota to two percent, Won't go down well with the other Governors.'

'Don't worry, the antis won't dare raise it in the present political climate, and he's a perfect case for a scholarship. There's only his mother, who's a war widow, and she has nothing.'

'OK, just need the bursar to take a look at him, say eleven tomorrow?'

'Thank you Howard.'

Having taken Green Line buses via Wells and Glastonbury instead of the more expensive train journey, Yann sat opposite the bursar. His mother was in the waiting room outside.

'Welcome young Morris. I gather you hope to join us in September.'

'Yes, sir.'

'So let's get on with the paperwork. Surname, Morris. First name, Yann.'

The boy interrupted him, 'No, sir, Ian.' A new name for a new start, neither foreign nor Jewish.

He didn't tell his mother.

Ruth's heart leapt when she opened the letter from Pitt College and read that a full scholarship had been offered.

Then she noticed that it was for Ian, not Yann Morris. This wasn't the first time that Yann's unusual name had been misspelt by different authorities. Ruth went to the nearby public phone box to ring the school about their error; however, when she got through to the bursar's office she was promptly informed that there was no error and that Yann had insisted on being called Ian.

Walking slowly back along the pavement to 36 Mafeking Street, Ruth felt a heaviness in her heart. The only memory of Tate, her dear lovely father, had been thrown away by his grandson's shame.

CHAPTER THIRTY-THREE

Unbeknown to Ian, and following a telephone call from his mother, the well-meaning matron of his House at Pitt College had arranged for the new boy to be given a lift home at the end of his first term.

Bradshaw, his House Captain, announced loudly, 'Charged with seeing you home safely Morris,' as they exited the school and he was guided towards the Rolls Royce parked nearby.

'You sit up front next to the chauffeur and tell him how to get to your place,' Bradshaw ordered.

As they came onto the London Road forty-five minutes later, he stammered 'Snow Hill,' over-awed by the huge car, the uniformed chauffeur and the wish to be anywhere else but here. He couldn't understand why Bradshaw was taking him home and vowed that it would be the last time it ever happened. Mrs Bradshaw, enveloped by an aroma of mothballs from her fur coat, sat next to her son. She expressed surprise when Ian directed the chauffeur to turn right off the London Road. She had never done this before.

The large car purred through the ever-narrowing streets of small shabby Victorian terraced houses. The silence inside the car was deafening as it turned into Mafeking Street and stopped outside the small two-up two-down numbered thirty-six.

The chauffeur unloaded Ian's case onto the pavement and got back into the car. His mother must have been watching through the front window, and came into the street, dressed in a frock, but without the usual pinafore apron, and her hair was neatly coiffed. She smiled and held her hands deferentially in front of her as she began to speak.

'Would you like -' but the car had sped off before she could finish and the warmth faded from her face. Ian gave her a hug, picked up his case and led her into the house, conscious of the twitching net curtains of nearby houses.

Wordlessly she sank onto a kitchen chair and reached for her cigarettes. The best china, with its five cups nestled around the teapot, were laid out on the table next to a splendid caraway seed cake.

Bradshaw must have shared the incident with his fellow prefects. Required one afternoon to take the hated pink lateness slip Ian noticed it read 'Poire – late for games' as he handed it over to Bradshaw.

'You're doing Pliny as your set book aren't you?' the older boy asked. Ian nodded. It was customary for the type of punishment to follow the nature of the offence, so was expecting Latin.

'One hundred lines by assembly tomorrow. *Puer poire est.*'

He knew that *'puer est'* meant 'the boy is', but did not recognise the word *poire*. Later he opened the dictionary end of the Latin text book:

> POIRE (noun masculine): a person who lives in absolute
> abject poverty (used by Pliny in the second campaign).

Bradshaw chuckled as Ian handed over the lines the next morning. He tossed the papers unchecked into the waste paper bin.

'Empty that will you, *Poire*.'

Within a week all the House Prefects were calling him *Poire* and then the deputy prefects, and it was not long before only the masters used Morris.

It had all been a doddle at first. Ian was bright and Beaconsfield had done its job well. Too well; Ian started at least a year ahead of his classmates, so he didn't have to work. He just cruised along, and still came top in most subjects at the end of year exams. It was all so easy, it made him feel superior and, stupidly, he didn't hide it.

At least the rest of the 'Hebrew Tribe', as the few other Jewish boys from Beaconsfield were referred to in the school, attempted to mix in; he made no effort, worse still, he thought sport was a waste of time.

He returned to his second year, unpopular and friendless. New subjects had been added and just cruising through the old ones was no longer possible. Soon he was struggling and he steadily lost ground over the second year, so much so that he gave up trying.

Seeing his lack of effort and enthusiasm, his teachers lost interest.

CHAPTER THIRTY-FOUR

Ian pretended to read as the train drew into Bath's Green Park Railway Station as the five other boys excitedly moved cases and parcels from luggage rack to corridor.

'Come on, Poire, Bath awaits,' said Yardley.

'Don't worry about me – I'm staying on.'

'The train doesn't go any further.'

'That's where you are so wrong, Yardley, it goes on to Bristol in about twenty minutes. Mater is insisting we do the dreaded Christmas shopping and is meeting me there.'

The train came to a halt; he had used a similar excuse every term end for the past two years and it had always worked.

With a parting chorus of 'Merry Christmas' Ian was forgotten as luggage and boys spilled on to the platform into the melee of parents and uniformed chauffeurs.

The last train door slammed shut. Ian opened his suitcase, took off his school tie and blazer and put on a plain grey jersey. He stepped down onto the now empty platform, made his was out of the station and walked to Manvers Street. He sat on his suitcase at the bus stop; there was a while to wait.

As the bus went through Queen Square, down George Street and into London Road, he contemplated the large high tea waiting for him. He loved his mother, despite being embarrassed by her foreign accent and grammatical errors, and she went to such trouble to have his favourite food waiting for him when he got home. It had been an up and down couple of years since Beaconsfield had closed. She had been very upset that Uncle Sebastian's *Magen David* had been taken off and relegated to his sock drawer before he went off to Pitt College. Then came the tears when he refused to be *bar mitzvahed* eighteen months ago. But all in all, he thought that things were turning out all right. He looked forward to the time, after he left school, when he could make things up to her.

The more he thought about his mother, he could almost smell the meal waiting for him. There would be sausages, baked beans, fried bread so crispy it didn't go soggy, with a fried egg on top and square chips to the side. He didn't mind the absence of bacon, and there would be a big mug of tea, bread cut thickly from Hovis, with real yellow butter, not margarine like at school. For afters, there would be tinned half peaches in syrup, all the way from America, with evaporated milk and she would have put out her 'lucky spoon' for him to use. Already he could feel the warmth of the kitchen fire and smell his holiday wear airing in front of it on the wooden clothes horse.

Stepping off the bus, he carried his suitcase up Snow Hill and turned into Mafeking Street, but the house was in darkness. Surely his mother had not forgotten that this was the day he broke up, after all he had written.

Disappointed, he put his suitcase on the ground, felt through the letterbox for the key hanging on the string inside, pulled it out and inserted it into the lock. The front door moved about six inches and then stuck. He pushed harder and it opened a little further; the gap was just wide enough for him to squeeze through into the small hall. A number of unopened letters were wedged under the door. He tugged them free, pulled the door open, rescued his suitcase from the street and closed the front door. It was pitch dark.

He pushed the light switch down. Nothing happened. Feeling his way to the small hall table, he found the candle in its tin holder with the box of matches in case the electric meter ran out, and lit it. He shivered, the house was cold and damp. Shielding the flickering candle with his hand, he glanced into the sitting room. No fire, just a grate of grey ash. Perhaps she had just popped out to get some change for the meter. No note, the kitchen table was bare, clearly he was unexpected; this had never happened before.

'For God's sake Mum, where are you?'

He picked up the candle, wandered back into the hall, and glanced at the pile of envelopes on the floor. The top letter was his, unopened. Instantly all was explained. His mother, unaware of his homecoming, had stayed over at work; she often worked overtime to earn a little extra for the Christmas luxuries. Not for a moment did he question why the letter had lain there for several days.

Reassured, he climbed the staircase to his bedroom over-looking the street, and laid his suitcase on the bed. Despite his absence at school, as 'the man of the house' his mother had insisted he have the larger front double bedroom. Then he heard a sound coming from the other end of the landing.

'There it is again,' Ian said aloud as, candle in hand, he walked down to his mother's single bedroom at the back of the house and opened the door.

Shit – the smell of human waste was overpowering. Something live ran over his feet and out to the landing. Lying across the unkempt bed was his mother, her long silver hair, usually immaculately pinned up in a bun, hanging down to the floor. There was a dry trail of vomit from her half-opened mouth, her face was ashen, contorted with pain.

Ian fled down the stairs, yanked open the front door and ran out into the street. He sprinted to the telephone box on the corner of Snow Hill, only to find it occupied by a teenage girl. A number of the small panes of glass were missing from the red cast-iron call box and he could hear her conversation.

'Yeah, well Mary said she saw you with that tart at the Scala last night,' the girl snapped into the receiver. Ian moved round the box, so that the girl could see him waiting. She couldn't have been much older that him, maybe sixteen, but she was buxom and heavily made up.

'You lying sod.' She was still talking on the telephone, but she pushed open the heavy door and glared at Ian. 'What do you want?'

'Look, I'm awfully sorry, but I need to use the telephone, it's an emergency.'

'You may be offaly soree,' she sneered, mimicking his accent, 'but so is this, so get lost.' She turned her back on him and resumed her conversation.

Ian grabbed open the door, snatched at the back of the girl's blouse and pulled her out onto the pavement.

He picked up the dangling telephone and slammed it back into the cradle, before immediately picking it up again. He dialled 999.

'What service do you require, fire, ambulance or police?' A voice asked, but before he could answer, the girl was screaming and grabbing at the door.

'What service do you require, fire, ambulance or police?' Ian stuck out his leg, pushed his foot into the girl's stomach and sent her sprawling. Supporting the telephone receiver on his shoulder, he held the door shut.

'What service do you require, caller, fire, ambulance or police?' The voice started to sound irritated.

'My mother's dead, I just came home and found her.'

'Where are you calling from?'

'Snow Hill,' responded Ian.

'Please read the notice above the telephone.'

'You don't understand. She's dead.'

'I must know where in Snow Hill.'

Ian looked at the small printed notice facing him under the small mirror.

'The junction of Mafeking Street and Tyning Lane.'

'Thank you, caller. What is the nature of the injury?'

'I already told you – she's just lying there dead!' he shouted.

'Calm down. Where is "there"?'

'At our house, 36 Mafeking Street.'

'36 Mafeking Street, thank you. Return there and wait.'

The girl was sitting on the pavement sobbing. Streaks of black mascara mixed with make-up ran down her face, and she clutched the torn blouse around herself.

He knelt down, and was horrified to see blood on the pavement.

'Look, I'm sorry, but-'

'You stuck up sod.' She suddenly stared at his right hand, which was bleeding profusely. Ian saw small shards of glass embedded in the palm, where he had clutched through the broken window at the telephone box door to keep her out. He felt no pain as he bound it up with his handkerchief, and ran back to the house.

He stood outside waiting for the ambulance. He could not go back in to see his mother. Suddenly the darkness of the small street was bathed in blue flashing light, as a police car, not an ambulance, turned the corner, slowed and stopped by him.

A policeman got out of the front passenger seat of the black Wolsey. 'Did you call an ambulance?' He was eyeing the open front door, unlit house, and the blood soaked handkerchief.

Ian nodded.

'What happened?'

'My mother's dead in the back bedroom.'

'What happened to your hand, and why have you turned all the lights out?'

The boy just stood there.

'Jack, give me the torch, and look after the lad while I have a look.' The driver got out of the car, handed over the torch, and opened the rear door.

'You just sit quietly.' The driver pushed Ian's head down and manoeuvred him into the back seat, before closing the door. He returned to the driver's seat and unhooked the microphone hanging from the dashboard.

'Control, Alpha Tango at 36, three-six Mafeking Street, male, minor injured and in custody, investigating fatality.'

Meanwhile the first policeman switched on the torch, and gingerly entered the house, only to return quickly. He ran out of the front door, and stuck his head into the car. 'What a mess. She's alive, but only just – where the hell is that ambulance?'

CHAPTER THIRTY-FIVE

Ian opened his eyes and looked around the bleak dormitory with its bare walls, uncurtained windows and eleven empty beds. Yesterday, at the end of the Easter Term, every boy in the school, except him had gone home. The rolled up mattresses and each boy's wooden locker had been placed across the bare metal springs. Nothing and no one had woken him; no bell rang and no prefect was shouting at him to get up. He was entirely alone, the only boy in this vast empty school mansion. He could just lie here all day and no one would know or care. In fact, he could probably stay in bed for days without anyone... Then he remembered the Head. He had been a brick.

His thoughts went back to his return to school three months earlier. Somehow he had got himself back for the start of term, fares and laundry paid out of what he had earnt at Sally Lunn's. But no sooner had he got off the coach, when the headmaster, Howard Edgington, had summoned Ian to his study.

The Lady Almoner at St Peter's hospital had been sympathetic and telephoned during the holidays to let him know of Ian's plight. Yes, he had cleaned up the house and done well to get the job washing up at the restaurant in North Parade Passage during Christmas and New Year, but the reality of the situation had to be faced and the school informed. For a start there was the house in Snow Hill and the rent to be paid. The doctors had confirmed that Ruth Morris was likely to be in hospital for a long time, and the almoner was concerned about Ian and the forthcoming Easter holiday. Not yet fifteen, he was too young to be left to his own devices, and she was aware that there were no other relatives to care for him. The only alternative was for Ian to move to the Bath Orphanage in Walcot Street until his mother recovered.

'I told her that will be unnecessary,' the Head explained to Ian. 'The governors have agreed that you can stay at the school when the term ends, and until your mother gets better. The almoner has also arranged for you to see your mother outside of hospital visiting hours, so you can cycle to Bath every Sunday morning.'

'What about Sunday chapel?'

'You are excused, but surely as a Jew you don't attend?'

'I do, sir, otherwise everyone would think I'm a Catholic!'

So tomorrow, as he had done on the last dozen Sundays, he would ride over and see his mother.

Silence, not a sound. It was so weird. No one to talk to. Then it occurred to Ian that apart from his mother, there was nobody, not a single person outside the school who knew where he was and cared what happened to him. I am on my own, utterly alone. Frightened, Ian pushed the thought away. He needed nobody, not to wake him up, love him, or for anything else. He could fend for himself.

He got out of bed, snatched up his sponge bag and headed for the washrooms. His footsteps on the parquet floor echoed in the long and deserted corridor, reminding him again how alone he was. But he would get used to the silence and loneliness. He had no choice. He turned on the shower.

He went to step out of the shower to make way for another

boy after the stipulated two minutes. 'Stupid,' he said aloud and got back in. Then feeling guilty about wasting hot water, he turned off the tap and reached for his towel. Absolute silence.

'Mustn't start talking to myself, the first sign of madness.'

Back in the dormitory he dressed in his school uniform, and he worked out the day's routine. 'Yes,' again he spoke aloud, 'everything will be fine.' He would make a timetable so that, as in term time he would be occupied every single minute of every day.

He went down the grand front staircase, normally a prefect's privilege, and knocked on the Head's study door. After a moment it opened.

'Good morning, sir.'

'Morning, Morris, come in.' The Head led Ian across his study and through another door into the private accommodation occupied by him and his family. The inner sanctum, holy of holies, yet another tale for the boys upon their return next term.

They entered a large dining room. 'Ah, Elizabeth, dear,' he said to his wife, 'you know young Morris here. He will be joining us for meals during the holidays.'

Ian surveyed the silver dishes of porridge, eggs, bacon and kedgeree lined up on the Regency sideboard. They looked even better than the fried teas his mother made, never mind the usual school breakfasts.

'Now, Morris, I want to talk to you about the extra studies I have organised for you. I have timetabled two sessions every day from breakfast to lunchtime, and then from two to four o'clock. Today, we will start with Maths, your weakest subject, and then move on to…'

And so began a holiday routine that continued for fifteen months.

During that time Ian never missed a Sunday. Whatever the weather, he cycled over to see his mother, not because he wanted to, but because the Head had told him to.

He didn't dare question why he went and why his life was so different to everyone else's, it just was.

Just as he had blanked out the reason for going, so did he deal with the visits themselves. He would rehearse what he would tell his mother on the journey over, and ramble on to her about meaningless school events. Sometimes she was alert and keen to listen and at other times she was barely awake. There never seemed to be the right time to have a proper conversation and gradually the relationship became perfunctory. Ian tried hard not to think about the love his mother had lavished on him as a young child and the affection of his Uncle Sebastian, Uncle Isaac or Auntie Naomi.

As his fifteenth, and then his sixteenth birthday passed with just a single card awaiting him at his mother's bedside, he became ever more isolated. Nevertheless, the role of dedicated and dutiful son had its reward: everyone stopped calling him Poire.

CHAPTER THIRTY-SIX

Howard Edgington had been involved with scholarship throughout his working life and was pleased to get back to teaching. It was good to get away from the endless politics involved with the running of a large public school.

He enjoyed his holiday sessions with Morris and was pleased that in contrast to his past lack-lustre performance the boy was finally starting to apply himself. Morris was responding to this one-to-one relationship, and Edgington was pleasantly surprised at the rapid improvement in the regular tests he set every Friday afternoon. Ian achieved ever better marks at the mock examinations Edgington set him the weekend before everyone returned from the Easter holiday in 1958. Passes in Maths, English and History were particularly good, and the headmaster pondered how to reward this endeavour.

The answer came a week into the summer term, when he had a visit from a wartime colleague and friend. Colonel Marcus Rose came to see him about the Hope Venture. For the previous ten years, starting with a single purchase in 1947, the Venture had been buying up large old houses, into which it settled displaced children and youngsters rescued from the refugee camps of war-torn Europe. Now it had acquired a Victorian building in nearby Norton Fitzwarren that needed a modern classroom for the twenty Polish teenagers in residence. Rose explained that the necessary pre-fabricated building had been bought and delivered. All that was required was an appropriate person to co-ordinate its erection and an unskilled labour force to carry out the manual work.

A few days later, Edgington enthusiastically introduced the project at morning assembly. The workshop master, Mr Longfellow, would run the project, but to everyone's surprise, the Headmaster announced Morris's appointment as Labour Organiser, charged with arranging the timetable and process, whereby every boy in the school, from the highest to the lowest, went into a squad and worked on the project for at least one afternoon every week.

They started digging the foundations on the first day of June 1958 and within less than a fortnight the strongest twelve boys in the school had completed the last and biggest of three service trenches: the one to carry the main sewer from the road to lavatories in the new classroom extension.

As they had done with the earlier two trenches, 'Tom' and 'Dick', the 'Dirty Dozen' stood to attention in a straight line, unbuttoned their flies, and to the count of three, simultaneously peed down into the trench, solemnly baptizing their latest effort, 'Harry.' Longfellow was nearby and must have seen the ritual but made no comment. Later he would talk proudly of the incident using phrases such as 'team spirit', 'moral fibre' and 'bonding' in the masters' common room and when the headmaster visited the site. None of these words had any relevance to Ian the following afternoon, stretched out on his back in 'Harry' and looking up at the thick concrete slab which formed the floor of the new lavatories. He was lying in three inches of cold and rather smelly water.

'Throughout life you will find that with power and privilege comes responsibility,' Longfellow had droned on as he handed over the cold chisel and hammer. 'The sooner you learn this, the better you will be able to lead others. So down you go Morris, and break through the concrete slab for the sewer access.'

Longfellow had made clear that he didn't think much of Ian, or that he was up to the job given to him by the headmaster. But Ian was a born organiser. He realised that the secret was picking the right squad leaders, the teams of boys and allocating the work. Everything had gone like clockwork and stayed on schedule, until now. He had considered confessing about the tape measure.

They had finished laying the concrete base for the new classroom as dusk fell the evening before and Longfellow had decided to check its overall size one last time, despite the rain. He unwound the large one hundred foot surveyor's linen tape from its blue circular drum and, oblivious to the downpour, stretched it across the concrete foundation.

'Right to a tenth of an inch,' he grunted with satisfaction, before walking off.

Early the next day, Longfellow started to chalk out the critical pipe and sewer points on the now solid base. Three times he checked the measurements and puzzlement soon turned to disbelief, when it became apparent that overnight the whole concrete base had grown by three inches in length and slightly less in breadth. He tossed the tape to Ian and stormed off, unfurling the surveyor's plans as he walked.

'Morris!' came the angry roar across the site ten minutes later. 'Bring that bloody tape here!' Longfellow had decided to check one last time, and picking up a different tape, found that everything was absolutely correct. Quickly he compared the two tapes.

'Well, I'll be dammed, look at that. The bloody tape has shrunk – not just a quarter inch, but three inches! We'll have our money back on this one.' He tossed it to Ian. 'Put it in my study when you get back. Never seen anything like it.' He walked off muttering to himself.

But Ian knew what had happened. Unwittingly, after washing off the muck the previous evening, he unwound the whole tape and wrapped its entire length around the radiator to dry overnight.

Now under the concrete, Ian took a deep breath and pushed back a wave of claustrophobia. He ran his fingers across the rough surface above him until he located the protruding pilot pin bedded into the concrete. Gingerly, he placed the chisel next to the pin and tapped it with the hammer. A shower of concrete chips fell onto his chest but when he ran his fingers around the area again, he could barely discern the indentation he had made. With so little room to wield the hammer he knew he would be stuck in this dark piss stinking trench for a good while yet, and all because of Longfellow's antagonism towards him. Still he would not give him the satisfaction of asking to be relieved until the job was done.

A small mound of concrete chippings had accumulated on Ian's chest, when he felt something strike one of his feet that was protruding from under the concrete raft; he looked down to see some earth had been dislodged from the trench wall. Then it happened again, and then again and he realised that someone was tapping on his Wellington boot. Grateful for an excuse to stop, Ian wriggled his body backwards down the trench, anticipating a harangue about lack of progress. He started to mouth an excuse as he emerged into the daylight.

'Sorry, sir, but it's a-' But it wasn't Longfellow looking down on him. It was a stranger.

The man was old, really ancient, about sixty. He was holding a shooting stick, clearly the boot-tapping instrument.

He towered over Ian, who took in the smart clothes the tall man wore as he scrambled out of the trench. First the brown leather brogues with their embossed patterns, then the razor-sharp creases up the fawn trousers before the yellow waistcoat, lowest button undone, the gold watch chain, and the striped blue tie. The man's fawn trench coat was unbuttoned but he had on brown leather gloves, and when Ian's gaze finally reached the face , it was like the leather of his shoes, brown and wrinkled.

Long, thick grey hair, almost silver and perfectly brushed, was matched by a large handlebar moustache below a fine aquiline nose; strangely the bushy eyebrows were jet black.

Ian was conscious of a smell of cleanliness, eau-de-cologne and soap, sharp not sweet and sickly like his mother's scent. The man sniffed and Ian thought he had probably noticed the smell of urine emanating from the grit and mud caked overalls. He reminded Ian of someone but he wasn't sure who – probably one of the fathers who turned up on Founders Day – retired professional soldiers, dark skinned from years in the Indian Army and wives with voices like cut glass.

He was certainly very distinguished looking, and seemed somehow familiar.

'Hello young fellow and who might you be?'

The gentle voice took the boy completely by surprise. It was warm, soft, not at all army-like.

'Morris, sir, I am the Labour Organiser.'

'That's a very grand title for a small chap.' He seemed to be about to say something more when Longfellow rushed up.

'Colonel Rose,' he beamed, 'this is an unexpected pleasure.' Clearly it was not, thought Ian, knowing that false smile only too well.

'Headmaster said you might pay us a visit, following your very generous donation. What can I do for you?'

'I thought I would see how you were getting on. Young Morris and I were having a chat, hopefully you can spare him to show me around?'

Clearly he could but was reluctant to replace Morris. 'Oh, I should be delighted to show you around myself,' replied Longfellow.

'I wouldn't want to hold you up. I am sure your young Labour Organiser will do admirably,' and before Longfellow could object he had placed a hand gently on Ian's shoulders. 'Now, Morris, give Mr Longfellow back the cold chisel and hammer, and explain to me what is going on and your part in it all.'

Unrecognised and unremembered by Ian, Marcus Rose had re-entered his life.

CHAPTER THIRTY-SEVEN

Some days later Ian was surprised to see his name, the third after two persistent offenders, on the headmaster's interview list pinned to the school notice board. The list was generally used for misconduct that was too serious to be dealt with by the school prefects or the housemasters and he couldn't think what he had done wrong.

He waited anxiously outside the study as the second boy exited grimacing, no doubt due to the harshness of the Head's displeasure. He knocked.

'Come,' Edgington's voice boomed.

Ian entered the room and saw that the Head was studying some paperwork on his desk.

'Ah, Morris.' The man looked up. 'Colonel Rose came to see me yesterday; I gather you and he met last Friday and had quite a chat.' He shuffled his papers and set them straight.

'I hope that was all right, sir.'

'More than all right, you made quite an impression,' the headmaster smiled, 'and he has invited us over to tea tomorrow afternoon at his home outside Bath. Meet me at the main doors at 1.30 pm, and make yourself look smart, I think it could be quite an interesting visit.'

Ian was waiting at the appointed hour and in an effort to 'look smart' he had decided to wear his mufti coat.

The headmaster brought the large Daimler to rest next to him and leant across to open the passenger door.

'Good gracious Morris, what are you wearing?' Edgington said, looking appalled at the brown half-length coat with its fur collar. 'Take it off! You look like a bookmaker!'

Shaken, Morris did what he was told, climbed in and placed the folded coat onto the back seat with the bookmaker comment tucked into his memory for later consideration.

They turned right between two stone pillars just after two. The headmaster drove slowly, even reverentially Ian thought, as the Daimler glided up the gravel drive, bordered on each side by immaculate sweeping lawns, purple rhododendrons and orange azalea bushes. He decided that he would never wear the brown coat again.

The drive ended in a perfect circle of apricot-coloured stone chippings, raked smooth and surrounding a large marble fountain of four vertical dolphins, eyes open, heads down, water gushing from smiling mouths. The symmetry of the large Georgian house was perfect.

New images and thoughts assaulted the boy as a butler ushered them into Widcombe House. They had literally stepped up onto the wall-to-wall carpeting, so thick and luxurious was the pile. They went into the massive study, lit with the bright summer sunlight from half a dozen full length windows overlooking the formal lawns that swept down to parklands and a lake. What was the smell? He didn't recognise it at first. Then he placed it; the odour of the very rich – good quality cigar smoke.

'Welcome Howard, and you too young Morris.' The colonel had quietly entered from the other end of the room. Cleverly, in one of the glass cabinets of old books stretching from floor to ceiling, was a concealed door. He walked towards them from behind a large dark wooden desk and gestured to the deep brown leather armchairs arranged around a low table made ready with tea cups, plates and napkins for afternoon tea.

The butler reappeared with a tea trolley covered by a white cloth, on which stood a silver service; teapot, strainer, hot water and milk jugs, each ornately decorated with matching small silver oak leaves and acorns. Old and very valuable, Ian thought. Deftly the butler raised and secured the side wings of the trolley so that it became another table, and reaching below it lifted out plates of crustless white triangular sandwiches and small cakes.

'Shall I pour, sir?'

'No thank you Jennings, we'll manage.'

Colonel Rose waited until the butler had closed the study door and smiled broadly at Ian, clearly trying to put him at ease but with limited success.

'Do help yourself to whatever you fancy,' he said and leant forward to pour the tea.

The two men spent time discussing progress of the classroom construction and the Hope Venture generally. Ian took the Colonel up on his offer and helped himself to the tiny sandwiches, iced cakes, jam tarts and coconut cake. From time to time, and to Ian's surprise, the colonel invited his comments and listened carefully to the boy's answers.

After Jennings came back and left with the tea trolley, Colonel Rose stood up and walked to one of the French casements.

'Now Howard, can I tempt you to a walk in the garden on this beautiful afternoon?' he said as he opened the glass door. 'The Harkness roses are particularly impressive this summer.'

The Head stood up, looked at his pupil for a long moment – 'Take care' the look signalled – and then walked out into the garden.

Colonel Rose smiled broadly at the boy.

'Now Ian,' he said, using his first name for the first time, 'why don't you tell me all about yourself?'

Ian considered Colonel Rose's question, then after a moment, hesitantly launched into a litany of school activities, his duty as Labour Organiser for the Hope Venture and his role as a squad leader in his house. He mentioned his favoured subjects and as his confidence grew, the monologue flowed faster, encompassing his rank of corporal in the Combined Cadet Force, manoeuvres, and summer camp with its thrill of flying in light aircraft. He ended with a strange little tale about an escapade involving his membership of the School Photographic Society and the local girls' school, and how he built a crystal wireless set in the Radio Club. He eventually fell silent, mindful of the Head's warning and got worried by how long he had held forth. Man and boy regarded each other.

'All very interesting, Ian, but it was not what I asked.' The colonel was no longer smiling. 'What you get up to at school is all very well, but you have told me absolutely nothing about yourself, or your background? I understand you are Jewish, what part does your religion play in your life? How do you feel about the present difficult situation of living all the time at school while your mother remains in hospital? And, perhaps most importantly, what do you plan to do after you leave Pitt College?'

Ian was shocked. These things were personal, especially the bit about his mother. As to how he felt about it all, the short answer was that he didn't.

Suddenly his eagerness to please for the headmaster's sake vanished. He didn't care how much money this old man had contributed to the Hope Venture. The enjoyable tea party was forgotten.

'I don't think that is any of your business, sir.'

'I don't blame you for being suspicious, Ian, or should I say Yann,' he paused before continuing, 'but what happens if your mother has to stay in hospital for a long time? You can't live at the school forever. What will you do after you leave Pitt College? Where will you go, and more to the point how do you propose to earn your living?'

'Why do you care?' Ian blurted out, surprised by the use of his real first name. 'I'll manage. I'm thinking about joining the Royal Air Force as a pilot.'

He already relied on a bursary from the school for every stitch he stood up in but one thing he didn't want was more charity.

'So you're thinking of a military career?'

'My CCF Commanding Officer thinks it would be a good idea rather than going to university.'

'How and what as?'

'Through Cranwell, as a pilot fficer. I am going up to Hornchurch at the end of term to sit for a flying scholarship.' He defiantly returned the colonel's questioning look. And once I've passed, he thought, the RAF will teach me to fly, and with my student pilot's licence in the bag, Cranwell will welcome me with open arms, so, I don't need any help from you, or anyone else.

'Clearly I was mistaken and you obviously don't need my advice or assistance. I wish you the best of luck for the future.' Colonel Rose said sharply and stood up. 'Let's find your headmaster.'

'Well how did it go?' the head asked Ian during the drive back. Their departure had been rather sudden.

'Fine, sir.'

Howard Edgington had thought it best not to press the boy.

He and the Colonel had seemed to get on well together and hopefully he could help solve the problem of Ian Morris's future. He wondered if they had got around to talking about their shared religion.

Later that evening, Edgington lifted the handset off its cradle and dialled Widcombe 230. Jennings answered the telephone and put him through.

'What can I do for you?' Unlike his usual friendly tone, Marcus Rose sounded brusque as though dealing with a business matter.

'I thought I would ring to see what you thought of young Morris.'

'Very independent young man. He told me in no uncertain terms that he did not need my or anyone else's help. Resented my questions and said he would go into the Royal Air Force. I get the impression that he is crazy about flying.'

'What?' It was the first Howard Edgington had heard of the idea.

'Oh yes, no doubt about it. I fear there is nothing I can do for the boy despite my desire to help because of his mother's misfortune. It's a pity but thank you anyway for bringing him over to see me.'

The headmaster was quite shocked when he replaced the receiver, but upon later reflection thought it not such a bad idea. Why had he not thought of the Armed Forces? The Royal Air Force could provide the boy with the career, stability, and most importantly, fellowship. Howard Edgington had witnessed this often before – the ideal haven for popular young gentlemen, the offspring of stable upper and aspiring middle class English families. The complete opposite of Morris.

CHAPTER THIRTY-EIGHT

The week at Hornchurch had been wonderful. Proud in his Combined Cadet Force uniform, and armed with the all-important looking official rail warrant, Ian had travelled down from school by train on the Sunday to arrive at the Royal Air Force fighter base on the outskirts of London. Once through the gate, he had been absorbed instantly into service life with nineteen other hopeful recruits.

Gone was the desperation of war. Flying and the Officer Corps was attempting to revert to the preserve of gentlemen from good public schools. Ian was addressed with the pseudo-respect of 'young Mr Morris, sir' by the sardonic NCO instructors, and as an equal by his fellow students.

'Corporal Morris, isn't it?' the grey-haired commanding officer had asked in the officer's mess on the third night.

'Yes, sir.'

He held out his hand. 'My name is Shores. You are from Bath aren't you?'

'Yes, sir, do you know it?'

'Only from a few thousand feet in the dark. Bagged my first kill there as a pilot officer in April forty-two with 255 squadron. I was flying a Beaufighter when we stumbled across a lone Junker 88 climbing away from the city. Flying straight and level five hundred feet below us. Sitting duck. Came in from the starboard.'

The squadron leader demonstrated by using his left hand as the bomber going along on the horizontal, with his incoming right hand as the fighter.

'First time I saw what twenty millimeter cannon shells could do at close range. Ripped through the whole length of the fuselage, black cross and all. The wing disintegrated. Only the pilot got out – found hanging unconscious from a tree. Survived, I heard later, in a POW camp at Bridgwater. Only German bomber that didn't make it back that night.'

This was for him, Ian thought, very much so – forget going to university. Strangely, the unlikely events surrounding his birth had never been mentioned, so he was unaware that the story the squadron leader had just told, happened two days before he had been born.

The whole Hornchurch experience had been intense, and although in good physical shape, Ian had found the dawn ten-mile runs and forced marches boring. Jumping from the high diving boards into the swimming pool as if abandoning a bomber ditching in the sea, and then swimming under water covered by supposedly burning fuel, were better. The aptitude tests had been conducted in the blacked out cockpits of Second World War fighters and bombers. Whilst these never left the ground, their complex instruments, engine noise throat microphones, flying helmets, and gun and cannon sights made it very realistic.

Now, on the morning of their departure, the ten remaining candidates – half had not completed the course for various reasons ranging from colour blindness to hay fever – were assembled and sat outside the CO's office. Their number rapidly decreased as one by one, they were summoned by the adjutant in alphabetical order. The door would shut and a few minutes later they would emerge, their demeanour revealing all.

Finally it was Ian's turn. He went in, shut the door and Group Captain Shores motioned him to sit down. He picked up a buff folder and opened it to reveal bundles of various signed chits of different colours, held together by a large brass staple. Morris recognised these as the forms completed before, during and after every exercise.

'Now, Corporal Morris, let me see,' the officer said, glancing down at the first of the two foolscap evaluation sheets pinned inside the front cover. 'Physical fitness, excellent. A1 G1 – suitable for air and ground crew, not that the latter is of any interest to you.'

Ian sighed, the worst was over. Shores lifted up the top sheet, looked at the second and continued.

'Sorry old chap, you have failed the aptitude test – it wasn't even a near pass, so there is no doubt about the matter. I am afraid you do not have the aptitude to fly one of Her Majesty's aircraft and we cannot offer you a flying scholarship.' He stood up and extended his hand. 'Goodbye, Corporal Morris, and good luck.'

CHAPTER THIRTY-NINE

'It now gives me great pleasure to declare this magnificent new classroom annexe, built for the Hope Venture by the boys of Pitt College, officially open.'

Her Royal Highness, Queen Elizabeth the Queen Mother, picked up the pair of gold-plated scissors from the crimson cushion and cut the coloured ribbon, which Ian had fixed across the front entrance two hours earlier. She walked along the red carpet and into the building: at one end the college quartet was singing sea shanties.

Standing in a line along the side of the carpet were Mr and Mrs Edgington, Bradshaw, now head prefect, and Ian Morris. Next to Ian was a very attractive sixteen-year-old Polish refugee, who was introduced to him as Katrina. She was the resident representing the Hope Venture. Ian was aware of her watching him as they waited their turn. He had never seen her before so she must have only recently moved in, because all of the girls, even the unattractive ones, were the subject of endless dormitory fantasies by the boys of Pitt College.

The Queen Mother's aide, the Lord Lieutenant of the County, Malcolm Austwick, first presented the Edgingtons to Her Majesty and then the two schoolboys, explaining Ian's role as Labour Organiser. The Queen Mother paused in front of him and, as he raised his head from the bow, he noticed that the Lord Lieutenant was speaking quietly into her ear.

'Ah yes, I remember,' she said, nodded and turned to him. 'My aide has reminded me that you come from this City of Bath and the quite extraordinary circumstances surrounding your birth during the bombing in 1942.'

'Ma'am?' Yann replied hesitantly, puzzled by the reference to his birth.

'How is your mother, she was so very brave.'

'Not very well ma'am, she is in hospital.'

'I am sorry to hear that, I do hope she gets well soon.'

'Thank you, ma'am.' And then she was gone, addressing the Polish girl next to him.

What was all that about when I was born, and my mother's bravery? he wondered. He would ask his mother when he next visited the hospital; she had been very poorly the last time, but was delighted when he had told her about the forthcoming royal presentation.

'Enjoying yourself, Morris?' a familiar voice asked a little later. Ian turned to see Colonel Rose, saucer in one hand and a delicate china cup half raised to his mouth in the other. Howard Edgington was beside him.

'Yes, thank you, sir.'

'I was sorry to hear about Hornchurch, You must be very disappointed. What are you going to do now?'

'I don't know.' Suddenly he felt deflated. 'They have offered me a place as a navigator, which means I could still go to the Staff College at Cranwell. But I so wanted to fly.'

'Well you know my door at Widcombe House is always open, if you ever want some advice.'

'It's very good of you, Colonel,' the headmaster interjected, looking hard at Ian, daring him to reject this offer. 'Morris could take his bicycle on the train to you on Saturday, if that is convenient, can't you Morris?'

'Yes, sir.' Well, there goes my free Saturday, he thought.

'Good, look forward to seeing you.' The colonel nodded to Ian and turned to walk away with the headmaster. 'Now, Howard, what's your next project?'

'They say you are Polish.' It was the pretty Polish girl, Katrina, who had stood next to him in the presentation line. He wondered how she could have known but didn't mind, because the way she spoke reminded him of his mother, softer but yet the so familiar accent.

'No, but my mother is. I was born in England.'

'Where did she come from, and what about your father?'

'A town somewhere west of Warsaw which began with an L, Lodge or something like that. My dad was killed in the war by the Japanese.'

She didn't say anything for a moment but just stared at him; it made him feel awkward, horny. He looked into her big brown eyes but was conscious of her breasts under the tight white blouse.

'Was it Lodz?' she said, pronouncing it *woodge*, just like his mother did.

'Yes, that's it.'

She smiled. 'That's where I was born.'

Suddenly she grabbed his arm. 'Come on, I'll show you round the rest of the house.'

This had always been strictly out of bounds to all Pitt College boys. Before he knew it, she had manoeuvred him out of the crowded new classroom, down the covered walkway and into the stillness of the panelling and mosaic tiles of the gloomy Victorian entrance hall of the original house.

'Where is everyone?' Ian couldn't believe they were the only two people there. It was so busy outside.

'Oh, don't worry, they are all in the assembly room with the Queen.'

'Queen Mother,' he corrected.

'Queen, Queen Mother, what does it matter? Come, I want to show you something,' she said, urgently pulling him up the wide polished wooden staircase.

First they went down one shadowy first floor corridor and then another before she opened a door into a tiny bedroom. She followed him into the room and closed the door with her bottom while using her hands to push him down onto a wooden chair, which stood at one end of a narrow single bed. At the other was a small window allowing a little daylight to penetrate through thin curtains.

In an instant she straddled him, her arms around his neck, open mouth hard pressed to his, her tongue fishing inside his mouth for his. Then he felt her hands at the top of his trousers and she quickly undid his buttons. His erection was instant, faster and bigger than any experienced in his dormitory. Without knickers, expertly she guided him straight into her, moist and warm. Wonderful, wonderful, he thought. So this is what it is like, as she raised and lowered herself, ever quicker, on his lap. But it was all over so quickly and she lowered herself gently onto his failing erection and held his head between her hands. 'Your first time, yes?' she whispered.

Ian nodded, too embarrassed by the speed of events to speak.

'My first English virgin gentleman,' she giggled. 'Next time will be better. I will teach you,' she said softly.

Katrina kept her word, often in the shed housing the school's extensive collection of lawn mowers. The smell of warm freshly cut grass always proved erotic for Ian, reminding him of the hot and very educational summer of 1958.

CHAPTER FORTY

Ian gently laid his beloved Raleigh bicycle, gear side up, on the gravel to the left of the front doors of Widcombe House, and pulled off the two bicycle clips securing the bottom of his trousers. He wrapped his hand around the patina of the bell pull, and pulled it downwards.

In his study Marcus Rose recalled the critical telephone conversation with Howard Edgington earlier that morning.

'Are they sure?'

'Positive, I'm afraid, the hospital almoner called me last night, no further operations are feasible; the original cancer of the stomach has spread everywhere.'

'How long?'

'The surgeon says certainly not more than twelve months, probably less, she has been weakened by so much surgery.'

'Have you told Ian?'

'No, not yet. Morris still believes she will make a full recovery, and his exams are still a year away.'

Marcus thought about the headstrong teenager. 'Leave it with me, Howard. If nothing else, it's the least I can do for a very courageous woman. I will call you after our meeting this afternoon – I assume he is still coming?'

'Yes, he should be with you soon after lunch. Thank you, Marcus.'

The colonel decided the drawing room was more suitable

for the forthcoming encounter, and was still thinking how best to tackle the subject of Ruth's prognosis when Ian arrived. He rose to greet him and they both settled, facing each other in the beautiful French chairs, as Jennings left, quietly closing the door after him.

For a moment he regarded the boy in silence and then he came to a decision.

'Ian, I would like to ask you a very important question.'

The boy did not answer, but grudgingly nodded.

'Following your failure at Hornchurch, the matter of how you propose to earn your living is both relevant and urgent.'

'What do you mean? There's ages before I have to think about that. Why worry about a job until after I have graduated from university? That's another four years away.'

'You are sixteen?'

'Sixteen and a half. I will be sitting A-Levels next year and then go on to Cambridge to read Physics.'

'And how on earth are you going to afford living in a Cambridge College, where is the money coming from?' Rose was becoming impatient with the boy's lack of reality.

'Oh, I hope to get a scholarship, and I can always work in the holidays.'

'And then what?'

'Oh, I don't know, I haven't really given it any thought, but there must be plenty of good research jobs around for someone with a Cambridge physics degree.'

'And what about your mother while you study and earn nothing over the next four years?'

'No problem, the Lady Almoner has spoken to the St John's Charitable Trust in Bath, and they will find us a small rent-free flat when she leaves hospital. There is the money from the Employment Exchange until she goes back to work, and her widow's pension. That will be about £2 per week.'

The silence was broken as the small brass carriage clock on the mantel piece over the fireplace chimed the quarter. Marcus Rose trod carefully.

'What do you think are your chances of getting a Science Scholarship to Cambridge?'

'Pretty good, I reckon.' Ian blushed. 'I've always managed scholarship exams before.'

'Young man, for your own good, stop daydreaming!' Rose had lost patience with the boy. 'Firstly, you stand very little chance of getting into Cambridge, and secondly, there is absolutely no way you could get a scholarship. Cambridge isn't an English public school, but perhaps the finest university in the world.'

'How can you say that?' the boy snapped back. 'You don't know what I can achieve academically.'

'You are right. These are not my opinions but those of your headmaster. He says that you are a bright boy and that you now work hard, but it takes much, much more, even brilliance, to win a science scholarship to Cambridge. Both of us only have your welfare at heart, but you must face reality. Not only Cambridge, but even the newer ones like Nottingham or Birmingham are out of the question.'

Marcus Rose was aware that Ian could probably stay on at Pitt College and would be eligible for one of the new education grants introduced for children from poor backgrounds to enter university, but didn't feel this was in Ian's best interest. Rose believed that a professional qualification was what he needed to get on in this world, not an academic one.

'I don't think you can or should stay at school for much longer. You need to earn a living and can't rely on living with your mother.'

'What do you mean by that?' Ian asked.

Colonel Rose took a deep breath and wondered if he ought

to mention his friendships with Sebastian Cassofiori and Isaac Abrahams. But he knew that it wouldn't lessen the blow, only delay it. Instead he replied in a softer tone.

'Sadly Ian, your mother will never leave hospital; you must prepare yourself for the worst. She has less than a year to live.'

The boy said nothing but the colour drained from his face, and he dropped his head into his hands.

Marcus pushed the bell at the side of the fireplace and a moment later Jennings quietly entered the drawing room.

'The drinks trolley if we may.'

'Yes, Colonel, and for the young man?'

'Oh I think we can stretch a point, he is not at school now.'

Ian, obviously shocked, looked up with glazed eyes. Marcus decided to take the opportunity to leave him for a moment to return to his study and telephone Howard Edgington.

'How is it going?' the headmaster asked.

'Badly, he had no idea. But I have had a thought. My wife, Susan, is due back from London any moment, and I would like Ian to meet her so she can add a woman's touch, so to speak. If he stays for supper, my chauffeur can drive him back to school about nine. How does that sound?'

'Good idea, but are you happy to become so involved?'

'Yes.' Marcus paused. 'I haven't mentioned it before but I met both mother and son about twelve years ago at Cassofiori House; I was on the board that ran the place.'

'What, the blind home out at Box? I didn't know that there was a sight problem, on top of everything else.'

'There isn't. His mother was the live-in housekeeper, so Ian grew up there. He doesn't remember. He was only about five, but the boy and I go back a long way. Two friends of mine, the doctor who delivered him under the Bath rubble, his wife and the blind Cassofiori youngest son, nurtured them as their own, but sadly, all are now dead. Yes, he is an awkward so and so, but the more I get to know him, the more I think I can make a difference. Actually, why don't I ask him to stay the night and Jennings will drive him back early tomorrow morning?'

CHAPTER FORTY-ONE

Only after he had left the train and was standing at the bus stop outside Victoria Station did Ian begin to fret. Even though the school secretary had written out the directions for his trip to London, and he had read and re-read these until he knew them by heart, he was nervous that this wasn't a number seventy three, as he was swept on board the bus by other waiting passengers. He sat down on the bench adjacent to the open platform as the conductress, standing in front of him, with her bosom in his face, pulled the overhead bell cord and the bus moved off.

'Where to, luv?'

'Park Lane, and can you tell me when to get off please?'

'That'll be a tanner. Whereabouts are you wanting?' She spun the handle of the aluminium ticket machine hung from around her neck, and it spat out the thin paper ticket which she handed to him.

'Berkeley Square.'

Nervously Ian twisted the ticket between his sweating fingers. What was he doing amongst this crowd of jostling strangers? Less than a month ago, he was among boys he knew, learning and preparing to go up to university. Now he was on his way to see a complete stranger to get a job in property surveying, whatever that might be. Why the mad rush to earn a living?

'Park Lane, for Berkeley Square!' he heard the sing-song voice of the conductress and the bell before the bus slowed down.

He stepped down on to the pavement and crossed over Park Lane and headed down Mount Street. He was fascinated by the specialist shops, with their nineteenth-century South American bank notes or rows of unplucked pheasants, until he came to Berkeley Square, and saw number twenty-three.

The gold lettering of 'Woods & Parker, Established 1763' stood proudly above the building's stone entrance. Ian's heart was pounding as he climbed the impressive semi-circular flight of steps that led up to a glass revolving door set between a pair of bow windows with odd panes of bottle glass that gave the effect of age.

He pushed at the door. Nothing happened, so he exerted more pressure but it still didn't move. A large red-cheeked man standing inside looked at him for a moment then stepped forward and mouthed something. Ian didn't understand, and was on the point of giving up when the man stepped forward and gave the doors a shove.

'The other way, stupid boy!' The doors revolved rapidly and Ian, facing the wrong way, was swept inwards and landed in a heap at the man's feet.

'Silly bugger.' The man laughed and strolled away into the depths of the building.

'That was a dramatic entry, young sir,' a different voice commented. 'I see you've met the senior partner's son. Don't mind Master Paul, hasn't been quite right since he was shot out of a tank on D Day.'

Embarrassed, Ian picked himself off the floor and looked up at the large, heavily bewhiskered Commissionaire in his immaculate black uniform with brass epaulettes and three golden stripes on each sleeve.

'And who might you be?' the voice added.

'Morris, sir.' He wondered why the middle aged man, who

had walked away into the building, should be referred to as 'Master'.

'Not sir, Mr Morris, but Sergeant, Sergeant Baldwin.' He looked down at an open diary on the pedestal desk in front of him.

'Ah yes. You've got an interview with Brigadier Sale. I believe he's running about half an hour late but you can wait in the small client waiting room. Follow me.'

Puzzled that size determined where you waited, Ian followed the Sergeant up a broad stone staircase to the first floor and into a sizeable waiting room, with circular walls and a surprisingly high and ornate ceiling; it reminded him of the school side chapels. He perched on the front of one of the deep leather-backed chairs that surrounded a round table in the centre of the room and looked about him.

Hanging on the walls were a dozen or so auction posters, announcing the sale of various country estates; they reminded him of the billboards outside the Theatre Royal in Bath. The most impressive appeared to be the sale of the Palle Estate. It included a 'gentleman's country residence and parkland with eight villages, thirty thousand acres of farmland, with diverse mining, fishing and shooting rights'. There were posters advertising sales that stretched back seventy-five years. In the one dated 1872 the firm was simply called Woods, with, to his surprise, an address of 17 Wood Street, Bath. Many of the sales had taken place during the 1920s and 1930s.

Despite the time of day the room was dark with its net curtains and heavy brown ornamental drapes covering the only window. Brass table lamps with green glass shades threw circles of light onto the side tables, and a thick biscuit-coloured carpet added to the tranquil atmosphere. Ian detected the faint lingering smell of cigar smoke, which always made him think of affluence.

Sergeant Baldwin returned and together they went down a panelled passageway, again decorated by posters of past sales, into the depths of the building and a door with the name of Brigadier Frank Sale embossed in gold on its polished wood.

The sergeant knocked and ushered him into another dark room that was dominated by an enormous desk. Behind it was a portly man with a large red nose on a purple face of broken veins.

'Sit down.' The man indicated a small low seat in front of the desk as the sergeant left the room and Ian wondered why he was being interviewed by an army officer for a job in civvy street.

'Ah, Morris, yes,' Brigadier Sale said, looking down at the single sheet of paper on his desk. More used to interviewing the offspring of the minor aristocracy and old military families, his interviewing procedure faltered. The name Morris was unknown to him; there were no social links that he could bring into conversation.

The interview sheet was signed by his senior partner, Gordon French. But who the hell was 'Rose' – there had been a chap in the Intelligence Corps called Rose – a strange bod, friend of Churchill, a Hebrew by all accounts. Morris, wasn't that his tailor's name? Another Jew. Why would French want a Jew in the firm?

'And what makes you think that you are good enough to join Woods and Parker, Morris?'

The boy looked so taken aback by the question that Sale wondered if the boy had suddenly realised that an old English professional firm like Woods and Parker was an inappropriate place for a Jew boy. When Morris didn't immediately answer, Sale pressed on. 'Well, let me tell you how to get on, if you are lucky enough to join us. Same as in the regiment. Trust the Lord and keep your bowels open, and-'

To his relief the long intercom box on his desk buzzed and a light marked 'Senior Partner' flashed.

He pushed down the switch, leant forward. 'Brigadier Sale.'

'Corporal French here, Sale.' The voice coming out of the loudspeaker had a hint of mockery, because of his junior partner's continuing use of wartime rank. 'Is the boy recommended by Marcus Rose with you?'

'Yes, why?'

'I want to meet him. Come into my office. Both of you.'

To the brigadier's horror, Gordon French had offered Morris a job, starting as everyone entering the firm had to, in the filing room at £4 per week for a trial period of six months. To French's surprise the boy seemed reluctant to accept, and asked if he could let them know.

Ian still hoped a way could be found for him to stay at Pitt College. It had been agreed that after the interview he would return and stay the night at Widcombe House. On the train from Paddington Ian racked his brain for a reason not to take the job.

Marcus Rose was none too pleased to receive the phone call from Gordon French, telling him of the boy's procrastination. After all, he, the senior partner, had put himself out and overruled a fellow partner to do Marcus a personal favour, on the understanding that young Morris would jump at the opportunity to join the firm. Many requests for a job came, few even got through the front door, and only three a year were chosen.

They had been at loggerheads for over an hour. Face to face across the desk in his study, Rose had dismissed Ian's excuses one by one, knocking all props away.

Ian, desperate, played his last card. 'There's also the problem of finding somewhere to live in London on £4 per week. Where can I afford?'

'I think I might be able to help.'

Ian interrupted. 'I won't accept your money.'

Marcus laughed, 'I'm not offering it. But there's a maid's room, which goes with our flat in Grosvenor Square. It's a single room, up on the top floor, and you'll have to share a bathroom with the other domestics.'

'How much would it cost?'

Again Rose laughed. 'For you, nothing, just some promises.'

'Which are?'

'First, you start your correspondence course for your exams the day you join Woods & Parker. Second, Susan and I expect you down here in Bath every Friday night for dinner, and I will send the car to collect you. After dinner, you and I can discuss how the work and studying are going. I will make a room available here for you to study in over the weekend, and the car can take you back on Sunday night.'

Ian was taken aback by Rose's insistence in being involved. Why was that? He was being dragged into more than just a job with a room.

'Why are you doing this, you know, helping me? It's not as though we are related. You don't know my mother, and you are trying to interfere.'

'That's where you are wrong. I first met your mother after the war in 1946, when she was the housekeeper at Cassofiori House. I met you once, it was Chanukah, you were nearly five, do you remember?'

'No,' Ian said uncertainly.

'Not even the silver sixpence, the *gelt* as you described it to Sebastian?'

'You knew Uncle Sebastian?'

'Yes.'

'And Isaac and Naomi?'

Rose nodded. Ian did not remember, and continued to look blankly at him.

'By the way, when did you last see your mother?'

'Ten days ago, why?'

'That explains it. I took the liberty of visiting her last Thursday. Of course she was very surprised to see me again after such a long time, but once I told her everything, she seemed greatly relieved.'

Ian was dumbfounded. 'Why you are doing this, really?'

Marcus thought for a moment and decided that the boy deserved an honest answer.

'In 1940, Susan was pregnant with our first child, and we visited her two sisters in the East End of London. They were her only family still alive who had got out of Russia. We wanted them to come back with us, but they wouldn't hear of it. They were happy as they were. As usual they would sleep in the underground station if there was a raid. That night the station received a direct hit. Those two weren't killed by the bomb; they drowned when the burst water main flooded the whole tunnel. It took three weeks for the bodies, or more to the point, what was left of the bodies, to be brought out. I spent days going from mortuary to mortuary, trying to find her sisters. Often I was just shown an unrecognisable piece of mildewed flesh. It was hopeless. Susan miscarried. That miscarriage was followed by five more. Then you turn up, much the same age as the child we never had, a Jewish boy, appearing from my past. Destiny – it's not as though I had gone looking for you, or you for me.'

Marcus stopped talking and let the silence linger, before asking, 'Do we have a deal?'

'On one condition.'

Surprised at his chutzpah, Marcus asked, 'Which is?'

'I can pack it all up anytime, if I don't want it; just leave the flat, the job, you, Susan, everything?'

Marcus nodded. 'Deal. The head porter is Stafford, ex-army, and very pompous, but I will call and tell him you will move in next weekend, so that you start at Woods and Parker on Monday.'

'If I must.' Ian grudgingly gave up the struggle. It never occurred to him to thank Marcus.

Ian pushed open the plate glass door to 37 Grosvenor Square and stepped into an immense marble hall with thickly patterned carpets and antique looking furniture. A tall, well-built man dressed in a tailcoat and winged collar stood up from a small desk in an alcove and walked towards him.

'Can I help you?' He looked at Ian disdainfully.

'My name is Ian Morris, and-'

'Ah, yes, Colonel Rose told me to expect you. Wait here a moment.'

He collected two keys from his desk and led him to the back of the hall. Here he pulled open a cleverly concealed mirrored door. The dark bleak concrete stairwell contained an iron-caged lift and smelled of dustbins. Stafford handed him the keys.

'Room twenty-four, eighth floor. You will find the rules for domestic servants on the back of the door to your room, and you will abide by them.'

He turned to go back, then stopped and pointed to a door at the other side of the lift cage.

'The second key is to the tradesmen's entrance in Adams Row. It's locked at eleven every night, and I should be obliged if you would use it at all times instead of coming through the front door. What little mail you might have should be addressed "c/o the Porter's Lodge".'

He turned and left Ian to find his way to the maid's room, number twenty-four.

CHAPTER FORTY-TWO

He stared at the crucifix on the wall; it reminded him to take Uncle Sebastian's *Magen David* out of his pocket and place it around his neck. He had resumed wearing it when visiting the hospital, as he knew it pleased his mother. Below the crucifix was his mother's name chalked on the small blackboard showing the ward's bed positions. Over the last three years she had moved up to occupy pole position.

Sister O'Brien came in to the ward office and, unusually, closed the door behind her. He wondered why, as she sat down with the habitual smoothing of her uniform.

'I wanted to see you, Ian, because I'm afraid your mother had a turn for the worse this morning. She's quite poorly, and you don't have to leave when you hear the bell at the end of visiting. You can stay as long as you like.'

He nodded slowly.

'Isn't there any other family at all? Even back in Poland that we could try to contact?'

He shook his head.

'No.' He finally spoke. 'There's only me left.'

The floral curtains were drawn, completely screening his mother's bed from the others in the ward. He knew that this wasn't a good sign, but occasionally it had happened before over the last three years, after the numerous operations and setbacks. He was sure Sister would have said something if it was really bad.

They went through the curtains and he bent down to kiss his mother. The *Magen David* around his neck brushed her cheek. Her gaunt pinched face was flushed, and she was breathing in short shallow gasps.

Sister took the chair from the head of the bed and placed it behind him before slipping back into the ward. He sat down and clasped his mother's hand, its back bruised by the continuous punctures from intravenous drips.

Visiting was soon over. The supper trolley came and went. He sat there.

Sister O'Brien gently shook him. He had fallen asleep in the darkened ward.

'The next bed is empty. Why don't you stretch out on it? I'll draw the curtain back between the two beds so that you can still see your mum.'

She helped him unlace his shoes, and climb onto the adjoining bed. He lay on his side exhausted. 'Goodnight Mum,' he whispered.

CHAPTER FORTY-THREE

The bustle of the breakfast trolley woke him. It was six in the morning and Ian rolled over to check how his mother was.

The bed was empty and stripped.

CHAPTER FORTY-FOUR

Sister O'Brien looked at the boy; not a tear, he was in shock, utterly bemused, lost – later she thought numb was the appropriate word – disconnected.

'You need to take this to the Guildhall, Ian,' she said, handing him the medical certificate which Dr Medlock had signed an hour earlier; it certified bowel cancer as the cause of death. 'Ask for the Registrar, Alistair Colston. I'll give him a ring in a minute to let him know you are on your way. He and his wife, Cathy, are good friends of St Peter's. They do great work, fundraising for the hospital in their spare time.' She stood up and held out a hand. 'Well, goodbye Ian, and the best of luck for the future. I was very fond of your mother, she was a very brave woman.'

Ian was alone in the cavernous and dimly lit waiting room. Its scant and threadbare furniture had made no concessions for the grief-stricken over the decades. Little piles of under-takers' business cards were scattered around the room.

Alerted by Sister O'Brien's telephone call, Alistair Colston had left his door ajar, so that in an instant, the Registrar had gathered the boy up and ushered him into his office,

'Have a seat, Ian. More paperwork I'm afraid, but I will try and make it as painless as possible. Let's start with the medical certificate.'

The boy handed the piece of paper over without a word.

Alistair looked down at the book of green death certificates open on his desk, the next blank one was number 415. He picked up his fountain pen and started to fill in the various blanks, speaking aloud as he went.

'Name, Ruth Morris, time of death, 3 am. I need your help with the next questions. Date of birth?' Silence. 'Your mother's date of birth?' No reply. Pen poised in mid-air, the Registrar waited. Still nothing. 'I must have this information,' he said, 'before I can allow you to bury your mother.'

'I don't know.'

'Well, let's work it out. How old was she?'

'I don't know, she never told me.'

Alistair decided to tackle it another way. 'What did her birth certificate say?'

'She never had one.'

'Why not, where she was born?'

'Woodge.' Ian remembered how Katrina had pronounced it.

'Where's that?'

'Poland.'

'How do you spell it?'

'L-O-D-Z.'

The Registrar wrote 'Unknown' in the first box and 'Lodz, Poland' in the second.

'How long was she in hospital?'

'For the last three years.'

He put 'St Peter's Hospital' against last address, and 'None' for occupation. He signed the certificate, blotted it, tore down the perforated edge and removed it from the book.

Next, he completed and signed the certificate of burial and passed both across the desk to Yann. 'The undertakers will need these. Have you decided who to use?' The boy looked blank.

'Try Thomas & Company, they are as good as anyone, and

right opposite on the other side of the High Street. Nigel is a nice man and does as good a job as anyone, at a reasonable price.'

The Registrar stood up and held out his hand. Ian shook it and left the Guildhall to cross the road.

'How much?' he asked incredulously ten minutes later.

'Seventy-five pounds,' repeated Nigel Thomas.

'I haven't got anything like that.'

'What about the others in the family, won't they help?'

'There isn't anyone.'

'No one?'

Ian shook his head.

'Well, there's always the pauper's funeral payment.'

'What's that?'

'Thirty-seven pounds, which the State provides for the burial of the destitute poor. When were you born?'

'April 28th 1942.'

Thomas mentally calculated his age. 'No good, I am afraid you're ineligible. A son has to be under eighteen to claim it. How much have you actually got?'

'Twenty-eight pounds and eleven shillings in the post office,' Ian replied despairingly.

Nigel Thomas felt sorry for the lad. The last time he had come across such a situation was after the bombing, but then public donations had paid for the mass burials of the countless unknown. He did the calculations in his head. Bury the body for fifteen pounds, using casuals, no ceremony. No headstone, that wouldn't be needed for a year, until after the ground had settled. Forget a hearse, collect the body in the van from the hospital, say three pounds. The cheapest coffin, reconstituted cardboard, twenty. No shroud and strip out everything else, flowers, adverts, church ceremony.

'The best I could do is thirty-eight pounds, twenty up front and the remaining eighteen at seven bob a week for a year. OK?'

Ian nodded.

Ashamed, he told no one about the funeral; Marcus and Susan were away on holiday and he was evasive with the few others who asked. Two days later Ian, the sole mourner, stood by the mound of earth after the grave diggers had finished. He had been shocked at how small the coffin had been. Ravaged by the cancer over the years his mother had been reduced to the size of a child. He didn't even bother to look for a rabbi, the ceremony had been perfunctory and brief, performed by what Mr Thomas had described as the cemetery's 'inter-faith chap' at no charge.

Aloud he started to recite, '*Yisgadal veyishkadash shemey robo.*' Ian got no further than the first line of the Hebrew prayer. It had been so long, years since he had last said, or even heard, the Kaddish, and he had forgotten the words. He tried again, but only bits of it came back, he gave up.

'Goodbye, Mum.'

The small parcel was waiting for him in the Hall Porter's office when he got back to London and Grosvenor Square. He unwrapped the brown paper to reveal a tin about a foot square, and six inches deep. Attached to it was a handwritten note:

St Peter's Hospital – 4th May 1960

Dear Ian,

Sorry, forgot to give you this. It belonged to your mother and was kept in my 'special' cup-board. As far as I know this is the only personal

effect she had for all the years she was with us.
From time to time she would ask me to add
things.

All the best.

Sister O'Brien.

'Peek Frean, makers of famous biscuits' said the faded red label on the lid. The tin had rusted in the corners where the label had been worn away by use. Gently he prised the lid off. It was crammed with papers; they were receipts.

He picked out the first, and unfolded it. It was a hire purchase agreement for a bicycle costing nineteen pounds one shilling and ten pence; four pounds as a deposit with weekly repayments at three shillings and four pence. It was dated March 1956. His beloved Raleigh, his mother's fourteenth birthday present – it had never occurred to him that it had taken her nearly two years to pay for it.

He delved deeper and out came more HP agreements and payment cards going back years. The few sticks of furniture for the cottage at Rowas Grange Estate at half a crown a week for two years. Then a rent book for the house in Mafeking Street at nine pounds and a penny every month. More furniture, on and on it went, everything 'on tick'. Year after year, the never-never was the only way his mother had survived on her meagre wages.

By now the box was only half full. Next came bundles of receipts for odd payments to Beaconsfield and Pitt College. He had always assumed that his scholarships had covered everything. Dozens of them for odd sums, always in guineas, starting in September 1947, and ending nine years later, that

Christmas when he had arrived home and discovered her barely alive.

He emptied the last inch and a half of the box and was horrified to discover that every single one of the thirty or so slips were judgements for debt, usually for a few pounds, issued by the Bath County Court going back years. In every case his mother had been ordered to pay back a few shillings every week.

Carefully, he sorted them into datal order, each year a separate pile on his bed. The plaintiff's name for the numerous rent arrears was Lundy, and in most other cases the orders were signed by Colonel John Bradshaw(Registrar).

It was then that he noticed the folded sheet of newspaper almost stuck to the bottom of the tin. He took it out and carefully unfolded the faded front page of the Bath 1942 Chronicle for Wednesday 29th April.

PREGNANT WOMAN SURVIVES UNDER RUBBLE
FOR THREE DAYS
MIRACULOUS BIRTH OF SON

Doctor Isaac Abrahams delivered...

'Dear God, Mum, I am sorry, so sorry, so very sorry. Forgive me, I was ashamed of you – I should have been so proud. All those years alone, how many frightening sleepless nights?' At last he let go and wept, the anger, the shame, the guilt. 'This should never, never, never have happened.' He sobbed uncontrollably, his head falling into the years of struggle and shame, piled on his bed.

CHAPTER FORTY-FIVE

Ian liked Jeremy Thring. Unlike most of the other senior partners of Woods & Parker, there was no side to the sixty-five-year-old who headed up the commercial investment department. Whilst the junior partners and staff indulged in long liquid lunches 'making contacts', when he delivered the midday mail Ian would find Thring sitting in the first floor bay window eating a sandwich and observing the comings and goings in Berkeley Square. Thring, in turn, took an interest in the youngster, especially when he learnt that Ian was studying for his surveyor examinations at night.

'You must be the first for a long time; I cannot remember when someone in this firm last qualified.'

'It was twenty-five years ago, sir,' Ian replied, 'in 1934. I had to look it up for my application form.'

'I'm not surprised. Youngsters then never had a chance. Immediately the Second World War started, they were called up. Then after it ended there was compulsory national service for everyone at eighteen. Six months basic training and off they went with the Regulars; the slaughter of Indian Partition, Malayan terrorists, the Mau Mau in Kenya, EOKA in Cyprus...' He paused. 'Remind me, when did conscription end?'

'The month after I joined the firm, sir.'

'That is fortunate. You are going about it the right way, practical work here in the daytime, and learning the theory afterwards is an ideal combination. How long does it take these days?'

'Nearly five years, assuming you pass each exam first time. Nine subjects in each exam, three exams, First, Intermediate and Final; one every eighteen months.'

'Tough, but worth it. Don't hesitate to come and see me if you think I can help.'

Thring knew that Gareth Notts was a good manager, but not a deal maker, so not perfect partnership material. Opening a branch office of Woods & Parker in Wales was the answer, with Notts's lack of flair pushed out to the provinces. A Welshman, he was destined and content to rule in his own fiefdom, and had found a suitable firm to buy.

'Okay, you can go to £50,000, payable over three years. And you'll need to make sure the annual turnover reaches £25,000,' Thring said to Notts over the telephone. 'Now do you need anything else?'

'What do you need an assistant for?' He listened for a moment but cut in before Notts could complete his answer. 'That's an office boy's job. There's a bright lad in the filing room called Morris. You can have him for four weeks. It will be good experience for both of you. Keep me informed. Goodbye.' He replaced the telephone before Notts could proffer any argument.

It seemed like a dream. Yesterday was just another day in the filing room, and now, he was sitting on the night Pullman to Swansea, with all his living expenses paid for four weeks.

He had never seen, or been on a train like it. You could actually have a meal while travelling. After a 'Good evening, sir' the uniformed conductor had picked up Ian's small case and shown him to seat Ten F at a table with a little brass lamp topped by a pink lampshade. Laid for five courses, the silver plated cutlery jingled as the train picked up speed leaving Paddington.

Ian was the only passenger to get off the train at Port Talbot. The rain was tipping down as he walked along the deserted and bleak platform and stared at the flames reaching up to the heavens from a series of towers about five hundred yards away. Guarded by Cerebos he mused, as he headed down the exit tunnel, under a sign welcoming him to 'THE HOME OF THE STEEL COMPANY OF WALES'; the smell of sulphur was augmented by the stink of urine. Skirting around the closed booking hall, he found himself in a cul-de-sac flanked by goods yards; not a soul in sight.

Notts had telephoned him earlier that day.

'Sorry I can't meet you, we are signing the deal off with dinner afterwards. You're booked into the Berni Inn, best place in town and only two minutes from the station.'

He turned into a road of mean Victorian terraced houses with pale lights showing in some of the upper rooms. Further along on his right, illuminated red letters three feet high announcing 'ERNI INN' had been fixed to iron bars spanning the first floor of three adjoining houses.

Early the next morning he waited in the street to escape the stink of stale tobacco and fried food, which oozed from every surface of the hotel. The drabness of the town, having been hidden by darkness on his arrival, came as a shock. Daylight revealed that thick dark smoke plumes had replaced the flames from the steelwork's chimneys, and a pall of it hung over everything. Notts strode towards him.

'Morning Morris, glad to see you made it.'

He was a dapper little man with a moustache, and gap between his front teeth that reminded Ian of the comic actor Terry Thomas.

'Morning, sir.'

'Don't call me sir, save that for the old fogeys in head office. Come along, there's a lot to do.'

Ian fell into step with him as they headed towards the town centre.

'The firm has bought a local estate office and it is to become our first branch in Wales. I heard about it through my fellow Freemasons at the Lodge, never came onto the market.' He lowered his voice to a conspiratorial whisper. 'It all had to be done very "r" and "h", rushed and hushed – the only partner died months ago, a drink problem they say. All the other staff gone. Only completed the negotiations and signed last night. Here to collect the keys,' he concluded as they entered the solicitor's office.

It was a twenty-minute walk from the town, where a private weed-strewn driveway ended in front of a substantial but somewhat forlorn looking detached villa. The brass plaque read 'THE ESTATE OFFICE'.

It had taken both of them to shoulder open the door against an accumulation of post and circulars. Inside was a shambles with piles of files from floor to ceiling, many of which had collapsed, spilling their contents everywhere. The staircase to the upper floors was completely blocked with boxes of papers, and when they eventually cleared a narrow pathway, they discovered even worse. There were broken and glassless windows, heaps of wind-blown papers, and bird shit everywhere.

Ian's suit stayed in his hotel room and was replaced by a blue boiler suit purchased from the local ironmongers. Over the following weeks, yard by yard, room by room, and floor by floor, he stacked and sorted papers for fifteen hours every day.

There was a constant flow of tradesmen. After five days the electricity was reconnected to replace the candles and paraffin lamps. For a week Ian had to piss in the garden until the water was reconnected and the lavatory came back into operation.

'Forget anything over sixty years ago and stack it into there.' Notts indicated the cleared back office previously used as a secretarial pool. 'It's all ancient history. I've ordered six incinerators for the back garden, and then you can start burning. Likewise, all the old expired leases and everything else vaulted in the basement; most of it goes back to when the office first opened over a hundred years ago.'

For the next ten days Ian moved tons of old papers and expired documents into the rear of the building, so that the decorators could move into the front.

The galvanised incinerators, dustbins with mesh bottoms and lids with chimney pots arrived.

'I reckon it will take a good week to burn that lot, so the sooner we get started the better,' Notts said. The 'we' was, in reality, Ian.

Later the old estate office sign was replaced by a large brass plate:

WOODS & PARKER
Established 1763
Regional Partner: Gareth Notts FRICS

Ian started the burning that evening. But it soon became clear that lobbing the whole files into an incinerator would not work because the edges just became singed and the fire would not catch. He reconciled himself to breaking up every file and feeding all six incinerators constantly. He cleared a space by the back door into which he could throw the contents of each broken up file and started with the vaulted files from the basement. He had never looked at these in detail before.

The files were of a type not used in modern offices, each was named in black ink on its outside, and comprised of a thick wad of correspondence with an envelope stitched into its back cover containing documents. He opened the first, labeled 'LLCHWR TENANCIES 1860 – 1861' and started to read. Llchwr was a village outside Port Talbot – he had seen it as a destination on the front of the town buses – and wondered how you pronounced a name without any vowels.

He tore out the paperwork from the file, threw it on to the floor to start the pile for the fire, and looked in the envelope on the back. It contained an indenture relating to a railway line, with copperplate handwriting on parchment and red wax seals, its inner edge cut irregularly where it had been separated from its duplicate counterpart. A separate handwritten receipt for the first quarter's rent was pinned to it. He had never seen anything so old before, and intrigued, he put the document to one side to look at later, before moving on to the next file. After he had stripped twenty files he started the incinerators again.

Ian left the office at 11.00 pm that night, taking six parchment documents back to his hotel to read.

Notts was impressed when he arrived the next morning at 8.00 am and found Ian hard at work with all the incinerators burning furiously.

'You are sure Mr Notts, that you don't want to keep anything before 1900?'

'Absolutely, don't care how you do it, just get rid of it all. You need only go back sixty years for good title, so burn the rest.'

Instead Ian continued to take the parchment deeds back to his hotel. Notts put his hand into his inside pocket and withdrew his wallet. 'Here's a fiver, all that matters is that the office is cleared by Friday morning, ready for Mr Thring's visit.'

It took Ian until 1.00 am on Friday morning to finish the clearout. He put all the deeds in the secondhand school trunk in his room that he had purchased with Notts's £5. He locked and addressed it, to await collection at Paddington.

Notts had stalled Jeremy Thring's visit from head office until everything had been returned to normal, for fear that otherwise his ambition to head up a Welsh office would be viewed as disastrous.

When the day arrived Notts cautioned Ian about his boss.

'Be a good chap.' He had a habit of smoothing his moustache with thumb and forefinger when he was anxious. 'Don't let on to Mr Thring about the shambles we found. I know the hours you have worked, and I will push for a little bonus for you.' He lifted his hand away from his face and smiled, revealing the Terry Thomas gap. 'Can't promise anything, mind you.'

'So, how was Morris? I couldn't get a word out of him,' Thring asked Notts as they waited at Port Talbot station for the London train. The trip had gone well and, relieved to have his contract confirmed, Notts was effusive.

'Excellent, very willing and worked hard all hours of the day. I think he deserves a small bonus.'

'Leave that with me, I have something more in mind for him,' Thring replied as he stepped on to the train.

The London dealer in Mount Street – the very same shop he had passed on his way to his interview a year earlier – arranged the dozen documents that Ian had left with him the day before into four separate piles.

'This one,' he said, indicating the first stack of documents, '£1 or so each. This,' he pointed to the second pile, 'say £20 each. The next pile, £40 each, and the single one is £100.'

Not wanting to show his surprise at the sums involved, Ian thought for a moment, then said, 'What's wrong with the deeds in the first pile?'

'Nothing.'

'I don't understand.'

'It's not the deeds, you can buy these for two a penny. It's the receipts, and the Victorian postage stamps on them.' He pointed in turn to each of the last three piles. '1840 penny blacks, 1840 twopenny blues and 1882 £1 brown.'

Ian picked up the deeds. 'I'll let you know in a day or so.'

Later that night in his bedroom, Ian sorted them out. Of the 130 documents, ninety had the black postage stamps with Victoria's head on, twenty-eight had other coloured stamps, and there were twelve documents with no receipts.

Ian tried two other dealers in Jermyn Street before returning to the original one and negotiated him up. He walked out of the shop with a cheque for £5,200 – twenty-five years of his weekly present wage of £4 per week.

On the following Saturday he went into the County Bank in Milsom Street and opened a deposit account into which he deposited the whole sum.

Christopher Johnson smiled at the morning 'Prayer Meeting' on the following Monday, when he noticed the name on his weekly list of new depositors – Isaac would be proud, he must arrange to meet the boy. Not such a boy he thought ruefully, as he viewed the size of the deposit.

CHAPTER FORTY-SIX

Two days after he returned to the London office he encountered Mr Thring in his usual place at lunchtime, looking out at Berkeley Square.

'Hello Morris,' the older man said, and turned from the window. 'I have been waiting to have a word with you. Notts told me about your good work in Wales. Well done. Now tell me, how old are you?'

'Eighteen, sir.'

'Right, well I think it's about time we got you out of the filing room. But is there a department you particularly fancy?'

Ian had realised months earlier that the greatest fees were earnt in the firm's two investment departments: one agricultural and the other commercial. Agricultural estates seemed to be staffed by middle-aged tweed-clad types, always muttering about walking around ploughed fields and prices per acre. The commercial boys, on the other hand, were in their late twenties and early thirties, confidently arrogant, flamboyant in manner and dress, with beautiful cars. Most became junior partners because the senior partnership seemed unable to resist their claims of an ever-increasing profit stream. The few who were passed over moved to lesser firms.

'I want to join your department Mr Thring,' he replied. 'Commercial investment is the only thing that really interests me, none of the others.'

'Why's that?'

'It's because that's how I can earn the most money, sir.'

'And is that the only reason?'

'Pretty much for the time being. Unlike a lot of the other boys in the filing room, I don't have the luxury of choice – to survive I must qualify and earn. That's all that matters.'

'And do you think money brings happiness?'

'Absolutely, the more money I make, the happier I will be!'

The certainty and single-mindedness was surprising in one so young, and rather refreshing to the older man, who felt detached from the drifting and indulged youth of postwar Britan.

'Fair enough, that's settled. I will tell the others. Report to the head of department, John Mulholland, here on Monday morning.'

Well satisfied, Thring returned his gaze to the square below.

John Mulholland had his *Financial Times* spread across the desk. His morning ritual always started with a check on his shares' closing prices on the previous day.

Slowly, he looked up from his beloved 'pink'un' and over his half glasses, as if appraising Ian before speaking.

'So, you are the little bugger Jeremy has decided should join us. You can sit there,' he pointed to the smallest desk in the room that was next to the door, 'but you'll need a decent suit, some proper shoes to replace those brothel creepers, a tie or two and some white shirts. We can't have you representing the department looking like a bookmaker's runner.' Ian remembered his headmaster's comment about his old fur coat and must have reddened because Mulholland went on.

'Don't worry about the cost, I will lend it to you against your first commission.' He pushed his chair back from the desk and stood up. 'Now follow me.' And off they marched to the wonderful world of the Burlington Arcade.

Ian's learning curve in Mulholland's office was steep and exhausting. As the only junior in the Investment Department, he was at the beck and call of all six of the valuers and negotiators, and sometimes the three senior partners. He was soon exposed to every form of commercial property investment.

Each night he would return to his small dingy room – often too tired to eat – for endless study and little sleep. He got up at six, arriving at the office with the cleaners every morning in order not to fall behind with the written papers, which had to be posted back to the College of Estate Management each week.

Jeremy Thring had been very good about Ian leaving early, and many were intrigued by the large Bentley which waited for him in Berkeley Square every Friday afternoon. He enjoyed the journey to Bath and after a few trips the chauffeur knew well enough to leave him alone, as, sitting in the back, he went through the past week's marked study papers.

He loved the weekends of delicious food, clean sheets and competitive games of Scrabble; the luxury of Widcombe House was such a contrast to the maid's room in London. Right from the first weekend, Marcus Rose had insisted that he bring the work marked by the college with him, so that they could go through it after dinner. It was more unwanted pressure but, keen to impress, these sessions kept him from falling behind in the relentless treadmill of study and work. By the last Friday before Christmas 1960 Ian could relax; Contract and Tort, Valuations, Law of Property, all had earned him an 'A' mark, with only a 'B' in Building Construction. Marcus should be pleased.

Sunday night, back in the maid's room, the next week's washing and ironing brought him back to earth. He had splashed out on a new-fangled 'drip dry' shirt, bought from Marks & Spencer at great expense. Its wrapper proudly boasted, 'needs no ironing, just wash and wear, your body heat does the rest: after only five minutes, not a wrinkle in sight'. His creases lasted right through the day. At the drawing board, jacketless one morning, Mulholland made a comment about juniors coming to work in shirts they had slept in. Ian went back to ironing.

One day, he fell into conversation with the old Etonian who had replaced him in the filing room; he had once been told Old Etonians were either totally charming or perfect shits. This one was the former, always broke, and was at the firm because his father nurtured 'the vain hope that his first born would learn how to take over the family estate when he fell off his perch'.

He explained his latest money-making racket in the filing room. It involved jamming the machine for franking the postage on the hundreds of letters sent out daily. Given money to buy stamps, the machine would magically and secretly resume working and the filing room boys would pocket the cash.

'How big is the estate?' Ian asked.

'Oh, I don't know, bloody great manor house, with six whole villages, in Yorkshire. Can you imagine?'

Ian couldn't, they lived on different planets.

'I will have to go into the House of Lords, when the title passes to me. Probably disappear and join the Foreign Legion.'

Ian was fascinated by his immaculate stiff white collar.

'How do you get them so smart?' he asked, conscious of his own limp efforts.

'Easy, old chap. Regency shirts in Adams Row. The branch at Windsor did the ones for school, and this one is designed for us impoverished wage-slaves. I'll take you down at lunch time, if you like?'

To Ian's dismay, the trip cost him his three shilling luncheon voucher, but it was worth it. A dozen detachable white collars that were starched like steel. At first, life was agony as they cut into his neck. Viewing the angry circular red scar in the mirror after a week, he looked as though he had just narrowly escaped the gallows. You could always tell a Regency man, scarred for life.

The practical daytime work, coupled with his academic studies, supplemented each other perfectly, and his knowledge grew exponentially. To his surprise, the more Ian learnt and did, the more he liked it, and the more he liked it, the easier he found it to excel. Most importantly, he had started to make money, which was his road to salvation.

CHAPTER FORTY-SEVEN

The work and study were relentless, often leaving Ian with no more than five hours sleep on week nights, and little more at the weekends. The lifestyle suited him, he was always busy and didn't have the time or inclination to dwell on anything other than work and study; using his specialist property knowledge from the latter at work, earnt him the nickname of 'the boffin in the Investment department'. Better than Poire, he mused.

It was obligatory for each department to be aware of the contents of the obituary column of the *Times* newspaper every day. Anyone who knew, or had any knowledge of an inclusion, however remote, had to attend the 'Graveyard' meeting at ten o'clock, where it was decided who would write to the widow. Usually it was the senior partner, and it followed a strict format. 'Very sad...', and if appropriate, 'only saw him... shared a drink at the club...', and always ended: 'If there is anything, absolutely anything at all I, in my role as your late husband's friend, can do to assist, please do not hesitate to be in touch.'

Handwritten, the letter would be delivered, not posted, by the office motor cyclist, an ex-army dispatch rider, nicknamed the 'Angel of Death'. Mandatory attendance at the funeral or cremation followed, which routinely bore rich pickings for the firm.

Thus it was that Ian found himself accompanying John Mulholland to the 'Graveyard' meeting in early June of 1961, following the announcement that morning of the death of Marmaduke, the third Earl Lundy.

The company had last acted for the family when the first Earl acquired the island of Lundy in the Bristol Channel at the turn of the century. Ian's connection was instantly and sniffily dismissed when he admitted his mother's role as housekeeper to the family. He did not mention his last encounter with Alistair, the son, now to be the fourth Earl, when he and his mother had been evicted.

Much more relevant was Brigadier Sale's connection through Poppy Day and the British Legion. His letter was duly delivered to the widow, Emily, at Rowas Grange Estate. As was hoped, Woods & Parker were appointed to handle the Probate valuation. John Mulholland was put in overall charge, and being from Bath, Ian was the natural choice as his assistant.

Mulholland explained what was to be expected as they drove down to meet the trustees.

'This is a big job, Ian, probably the largest estate the firm has handled for years. Rumour has it that the first Earl Lundy, the plain but by no means simple, Mr Michael Symons, bought his peerage for a political donation of about £1 million in the early 1920s, through a man called Maundy Gregory, who was Lloyd George's whoremaster in such matters. Can you imagine £1 million forty years ago? But this was a mere drop in the ocean of his vast fortune made in mining, shipping, banking, property. The grandson, Marmaduke, has not been too clever; lost a stack of money in some hair brain property venture in Bath. Neither he nor his father, the second Earl, did any death duty planning, as no doubt will be revealed later this morning.'

The estate was enormous. The first Earl had been very canny. Both son and grandson had been barred from selling any part of the estate. However, this had not prevented them from borrowing heavily over the last fifty years, in order to maintain their lavish life styles.

'So there you have it Mr Mulholland,' Malcolm Austwick, the principal trustee, summed up at the end of their first meeting. 'It encompasses at least ten per cent of Bath, with all sorts of commercial buildings. There are countless shops, factories, hotels, pubs, and other businesses, as well as thousands of freehold ground rents and rent charges, not to mention the swathes of working class terraced houses all let on weekly tenancies.'

Austwick stopped and looked directly at Ian.

'Do you drive?'

'No, sir.'

'You'd better learn. In the counties around the city are about twenty thousand acres of agricultural and woodland, and much of the Somerset and Bristol coalfields that produce over 8,000 tons a month. Then there are the Fuller's earth workings that are still profitable but the stone quarries, some dating back to Roman times, lose money – now either too dangerous or uneconomic to work.'

'Ian, how do you feel about moving back to Bath? The estate is much larger than even I expected, and the death duties are a disaster waiting to happen.' The meeting had been productive and Mulholland needed to work out how best to proceed. 'This job is going to take at least a year, probably longer, even two given the negotiations with the tax people. I need someone I can trust on the ground.'

Ian hesitated. He didn't want to do anything that could jeopardize his career, and Bath was over 100 miles from London, where the real decisions were made; mind you, it would be sweet to see Alistair Lundy brought down a peg or two.

'Don't worry about the money,' Mulholland continued, 'the estate will provide you with everything, accommodation, meals and even a car, given the distances involved.'

'That's not what bothers me,' Ian said, 'but away from head office… you know.'

'I promise you won't be forgotten and this is a great opportunity. Anyway, I will stay for the first few weeks while we get the show on the road, and then visit weekly until the job is finished.'

'Where will I work from, and live?' It was one thing staying at Widcombe House at weekends, but he didn't relish being subject to Marcus Rose's scrutiny every day.

'The trustees own a company called Lundy Enterprises Limited that is based at Cleveland House. They have agreed we can have the first floor, and a load of debbie secretaries under the control of the late Earl's eldest daughter, the Honourable Fiona Symons. As to a place to live, I'll have a word with one of the directors of St John's in Bath, which is a charity for whom we act. It's as old as Bath, and has amassed dozens of almshouses in the city over 800 years, which it lets to deserving cases – I will enquire to see if they can help. In the meantime we will put you up at the Francis Hotel in Queen Square, which, surprise, surprise, is linked to the estate. Another advantage, you will be much closer to your mentor, Marcus Rose, at Widcombe House – no more long drives to and from London every weekend.'

Ian doubted this last point was an advantage, but knew in reality he had little choice. He smiled; he hadn't seen Fiona Symons for years – how long had it been, ten, eleven years ago – but, unlike her awful brother, she had been kind when he had lived in the cottage on the estate.

'All right, but I want one last thing.'

'Which is?'

'The firm to pay for my driving lessons.'

Mulholland laughed. 'Agreed!'

Ian travelled up and down to London in a day to collect his few belongings. He rejoiced at exchanging the tiny maid's room in Grosvenor Square for the grand Lundy Suite in the Francis Hotel overlooking Queen Square. Not bad at eighteen, he thought.

CHAPTER FORTY-EIGHT

He really was fucking above his station, and the Honourable Fiona Symons beneath hers, in more ways than one. Slowly, so as not to wake her, he drew back the sheet to marvel at the long blonde hair and firm breasts which had been all over, under and around him for the previous eight hours. Clearly, like himself, this beautiful woman, ten years his senior, had been without sex for quite a while. He wondered why she had never married.

Feeling very much an outsider, he had tried to avoid the Christmas party at the Lundy Estate Office. Miss Symons – they were not even on first name terms after all these months – had spotted him leaving via the back stairs.

'Mr Morris, the dedicated always working Mr Ian Morris, where are you going? You must join us.'

'Sorry, I've got much still to do.'

'Nonsense, I insist, for one night, you can give it a miss. For goodness sake, it's Christmas Eve, or do what you want to live up to your nickname?'

'What do you mean?' He had no idea what she was talking about.

'Oh, I thought you knew, you must surely, the typing pool refers to you as "the monk of St Johns". They say you must be terrified of women, or worse still, a queer. Come on, show them what you're made of.'

Before he could protest, she had steered him into the hot noisy room and marched him straight to a group of young women circled around a young man of his own age, bryl-creemed hair and a sheen on his face, still the unmistakable bully he remembered.

'Alistair, you remember Ian Morris, you used to play together. Now he's back working all hours of the day and night to save us from financial ruin.'

'Ah yes, the housekeeper's boy. Hello Morris, I must say you've come up in the world.' Ian felt Fiona's hand tighten its grip on his arm.

'You never told me that you lived in an hotel,' Ian said as Fiona struggled, post innumerable large gins, to insert the key into the lock of the very large black front door of 12 Great Pulteney Street. She laughed, and the keys fell from her hand and dropped on to the step.

'That's the Carfax,' she said, pointing a few doors along. Ian bent down and picked up the keys.

'This is owned by the estate. I've got a couple of chums living here too, but they've both gone home for Christmas.'

He opened the front door and stepped aside to let her enter.

'Welcome, Mister Surveyor, I thought an early inspection would save you coming later.' The double entendre was not lost on him, as she threw her handbag onto the hall table, and he followed her up the magnificent central staircase.

Quietly, he rose from the large double bed and put on his underpants. This had to be the grandest bedroom he had ever slept in, even compared to Widcombe House. It was far more spacious than his whole flat. There was a trio of full length windows overlooking the street, with the pale yellow curtains, which she had been in too much of a rush to draw. The matching thick pale wool carpet stretched from wall to wall and was partly covered by a Persian rug.

He went in search of the kitchen and found it three floors below, at the ground level. It was the first time he had been inside one of these houses. The Lundy Estate owned about a quarter of the street, but he hadn't got round to inspecting them. They were large, very large, at least five floors, and Pulteney Street was over a thousand feet long. He walked down it to and from work most days, and out of habit, noticed that virtually all the houses had a single bell, which meant they were in single occupation. Good, he had thought as he passed by, easier to value. He knew they were all different inside. They would be a nightmare to maintain, but could be worth £10,000 each.

Again, the kitchen was vast with dark brown flag stones, a cream AGA cooker with a shelf of herbs over. There was a central highly polished wooden work unit, with four matching bar stools. With difficulty and much searching he managed to put together a mug of coffee, and took it up to the first floor drawing room which he had passed on the way down.

He opened the shutters of the three windows and looked across the street, reckoning that it must be all of a hundred feet wide. Good salesman, Thomas Baldwin, he thought, knew how to minimise risk right back in 1789, before the great property crash four years later. He only built the façade for Sir William Pulteney, then sublet the plots and let people put what they wanted behind.

Drawing room and withdrawing room had been combined and its elegance and size was astounding, from front to back the entire depth of the house. The grand piano, marble fireplace with its leather and bronze fender, the dark green carpet with its Napoleonic roundels and period furniture; it was as if he had stepped back into a Jane Austen novel. What must all of this be worth? He went over to the glass bookcase, and glanced at the titles, wondering about Fiona's literary taste.

Hands emerged from behind, sliding into his underpants and causing an immediate erection. He turned, and she climbed on to him, her legs off the floor, gripping him around the waist. He had never fucked or been fucked like this.

They didn't dress for two days. She found him a Japanese silk dressing gown and they rotated between bedroom, kitchen and drawing room, as hunger and lust took them.

It was Boxing Day night. He had got dressed, she sat on his lap while they shared a bottle of wine before he headed back to his flat. She placed a finger on his lips.

'Remember, Ian, silence,' she said. 'Not a word, look or a sign, when you get back into the office. Having seen us leave together, all eyes will be watching. But you must behave as you did before. Totally ignore me and I will do the same.'

He pulled her hand down.

'But I love you Fiona, and I don't care who knows it.'

'No, you don't.' She dismissed his earnestness lightly. 'Some monk! We've just had a good time and, anyway, I'm too old for you. It will fade into a pleasant memory, once you find someone else of your own age.'

'But-'

She cut him off and stood up. She was serious.

'Listen Ian, it's been great fun, but this goes nowhere. You understand? Nowhere. We live in different worlds. Can you imagine what my mother would say, if she ever found out? Worst still, my brother. Remember, now that Daddy is no longer around, Alistair can control my life completely. My trust, allowance, even this house. One word from him and it all goes, and there's nothing you could do about it.'

'Fiona.'

'Stop right now,' she commanded.

A few minutes later the Honourable Miss Symons, not his beautiful Fiona, was sneaking him out through the back door. He'd been used, he thought morosely, as he cut through South Parade on his way back home. The lights were blazing in both the Southbourne and Pratts, as they had done in peacetime for the last two hundred years since John Wood had designed them. Fiona was forgotten – first thing tomorrow he must check on the deal with Southern Counties. They were keen to add both of these Bath hotels to their others, the Royal in Southborough, and the Imperial in Exeter, and his introduction fee would come in very useful.

True to his word, Mulholland had persuaded St John's Hospital to let him use one of the St Catherine almshouses. On the site of the original wonderful medieval hospital, the little house, off Westgate, had been built in the 1700s, and was perfect for Ian.

Waiting for him was the letter from the Institution, advising him that he had passed the first examination.

CHAPTER FORTY-NINE

'Happy New Year, Ian. But god it's so cold!' John Mulholland, still clad in overcoat, scarf and gloves, had driven down on New Year's day and was sitting across from him on the first floor of Cleveland House. Six inches of snow covered the ground outside.

'Twenty degrees of frost, according to the thermometer by the front door, coldest January since 1940 they said on the radio,' Ian answered.

'The place is deserted, a morgue, where is everybody? Not even the formidable, 'The Honorable Miss Fiona Simmons."'

'She rang in and left a message. Apparently big New Year's Eve party at the Pump Room last night, didn't get home until four this morning, so saw no point in coming in. Great life for some.'

'Not invited?' Mulholland asked.

'Different world. Upper class of Bath only, not my sort of thing anyway.'

'The broke-class more likely,' the older man responded. 'Which brings us back to business, and the trustees meeting this afternoon. Tell me, how much does the tax man want for death duties?'

'I have got him down to half a million since our last meeting with him in November. That really is his bottom line. He won't be pushed anymore.'

'That much?' Mulholland was obviously surprised. 'What do you reckon the whole estate is worth then?'

'I haven't inspected it all. There's still the area around Great Pulteney Street to do.' Suddenly Ian had a flashback of a naked Fiona, and hesitated for a moment before continuing. 'Lotted properly and sold privately over say two or three years, I'd say around £2 million. Much less if the market knows, as it will be sure to guess, because at auction everything has to sell. Added to that there are very few buyers in the market with the money for such a large chunk of real estate. With a forced sale I would say £1 million before costs, net £900,000.'

Mulholland interrupted. 'Then there's the interest payable on the half million tax, since the old boy died. It must be around £500 a week and that's without the local banks hammering on the door for their overdue mortgages to be repaid. Remind me, what do they total?'

'£600,000, including unpaid interest.'

'But Ian, that means the estate is bust and it will all have to go. There's no choice. It will come as a terrible shock for the family, but they have been living beyond their means for decades. They went on borrowing without any thought as to how the loans could be repaid. A classic case of C to C.'

'C to C?'

'Clog to clog in three generations.' He stopped, sighed and then smiled at Ian. 'Ah well, not our problem and, quite the reverse, fee-wise. And on that note, it's time for lunch and a drink. Where do you suggest?'

'Sally Lunn's; its owner, John Overton, is very kind, gave me my first job, washing up when I was fourteen.'

'Lead on,' Mulholland replied. 'Anywhere, as long as it's warm.'

Mulholland had ordered a large brandy and looked around the tea shop.

'Unusual place.'

'One of the oldest houses in Bath, dates back to the fifteenth century. There has been a bakery here since Roman times. Gives you an idea of what medieval Bath must have looked like with its narrow alleys and overhanging gabled roofs. Used to be called Lilliput Alley, and hasn't much changed except they raised the street level about 300 years ago so that the original ground floor became a cellar.'

His boss had ordered the special, the Sally Lunn Bun with the recommended toppings.

'And the bun?'

'Recipe discovered in a secret cupboard in 1937. Named after a Hugenot refugee, a woman who fled France and came to work here in 1680. It's very different, I think you'll enjoy it.'

Rather you than me, thought Ian a couple of hours later, as John Mulholland stood, swaying slightly. The lunch had been good, possibly too good and too liquid, as his boss had fortified himself to deliver his dire message to the Lundy Estate trustees. Only three of the four were present. Alistair was absent, Malcolm Austwick explained; nothing was allowed to disrupt his two months skiing holiday at the family chalet in St Moritz. Unconcerned, the fourth Earl had signed the appropriate Power of Attorney authorising the remaining trustees to decide everything in his absence. Ian had not met the other two, Christopher Johnson and Peter Groves.

They listened carefully and occasionally noted figures down. Neither appeared shocked, presumably because their firms had handled the family's affairs for generations. John Mulholland finished and Austwick looked at the other two trustees, who nodded before he responded.

'We are most obliged Mr Mulholland; can you confirm you are authorised to accept instructions today?' John nodded in reply. 'We should be grateful if you and Mr Morris would leave us for a few minutes, while we discuss matters.'

They both lit cigarettes as they left the room and had barely finished them when they were called back. Austwick addressed John Mulholland.

'On behalf of my fellow trustees, we greatly appreciate the speed and professionalism with which Woods & Parker have addressed the estate's problems.' Now they all looked at Ian. 'We are particularly mindful of Mr Morris's diligence, and we do hope his involvement on a day to day basis continues. We are unanimous. Forthwith sign the deal with the Inland Revenue. Clearly everything has to be sold. Pay the death duties and then repay all the loans as soon as practicable. In the meantime, we would be grateful if you would take over the entire daily management, using the existing staff and accommodation for as long as you need. It's our wish that, to save time and avoid delay, your firm be given complete responsibility as to programme and method of sales. Naturally we expect you to do the best you can, and above all, discretion is paramount; we wish to avoid any unnecessary publicity. All banking will continue through Mr Johnson at the Bank of Bath, with Mr Groves handling all accountancy issues, and my firm will deal with the legals in relation to the death duties, sales and loan repayments. Naturally, all fees will be as per your institution's scale charges. We have already agreed the valuation fees for work so far, but now we propose two per cent of all sale proceeds plus ten per cent of all gross rental income. However, the position is so serious that we would like work to start immediately. Is that acceptable Mr Mulholland?'

'Yes.'

Mulholland decided to stay over in Bath that night, and during dinner explained how he wanted the job to be handled.

'This could be an excellent opportunity for you, Ian, based on the initial income flow and the base it will provide for years to come. The firm has no option but to open an office in Bath, and while Thring will want me to run it, I want you as my number two. What do you think of the idea?'

'This would mean a permanent move away from Berkeley Square, wouldn't it?'

'Yes, but if you play your cards right, you could have a local partnership in ten years. Before you're thirty. Now that can't be bad can it?'

'I very much appreciate the offer, but as tomorrow is Friday and I am going to Widcombe House, do you mind if I ask Mr Rose's advice?'

Mulholland hesitated for a moment, he had met Marcus Rose occasionally, and then only socially.

'Not at all but please stress the confidentiality, and I must have an answer when I go into Berkeley Square to see Jeremy Thring on Monday morning. Phone me at home on Sunday night.'

CHAPTER FIFTY

To Ian's surprise, it wasn't the butler, but Marcus Rose who opened the front door on that Friday evening. 'Susan had to go up to the Grosvenor Square flat for a charity do, and has taken the staff with her.'

After a cold buffet they retired to the study.

'Shouldn't you have started your Intermediate by now?'

'I am a bit behind,' Ian admitted.

'Is that just Christmas celebrations, or something more serious?'

'More serious,' Ian replied.

Marcus smiled. 'What's her name?'

Ian's first thought was that Marcus had heard about Fiona and his Christmas at 12 Great Pulteney Street.

'Don't look so worried. It was just a guess. Not a difficult one. Sooner or later you had to be distracted, young red-blooded male, it was inevitable. After all, you're not a monk.'

'How do you know my nickname?'

Marcus looked perplexed but moved on. 'Is she pregnant?'

Ian laughed, the thought had never crossed his mind. 'No.'

Even more puzzled, Marcus gave up and remained silent.

'Don't worry, it's nothing to do with a girl; it's work, Woods & Parker.'

Ian summarised the previous day's meeting and Mulholland's offer. Occasionally Rose interrupted to clarify a point, and it was nearly midnight by the time they finished.

'When do you have to let him know by?'

'I agreed to ring him by Sunday night.'

'So you've got two days. Let me think on it overnight. I have something I must do tomorrow and will be gone most of the day, but we can talk again at dinner. Turning to equally important things, Tell me, when do you intend to resume studying?'

'The application forms for the Intermediate are already in, so I should receive the study papers any day now.'

'Good. Let's get off to bed.' Marcus rose, and together they slowly climbed the stairs, Ian became conscious for the first time how this man, who meant so much to him, had aged since the Hope Venture project, when he already looked old. As though reading his mind, Marcus put his arm around Ian's shoulders. It was the first time he had ever shown such affection.

'Remember, the gods have clay feet, Ian. This particular god will stay the course for you. Good night and sleep well.'

'Good night, thank you,' Ian replied, touched by the physical contact.

More questions, more discussion, dinner over, they sat in the drawing room, the Scrabble board was opened and letters chosen. Both Susan and Marcus were fanatical about the game, playing every night. Susan usually won, Marcus very occasionally and Ian had never beaten either. He was always amused at the light-hearted banter between them as Marcus attempted to put down invented words which, to his feigned surprise, were never in the dictionary. Ian went first, putting down RAZED, and felt very pleased with himself at scoring 30. Probably because he was stuck, Ian thought, Marcus forgot the game and resumed their earlier discussion.

'Take the offer Ian, you can't afford not to. It's a great opportunity, no question about it.'

'Why are you so certain? I will be so far away from the centre of things in Berkeley Square.'

'That's the point. There's no competition locally for a bright boy like you, especially with the backing of one of the biggest firms in England. Pound the pavements in both senses. Just like a London cabbie, acquire "the knowledge". Get to know every square foot of the city, every street, every nook and cranny, and all on Woods & Parker's time and at their expense. Do it right and within six months, twelve at most, you will know the value and rent of every building and piece of land in Bath. Instinctively you will know what's cheap when it's offered. Every investor will be beating a path to your door when, as it will, word gets around the market, that you are the dealmaker. Very soon you will have the best contact book in Bath. Become indispensable in the branch office, squeezing for as much money and individual commissions as you can, until you qualify in four years time. Then-'

Ian interrupted him. 'Go for a junior partnership?'

Rose laughed. 'You're not stupid; leave the firm.'

'Leave Woods & Parker?' Ian was shocked. 'And do what?'

'Why, set up on your own, of course. You will never make real money working for others. First step, go on your own, you'll know when. You need to start as an agent, but this time you, not Woods & Parker, become indispensable to your clients as a deal finder and doer. Then the next step. They, the clients, will have no option but to take you into partnership. It is all very simple, and as old as the hills. Identify and create a unique property niche and know every inch of your patch. That's exactly how I made my last property fortune.'

This was the first time Rose had ever referred to one of his specific businesses. He had always side-stepped Ian's occasional questions by answering in generalities. Ian decided to push his luck.

'I would be very interested to learn more. What's the connection to Bath?'

Marcus thought for a moment.

'That's a story for another day, but suffice to say, substitute the Lundy Estate with that of the Grosvenor Estate, and the City of Bath for Mayfair, London. The wide streets, squares and crescents of Bath's Georgian architecture are even matched by the layout and early Classical architecture of the West End and Belgravia.'

'I have never thought of it like that.' Ian was intrigued with the analogy of Queen Square to Hanover Square; there was no real difference.

'Think about what I have said overnight, and we can talk again tomorrow.'

'No need. It all makes perfect sense. I'll call Mulholland in the morning and accept.'

'Good decision, but now more importantly,' Marcus looked down at the Scrabble board, placed a C in front of RAZED, and cleared all six of his remaining letters from his rack to make the word QUIXOTIC, with the X on a double letter, and the Q on a triple word score, 'I make that 170,' clearly having worked it out before putting the letters down. He sighed. 'If only Susan was here.'

The discussions with Mulholland took longer than Ian expected. Not wishing to sound too keen, he pretended hesitancy, so that more money could be squeezed out of the deal.

This approach got him a salary increase to thirty pounds per week, plus a personal introductory commission of one percent of all fees created by him. It also achieved the one thing that Ian had most wanted, participation in the firm's very generous house purchase scheme. Normally reserved for employees with at least five years' service, Mulholland agreed to an interest-free loan of £5,000 for ten years.

He relayed his triumph over Sunday lunch, and afterwards Marcus guided him into his study. He went to the large bookcase lining the longest wall and unlocked its glass door. At his direction, Ian unfolded the library steps and climbed up them.

'My Bath Bibles, I haven't taken them down for a few years. All ten with the red bindings on the top shelf,' Marcus instructed.

Ian handed down the large leather bound books, each one bearing a single Roman numeral on its spine. Rose arranged them on the large desk, opened the first and handed it to Ian.

THE LUNDY ESTATE
VOL. I : FIFTY-ONE CITY CENTRE FREEHOLD
AND LONG LEASEHOLD PARCELS OF LAND

'How on earth…?'

'The Lundy trustees. They wanted me to buy the whole estate when the second Earl died in the forties. I spent months and a lot of money exploring the angles, but it was all to no avail. The first Earl's bar on any disposal for fifty years was unbreakable. Now that's ended, I don't see why you shouldn't have the benefit of all my hard work, expense and experience twenty years ago.'

Ian was staggered by the detail in his perusal of the tome. Until now he had only the management department's rent cards to work from. But here there was tenure, coloured plans, dimensions and even the allowable use shown, as well as a value for every holding.

'Keep them in the library, and as always, you can come and go as you please, but please don't disclose their existence to anyone and never remove them without my permission.'

'I won't, and thank you very much.'

Marcus looked at the calendar on his desk. 'Remember this day Ian, I give you five, no four years, I bet by the twenty-first of February 1966, you will have your own business. The sooner we get started the better, and there's one site that demands our immediate attention.'

Ian noticed the 'we' and 'our'.

'That's where I went yesterday morning, after you had told me about Woods & Parker opening a Bath office. I couldn't resist having a look.' Marcus found what he wanted, the estate's ground lease of much of Southgate.

'It's crying out for re-development, and I think I know the man in London who would jump at it.'

CHAPTER FIFTY-ONE

Over the following three months Ian's numerous telephone calls were never returned by Fiona. Finally he cornered her after everyone had left the office. Angrily, she brushed off his hand from her arm.

'For God's sake, don't you get it? Stop kidding yourself. I am not for you, and you most certainly are not for me. It was just a fling, so for Christ's sake, stop bothering me. It's bad enough to see you here every day to remind me just how stupid I was. But it won't be for much longer.'

'What do you mean?'

'I'm leaving next week.'

'What are you going to do?'

'Not that it's any of your business, but I am going to the family chalet in Switzerland, no doubt for the last time before that goes in the destruction of the Lundy family. My brother Alistair was right about you, Ian Morris. You're nothing but a pushy little upstart. No breeding, only interested in money.'

Fiona never came back to Cleveland House, and when, three months later, all the estate's houses in Great Pulteney Street were being made ready for sale, Ian's instructions to the solicitors were driven by her rejection. Now it was his turn to inflict pain. There was no tenancy, so they could serve

Notice to Quit immediately on the privileged bitch and get the keys back, using forcible entry if necessary.

Despite a doomed attempt through her solicitor to gain time, the Honourable Fiona Simmons was evicted by court order. Now you know, thought Ian, as he altered the draft auction particulars to show number twelve vacant, how it feels to be forced out into the street. Not that the St Moritz chalet, to which, he presumed she had fled, left her homeless, but it was only a matter of time – the Swiss agents had been instructed.

The large brown envelope was awaiting him when he arrived home just after six, and made him feel even more sorry for himself. It contained the programme of study papers for the Intermediate Examinations and another eighteen months of solid grind.

Looking at the hundreds of hours of work involved, he wondered what it was all for? No one he knew was attempting to qualify. Everyone was swanning around with cars, plenty of money in their pockets, and some very pretty women. Was he stupid to listen to Marcus Rose? After all he hadn't qualified and had done very well for himself. For the first time since his mother had died two years ago he began to doubt.

His thoughts were interrupted by the telephone ringing.

'Ian?' It was Mulholland. 'What are you up to?'

'Just the usual, as I have done for the last two and a half years, studying. The Intermediate papers just arrived.'

'I need a favour, but I'm not sure this will be an improvement.'

'Anything must be better than,' he looked down at the first entry on the programme of studies, 'Advanced Domestic Drainage and Sanitation, paper one.'

Mulholland laughed. 'There you might just be right. *In Camera.*'

'I beg your pardon?'

"*In Camera*, a play by Jean Paul Sartre, opening at the Theatre Royal tonight in front of an invited audience, of which I am meant to be one. Looking at the blurb, it seems to be about a lesbian, a homosexual and a nymphomaniac, who have died and ended up locked in a room in hell for eternity. Good cast though, Constance Cummings, David Knight and Jill Bennett. Anyway, I am stuck out at Rowas Grange Estate with Lady Lundy and her solicitor. It starts with a cocktail party at seven and curtain up is an hour later – I'll never make it – can you stand in for me?'

'Sure, Sartre must be better than lavatories, but what's it all for?'

'Oh, the usual, like all provincial theatres, the Theatre Royal is struggling to survive and wants to lure the firm into the Refurbishment Fund. I'll call them and tell them to expect you instead of me.'

He was one of a group of fifteen men, the others predominantly middle-aged and partners in Bath's leading firms. Glass in hand at the rear of the private bar, Ian looked at the young woman addressing them. She was about twenty and very striking, with long thick brown hair falling down beyond her shoulders. Her clothes were unusual, a man's shirt, with its cuffs rolled up, hugging her ample figure, and well worn trousers, with chipped black boots that would be at home on a building site. It was all very masculine, and the 'I couldn't care less' statement attracted him, because it probably wasn't true.

'My name is Rachel, and being the A.S.M, Assistant Stage Manager, the lowest of the low, I get the job of trying to prise as much money as I can from you, because you are very successful and rich.' A few of the men laughed nervously, unused to being addressed in such a blunt fashion, especially

284

by someone so much younger. She's not shy in coming forward, thought Ian, full of admiration at her casual confidence.

'All of us love this beautiful old theatre, and will do everything possible to help it survive. Your evening is in three parts. First this little drinks party, when the theatre owner will give you a five minute history lesson. He'll be followed by Frank Hauser, director of tonight's play, and then the play itself. We have put you in the front two rows. Afterwards, if you want to stay on, please join us for a drink with the cast in the Garrick Pub next door. So,' she turned to the man next to her, 'over to you.'

'Welcome, most welcome,' the man started with a flamboyant flourish of hands. 'Theatrical life has always been precarious in Bath. Over 250 years ago, 257 to be precise, George Trim built the first theatre. It lasted for thirty-three years, apparently never made a profit and was demolished in 1738 to make way for the Mineral Water Hospital. Then there was the New Theatre in nearby Kingsmead Street, that lasted until 1751.'

Ian was watching Rachel move round the room, replenishing glasses. He wondered what an Assistant Stage Manager actually did, and guessed it was the first step on the theatrical ladder, like the filing room at Woods & Parker.

'...On 27th October 1750 we tried again in Orchard Street, opening with Shakespeare's Henry IV...'

Ian fantasised about the girl's figure hidden by the awful clothes.

'...And so the great day in 1768, 197 years ago when the Theatre Royal Bath was granted a Royal Patent, the first outside London, and the first stop for every famous actor outside the capital...'

Ian held out his glass; she filled it.

'Hello. You look too young to be rich,' she said quietly.

'I am just an understudy, as you would say.'

She laughed. 'Welcome to the club, me too. Rachel Jacobs.'

Close up he could see the large brown laughing eyes under the slightly arched thick brown eyebrows, high forehead and exquisitely beautiful face.

'Ian Morris,' he mumbled.

'… Then the final move, the year of the battle of Waterloo, 1815, we arrived in Beaufort Square, where you are now standing. Designed by George Dance, and built for £25,000 in just one year. On 12th October we opened with Richard III…'

'Nice to meet you Ian,' and she was gone, before he could say anything.

'… Then disaster, tragedy, the never to be forgotten 18th April, Good Friday 1862, the whole place burnt to the ground. Couldn't go back to Orchard Street, first a Catholic Church, followed by a Freemason's Hall…'

Those brown eyes, her face; vaguely Ian heard the owner.

'…In 1905, the most famous actor in England, Henry Irving, stood on this stage and made his centenary farewell performance…'

Next Rachel introduced Hauser, but this time stood close by him, hanging on his every word.

'What Sartre is saying is, "Hell is other people, and in this case, the perverted spinster, Inez, has to share a room with a tart, Estelle, and a coward, Garcin", for eternity after they die. I attempt to balance the scalding of the first with the revelations of the second, and the confessions of the third. I believe I have succeeded. Now Rachel and I must prepare for this night's offering. Please give generously for this wonderful theatre.' And then they were gone.

The curtain rose, showing a sparsely furnished room in the

style of the Third French Republic, with three settees, over which hung a dazzling glass chandelier, and incongruously, a live butterfly fluttered above it.

Ian had never been a pub person. He hated cold, uncomfortable and poorly lit bars, full of loutish men, who got louder and louder as they swilled vast amounts of beer. He felt pity for the women who felt compelled to accompany them. Despite this, after the play he went next door to the Garrick in the hope that Rachel would be there.

He felt self-conscious as soon as he stepped inside as he was the only person wearing a suit. The small salon bar with its faded red plush banquette seats and matching carpet was a replica of the theatre on which the visiting company, now out of costume, seemed to be putting on a noisy performance of self-congratulation. Thankfully Rachel came out of nowhere to rescue him.

'Well done,' she said as she settled them into a corner away from the raucous crowd around the coal fire.

'For what?'

'Turning up. All the others politely declined and went back to their Georgian firesides. Mind you, we did well money-wise out of them, raised about £500 in sponsorship, which reminds me-'

Ian held up his hands. 'Sorry, nothing I can do, remember I am only a stand-in at the last moment for my boss, John Mulholland. But I will have a word.' Then to change the subject he stood up. 'Now what can I get you to drink?' She pouted, feigning mock disappointment. 'A pint of Guinness.'

That's a first, Ian thought as he made his way to the bar, surprised by both choice and quantity.

'So what did you think of the play? Frank's brilliant isn't he?'

'Frank?'

'Frank Hauser, the director. Met him when *Beyond the Fringe* opened at the Fortune last year. He came out of the Meadow Players, you know, Oxford, the Uni Dramatic Society.'

Ian didn't, and wondered if her doting adoration meant she was sleeping with him. Lucky guy, she was even more fantastic close up.

'Great.' He didn't know what else to say, and then added, 'I thought the butterfly was a nice touch.'

'Butterfly?'

'You know, the one flying around the chandelier before they came into the room. Clever, how do you do that, do you have a supply of them?'

'You saw the butterfly,' she said incredulously. He nodded. Suddenly she was on her feet, shouting at the others.

'Hey chaps, the butterfly was in the first act.' Everyone stopped talking, looked over, and en-masse moved towards them. Ian found himself the centre of attention. At Rachel's prompting, he repeated what he had seen. A large cheer went up, and another round, a Guinness and a single malt arrived from nowhere. Bemused he looked at Rachel.

'You don't understand do you?' He shook his head. 'It means the show will be a success. Here's to good old Jean Paul.' She lifted her glass and clinked it against his. Her enthusiasm was infectious with her broad smile, with the perfect white teeth.

'It all started in 1948, during the dress rehearsal of the pantomime *Little Red Riding Hood*, after a scene with a ballet done by girls dressed as butterflies. A dead butterfly was found on stage, and then the producer, Reg Maddox, who had been there at the theatre for years, dropped down dead from a heart attack, while fixing the lighting.' Her earnestness was compelling. 'Well, you know how superstitious theatre folk are, you know, Macbeth, break a leg.'

He had no idea what she was talking about, but as long as she went on looking at him like that, he was happy.

'They immediately dropped the scene, believing the butterfly was a bad omen. Then just before curtain up on the opening night, a butterfly was seen fluttering around backstage. Hey ho, another omen, this time a good one, it's Reg, reincarnated, telling them to reinstate the ballet scene, and so they did, and the show went on to be a smash. So now, whenever there is a butterfly, which is not that often, it's a big hit!'

'Time gentlemen please,' shouted the landlord. 'Glasses please!'

'Can I see you again?' Ian asked this wonderful girl. Rachel paused for a moment.

'Oh, all right, you funny young capitalist. Tomorrow night, after the show at the stagedoor.' She laughed. 'Then I'll tell you the tale of the Theatre Royal's ghost, the Grey Lady in her eighteenth century dress, feathers in her hair and the smell of jasmine.'

Ian was too excited to concentrate any longer. He closed the book and looked at his watch, 9.30 pm. Redman's *Landlord and Tenant* could wait. Only another half hour and he would see Rachel. He had thought about little else since they had met the night before. He checked for the umpteenth time; kitchen, sitting room and bedroom, all clean and tidy. He was nervous. He had never brought a woman back to the house, and for Rachel it had to be perfect.

He got there too early, but ten minutes later she emerged, calling a goodnight to the old boy guarding the stagedoor.

'Hello Ian, that's better, you look almost human.' He had deliberately not worn his suit. 'Where shall we go?'

'I have booked a table just over there.' He pointed at Raphael on Upper Borough Walls.

'A bit too posh for me I think.'

'No don't worry, it's on me.'

'Nice thought Ian, but I pay my own way, then there's no obligation at the end of the evening.'

Yet again, the same corner seats in the Garrick, she with her Guinness, he with a small glass of the cheapest plonk, his normal Highland Park abandoned, because he knew she would insist on buying the next round.

'You are Jewish aren't you?' Ian was surprised by the question, never before asked, nor referred to.

'Yes, how did you guess?'

'Not a guess, it takes one to recognise one. Don't forget, my surname is Jacobs. Welcome to the club.' She lifted her glass in a mock toast.

'Not a practicing Jew, gave up five years ago. You?'

'Part-time, when I am at home, Reform not Orthodox. The whole performance at home on Friday nights, all the family, candles, gefilte fish, chicken soup, course after course, but I love it. Why did you lose faith?'

And before he could stop himself, he blurted it all out. The blind home, his mother, her struggles and awful death. Her eyes never left his, sitting perfectly still, she listened intently. Embarrassed, he mumbled, 'I'm sorry I have rather banged on, but I've never been asked that question before.'

'Why, should you have? I bet you don't go out with Jewish girls, do you?' Ian shook his head, it had never occurred to him, but to excuse himself, he said lamely, 'There aren't any in Bath,' and then added, 'What about you, do you distinguish? Do you go out with Jewish boys?'

'Only.'

'Last orders please,' the landlord called.

'Must go, matinee tomorrow,' she said, bringing the conversation to an end. 'I have enjoyed it. Thanks for the drink.'

Rachel thought about Ian as she lay in bed back in her digs on the Upper Bristol Road. He wasn't tall, although with his olive complexion, brown eyes and thick dark hair, he was certainly good looking. He was one of those young men who knew it, and she suspected he used women for only one purpose. At first, she had been put off by his manner, but the unexpected outpouring about his mother and difficult background masked an inner vulnerability. Although very attractive she decided it was best not to get involved.

CHAPTER FIFTY-TWO

Unarranged, Ian was waiting at the stagedoor on the following night when Rachel emerged.

'Fish and chips?' Surely that must be within her budget.

'Sorry, can't afford it.' She started to step around him.

'No more than a shilling each, I promise.'

He looked desperate, so against her better judgment, she changed her mind.

'Go on then, where?'

'Best place in town.' He didn't have the nerve to put his arm through hers, so muttered, 'Follow me, it's not been open long.'

He had let the shop to Seafoods in Kingsmead Street, and the little restaurant was doing a roaring trade. The heat from the bank of deep fat fryers, sizzling behind the white marble counter, and the smell of freshly fried battered fish and chips was irrestible. Soused in vinegar, covered in salt, they had both wolfed their suppers down, and now sat holding their mugs of tea.

'You sure know how to show a girl a good time,' she said, in an American accent.

'Of all the bars in all the world…,' using his best Humphrey Bogart accent. They laughed and suddenly Ian knew it was all right; they could be friends.

The play was to run for six weeks, and every night Ian would finish studying and walk round to wait for Rachel. They ran out of cheap eating places after the first week. Rachel finally agreed to go back to the small house in St Catherine's. She laughed at the bachelor kitchen, with its empty cupboards, and promptly sat down to write out a long shopping list before they went back to Seafoods.

The cooking utensils were the easy bit, and Ian just crossed the road from his office to Kitchens, where a helpful assistant assembled everything in carrier bags. The food items were more tricky, but Fortts in the High Street found everything, including some spices, pastas, and other obscure ingredients that he had never heard of.

Proudly he showed his purchases off to Rachel, who set him on scrubbing out and lining the empty kitchen shelves, while she sorted and stored. She then sent him off to the off-licence for two bottles of wine, preferably Italian, while she began to cook.

This was the night, in his cosy little kitchen, when he realised that he was in love with Rachel. She had her back to him, straining the steaming pasta, when he felt a physical joy of being with a woman, who made him feel so special and so happy. He walked up behind her, parted her beautiful brown hair, and kissed the nape of her neck. Slowly she put the food down, turned and kissed him for the first time full on the mouth. Passionately, he returned her kiss, grasping her body to his before she broke away, breathless and gently pushed him down into the kitchen chair.

'Whoa, slow down. Let's eat. We need to talk.'

The food and first bottle of wine finished, Rachel stretched over and took Ian's hand.

'Ian, I am not going to sleep with you.'

Ian held up his hand to protest at the suggestion. 'I wasn't-'

'Maybe not now, not tonight, but sooner or later you will

want to take me to bed, and our relationship will become one long wrestling match, you becoming ever more desperate for sex, and I warding you off. Despite what you think about the theatre world, I have never had sex with anyone. It's been a very close run thing, but I am still a virgin, and intend to remain so until, if and when I get married.' She stood up and looked down at him. 'I am going home now. I would love, and I mean love, to see you as usual tomorrow night, but only come to the stagedoor if you are prepared to play by my rules.' She kissed him lightly and left.

He was there the next night and she hugged him. 'Thank you for coming, I thought I wouldn't see you again.'

'No chance.' He kissed her gently. 'Dinner – my place?'

She nodded and, arms around each other, they strolled back to the house. He knew the rules, and accepted them. She was worth it.

CHAPTER FIFTY-THREE

Ian had hired the Pump Room for the three day auction sale of the six hundred or so lots, which formed much of the Lundy Estate in the city. Now, late on the second afternoon of 28th April 1962, the day of his twentieth birthday, Ian stood to the side on the rostrum, and watched Mulholland rattle through the sale.

'Lot 330...'

He was proud as he looked around the packed room, knowing that most of this was due to his hard work. He also knew that many London dealers had registered before the sale.

'Lot 333...'

Marcus had been right, the largest site, Southgate, had been snapped up before the sale by his London contact.

'Lot 336...'

No mention of the sale was made at the time, but when the intention to redevelop it, the city's largest block of business property leaked onto the front page of the *Chronicle*, dozens of the small traders involved were up in arms. They were fearful of what the future held when their landlords, the Bath City Council, refused to renew their leases.

'Lot 340...'

The estate's holdings around Broad Street had also been shifted quietly to a developer. Ian wondered how long it would be before that made the headlines. He became aware of his growing excitement.

'Lot 341, what may we say, £15,000, £10,000, who will start me, £7,500, £5,000 then. Thank you, sir,' as a numbered bidder's paddle rose halfway down the room.

'£6,000, £7,000, £8,000,' as more paddles appeared. Marcus made no move.

'£9,000...£10,000, thank you, anymore?' Still Marcus did not stir and Ian began to panic, his heart started to race.

'£10,100, for the first time then, thank you sir, a new bidder, £10,200,' as Marcus raised his paddle.

'£10,300, £10,400, £10,500 and £10,600. Number 12 Great Pulteney Street. Going for the first time, second...and... sold to Mr Rose, thank you.'

'Lot 342...'

Elated, Ian left the rostrum and caught up with Marcus as he signed the sale memorandum and paid the deposit.

'Thank you so much, Marcus.'

'You are very welcome. Now you are on the first rung of the property ladder. Susan has invited you for dinner tonight, to celebrate or commiserate, is how she put it, depending on how we got on.'

Ian paused.

'Problem?'

'Well, I'm a bit tied up.'

'All work and no play makes Jack, or in this case, Ian, a dull boy. Leave the studying for one night. I know it will mean a lot to Susan.'

'It's not studying.'

'Well, just tell Mulholland to find someone else, you give your all to Woods and Parker.'

'It's not work, it's social.'

Puzzled, Marcus paused. 'Don't tell me you've got a

date?' Ian nodded. 'Serious?' Again Ian nodded. 'Well, bring the young lady too, she will be most welcome. What's her name?'

'Rachel.'

'Good, I'll send the car for you both at 7.00 pm.'

Using the public telephone outside the Pump Room, Ian rang the stage door of the theatre, and asked for Rachel.

'Tell me.' She was breathless from her rush to the telephone.

'Got it, £400 less than my limit of £11,000.'

'You clever man, brilliant, something to celebrate tonight.'

'Oh.'

Rachel sensed his hesitancy. 'Something wrong?' nervous that she had presumed too much.

'No not really.' He paused, then made up his mind. 'Could you get the night off, it's important.'

'Maybe, tell me more.'

'Susan and Marcus Rose have invited us for dinner.'

Now it was Rachel's turn to be silent – Ian had explained their importance in his life.

'Great, love to, what time?'

'Need to pick you up just after 7.00 pm.'

Ian looked across the dinner table. Rachel was stunning; her beautiful smiling eyes, long brown hair tucked behind her left ear, and hanging down over her shoulder, resting on the firm breasts. How he loved this woman.

'So, tell me Rachel, where's home when you are not on the road with the theatre?' Marcus asked.

'Hampstead, in north London. Dad's semi-retired, but still goes into the city two mornings a week. He can't let go.'

'Stockbroker?'

'No, solicitor.'

Marcus thought for a moment. 'Jacobs, not John Jacobs?'

'Yes. Why, do you know him?'

'What a small world.' Marcus turned to his wife. 'You remember, Susan, John and Sarah Jacobs, lovely couple. He acted for Sebastian Cassofiori.' He looked across at Ian. 'John was instrumental in helping to get you into your first school, Beaconsfield, and was with Sebastian the night he died.' Ian vaguely remembered the story about the accident with the wheelchair that caused his uncle's death.

'How are your parents?' Susan asked.

'Sadly there's only my father, my mother died six months ago, but he's coping.'

Rachel had told Ian about her mother's drawn out illness, and although saddened by the story, he was secretly pleased that they had a common experience. Nevertheless, he wanted the meal to remain a celebration and promptly changed the subject to his new status of house owner.

CHAPTER FIFTY-FOUR

The Wednesday after the sale, Ian went up to Widcombe House and handed his cheque for £10,600 to Marcus. It had taken all his 'Welsh stamp money', bar £200, plus the loan from Woods & Parker, but to Ian it was so worth it. Rose looked at the cheque.

'What, no agent's buying commission? Where's my 2% then?' He sounded aggrieved, but then burst out laughing. 'Only joking, but seriously, it's a very big house. Why Great Pulteney Street, and what's so special about number twelve? There were plenty cheaper, even in the same street.'

'It has special memories,' Ian replied. 'I am going to live in the best floors and let the rest.'

'Well, here's to your first home.' Rose raised his glass. They were sharing a drink in the library with the early evening sun streaming through the long windows. So it had been the Lundy girl, he thought.

'Now, how's the lovely Rachel? Susan and I thought she was delightful.'

'Fine. She liked you too, and was amazed you knew her father. We are meeting up later.'

The telephone at Marcus's elbow began to ring and he picked it up.

'What a pleasant surprise, we were just talking about you, and yes, he's here.' He handed the telephone to Ian. 'It's Rachel.'

Surprised that she would telephone him during her busy working day, Ian assumed that a serious problem had arisen.

'What's wrong?' he asked.

'Nothing, quite the opposite.' She sounded excited. 'You know that I understudy Jill Bennett, well tonight's my big night. She's gone down with a throat infection, I'm to be the nympho for a night or more!'

'That's good news, really promising!'

'Can you come? They've got an unbooked box, which I can have free, if I want.'

'Love to.'

'That's great. Curtain up is 7.30 pm and you'll get a chance to meet my father, he's already on his way.' She paused. 'That still leaves two free tickets, do you think Susan and Marcus would like to come?'

'I'm not sure, let me hand you over.' He passed the telephone back to Marcus who listened.

'We would love to, and it would be a good opportunity to see your father after all these years.' He replaced the telephone back in the rest. 'She'll tell her father to meet us in the stalls bar at 7 pm. I'll book a table at Raphael for a meal after the show. I think she's growing very fond of you Ian. What about you? How do you feel about her?'

Ian was silent, conscious of a queasy feeling in his stomach. It was the first time he had been asked, or asked himself the question. He knew that she was only in Bath for a period of weeks and that she was ambitious about an acting career. The thought of losing Rachel was frightening and not something he wanted to think about.

'Due to illness, Miss Bennett's part will be played by Miss Rachel Jacobs.'

Ian removed the last minute insert from the programme and inserted the slip of white paper into his breast pocket. He wanted to tell everyone, this is my Rachel, but had arrived so early he had the bar to himself. Pride turned to nervousness as he read the programme again, and sipped the glass of wine – pace yourself, take it slowly, best not to drink too much in front of her father. Would she remember her lines, how would it go, her first time centre stage? All the walk-on extra one-line appearances of the past were nothing by comparison and he wondered if she could even act.

'Ian?'

He looked up at the tall thin man in his mid-sixties, Rachel had inherited the smiling brown eyes.

'Mr Jacobs, very nice to meet you.'

'And you after all this time. I worked it out on the train, it must be fifteen years ago. You don't remember me coming to Cassofiori House do you?'

Ian shook his head.

'Not to worry. I am pleased to meet any friend of Rachel's.'

'John!'

'Marcus, Susan.' Hands shaken, kisses exchanged, they barely had time to finish their drinks before the curtain up bell sounded, and they hurriedly made their way to the box, which overlooked the left hand side of the stage.

Ian need not have feared for Rachel. She was superb, and the audience, at first disappointed by the absence of Jill Bennett, warmed to her, understanding what was being asked of this young and inexperienced understudy. She was a natural, and the applause as the curtain fell recognised this. In true show-business style, her two fellow actors kissed and clapped her debut, and the crowd loved it. Rachel appeared overwhelmed, but blew Ian a kiss before finally leaving the stage.

Everyone met up in the stalls bar and Rachel introduced her co-stars, Constance Cummings and David Knight. A drink or two later they crossed the road to the Raphael Restaurant. Its owner greeted them enthusiastically – Jane Shayegan, tall, slim, blonde and beautiful in the classical English way. Her husband, Kambiz, was dark, handsome, with black hair, and built like a rock.

The stylish restaurant with its dark polished floors, wooden furniture and soft candlelight was noisy, atmospheric and itself pure theatre, into which they made an entrance. The whole group was soon seated on the long table as the staff busied themselves opening the bottles of Dom Perignon, and filling glasses. Jane and Kambiz raised theirs: 'All at Raphael salute the theatre's latest star.' Other diners and fellow playgoers, delighted to see the whole cast, clapped and cheered. Constance Cummings and David Knight rose and generously gestured to Rachel to join them, and all three acknowledged the applause.

Ian looked over the candlelight at this wondrous young woman, his woman.

'Do you know that this building dates back to 1730?' Marcus was telling John Jacobs.

Rachel caught Ian's eye, winked and spoke to her father, sitting next to him. 'Daddy, the show moves to Oxford, and I'll be coming home when it closes there. Can I invite Ian afterwards?'

'Surely, if that's what you would like.'

'Very much so. All right, Ian? Can you drag yourself away from your beloved firm for a few days?'

Ian, taken completely by surprise, nodded.

'You'll meet my friends in London.' Rachel turned away in answer to a question about the Oxford opening.

John Jacobs smiled at Ian. 'You are very honoured Ian, you

are the first young man she has ever invited home.'

The meal had been chosen by Marcus and Susan and was magnificent. English asparagus, picked that morning at Valley Spring nursery garden, on a rocket salad with mustard vinaigrette. Then Gressingham duck with chive mashed potato, and a cannellini bean, bacon and rosemary sauce. The elegance of the Puligny-Montrachet with the first course was followed by the ripe black cherry aroma of the Haut-Médoc, perfect for the duck. The fresh English strawberries picked and brought with the asparagus and a home-made meringue, finished the most perfect meal Ian had ever eaten.

Ian was surprised to see that Fiona's St Christopher, with her initials on the back, was still attached to the key ring. The power was off when he entered the house, and he had to feel his way along the pitch black hallway into the ground floor dining room, where he opened the shutters. Empty and with bare floorboards, it was even larger than he remembered.

He ran up to the top floor, opening more shutters along the way, and walked back down, marvelling at the architectural detail as he went. The fireplaces had marble surrounds with decorative brass handles nearby on the wall for calling servants in years gone by. The cantilevered staircases had curlicues on each landing, and he loved the rich feel and smoothness of the mahogany banister. Finally he reached the lower ground floor where he pushed down the main power switch for the lights to come on.

He smiled with pride at what he had achieved. The first tangible, touchable, enjoyable and endurable thing belonging to him, through his own efforts; his own house. And what a house. He analysed his emotions. Above all else, excitement at the realisation of not only what he'd got, but what could be achieved for Rachel and himself. The sky was the limit. He needed to just stay dedicated and on track. Nothing would get in the way. In five years, who knows, he might be worth £50,000, even £100,000, then the Lundys of this world would sing to a different tune.

What would his mother say if she could see him now? Surely she would be so proud. Mafeking Street to Great Pulteney Street in what, five years. 'Thank you mum,' he mouthed silently. 'Thank you so very much, if only you were here.'

Walking back up to the ground floor and the front door, he closed it and noticed the postcard lying in the wire basket behind the letter box. On the front was a picture of a large modern white building by a lake, and in the left hand corner was printed 'the Humanite Clinic, Geneva'. He turned it over; it was handwritten and addressed to him, and simply read, 'You owe me 900 Swiss francs.' Fiona had left it unsigned.

CHAPTER FIFTY-FIVE

It was the night before Rachel's play moved on to Oxford, and they had arranged to meet outside the Little Theatre, an art deco gem of the thirties, which had been converted to a cinema. Her high had been replaced by gloom, as Jill Bennett had recovered and was on stage, whilst Rachel returned to being Assistant Stage Manager backstage.

The film made things worse. They watched *Splendour in the Grass*, with Natalie Wood's sexual frustration driving her into madness as she defends her virginity against rich playboy Warren Beatty.

Much like our sexless relationship, thought Ian, and he knew that Rachel was thinking the same thing, as they kissed goodnight afterwards, and he headed back to his new house alone.

Rachel had only been gone three days. He had taken himself off to see *The Magnificent Seven*, the latest film at the Beau Nash, which had been fun, but he missed her dreadfully. They had spoken briefly each night, and he was surprised when she rang him again in the office.

'Ian, my darling, just had to ring you, great news.' She sounded bubbly and excited.

'Go on.'

'I got a call from Gerald Blake, he wants me to audition for television. The director was in the audience when I went on that first night at the Theatre Royal in Bath, and thinks I'm just what he's looking for.'

'What's the show called?'

'*Z-Cars* – cops and robbers stuff.'

'Like *Dixon of Dock Green*?'

'Don't be silly, not a sixty-year-old pensioner walking the beat, but fast cars, modern, you know, rough and violent. I'm going up to the studios this afternoon.'

'Break a leg.'

Rachel laughed. 'Thanks, probably will end up doing just that, if I get the part. I'll be in touch.'

It was two days before he heard. He had tried her digs first, and then the Oxford theatre; he was told that she had quit the company and wasn't expected back. In desperation, he called her home. Her father answered.

'Hello Ian, great news isn't it?'

'Sorry?'

'About the part.'

'Oh,' he said hesitantly. 'Is she around?'

'Fraid not. She left yesterday for Liverpool, Kirby, where they produce the show. She's got a contract for twelve weeks – nothing big, but a real start in television.' Then he added, 'It was all very sudden. Hasn't she been in touch?'

'No. I'm sure she has just been too busy.' Ian tried to hide his hurt. 'Do you have a telephone number in Liverpool?'

'Sorry, no. She didn't know where she would be staying, but,' Jacobs hesitated before continuing, 'I'm sure to hear from her soon and she is bound to be in touch with you too.'

'If she does can you tell her I called?' Ian's hurt was replaced by resentment.

He was asleep when she rang at eleven o'clock the next night. She was at a party, difficult to hear because of the music blaring in the background, and obviously drunk.

'Ian darling,' her speech slurred, 'all is wonderful; wonderful director, wonderful show, wonderful party, wonderful actors, Brian Blessed, John Thaw, and a fabulous woman called Judi Dench.' Some man was shouting her name. 'Just a minute, David. That's the wonderful David Mackenzie.' Then the phone went dead. He stayed up until the early hours but she never called back.

On Friday afternoon, she rang the office. No mention of the earlier call.

'How are you?' She didn't wait for his reply before adding, 'I'm a tart.'

'I don't understand.'

'A Liverpool prostitute, a bit of rough. It goes out live on Saturday night. Promise you'll watch, but must dash for the final rehearsal.'

He did, and she appeared for about three minutes. Afterwards there was a late night phone call, this time from a raucous pub, with 'darling this' and 'darling that' and 'wonderful this', and 'delicious that'. This was not the Rachel he knew. She was living in a different world – an unreal one. Ian felt dispirited, and incapable of having a meaningful conversation with her; he hung up. He then heard nothing for a week, before receiving a note, scribbled on the back of a page of a script that was waiting for him when he got home from the office.

My darling Ian,

It's been great fun, but it will never, never work between us. We are so different. You

with your obsession with money, and the
security and the happiness you think it will
bring. It's not for me. I am ambitious, but
only about acting and the theatre. That is
what is important in my life, something
that you find so alien. How could you possi-
bly understand? I've met someone else,
another actor, who does. I'm sorry.

Rachel

Stunned, Ian re-read the letter twice. This couldn't be right. Things may not have been good recently between them, but he loved her and she him. He understood about her acting, but she was infatuated with the razzamatazz of the glitzy world of show business and artificial people. All he had to do was wait, he told himself, and soon she would realise her mistake and come back, After all, he had the house in Great Pulteney Street, and, quite soon, he would make it and they would be very rich. How could she give all that up for some fling?

He turned to his studies, determined to use his evening effectively, but could think of little else. Surely Rachel was intelligent enough to see how shallow actors were and that the theatre can never offer a reliable income. He only wanted to provide for her and love her. Why was she refusing him? Denial turned to anger, and he pushed his papers to one side before reaching for the whisky. He downed a second drink, went for a third and turned on the television.

The screen was full of different images of Marilyn Monroe. Over each was superimposed:

JUNE 1st 1926 TO 5th APRIL 1962 R.I.P

FOUND DEAD IN THE BEDROOM OF HER U.S. BRENTWOOD HOME BY HER PSYCHIATRIST, RALPH GREENSON. INITIAL REPORTS SUGGEST SUICIDE FROM AN OVERDOSE...

Well, there you are, that's what happens to wayward actresses, Ian told himself.

He introduced numerous deals through the late spring and early summer, but Ian couldn't stop thinking about Rachel. As August drifted into September, he began to wonder if he could resurrect the relationship. He told himself that the contract in Liverpool with the BBC would be over by now, as probably would the relationship with the actor boyfriend. He arranged for a dozen red roses to be sent to her London home, writing, 'Come back darling, all is forgiven. Love Ian'. He too could do the glitzy show biz thing, if that was what she liked, and he waited for her reply.

The response however was not what he expected when the phone rang the next evening; it was her father.

'The roses arrived for Rachel. They are lovely, but she's gone away I'm afraid.'

Ian tried to keep the disappointment from his voice. 'For long?'

'Yes, at least until next year. Her actor friend got her on to the liner circuit when the *Z-Cars* contract ended. Look, I'm really sorry it didn't work out between the two of you.'

'Me too. Enjoy the roses, Mr Jacobs. Goodbye.'

He finally accepted it was all over and vouched never to trust a woman again. Forget love, sex was all he wanted. And as one of his wealthy American clients put it over lunch, 'if it flies, floats or fucks, rent it.' All he had to do was earn the rent. Making money is his vocation. It can bring happiness, lots of it; people who said otherwise were only excusing their inability to make it.

He was walking home through Orange Grove when he heard music unlike any he had ever heard; electric guitars pounding out a frenetic beat. He followed the sound left down North Parade. It was deafening by the time he reached its source, the Pavilion. Hundreds of youngsters had spilled outside dancing in the mild October night. The amplifiers now pushing the sound of a harmonica harshly over the guitars, played as never before.

'Love, love me do.' Rough Liverpool voices sang over the instruments. He leaned over the stone balustrade from the bridge and looked at the mass of wildly gyrating, arms raised as if in prayer, screaming the lyrics.

'You know I love you...'

'You like the Beatles, yes?' she shouted. The accent was German and the hair blonde. A true Aryan, he thought, not more than eighteen, wide-eyed, the pupils enormous. Acid, he guessed. Only yesterday he had read the interview in *Playboy* magazine by Tim Leary, the weird psychology lecturer conducting experiments at Harvard. He recalled bits of it, as he looked into the enormous eyes. First, the mushrooms used by Native Americans, which had led Leary on to LSD with its mystical experiences, the strange catchphrases: 'turn on, tune in, drop out.' Not for him, all too much like those nutters in their thousands who wasted their time every Easter marching, protesting about nuclear bombs. Mind you, Leary had said LSD was the most powerful aphrodisiac he had ever tried.

'Fantastic, first time I've heard them,' he shouted back. 'We dance?'

She took his hand, guiding him off the bridge into the narrow little stone tower and down the circular staircase into the young crowd below.

After hours of dancing and drinking, and back at Great Pulteney Street, he learnt that Uta was from Hamburg, where she had first seen the Beatles. She followed the band, hitch-hiking all over Europe and now England.

He fed her before she consumed him in bed, impatiently waving aside the condom because of 'das pill', as though she were eating a second meal, and groaning 'gut, so gut' when he entered her. He came instantly, because of the months without sex, but it didn't matter, insatiable, reveling in her willing body, time after time, exorcising Rachel.

His half-hearted attempts to embrace and kiss when they woke were brushed aside, so they dressed in silence and he walked with her to the station.

Uta simply kissed him on the cheek, and without a backward glance, boarded the milk train to the band's next venue in Exeter.

He was ravenous, and it was still too early to go to the office so he went for a full English breakfast at the Francis Hotel. He bought a copy of the morning *Chronicle* from the paper stand on the north side of the Abbey, by the Rebecca water fountain; the Sicilian marble now much disfigured with moss, algae and staining.

Two headlines, presumably placed next to each other by an editor with a sense of humour, caught his eye.

**CONTRACEPTIVE PILL
NOW WIDELY
AVAILABLE IN
MAINLAND BRITAIN**

**MOTHERS MOURN BBC'S
ANNOUNCEMENT THAT
DAILY CHILDRENS' HOUR
BROADCAST TO CEASE**

The dull pain of a hangover persisted. What would the Bath Temperance Association, who had erected this statue in 1861, make of modern Bath, he wondered.

CHAPTER FIFTY-SIX

Ian and Mulholland sat alone on the first floor of Cleveland House. It was December 1962, and the whole building had been emptied, apart from the table and two chairs on which the men sat.

'Well done, Ian, three months ahead of schedule, and half a million pounds of death duties paid in full. That will make Her Majesty's Inspector of Taxes happy.'

'He is one miserable sod. Did you see him? Front row seat at all three days of the auction, noting down every price achieved. Believes he settled too cheaply, and he's not wrong!' Ian continued. 'Now all we have to do is raise a mere £600,000 to repay outstanding loans, plus interest!'

'When do we complete the sale of this place?' Mulholland asked, looking around him before standing up and walking to a nearby window. Below him, Mike Godwin was loading the last of the office furniture into the large black removal lorry emblazoned 'Me and My Van.'

'Close of business tomorrow, Friday.'

'And the new place opens?'

'Monday. Everything went across yesterday, and I will use the weekend to fine tune. What time are you driving back to London?'

Mulholland looked at this watch. 'Couple of hours, why?'

'Time for you to see your new office.' Ian was proud of

what had been achieved in the prestigious location. 'I think you'll like it.'

Ian had designed the brass plate, identical to the one that Notts had used in Port Talbot, and arranged for it to be fitted on the corner of the building in Wood Street. Importantly, it was visible from Queen Square, where many of Bath's most influential professionals were based. Mulholland was clearly moved by the surprise, and ran his fingers across it.

WOODS & PARKER
Established 1763
Partner: John Mulholland FRICS

'Not bad, Woods of Wood Street has a nice symmetry to it, eh? I never thought I would see the day, my name on a brass plate outside the place where the firm started two hundred years ago.' He laughed. 'They don't even have that privilege at Berkeley Square. All they get is their name at the bottom of the notepaper.' He turned to his young colleague. 'Thank you Ian. One day your name will be on there with mine.'

Ian quickly changed the subject.

'There's a great story about how this corner got named,' he said, pointing to the junction of Quiet, John and Wood Streets. 'Just as today, the city builders were hated by the city council-lors, who had to approve every new street name. When John Wood the Elder built them, the councillors made him wait until "Any Other Business", always the last item on the agenda of their meetings. John Wood became ever more frustrated. Finally, come eleven o'clock at night, he banged his walking stick on the floor and cried out, "What about my street names?" "Quiet, John Wood", responded the Mayor. The

314

builder left without a word. Next day up went the three signs, Quiet Street, John Street and Wood Street.'

'Is that true?' Mulholland looked at the familiar street names around him with new interest.

'Probably not, but it has made a good story for the last two centuries. Come on, you can tell me what you think of your grand new office.'

The opening of the Wood Street office went well, and Ian, for the first time in his working life, had his own office space, with his name printed in gold leaf on the door. He slid the sign on it from 'Free' to 'Engaged' and closed the door once things were quiet; the moment was to be savoured.

The room was bathed in autumn sunlight from the full length windows overlooking Wood Street, with Queen Square beyond. He sat down behind the Victorian desk, bought two weeks ago at the Aldridges furniture auction. In front of him, neatly stacked into three separate piles, were all the lot pages from the recent auction of the Lundy Estate in the city. On each, his newly appointed secretary, Trish Traynor, had printed in her bold neat handwriting the name, address and telephone number of each successful bidder, together with the price paid.

He had only asked her to do this on Friday and realised that she must have worked through the weekend. His instinct had been right about this local girl, who could have probably made university. Instead, the eleven plus had got her into Hayes Grammar School and then on to Pitman's Secretarial College in Bath, founded by the inventor of shorthand, Sir Isaac Pitman in 1842. She had only qualified four weeks before he advertised the vacancy in the *Evening Chronicle*.

Ian pressed his intercom. 'Come in Miss Traynor.'

He handed the pages back to her. 'Well done, exactly what

I wanted. Thank you Miss Traynor.' He always hid behind formality with female staff, and even more so when the age gap between them was so narrow. Having made the mistake with Fiona, Ian had no plans to become overly familiar with anyone at work ever again.

'Now I would like you to contact Stanfords, the map shop in London, and get them to send down a set of maps covering the whole central area of Bath. Then I would like you to telephone Martin Tracey up at the Framing Workshop in Walcot Street, best craftsman in town, and get him to make a cabinet for that wall.' He pointed to the one facing his desk. 'Let's see. At 50 inches to the mile, the map will need a square 8 feet by 8 feet. It must have wooden shutters, and most importantly, be lockable. Only two keys, one for you and one for me. It must remain closed and locked at all times when I am not here.'

'Yes, Mr Morris.'

'That's all for now.'

Soon afterwards Ian walked round to Jack Hare's bicycle shop in Orange Grove and bought the latest model, a Dawes, personalised with a map holder incongruously attached to its dropped handlebars.

Ten days later map and cabinet were up, and Ian sat in the deserted office early on a Saturday morning working through the list of buyers. He used a series of different coloured pencils to show the different owners of every property sold in the auction on the map. It took three weekends, and what emerged surprised him. Whole blocks of the city centre were coloured. He looked at the largest colour, red, and apart from a few gaps it involved Monmouth Street and four other roads. He realised why he hadn't spotted it before; each day of the three day sale had involved the same type of property, but this block contained everything. There were Victorian shops from day one, houses from day two, and even some of the blitzed sites from day three.

Who's red? he wondered and then saw it was A.I.P. Limited.

One of the up and coming, and most aggressive London property developers. There were a few uncoloured properties in the block and he became excited as he noted down the buildings involved.

Just after dawn next morning Ian cycled over to and around the Monmouth Street block, before anyone was up and would notice his interest. By the time he got into the office, he had identified the properties which were uncoloured and therefore A.I.P. did not own but were essential for any development.

A telephone call to the town planning office provided the final piece of the jigsaw. Permission was being sought to flatten the whole area and build 50 homes and 6 shops – the largest residential scheme since the war.

Over the next week he repeated the early morning cycle rides to each of the large different coloured blocks shown on his plan, thus identifying seven other would be demolishers of large parts of the city. He knew the local builders concerned, and recognised most of the others as opportunist London operators. In each case, he listed and put a value on the unbought individual properties needed to complete a block. Trish handed him two copies of the typed list of addresses and values on Friday evening, as the office was closing. There were 19 properties, with a total value of £500,000. He put the list in his briefcase, ready for his meeting in one hour's time.

'So, how much do you need?' Marcus asked. They were in the study looking at the list.

'I'll start by offering each owner 25% less than my value,

then gradually "be driven up" to say a maximum of 50% more, say £750,000. The secret is speed, buy as much as possible before the London boys know what's going on. Once bought, string them along.'

'And your profit forecast?'

'Well, not all of the developments will take place, but I reckon we will get all our money back, plus a third, say, £250,000 within two years.'

Marcus thought for a moment. 'All right, I'll do it. Susan's trust fund needs a top-up, and it's top heavy with shares and short on property. What would Woods & Parker expect?'

'Scale – say, 1% on the buying price, and the same again on the sale.'

'Agreed. Get the paperwork to me by Monday night. Drink?'

Ian nodded. As he lifted the decanter, Marcus posed the question, which Susan had recently asked after they had learnt about the Rachel break-up.

'Tell me Ian, when did you last attend synagogue?'

Surprised by the question, religion had never come up before, Ian had to think for a minute. 'Must be 1960 for a wedding.'

'Not since?'

'No. No point.' He sipped the malt whisky. *'Gott ist tot'*, Nietzsche was right, God must be dead after what happened to my mother. She took three years to die in agony. Judaism is just a tribal history of a people who have paid far too high a price over thousands of years of suffering, and can't, or won't accept it was all for nothing. All the organised religions are the same. A massive con to control millions of people by spreading mystery and fear. For instance, look at the Catholic Church's position about condoms.'

'Do you believe in anything?' Marcus was concerned; the young man sounded so angry, his disbelief brutal.

'Of course, I have learnt from you what really matters.'

'Which is?'

'Absolute financial security, total independence, needing nothing from any living soul, ever. Money is everything. I won't stop until I have made so much that I don't have to depend on anyone, not even you. That way I'll never be disappointed, let down or be humiliated again, like at my mother's funeral, when I couldn't even afford to bury her.' His tone was hard, abrupt, although his last words caught in his throat. Marcus noticed the trembling hand as he reached into his pocket for cigarettes and lighter.

'But what about friends, Ian, relationships?'

'Life's too short. They just get in the way.'

'And girls? Hasn't there been anyone since Rachel, or have you become celibate?'

'Good God, no.' Ian laughed, and his composure returned. 'Quite the opposite. Sex is like food: I eat whenever I am hungry, which is often. Give me women who just provide good sex when I want it, with no strings attached – the more the merrier. Sex is not a problem if you're rich.'

'It all sounds rather bleak, Ian.' He thought about his long and happy partnership with Susan. 'Don't you ever feel lonely?'

'No.' He took a drag on his cigarette and picked up the list of properties again; nothing more was said.

Later, after Ian had gone home, and they were going to bed, Marcus discussed the earlier conversation, and as usual, Susan summed the situation up succinctly. Ian wasn't short of female company and used the fairer sex when it suited him. That wasn't difficult because he had inherited his mother's slightly olive complexion, brown eyes and thick dark hair, which women found attractive. These traits could have been his father's too, as his naturally muscular build and somewhat arrogant nature were not qualities that his mother had portrayed when she had met her with Marcus all those years ago at Cassofiori House. Susan went on.

'He'll be twenty-one in a few months, and he needs to grow up, without being so angry with the world and women in particular. It is a pity that Rachel moved on, but I don't think she is responsible for his inability to have a mature emotional relationship with a woman. It's as if he blames all women for the death of his mother, and treats them simply as objects, whether for sex, cleaning his home or being at his beck and call in the office.'

Marcus pondered his wife's remarks after turning out the bedside lamp, and wondered how he could help his young protégé's attitude to women.

Ian set about quietly buying the nineteen key properties for Susan Rose's trust. He used the electoral register to establish ownership, and one by one the owners succumbed and were seduced by his 'once in a life time' offers.

First to be resold by the trust was the site of St James's Church, destroyed in the 1942 air raid; it had been a place of worship for 800 years. Next to go was Weymouth House School which was demolished, and like the first, became a new department store. One by one the old family businesses were falling, Ian thought as the deal was done on Westgate Buildings, and the Bush became part of the Co-op.

Within a year, Susan's trust was in profit to the tune of over £1 million.

'Better than the Great Train Robbery, and more importantly, all completely legal,' Marcus said light-heartedly over dinner, referring to the gang who had recently held up the Royal Mail night train and got away with the same sum; the largest robbery in history.

CHAPTER FIFTY-SEVEN

Ian took his seat at the table for the usual leisurely breakfast, but unusually, neither Susan nor Marcus Rose were immersed in the Sunday newspapers. On his side plate was an envelope with his name on. He opened it and took out a birthday card on which Susan had written: 'On your twenty-first birthday, to our son without tummy ache.' Underneath in Marcus's hand was: 'And hopefully not too much heartache!'

Susan stood up and came round the table and kissed him. 'Many happy returns, Ian.'

'Thank you, Susan.'

'I imagine you are expecting a big present?'

Ian had spent the night at Widcombe House because it was his 'coming of age', but despite his closeness to the elderly couple, he had no expectations. It had been many years since he had been made a fuss of on a birthday, and he hadn't been sure what to anticipate when Susan had requested his presence.

Marcus continued. 'Well my boy, no car I'm afraid, but there is this,' and he reached across the table with another thicker envelope. For a moment Ian thought that it might be money as he opened it, but out came a crocodile wallet with 'Howard Travel of Trowbridge. Travel Agents of Distinction' printed in gold letters on the cover. Inside was an air ticket, headed BOAC. Ian flicked through the numerous detachable dockets. The first one read 'London to New York', the next

'New York to Miami', the third 'Miami to Montego Bay', the fourth 'Montego Bay to Kingston'. Then followed four more in the reverse order.

Ian looked up. 'I don't understand.'

'Quite simple, my boy. I have got a job for you – possibly a big one – in Jamaica in the West Indies. Woods & Parker have agreed to release you on the basis I pay them a retainer of a thousand pounds.'

'But-'

'No buts, you leave next Saturday. No fee, except a wonderful experience, to broaden your horizons even if the deal does not happen. Now eat your eggs before they get cold and I will explain everything after breakfast.'

In his study Marcus had placed a large coloured aerial photograph on the table, showing a long coastline of blue sea, bright yellow beaches and dense green vegetation. A road ran across the top and a river ran down the right hand side.

'The James Plantation. Two square miles of sugar cane next to the Yallahs River, about fifteen miles east of Kingston, Jamaica. It has been in the James family for about two hundred years, when they settled there early in the eighteenth century. Sugar beet has knocked the bottom out of the sugar cane market, so it's no longer viable. You met the owners, Jan and David James, the attractive young couple at our drinks party last Christmas. They need to sell to get their capital out, so that they can start again here in Bath.'

'But I know nothing about property outside of England, let alone in Jamaica,' Ian protested.

'You don't have to. I have arranged for you to be introduced to the right people on the island. I just need someone I can trust completely, and that trust is my birthday present to you. I'd go myself, but I am not as young as I used to be and the time limit is too tight.'

Ian felt flattered, but doubtful. 'What do you mean?'

'I signed an option for £5,000 ten days ago. If I don't go ahead by May thirtieth, the James's keep the money, but if I buy, £5,000 is deducted from the purchase price.'

Now even more nervous about what was being asked of him, Ian retorted, 'But what do you know about growing sugar cane?'

'Don't be naïve Ian. I don't want to grow sugar cane, I want to build low-cost houses and for this I need you to establish if I can get planning permission, and if there is the demand for such houses. Also important is political stability. The agreed price is less than fifty pounds per acre, with consent the purchase price of fifty thousand pounds will become a million pounds, before tax – better still, there's no capital gains tax in Jamaica, so a million before tax stays a million after tax.'

'I know nothing about Jamaican law or planning.'

'Law – don't worry about it, I've already sorted that side of things through Malcolm Austwick. He has got a very good contact on the island. Used the firm many years ago for a chap called Peter Knee who went to live out there after the war. Regarding planning, as part of the Commonwealth the island has inherited our entire system, but much simpler. More like the local town council byelaws, I'm told. You did all of that in your first exam?'

Ian nodded. He was still doubtful. 'But I haven't got a passport. Remember, you asked me about this when we talked about going to the Venice Film Festival. Having no legal guardians I couldn't get one until I reached twenty-one.'

'Yes, I apologise; the Venice Film Festival was a blind, after I did the deal and started thinking about this matter. Now you are twenty-one this problem goes away. You will need to go to London tomorrow first thing, and see this man at the Foreign Office.' Marcus handed him a piece of paper. 'He is an old friend from the war and will organise everything. Luckily you don't need a visa for Jamaica. Any other problems?'

Numbly, Ian shook his head.

'Now let's enjoy the rest of your birthday.'

CHAPTER FIFTY-EIGHT

It had been an extraordinary week. As promised, the passport arrived by special messenger on Wednesday night.

Thursday was spent with Susan Rose as she dragged him around Jolly's buying a set of leather luggage and several outfits of clothes.

'Must look the part,' she said as she chose what she perceived to be appropriate for 'an agent from the home country representing a wealthy would-be investor'. She told him about her last visit to Jamaica. A leisurely two months sojourn away from the English winter with wonderful hotels, sandy beaches and endless drinks parties. She had met Noel Coward, Ian Fleming, members of the Kennedy family, and Lord this and Lady that. Montego Bay and a place called St Anthony's, apparently Errol Flynn's hideaway, figured large in her memories.

'Colonial life is a time warp from the old empire. It is a million miles from what you are used to, or have ever encountered before. The Caribbean is unique, because it is so close to the United States. It is a playground for the Americans, so piled on top of old money and privilege is the yankee exuberance of vast wealth and success. It can be overwhelming. Take it in your stride, observe and learn how to handle this; you will be constantly surprised. Once mastered, you will be cosmopolitan, fit to travel anywhere in the world.'

After a frantic few days tying up various deals he had

promised Trish a farewell lunch on Friday. She had chosen the Francis Hotel, designed by John Wood in 1739, its seven houses joined as a single residence in 1884. On his last day in England, they sat in the Regency styled dining room, enjoying a leisurely lunch. Using her usual initiative, she had obtained the island's official handbook from the Jamaican High Commission and presented him with it. It ran to more than three hundred pages and dozens of graphs, charts and tables. She assured him that she was more than capable of looking after everything in his absence. He trusted Trish but remained nervous, reminding her about the existence of the international telephone and cable services for emergencies. Unexpectedly, she kissed him on the cheek as they parted.

'I just want a cable saying yes or no,' Marcus said as they settled in the study armchairs after Friday's supper. 'Not even a telephone call. No explanations or reasons why or how you have arrived at the decision, I will trust your judgement. This must reach me by no later than noon, UK time, on the twenty-eighth, just twenty-four days from now, so I can exercise the option in time. Don't forget the time difference. We are six hours ahead. In the meantime all I want is a cable to say you have arrived safely. And afterwards…'

'Yes.'

'One last thing. Drink?'

'Yes please.'

Now what, Ian thought. Marcus went to the cabinet, poured two large Highland Park malts. 'You will have some free time once you have finished the work for what across the pond they call R and R.' He handed Ian five crisp new American one hundred dollar bills.

'That's very generous.' It was the first time Ian had seen or handled a foreign currency; the notes had a slightly waxy feel and smell.

'I have no doubt you will have earned it. After the job is over I want you to deliver this gift to a friend of mine. I've dropped him a line, so he will be expecting a call.'

Marcus handed him a small box wrapped in brown paper. Ian recognised the crested label and name of the renowned maker of handmade shoes in St James's, London. It was addressed to I. Fleming, Esq, 'Goldeneye', Uracabessa, St Mary, Jamaica.

'Is this the *James Bond* author?' Ian asked in amazement. Marcus nodded. 'How do you know him?'

'We met in British Naval Intelligence, setting up a special commando unit called 30 AU. Our commanding officer was Admiral Godfrey, and everyone reckons he's M in the books. Fleming has lived on the north coast of Jamaica for many years now. You can fly into Boscobel Aerodrome. There is a beautiful small hotel called Changs nearby that will suit you. It's exotic and unspoilt, one of the more beautiful places in the world.'

Marcus stood up. 'Now, you have an early start tomorrow. What time have you arranged to leave?' Ian was spending the night at Widcombe House

'Flight takes off at eight, so Jennings is waking me at 3 am.'

Marcus held out his hand and grasped Ian's. 'Have a safe journey. Good luck Ian, I know you won't let me down.'

CHAPTER FIFTY-NINE

The plane was huge. How could something this large actually fly? Ian had been impressed by the Shackletons at RAF St Mawgan where, as a CCF cadet, he had been based for a week when fifteen but this, the Boeing 707, was a whole new world.

The air stewardess greeted him at the top of the steps, took his boarding pass and showed him to his first class seat, number one by the window. The aisle seat next to him was empty. Ian opened the handbook which Trish had given him and started to read:

> *Jamaica lies ninety miles south of Cuba and a hundred and eighteen miles west of Haiti. It is one hundred and fifty-four miles long and fifty-two miles wide.*

'A Buck's Fizz or fresh orange juice before we take off, sir?'

The 'sir' from the older smartly uniformed woman, surprised him. 'Orange juice please.'

> *It is the largest of the Commonwealth countries in the Caribbean and has an area of four thousand two hundred and thirteen square miles. About a quarter of its population of over two million people live in the capital and largest city of Kingston.*

He rose and removed the notebook from the shiny new leather slipcase in the overhead baggage locker, bought from Jolly's two days earlier. He sat down and wrote his first note: (1) Pop = 2.5m+ ? house owners/tenants.

'May I check your seat belt, sir?'

He lifted the book off his lap and felt rather stupid – he had forgotten to refasten it, and quickly did so. Fascinated, he looked at the life jacket and oxygen mask drill being demonstrated by another attendant nearby. He could not resist watching the airport and the adjoining reservoirs recede beneath him after the plane took off. Again he marvelled at the ease with which this massive piece of complex machinery left the ground. Reluctantly, he returned to the guidebook:

> Ninety per cent of the population is of mixed black origin and less than one hundred thousand white people live on the island. The multi-racial nature of its people is possibly unique. Of the large numbers of original Tainos and Arawak Indians that existed when Columbus first came to the island in 1494, none survived the Spanish settlement.

'Good morning ladies and gentlemen, this is your captain, James Beer, and on behalf of BOAC may I welcome you aboard this Speedbird Flight to New York. Our flight time is nine hours and ten minutes.'

> The English captured Jamaica in 1655 and over the next one hundred and fifty years hundreds of thousands of black slaves were transported into the island from Africa. Indians, Chinese and Jewish traders followed from other countries. English plantation owners, Irish slave overseers, south American middle-

men, all interbred with each other, to produce descend-
ants of every possible shade, race and religion.

Ian added a second note: (2) Mixed races = difficult to
segregate = ? political stability.

'Breakfast sir?'

He put the guidebook and notebook on the seat next to
him. White linen, tray cloth and napkin, silver plate cutlery,
glasses and chinaware, all with the BOAC swallow emblem,
were placed before him. Newly baked rolls, fresh orange juice
and percolated, not instant, coffee as well as a traditional full
English breakfast appeared with slick efficiency.

I could get used to this Ian thought, and moved on to
Geology and Land Forms. The twenty or so pages yielded only
a single further note in his book, about the presence of the
limestone, known as karst, which covered two-thirds of the
island, with a query about its suitability for building foundations.

Wearily he went on to *Coastlines* and then *Climate*. He felt
compelled to read absolutely everything in case he missed
something important.

Lunch, another sumptuous affair of smoked salmon and
steak, came and went. He wondered how they produced such
food, and yielded to a glass of claret.

Now, drowsily, he ploughed through *Vegetation* and finally
Wild Life. This was all condensed in his notebook to three
pages of one-liners covering such diverse topics as hurricanes,
flooding, bauxite, gypsum and limestone mining – all to be
followed up.

He finished the general section of the guide book just
before tea arrived at 9 am because, on Marcus's advice, he
had turned his watch back seven hours to New York time. He
turned to the section headed 'Yallahs'.

Located on the south eastern coast of the Parish of St Thomas, in the county of Surrey, the town was founded in 1671 by a privateer called Captain Yallahs. It has an estimated population of a few thousand, and is made up of numerous districts, communities and villages named Poor Man's Corner, Heatese, Norris and Hampstead. All surround the Yallahs River, from which gravel is extracted.

These five pages produced more entries in the notebook, including water table, electricity supply, drinking water, sewerage, shops, etc.

Completely read out, he put everything into the briefcase. He'd been reading virtually non-stop for eight hours. He closed his eyes.

'Ladies and gentlemen, we are now starting our descent into New York, where the local time is five minutes past ten in the morning.'

Flying, he mused, travelled three thousand miles, and the time here is only two hours and five minutes after I left London.

CHAPTER SIXTY

'Pan American Airlines regrets to announce that its flight zero six five to Miami, Montego Bay, Kingston and Caracas is delayed due to tropical storm conditions in the Caribbean. At this time we are unable to estimate the delay period but we expect it to be not less than six hours.'

A groan went round the hush of the first class lounge. Someone near him muttered in an American accent, 'Time to spare, go by air.'

Reluctantly Ian fished out the first of a number of books from his briefcase, the rewards of an hour long search in his Institution's library at Parliament Square after his meeting at the Foreign Office. Entitled *The Town Planning Code of Jamaica*, it was written by a Frank Knowles FRICS of the Fédération Internationale Géometrique – the professional body for all surveyors worldwide.

He started to read:

> *Like most of the Commonwealth, over many years, the Privy Council has approved a system for this island, assuming it to be an English County Council, with full delegated authority, similar say to one of the Home Counties around London. Thus, anyone familiar with the basic legal framework and town planning system in the United Kingdom, will have no difficulty in*

*understanding and operating in the Jamaican environ-
ment.*

If only, he thought. Six hours later, just as Pan Am announced
a further five hour delay, Ian had finished the book and knew
the opening paragraph to be true.

Over the twenty-four hours it took him to Jamaica, he read
everything in his briefcase. Wearily, at two in the morning,
he came out of the Kingston terminal; it was deserted. He
stood there wondering what to do. He looked back into the
building. With the arrival of the long delayed flight, the
airport had closed down; even the sole immigration officer,
who had wearily stamped his passport, had disappeared.

In the stark neon light of the airport building, there was
nothing resembling either a taxi or even a rank. Then, a tall
black man of about his own age suddenly appeared out of the
ring of darkness.

'You looking for a lift, man?'

Doubtful, Ian nodded. 'Yes.'

'Where to, man?'

'The Courtenay Bay Hotel.'

'No problem, man,' and before Ian could ask the fare, he
had disappeared around the back of the terminal.

The large Cadillac that drew up was unlike anything Ian
had ever seen before except in a Hollywood movie. A vast
thing, not a recent model, it was a white convertible with
chrome everywhere and two massive tail fins more suited to
an aircraft than a car. Leaving the engine running, the man
languidly stepped out and around the car, and opened the
front passenger door. He took Ian's suitcase and tossed it on
to the back seat, shepherding him into the front.

'Call me Danny. First time in Jamaica, man?'

'Yes.'

'Where you from?'

'England. What's the fare to the hotel?' he asked anxiously.

'No worries man, talk about it later. What do they call you?'

'Morris, Ian Morris,' he said, unused to such informality.

'Well, you just relax Mr Ian and welcome to paradise.'

The driver talked on. Ian, exhausted, closed his eyes. Next he knew, he was being gently shaken.

'The Courtenay Bay Hotel, Mr Ian.'

Half asleep, he climbed out of the car following Danny with his suitcase. The hotel was stunning. It was floodlit, a white colonial with long balconies and an illuminated blue swimming pool, surrounded by tall palm trees, like something out of an Esther Williams film set. The velvet night was reverberating to the constant chirping of crickets. Unreal. They were let in by the night manager, who had clearly been expecting him.

'Good evening, Mr Morris. The paperwork can wait until the morning. You must be tired after the flight delays. When did you leave England?'

Ian looked at his watch, and made a quick calculation. 'Over twenty-four hours ago!'

The manager took the suitcase, impatiently waved the taxi driver away, and showed Ian into a large ground floor suite. Ian took off his shoes and sank on to the four poster queen size bed. Still clothed, he fell asleep.

The ringing telephone woke him.

'Hello, Mr Morris?'

'Yes.'

'My name is Phillip Cameron, Marcus Rose's solicitor. Welcome to Jamaica. We were expecting you yesterday, but I gather it was a rough flight. When would you like us to get together?' The accent was very upper class public school.

'What time is it?'

'Five o'clock.'

'Morning or afternoon?'

Cameron laughed. 'Afternoon. You have slept for over twelve hours. Shall we say six o'clock in the residents' bar?'

Ian should not have been surprised, but was; he had not expected Phillip Cameron to be black. Over six foot tall, this handsome man who held out his hand was in his late fifties, greying hair and immaculately dressed in a white flannel suit, and sporting an MCC tie. The piercing bright grey green eyes behind the tortoiseshell glasses twinkled. He laughed.

'Don't look so worried. Mr Morris, you are young, and hopefully you will soon get used to the way things are done here.' He paused before continuing. 'As I am sure you appreciate, time is of the essence and very tight if we are to exercise Mr Rose's option. It gets too hot to work in the middle of the day, so most people rise early, at say dawn, work until about ten thirty or eleven, and then start again at four in the afternoon until about six. To inspect the property I have arranged for a jeep and a driver to collect you here tomorrow at six thirty and take you to the James Plantation.' Over the next two hours Cameron set out the gruelling schedule needed to bring Ian up to speed.

Consulting his notebook from time to time, Ian asked a number of questions of Cameron, who was clearly impressed by how much preparation the younger man had done.

'The key thing here is the planning consent, and the person who can solve that is Emanuel O'Hara.'

Puzzled, Ian said, 'What, Irish?'

Cameron smiled. 'No, just the great, great, grandson of a randy and notorious Irish slave overseer. He can be tricky, so be careful what you say, and don't agree anything with him without me.

'As you will appreciate, the Jamaican government is very keen to see this development go ahead, and you are invited to meet with the Prime Minister and his Cabinet for a private drinks reception in ten days time.'

Ian's eyes widened and Cameron smiled.

'Don't worry. This is a very small island and it's all very usual. Someone from the British Embassy will also be there, and I will brief you nearer the time and be with you on the night.'

By the end of the meeting they were on first name terms, and Ian walked him to his car. As he turned to return to the hotel he noticed the Cadillac, hood down, with Danny lounging in the back seat.

'Hi, Mr Ian.'

'What do I owe you for last night?'

'Nothing man, treat it as a complimentary introductory ride,' he said grandly. 'What are you doing now?'

'Nothing, I was going to go to bed because I have an early start tomorrow.'

'You can't do that man. Let me show you Kingston town.'

Why not, Ian thought, as he clambered into the front seat of the outrageous car.

CHAPTER SIXTY-ONE

Danny had a great sales patter, doubtlessly fine tuned from escorting countless naïve tourists.

'Our mighty capital, Kingston, was begun in 1692 for survivors of the earthquake that destroyed Port Royal...'

First he showed him the Governor General's place, Kings House on Hope Road, then Devon House, an old colonial mansion next door, and so it went on.

Ian yawned. 'What about a bit of night life and you drink some of our famous rum, Mr Ian?'

'All right, but only a quick one, I want to be back at the hotel in about half an hour.'

'No problem Mr Ian.'

Two hours and four bars later, it dawned on Ian that they were on a brothel tour. Rough old places to start with, but growing ever smarter as the night wore on. Having never knowingly been in the company of a prostitute, Ian had naively dismissed the girls who seated themselves between Danny and himself as a management business plan to encourage him to buy exorbitantly priced drinks.

Feeling very sophisticated, he used the same technique as had worked in the Soho cocktail bars, thousands of miles away in London. Standing up suddenly, he would shout 'Let's go' to Danny over the booming ska music and then proceed to walk out. Fierce argument inevitably then ensued between the management and Danny. It seemed to involve money, but Ian couldn't understand anything said, even though odd words of the patois sounded like English. In the end Danny would shrug and they would climb back into the car. Danny would then assure him that they were on their way back to the hotel, but then suddenly stop, and with 'You'll love this one Mr Ian,' in they would go. The penny dropped as, under protest, he entered the fifth so-called club.

A quieter and sophisticated place with a dimly lit bar and a small dance floor on which a couple were glued to each other, making a gesture of minimum movement to the jazz combo.

They were shown to a table and drinks were ordered. Ian looked at the stunning tall black woman who had silently slid in next to him. She had white hair, cropped very short, and a low cut black cocktail dress.

'My name is Chantelle, what's yours?' To his surprise the accent was pure cockney.

'Ian,' he answered nervously.

'How about a dance, Ian?'

He shook his head. 'No thanks, just a quick drink and we're off.' Chantelle shot a questioning look at Danny. Suddenly a hand grabbed him under the table, between the legs.

'My, my, what a big boy, why don't we find it some action?'

Ian was terrified. She had him in an iron grip. He couldn't move. In desperation he looked at Danny, who just grinned.

Suddenly there was a man standing at the table, barking something at the girl, who started to argue. The grin had left Danny's face. The girl squeezed so hard that Ian felt faint, but then she let go and muttering, glided away from the table.

The man slid in next to him. He was of mixed race, clean shaven with a crew cut, lean, fit, and with Chinese eyes. He held out his hand.

'Hi, Peter Green.'

'Ian Morris, how do you do? Thank you for rescuing me.'

Green laughed. 'Don't mention it, Big Bertha is a man-eater. That really would have been a fate worse than death.'

'What did you say to make her leave?'

He laughed again. 'Don't you mean let go? I just reminded her that prostitution is illegal in Jamaica. Have a drink while I find someone of your own size. I think I know just the girl. Expensive, as is all good private education in this island!'

CHAPTER SIXTY-TWO

The Land Rover and driver were waiting for him as he came out of the hotel at six thirty the next morning. Feet up on the dashboard of the Cadillac, Danny smirked and waved him off. He had dragged Ian out of the girl's bed and returned him to the hotel barely an hour earlier, with a 'see you tonight, boss.' The memory of what the Eurasian girl had done to and for him lingered as he headed out of the city on the A4 to Yallahs.

He had always felt contempt for men who paid for sex, believing them unable to score for free. After the last few hours, he realised there was more to it than that. Amateur versus paid professional – a world of difference – like football. Hopefully Danny could get her over to the hotel when he got back.

With an effort he stopped thinking about what she had done with that string of pearls around her neck, and concentrated on what Marcus had sent him thousands of miles to do.

The potholed road soon deteriorated, becoming little more than an unmade track. They had stopped by a white corner post.

'It starts here,' the driver said. All Ian could see was a vast sea of green.

'Mr Cameron said to first show you how far it stretched along the road, and then take you down through the planta-

340

tion to the beach. After that it's back to his office for a meeting over breakfast.'

'Fine, but before we start, tell me what are the numbers on the milometer in the speedo.'

Shrugging his shoulders, the driver leant forward and read, 'two point one.'

'Ok, let's go, but take it slowly.'

By the time they reached the Yallahs River which, with its wide mud flats, formed the eastern boundary of the plantation, the milometer read four point six. Ian put this in his notebook and the driver turned the car round and started back. After about five minutes he turned left into what seemed little more than a path, and stopped. Anticipating the question, he read out, 'five point three.'

'Good, let's go.'

Gingerly and very slowly, the driver steered the Land Rover southwards, never getting out of second gear. The sugar cane grew in vast blocks, and they turned left and right as the path wove around them. The plantation was enormous and the cane reaching up above the Land Rover made Ian feel claustrophobic. After about twenty minutes they emerged from the gloom into the bright sunlight and on to a beach of white sand. Ian got out. The beauty of the place was breathtaking. At least a quarter of a mile wide, down to the blue glistening sea, the beach stretched as far as the eye could see in each direction.

'Six point five,' the driver called out.

Ian got back into the Land Rover. So, he thought, it's two miles wide by, say, a mile deep, if you adjust for going around the blocks rather than straight through. He took out a small slide rule and adjusted the cursor for the various measurements. Used to tiny UK building plots, he converted everything to feet, and read out the result. Always nervous about putting the decimal point in the wrong place, he re-checked his calculations; they were right, sixteen hundred acres at what, say, four plots per acre, after allowing for service roads, that's over six thousand houses. That means that the cost is more like thirty pounds, not fifty pounds per acre. He whistled. Each house plot would cost four pounds. As Marcus had said, it could make millions.

CHAPTER SIXTY-THREE

Little by little the deal came together, as Phillip Cameron skillfully put each part of the jigsaw in place for Ian to handle. One by one he introduced Ian to the people that mattered and were capable of answering his searching and wide-ranging doubts and questions. The two men would meet each evening to plan what was needed for the following day. Ian had been on the island nine days.

'I am happy on the construction, geological and site costings, Phillip, but I am left with three fundamental questions. Firstly, can we get planning consent to build at least five thousand houses? Secondly, are there five thousand potential buyers of such houses? Lastly, is Jamaica politically stable, or will it produce a Fidel Castro and go communist like Cuba did in fifty-nine? Alternatively, might it lurch to the right under an army general like so many of its Central and South American neighbours? Either of these two would be disastrous for the scheme.'

'We will know the answer to the planning after our meeting with O'Hara tomorrow morning. The third is not so straightforward. You know my own view. With such a strong middle class and multi-racially integrated society, I think both scenarios are unlikely. But you will have a chance to make your own mind up at tomorrow night's reception at Government House when you will meet the politicians who run this place. My main concern is your second point. These houses will be built in a rural unknown location. What's more, they will be too small and so basic that they will only appeal to the working classes. Sure, every native-born Jamaican aspires to one day owning his own house, but aspiration is one thing, having the money to achieve this is quite another matter. Frankly, I think this could be the killer of the project,' Phillip ended glumly. 'Anyway, let's see if we can get planning first – without it you might as well get on the next plane home. Either way I promise you a good lunch at my favourite restaurant after the meeting tomorrow.'

Ian was shocked. Phillip had chosen a booth in the restaurant so that they could not be overheard.

'100,000 US dollars for miscellaneous expenses,' he said. 'It's nothing more than a bribe.'

'Ian, my friend, if you are going to do this deal you have to swallow your righteous indignation and get used to how things work here. Corruption is endemic on this island, as it is worldwide. You will learn as you get older that it is just more subtle in England, I promise you. Now drink your beer and let's order.'

Over lunch Phillip briefly explained the mechanisms for paying the backhander, only when the consent was granted, and in such a way that it could not be traced back. It involved banks and trusts in the Cayman Islands. A different world Ian thought, but clearly something that had been done many times before.

'Can you be sure they will deliver?'

'Oh yes, the operation is well tried and tested. Each side has the other firmly by the balls and the slightest squeeze ensures compliance.' Ian smiled as he remembered Big Bertha.

Later, as had become his afternoon practice, Ian retired to the pool and read the *Gleaner*. It never ceased to surprise him that the country's only national paper, serving two and a half million people, resembled the *Bath Chronicle*, with its twenty-five thousand readers. There was little international news, but acres of print covering the trivia of Jamaican life. The sheer number of Christian churches and religious denominations announcing the times of their prayer meetings, services and masses was mind blowing. As in England, middle class values, concerns and aspirations dominated, with numerous articles and comment about education, crime, health and employment.

Yes, Phillip was right, all the institutions preventing violent political upheavals to right or left were in place, and were established. He turned to the business page. Even the various trade unions seemed more moderate than their militant counterparts back home. Next he checked the real estate adverts, the asking prices and sizes of the home lots for sale all seemed to be in line with what he had been advised and used in his calculations.

He was about to put the paper down when his eye was caught by a photograph. It was of about twenty black men, all incongruously dressed as English bus conductors, complete with aluminium ticket machine hung from around their necks, and standing in front of a passenger ship. Intrigued, he read the caption: 'The LT Academy of Kingston celebrates its tenth anniversary with its latest qualified recruits bound for London.'

Ian read on to discover how thousands of Jamaicans had been recruited and trained on the island by London Transport to work on the buses and underground services in the British capital. With the kernel of an idea developing, Ian went back to his room and rang Phillip.

For the first time since his arrival Ian wore a suit, and he and Phillip were in the back of the limousine on the way to the private reception at Government House.

'Ian, I have arranged for us to see a Mr David Cowles at nine tomorrow at London Transport. He is the top man in charge of the entire overseas operation run from London. Luckily he happens to be on the island for a few days as part of his Caribbean review. Do the figures work?'

'Yes. Using a sale price of two hundred pounds per plot, payable over four years, that's one pound a week for us, plus a shilling a week collection fee for London Transport. That means one and a half million for the land alone, even before you take any profit on building houses.'

'I can see why Marcus sent you; let's hope Cowles buys in.'

'He ought to,' Ian replied. 'The £50,000 London Transport will make from the collection fees alone in the UK would probably cover the cost of their entire recruitment programme here on the island, and there is another great advantage.'

'What's that?'

Ian knew that London Transport suffered from very high rates of staff turnover. Even among those workers recruited from the West Indies, once they got to England and discovered other, better paid jobs, they moved on. But the deal he was going to suggest would lock the employee in for four years. It would be a condition of the deal that if they leave London Transport before the land is paid for, the loan would be withdrawn.

The car slowed to a halt and the two men stepped out into the splendor of Government House.

'Hello Phillip, how are you?'

'Good evening, Prime Minister. May I introduce Mr Ian

Morris from England. Mr Morris is the agent to Mr Marcus Rose.'

'Ah yes, how do you do Mr Morris? It must be a sign of age because not only policemen and soldiers, but even agents grow ever younger.' Prime Minister Bustamante spoke with a gentle Caribbean lilt in his voice, and had an engaging smile as well as a shock of white hair. 'I met Mr Rose last year during our independence celebrations. I understand you are advising him on the Yallahs scheme. How is it going?'

'Well, thank you, sir, but there are still issues that need to be discussed.'

'Can I or my colleagues be of any assistance? The provision of affordable working class housing is a very important plank of our policy.'

'Well, sir,' Ian chose his words carefully, 'as you appreciate, Mr Rose's investment will be very considerable if the scheme goes ahead. Whilst I believe that Jamaica is a stable democracy, not at political risk, I have, after all, only been here ten days, and some comfort on the point would be greatly appreciated.'

'Of course. I think I know just the person, the man who advises the government on security, anti-vice and drugs.'

The Prime Minister turned and spoke quietly to his aide, who a moment later reappeared with a man in unfamiliar uniform.

'Mr Morris, may I introduce Colonel Peter Green.'

'Oh, haven't we met before?' Ian said, recognising the man from the brothel.

'I think not,' Green said, winking.

The Prime Minister continued. 'Peter, I want you to convince this young man that we are not all going to be murdered in our beds by men from Moscow or generals from Argentina.'

'A pleasure, Mr Prime Minister.'

Green took two days to satisfy Ian, visiting some very unusual places, including a flight in a Tiger Moth – one of three owned by the Jamaican Air Force – over the illicit marijuana plantations in the Blue Mountains. Although much of what he saw was foreign on a variety of levels, Ian was impressed by Peter Green's objectiveness. As Cameron had indicated, Jamaica was a young, independent nation with a sharp divide between rich and poor, but it appeared stable.

Ian's belief with regard to a deal with David Cowles of London Transport was justified, and the heads of agreement prepared by Phillip Cameron's firm were signed on day fifteen.

As a result, and with days to spare, Ian sent the one word cable to Widcombe House. Twelve hours later Cameron exercised the option and purchased the James Plantation for Marcus Rose.

For the first time since he had arrived on the island, Ian had nothing to do, and sitting in his hotel room after the conclusion of everything with Cameron, he felt a sense of anti-climax. He considered simply packing and heading back to England when he remembered the shoe box. No better time he thought. He picked up the telephone.

'Operator, can you connect me to Mr Ian Fleming at Goldeneye Oracasbessa?'

CHAPTER SIXTY-FOUR

The bungalow was quite modest. Ian was expecting something much grander than a simple white house tucked into the edge of the forest.

'Welcome dear boy,' the famous author said on Ian's arrival with the gift. 'Welcome Marcus's protégé, and many thanks for the shoes.'

Fleming also came as a surprise, but then the expectation was for James Bond, not his frail, rather gaunt creator flourishing a long cigarette holder.

Fleming guided Ian out to the terrace where tea was laid for three. Perched on the cliff top, the view over the turquoise sea was spectacular, and there were steps down to a little cove of pristine white sand and clear water. Rising from one of the high backed cane chairs by the tea table was a most unusual looking woman, even for Jamaica, where Ian had become used to the variety of racial mix.

'Hélène, may I present Ian Morris.' Fleming turned to Ian. 'Hélène Chang is my neighbour and very good friend. I have booked you into her hotel for the next few days, a most wonderful place that I am sure you will enjoy.'

No more than five feet three inches tall, of a background probably including European, African and Asian, this petite woman in her late thirties, with Chinese eyes and jet black long hair, proffered a hand

'You are most welcome, Ian.' The accent was deliciously French.

'Now, dear boy, you must tell me all about Marcus's latest project, but first do you take milk or lemon with your tea?' Fleming asked.

Ian was delighted to discover he was Hélène's only guest as he sat on the verandah of the small wooden hotel, encompassed by trees and lush vegetation set back a short way from the quietly lapping sea. The sun was setting and there wasn't another soul in sight. She had prepared a simple Chinese meal of noodles and snapper caught that afternoon, and they had swapped background stories as they ate. She spoke of her early life in Martinique, how she then went to study at the Sorbonne in Paris, before the untimely death of her parents when their Cessna crashed over the Blue Mountains of Jamaica. Following the accident, she felt unable to leave the place where her parents had last been alive, and was happy with the uncomplicated lifestyle she led. Ian felt so relaxed and comforted by her honesty and kindness that he responded with telling his own story. How he was sent away so young, the loneliness, the death of Sebastian and others, the shame of early poverty and the agony of his mother's passing.

'And what of women, Ian, have you loved?' Hélène asked. For the first time he disclosed his feelings about Fiona's rejection and abortion of their unborn child. Then he spoke of the loss of Rachel. It was easy to talk to her and it seemed so natural when she stretched her hand across the table to cover his.

'Come,' she said quietly and took him to her bedroom and into her bed. Ian felt a bond with Hélène that made him certain that whatever happened in the future, they would endure. The sex was as fulfilling as she was beautiful, and despite their difference in age, the following days and nights were perfect and unconditional. A genuine friendship was born.

'Watch the eyes,' she said to him as they lay together under the starlight. 'You can always tell if a woman is faking, the pupils dilate with a real orgasm.' He knew how fortunate he was to have met and loved Hélène Chang and that their time together was beyond value.

Gritty eyed and sleepless from flights delayed by twelve hours, Ian returned to reality. Gone was the glorious warmth, the bright sunshine, the easy Jamaican way of life and the beautiful Hélène. Instead it was July in England, a summer's day, Ian thought as he looked out of the car's window at greyness, buildings, people and sky, as the car drove away from the airport and headed back to Bath.

The ever efficient Jennings had guessed correctly. He had taken a single glance at Ian's lightweight clothing and handed over the overcoat. 'Welcome back to sunny England, Mr Morris. I think you will be needing this.' The warm glass cocoon of the terminal was brutally replaced by the cold and a light drizzle, and he had turned the heating up to full once the engine had warmed.

'Successful trip, I understand. Mr Rose seems well pleased. I expect you are glad to be back home.'

Ian wasn't so sure. Forget raw materials and markets for finished goods, the real reason for the British Empire had been the bloody awful English weather. The Caribbean was irresistible. Why would anyone want to live in England, he thought as he dozed fitfully. But he knew the answer after only his first trip to a faraway place – money, finance, power and vitality, all lay in the northern hemisphere, in London and New York. Live in the heat of the unsophisticated tropics and you would always be coming from behind.

Ian was very moved by the homecoming awaiting him at Widcombe House. For that was what it was, he had come to a home, to be greeted with much affection from two people who greatly cared, dare he admit it, even maybe loved him.

After a 'Well done', and his proffered hand ignored for a bear hug, the first ever from Marcus, Susan kissed him and ushered him up the stairs. 'You don't want to go back to that big empty house today – go and have a good sleep and we'll wake you for dinner.'

Dinner was wonderful and exciting as they reminisced about past experiences; the memorabilia of Jamaica. There was much laughter and a closeness between them that marked a change in his relationship with the couple. It was no longer mentor-cum-benefactor and grateful recipient, but more balanced and equal. Their trust in him had proved well justified and been rewarded. Nothing was held back. They treated him as special, an individual in his own right, his opinion sought and listened to. They cared about him for himself, true friends, more, he pondered, than friendship, like family. It was a strange thought, even frightening. He wasn't sure if he wanted to feel vulnerable.

Susan departed for bed at ten-thirty but over countless malts in the study the two men discussed the plans Marcus was putting in place to sell the plots and build the houses.

Eventually, as the mantel clock quietly chimed one, and after another chuckle about the bus conductors, Marcus stood up. 'To bed, tomorrow is another day. Well done, Ian, we are going to have great fun working on this together.'

'By the way, I received this this morning.' Marcus handed him the telegram across the desk.

CUCKOO C'EST MOI STOP
MERCI MARCUS ET BONNE CHANCE STOP
HÉLÈNE

Heléne had told Ian that she knew Marcus, and as he set his alarm clock for an early start at the office the following morning, he thought of her and that first magical meal together. What he wouldn't give to be back with that beautiful woman on the balcony of her tranquil little hotel overlooking the Caribbean sea.

On the floor below Marcus gently lowered himself into bed next to Susan's sleeping form. Whilst Hélène was a fleeting pleasurable memory from his past, he had called it right in organising the trip to Jamaica for Ian and his excursion to the north coast. As an older woman who had a different philosophy on life, their liaison may have been short but it would have broadened the boy's horizons beyond simple material wealth, perhaps not by much, but it was a start. She had shown him what his obsession with money was costing him. Too many whiskeys, but exciting times; he's growing up and just as well, thought Marcus. We have a town of two thousand houses to build in a far away place.

CHAPTER SIXTY-FIVE

Three hours after Ian had got into the office, he knew that Trish Traynor had done a superb job during his absence. She had anticipated his early arrival, and to his surprise and pleasure, was seated at her desk as he stepped through the door at quarter to six in the morning. Once again, he congratulated himself for choosing her. Little did he guess that, unsure of the flight's arrival time, she had stayed in Queen Square until ten the night before, not putting it past him to come to the office, straight off the aeroplane.

'Well done, Trish,' Ian said, purposely using her first name, as he handed her back the last of the 'Follow Up' books containing copies of every letter written in his absence. What would I do without you, he thought, and that worry immediately crystallised into pounds, shillings and pence. He would suggest a rise when he met Mulholland at lunch.

As expected the final proofs of three glossy Auction Sale brochures were laying on his desk awaiting his approval. How long had it taken? It must have been a year to sort out that bloody Lady Lundy and Alistair. Still, nothing could stop it now. He opened the one for the first day of the sale; David Ghent's people at Walcot Street had done a good job.

The second brochure for days two and three was an even more lavish catalogue, listing the entire contents of the

The Rowas Grange Estate Wiltshire

One mile from Limpley Stoke Station, SEVEN MILES FROM BATH,
450-ft up, on the dry and healthy Bath
stone formation.

Commanding Magnificent Views.

AS A WHOLE OR IN THREE LOTS

AN EXCEPTIONALLY WELL PLANNED &
FITTED MODERN

William and Mary Residence

in picturesque **FORMAL AND WILD GARDENS**, together with
SQUASH RACQUET COURT,
Stabling, Garage and three Cottages. The majority of
Conkwell Wood
Upper Haugh Farm, Accommodation and Brook Land,

In all about
400 ACRES

Grange in 507 lots, complete with coloured photographs of 'much fine antique furniture, pictures, clocks, silverware and other valuable items collected over three generations of the family.'

The farm machinery and livestock were covered by the catalogue for the fourth day. The final humiliation, Ian thought with pleasure. Sweet revenge for his mother's eviction from the cottage years ago.

The second brochure for days two and three was an even more lavish catalogue, listing the entire contents of the Grange in 507 lots, complete with coloured photographs of 'much fine antique furniture, pictures, clocks, silverware and other valuable items collected over three generations of the family.'

The farm machinery and livestock were covered by the catalogue for the fourth day. The final humiliation, Ian thought with pleasure. Sweet revenge for his mother's eviction from the cottage years ago. He knew the figures and that there would be nothing left for the Lundys after this final sale. However much it all raised, every penny would go to the banks and other creditors.

What if he could find a buyer and bid on his behalf? That would be the icing on the cake. He smiled and relished the thought of Lady Lundy's reaction when she discovered 'the housekeeper's son' hammering in the last nail into the Lundy coffin. He pushed the intercom button down.

'Trish, can you let me have the applicants register for country estate enquiries for the West Country; give the London office a ring and make sure it's up to date.'

'Yes, Mr Morris.'

Ten minutes later, the precious list was with him. The life-blood of every good agency, highly guarded, the register listed everyone seeking country property, from cottage to vast country estate. Buried in the bowels of Berkeley Square, six people continually categorised the hundreds of telephone enquiries and letters from eager buyers, be they ex-pats returning home, the newly wealthy captains of industry, or the downsizing dowagers. Unsuccessful bidders in previous sales were also a rich vein of future purchasers; removal from the list only happened when interested parties bought something or died!

Unfamiliar with the country market, Ian was staggered by the sheer size of the list. The section 'within twenty-five miles of Bath and Bristol' ran to eleven pages of names and requirements. One in particular caught his eye.

'Within ten miles of Bath or Bristol, Country House and estate of up to 500 acres – price no object for right one. Not an m.h.s. situation. All enquiries to JT, ref L' had been added under 'special notes'. JT was Jeremy Thring.

Puzzled, Ian wondered why on earth his boss in the commercial investment side was involved. He dialled the private number.

'Mr Thring, Ian Morris.'

'Hello Morris, how goes it?'

'Fine sir, I'm calling about L in the applicants register.'

'That's Country Estates, a bit off your patch?'

'Yes, but I think I might have something that fits. What's an m.h.s. situation?'

'Manor House Syndrome. Self-made man builds a business from scratch, works day and night for umpteen years to the exclusion of everything else, and usually wrecks his health and marriage in the process. Makes a packet by floating it on the Stock Exchange, and stays on as Chairman on a fantastic salary. Only problem, wakes up one morning and discovers there is more to life than just work; wants out of nasty 'trade' and become a respectable country gentleman. Essential ingredient country house and all the trappings. The impecunious local fox hunt, golf club and others pounce like kamikazes. Manor House Syndrome: very bad news for his new shareholders. Nothing changes, a hundred years ago Surtees wrote a very funny book about a tea merchant from the East End of London; *Handley Cross* said it all.'

'And why is L different?'

'There are two Ls: father's money, and son's talent. Father made a fortune and happy to wallow in trade. His son, that rare thing, a product of our public school system, but a born trader. Left school early for some reason, and noticed how many of the big country houses continue to come onto the market. Same thing happened after the First World War. Then it was no one to inherit, all killed, and death duties. Now the old families who have lived in them for hundreds of years have thrown in the towel, mostly they are broke, a few fled abroad to escape the spite of the Attlee Government.'

'So what do the two Ls do?'

'They are break-up merchants. They buy off-market, divide them up into separate smaller lots, and sell them on.'

'I wouldn't have thought there's enough profit in it, to make it worthwhile?'

Thring laughed. 'They doubled their money in six months on the last one I did for them in Yorkshire. Very slick operation. They always use the same auctioneer who was originally selling, so they save money by using the original auction particulars to re-sell very quickly. Agents love them, two sale fees for the same property. What have you got?'

That's what I like about Thring, Ian thought, straight to the point.

'It's the Rowas Grange Estate, about seven miles from Bath,'he said.

'I noticed that in the forthcoming sale sheets at the last

358

partners' meeting,' Thring replied, 'but given it's a trustee sale, surely you have to go to auction? My chap will never do that, avoids publicity like the plague.'

'No problem, the trustees will do what the bankers want, and they will jump at an off-market single deal that is quicker, cheaper and quiet.'

'When is the sale date?'

'In two months, at the end of September.'

'What about vacant possession, is someone still living in the house?'

'Yes, the widow, Lady Lundy, absolutely no problem, quite the reverse.' Ian was tempted to add how much pleasure it would give him to serve her notice.

'Ok, sounds like a runner. I'll send the dispatch rider down to collect the draft particulars. Have two copies ready in four hours.'

'Yes, sir. By the way, who are the two Ls?'

'Sorry, you'll only know that if they bite – I'll be in touch. In the meantime, well done for spotting the chance. Goodbye Ian.'

'Goodbye sir, and thank you.' It was the first time Thring had used his first name.

CHAPTER SIXTY-SIX

Trish was waiting for him, as he entered the office reception. 'Urgent message from Mr Thring, Ian,' she said. 'It came in after you left yesterday afternoon, and I couldn't reach you. Can you and Mr Mulholland meet him and the client 'L' off the London train getting into Bath this morning at 10 o'clock? They want to see the whole estate today and tomorrow.'

'Where will they stay?'

'L is very particular and will make his own arrangements.'

'Is Mr Mulholland in yet?'

'No Ian, he's away for two days valuing the villages on the Penrith Estate in Wales. I've booked the company Land Rover and I can drive you if you wish.'

'Let's see,' Ian looked at his watch, 'we have just two hours. Please ring Lady Lundy and tell her we will be doing a private viewing of the house starting at about half past eleven. Then the estate manager, I will require him to show us around the farm, cottages woodlands, everything.'

'Yes, Ian.'

Ten minutes later she was back. 'The estate manager was very helpful, he will make himself available all day. Lady Lundy says it is not convenient. I did my best, explained that people were coming down from London, but she flatly refused, she says you must give at least two days' notice for anyone to view. I am sorry.'

'Don't worry, I will speak to her.' A few moments later he heard the haughty voice from his childhood at the other end of the telephone line.

'Lady Lundy, Ian Morris here,' he said. 'Let me make the position crystal clear. I am not requesting a viewing this morning. Out of courtesy, I'm telling you that it will be taking place. Your permission is neither sought nor required.'

'You impudent young man, how dare you talk to me in such a tone.'

'Let me remind you,' he responded, 'that you only remain at Lundy Grange because of the goodwill of your long suffering creditors, to whom you owe vast sums of money, and for whom I act.' She attempted to interrupt, but Ian continued. 'As has been made abundantly clear to you on a numerous occasions, you are merely an unpaid caretaker. Do anything to obstruct or hinder the sale process, and I will not hesitate to arrange for you to be immediately evicted. Do you understand?'

Silence. The phone was put down, and the dialling tone returned.

Ian stood at the back end of Platform Two, where he knew the first class carriage would stop, and watched the London train come into the station. What would 'L' be like, he wondered, and what approach should he take. Don't try to oversell, he decided, the estate would speak for itself – stacks of potential. Ah well, here goes. The train stopped, and just six feet away, the carriage door opened to reveal Jeremy Thring, followed by another man, momentarily hidden from view.

Stepping aside on the platform, so that Ian could see his companion, Thring said, 'Henry, may I introduce our man, Ian Morris, Ian, our client, Henry Lieberman.'

'Lieberman! What's it been, nine years?'

Without hesitation, Lieberman threw his arms around Morris and hugged him. 'Ten actually. I was a bit thrown when Jeremy said your first name was Ian, but then I thought it must be Yann Morris. How are you?'

'Gobsmacked, but it's great to see you.'

Jeremy Thring was momentarily taken aback. 'Obviously you two know each other?' he remarked as they climbed into the car.

'Very much so, we were at school together at Beaconsfield, shared everything, even the beatings, didn't we Morris?'

'You bet.' Ian wondered how he should handle his sales pitch, given the change of circumstances. Gone were the restraint and soft sell. He trusted his instincts.

Thring, who was in the front seat, turned to Trish Traynor. 'Would you be kind enough to drop me at the office?' He turned to the two in the back, who had begun to reminisce. 'I'll leave you two to it. You don't need me. Shall we meet for drinks and dinner?'

'Good idea Jeremy. Hopefully I'll have seen enough and made a decision by then.'

'All right Ian, let's call it a day. Can you drop me at my hotel Trish?' It was only 4 o'clock but they had visited all that was relevant of the Rowas Grange Estate and Lieberman obviously wanted some time to consider what he had seen.

'Certainly Mr Lieberman, where are you staying?' Trish asked.

'Where else but Sharon Love's guest house,' Lieberman chuckled. 'My wife and I always stay there.'

'I beg your pardon?' Ian knew that Lieberman had made an early marriage but had never heard of Sharon Love or her guest house, and he thought he knew every hotel in Bath.

'One of Bath's oldest boarding houses, been there some say since the 14th century, now called the Royal Crescent.' Lieberman smiled as he looked across at Ian. He should have guessed, nothing but the best, one of the grandest hotels in the country, let alone Bath.

Trish parked the car and they stood for a moment outside the two houses in the exact centre of the perfect elliptical curve of thirty identical buildings. John Wood the Younger's masterpiece of over 200 years earlier, nearly fifty feet high and over 150 yards long, was bathed in the late afternoon sunshine. It never ceased to impress Ian and for the umpteenth time he marveled at the architect's scrupulous attention to detail, the total uniformity, under-rated gracefulness, and it's sweeping vision over most of the city.

'Welcome, most welcome Mr Lieberman.' A slim woman with blonde hair, in her early thirties greeted him. Attractive and elegantly dressed, she seemed genuinely pleased to see the businessman. 'It's been far too long.'

'May I introduce Trish Traynor and Ian Morris,' Lieberman said and they all shook hands. 'Give me fifteen minutes and stay for tea in the garden. Is it the usual Sharon?'

'As always, the Duke of York, Mr Lieberman.' She explained to the other two that his suite was named after the hill of marching fame in the nursery rhyme, the Grand Old Duke of York, who was the second son of George III who rented the whole house for £5,000 in 1797.

Ian had never been inside the hotel before and admired its pale colours, Regency stripes, and black and white chequered floor. He had stepped back 200 years into the luxury and calm of Georgian England, he thought as he walked between the deep purple sofas, with the gilt mirrors, under the ornate chandeliers and out into the garden to await Lieberman. He had heard about William Bertram's design of the newer buildings surrounding this oasis of tranquility, but now in the fading July heat and sunlight, the genius of this young architect's use of Bath stone was magical.

A few minutes later there was something incongruous, watching this large no-nonsense man grasping the dainty rose painted china cup in one enormous hand, a quarter cut crustless cucumber sandwich in the other.

'It all comes down to the figures.'

Ian knew it always would. It had to be cheap enough to tempt.

'Forget your clients for the moment. You and I both know that they are just a load of creditors, chasing a bad loan, and within reason will take what they can get. Let's start at the other end of the deal and work backwards. Say I wasn't on the scene and the auction takes place, what would the auction realise? Everything, house, cottage, land, contents and farm, the lot?'

Ian had been ready for the questions, but paused, pretending to give the matter thought.

'£250,000, selling individual lots to different buyers.'

'And as one single lot?'

'If you could find such a buyer, less – £200,000.'

'Less your fees and the total expenses of selling, you know, everything, advertising – how much?'

'£15,000.'

'And what would it cost me if I bought the whole lot, and I instructed you to hold the auction and do the resales?'

'Probably £10,000, including Woods & Parker's re-sale fee.'

Lieberman put the cup down, took out the small pad from his pocket – later Ian was to remember that it was no bigger than the proverbial cigarette packet – took out the gold Parker pen from his inside jacket pocket, and started writing figures, saying them aloud as he went.

'So break up sale proceeds, you say £250,000. Just let's be conservative. You don't sell everything, get left with some of the rubbish in the house and on the farm,' he wrote £225,000 at the top of the sheet, 'less your sale costs for the break up,' he deducted £10,000, leaving £215,000. 'For my risk, I am looking for a profit of at least £65,000.'

'As much as that?' Ian asked, doubtful if the deal would bear such a high traders margin.

'Afraid so, remember I don't make a penny until you've sold at least £150,000, and then there's the interest I am paying on the money borrowed to do the deal.'

'You borrow the money, how much?' Ian was surprised. 'You don't use your own cash?'

'Not a chance, far too risky. I borrow every last penny from the banks, that's what they are there for. So that makes my best bid £150,000. Can you accept that on behalf of your clients, the creditors?'

'Doubt it. Can't you get to £200,000?'

'Nope, not a penny more. I am afraid it's a take it or leave it situation.'

One tough cookie, Ian thought, for he knew Henry meant it.

'Who do you have to talk to, to make the deal happen?'

'Just my boss, John Mulholland. Woods & Parker have complete delegated authority from the creditors.'

'So when can you do that?'

'Tonight, he's joining us for dinner.'

'Good, because I'm only prepared to leave it on the table for twenty-four hours. I can't have you going round using it to find another buyer who will outbid me. I am not into Dutch auctions. If we aren't signed up by this time tomorrow, the deal's off.'

'But that's impossible, we don't even have solicitors, let alone a contract.'

365

'Ah, but you do,' he held up the proofs of his four auction catalogues. 'We'll use these. Each party can sign, I'll give you the ten per cent cash deposit, and, hey presto, Ian, we have a binding contract, completion in a month!'

'What about your solicitors, don't you need to talk to them?'

'Nope.'

Ian realised there was nowhere to hide. He remained silent, thinking.

'Go, talk to your boss, Ian. That will give me time to wash and change. See you all in the bar in an hour, and don't look so worried, one way or another it's been great to catch up with you. If nothing else, we will have a great dinner here.'

To Ian's surprise, John Mulholland didn't hesitate.

'We'll deal at £150,000.' He listed the reasons on his fingers. 'One, Jeremy knows him, says he's good for the money. Two, quick sale of everything, and three, Woods & Parker gets double fees. No need to wait until tomorrow, get two sets of the auction particulars and we can exchange contracts tonight. I can sign on behalf of the creditors.' He paused. 'And bring a letter instructing the firm for the resale on the original auction date, which Liebermann can sign.'

Deliberately early, Ian had gone straight up to Henry's suite and now he sat facing his old school friend. He knew, he just knew.

'Henry, I am afraid there's no deal. £150,000 is just too low.'

'Too bad.' Lieberman stood up. 'So, let's go down and drown our sorrows.'

Ian stood up. His heart was pounding, Lieberman was calling his bluff. The whole deal would fall through. He picked up his briefcase and started following him to the door. Lieberman opened it and turned towards him.

'How much, absolute bottom figure?'

'£165,000.'

'And we sign within the next twenty-four hours?'

'Tonight, now. I have the papers with me.'

'You have yourself a deal,' Lieberman said, slowly shutting the door and returning to the table.

Fifteen minutes later, Ian joined Jeremy Thring and John Mulholland in the bar.

'All signed, and I have the deposit for £16,500. Henry will be down in a few minutes.' He patted his briefcase.

'But ten per cent of £150,000 is only £15,000; why the extra?'

'Oh, I got him up another £15,000.' His manner was offhand and casual, unlike the inner turmoil he was still feeling – he could have blown the whole thing.

CHAPTER SIXTY-SEVEN

Wearily Ian folded his handwritten answer sheets, printed 'Advance Valuations/ Compulsory Purchase Orders' on the outside and placed then in the envelope addressed to the college. Only four months more, and he would be so pleased when the Intermediate Exam was finally over. It was only his promise to Marcus Rose that kept him striving for a qualification. He knew that Marcus could sense his frustration and continually assured him that it would be worthwhile in the long run. Ian didn't believe it, but out of loyalty to Marcus and Susan, he would keep going.

It was dark outside as he rose from his desk, stretched his arms and checked his watch. Ten o'clock. He picked his jacket up from the back of his chair and made his way out of the house, locking the front door. Great Pulteney Street was deserted. He walked down to the postbox at Laura Place, with its quirky little fountain; he smiled as he remembered the story about when it was first built and the local residents had baulked at the cost of the tall column originally intended.

Since the sale of the Rowas Grange Estate a couple of months earlier, Ian had developed the habit of working most evenings before making his way across Pulteney Bridge for a pasta at Joya's on Grand Parade. He had grown fond of

Lydia Crestani, a soft spoken Italian woman in her early forties, elegant, smart and exotic, who always welcomed him warmly.

She held his chin and kissed him full on the lips when he arrived. 'What's it to be?' she asked.

He loved the taste of her.

'Stop thinking it,' she laughed. 'It would be a wonderful diversion, but I am old enough to be your mother. Anyway, there is a girl you should meet. She deals with property just like you.'

'The usual, glass of Valpolicella and carbonara,' he muttered, resigned to his rejection. The restaurant was nearly empty and Lydia led him to a table in the window where a young woman sat alone with a book propped up against a wine bottle.

'Tanya, this is the young man I was telling you about. Ian Morris.' The girl stood up and shook his outstretched hand. Luxuriant red hair fell to her shoulders. She had a pale face with mischievously bright eyes, and a smile that regarded him with interest. There was an inviting warmth and openness. Ian guessed that she was of a similar age to himself, but the black, rather school-girlish tunic made her look younger. She was very different to Rachel.

'Join me,' she said, closing the book and staring straight into him with her violet eyes. 'Lydia tells me you run Woods & Parker's new office in Wood Street?'

Ian laughed. 'Not quite, that's my boss, John Mulholland.'

'Yeah, yeah.' She picked up a pack of Benson & Hedges, and offered him a cigarette before taking one herself. 'But they say you're the one that does all the work. I must say you are much younger than I thought.' Ian ignored her comment about his age, but reached for his lighter and lit both cigarettes before replying.

'And what do you do?'

'I work for The Bath Town Planning Consultancy.'

'What's that?'

'The private company that Bath City Council has retained to advise on the redevelopment of the whole city. We are based behind the Guildhall.'

Sitting at his desk the next morning, Ian felt sure he had been right to keep sex out of it. Instead of inviting Tanya back to his place and bed, he had walked her to the steps of her bedsit in nearby Henrietta Street, ignored the proffered lips, kissed her lightly on the cheek and departed, promising no more than he hoped to see her in Joya's again. Gorgeous body or not, she would be much more use inside the Council rather than in his bed.

A week later his hunch proved to be correct when Tanya poured her heart out to him over more Valpolicella. After a three year affair with her middle-aged boss, he had tired of her, as her demands that he leave his wife became more strident. She felt used and let down by someone she thought had loved her. 'And the bastard has bought my silence with a promise of promotion and more money, but I'm still waiting for it to happen.'

'What do you want to do about it?'

'Revenge, tell his wife. Make him suffer.'

'The wife probably already knows – they often do – and why hurt her? No, we'll find a better way to make him pay, rather than his poor wife.' He put his hand across the table and covered hers.

'Look, you are very attractive, there will be other men, more your age.' Her eyes lit up.

'No, not me Tanya,' he laughed and patted her hand. 'I have other fish to fry.'

'What's the lucky girl's name?' She took her hand away.

'Money, wealth, power.'

She was silent for a moment.

'Don't get angry, get even,' Ian tried to make her smile with his Humphrey Bogart impression, but it didn't work. 'Ok,' he became serious again, 'let me think about it for a day or so, but in the meantime, be nice to your boss. Lull him into believing that you still love him, and would never do anything to hurt him, but are happy to move on.'

'I'll try.' She pouted and didn't sound convinced.

'It's not for me,' he lied, and stood up. 'Now, let me walk you home.'

He deliberately stayed away from Joya's until he had worked out how Tanya's position could be of use. It took him a few days, but when he thought he had a plan, instead of waiting until the evening, Ian telephoned her office.

'You being nice to him?'

'Yes, but it's driving me mad. Anyway stranger, this is a first. Talking in daylight, what can I do for you?'

'Can I buy you a sandwich for lunch?'

'Well, you certainly know how to show a girl a good time. Where?'

'In my office, so we can talk in private. Pretend you are looking for a flat and then ask for me. One o'clock?'

'Trish, move the sign to Engaged as you go out please, and see we are not disturbed.'

'Yes, Ian.' She placed the sandwich bag on the table, and eyed this girl, with her violet eyes and a figure to die for; she must be someone special. Her boss had never done this before. Ian moved from behind his desk to where Trish had sat Tanya, and waited until the door was closed.

'So, how are you doing?' He bent down and gave her a kiss on the cheek.

'Well, I must give you your due. Being nice to the bugger has paid off, even though it makes me want to throw up.'

'How come?' He tore open the brown paper bag and laid it flat on the table, so they could both help themselves to the sandwiches.

'He has made me his personal assistant for real.' Without waiting, Tanya reached for something to eat. 'He has been talking about helping me move on from straightforward secretarial work for ages, and now suddenly it's happened. Perhaps I should have stopped letting him shag me earlier. More money as well. My own office, not much bigger than a cupboard, but my own space.'

'Tell me Tanya, what exactly do you do in the Bath Town Planning Consultancy?' Ian, too, reached for a sandwich and munched through it while Tanya put hers down and explained her new role and areas of responsibility.

'You still want to get even?' he asked.

'Yeah, maybe even more than I did before.'

'Why's that, now you've got your promotion?'

'My replacement.' She picked her sandwich up again. 'She can't be more than nineteen, like I was at the beginning. He hasn't wasted any time. The letch has already got his claws, or should I say, something else into her.'

'Stupid bugger. All his brains are between his legs. Anyway so much the better as far as we are concerned. Now eat up and I'll explain a perfect revenge. It won't happen immediately, we need to make sure that he is relaxed with you and trusting enough to make a mistake. But trust me, he will, and then he'll wish he'd been born without balls.'

They were sitting in front of the television, she invited to his house for the first time, about to discuss the sexual honeypot he had dreamt up, when the pictures flashed up. The motorcade, and later the First Lady in her blood soaked dress, grasping her children's hands. November 22rd 1963. The day when everything else was forgotten, and everyone would remember for the rest of their lives where they were when it happened.

Five days later in Bath Abbey, Ian stood before the High Altar draped in the United States flag, a gift of the American Embassy, as the buglers of the Somerset Light Infantry played 'The Last Post', or 'Taps' as the group of US Navy officers next to him called it, their dazzling white uniforms mingling with the dark blue of their colleagues from the Admiralty in Bath.

He felt he had lost a close friend as he walked back to the office. 'A prophet in his own land' came to mind. What was it with Americans and their love of guns? He supposed this is how it felt after Abraham Lincoln had been shot.

CHAPTER SIXTY-EIGHT

He looked through the thirty or so index cards which Trish had selected showing every residential lot sold at the Lundy Estate city auction. Each one related to whole streets of low quality artisan houses, let on weekly tenancies. They were in poor locations all over the city, and each had the same buyer, Zebrae Holdings Ltd, with a PO Box address in George Street.

'Trish, get me Malcolm Austwick on the telephone please.' It took a few minutes until he got through to the elderly solicitor, went through the necessary courtesies, and to ask for what he wanted.

'One of the big buyers at the auction was a company called Zebrae Holdings Ltd, with only a PO Box number and no telephone number. Given that you acted for the estate in the sale, and were in touch with all the purchasers' solicitors, do you know who is behind them?'

The line was silent.

'Mr Austwick?'

'I am still here Ian. May I ask why you want to know?'

'Future business. I have an idea that might make them and us a lot more money.'

'Us?' Austwick said quizzically .

'Yes, I was hoping you would act for me, if I can pull it off.'

'Why don't you put it in writing and I can then send your letter on to their solicitors?'

'It's not something that I want to put pen to paper about.'

'Why, is it illegal?'

'Good Lord no, just an idea that I want to get going before Christmas. I don't want someone else to get there first.'

'Leave it with me.'

Austwick telephoned him back mid-afternoon. 'The men behind Zebrae are Brian Palmer and his son, Roger, and they keep a low profile. I have never met them, they are not Bath people, but came here about five years ago from somewhere in South Devon. Made, and still make their money from abattoirs all over the West Country. They have been big buyers of property ever since but the whole operation is very secretive. Their telephone number is ex-directory, but their solicitor, a very bright young man, is Patrick McCloy in Bradford on Avon. I have spoken to Mr McCloy and he has got his clients' approval for me to give it to you.'

After noting the number down, Ian discovered from Austwick that the Palmers were interested in the new bus station, as well as some slum properties in Snow Hill, and the skyscraper block of flats that took their place.

'Do you know where I mean?' the solicitor asked.

'Yes, very well.' Instantly the memory of his mother and the house in Mafeking Street sprang to mind.

'I think they also have a finger in the awful redevelopment of the new police station in Manvers Street,' Austwick added.

Ian then asked for an outside line and dialled the number. A male voice answered, with a rich vowel register that reminded him of the kitchen and grounds staff at Pitt College.

'May I speak to either Mr Brian or Roger Palmer?'

'May I ask who wants him?'

'Ian Morris from Woods & Parker.'

'I am Roger Palmer, and gather you have some bright idea regarding the lots bought on our behalf at the Lundy Estate auction. What's on your mind?'

'I would prefer to meet, sir.'

'I am sure that you would.' Despite the familiar manner of the regional accent, the man wasn't for doffing his hat to anyone. 'But I want to know what it's about first.'

'I am sorry sir, but I am only keen to work on this if we can meet and talk.'

'Well, I am sorry Mr Morris, that doesn't work for me. Perhaps another time. Goodbye.'

He resisted the usual bluff of threatening to go elsewhere, and left with no alternative, said goodbye and hung up. He was tempted to ring again over the next few days, but decided against it.

Just as Jeremy Thring had predicted, Henry Lieberman completed the purchase of the Rowas Grange Estate without a hitch. A week later he returned to Bath for the four day auction sale originally planned. When all the lots were added, it fetched a total of £255,000, to give Lieberman a profit of £90,000.

After the sale Henry held a private dinner at the Royal Crescent for all concerned. Everyone, even Woods & Parker's auction porters brought down from Berkeley Square for the sale, had been invited. It was a clever gesture, and worth remembering for the future, Ian thought as he glanced around the Montagu Room. Forty people were enjoying the best the hotel could offer. Never forget the small people, he mused, even though the filing room of four years earlier was light years behind him.

Neither Henry nor Ian had drunk during the dinner. Alone afterwards, the two of them were in something mysteriously called 'the Club', deep in the bowels of the hotel, with a rowdy group of four or five men who all knew Lieberman.

Now as the drink flowed, his newfound 'bar mates', John, Dudley and Michael, seemed more and more familiar, but he couldn't for the life of him remember where he had met this flamboyant mob of the hotel's residents before, nor the numerous toasts to *The Wrong Box*. Henry insisted on one last nightcap in his suite. 'He had a present for Ian,' he said, so the two of them staggered up the stairs.

'Do you forgive me?' Ian slurred, as they sat opposite each other, with their malt whiskeys.

'What for?'

'The extra £15,000 I screwed out of you for the Rowas Grange Estate.'

'Good God, yes. Got it all back, and more, even before the resale.'

Now it was Ian's turn to be perplexed. Henry raised his glass.

'Here's to the bear skin rug.' Ian remembered the entire polar bear skin, complete with head and glass eyes, which covered the floor of what had been always known as the first Earl's Gun Room. He thought the hunting trophy from Nantucket was bizarre, and was surprised when his friend had successfully bid for it in the auction. He was even more surprised he had sold it on for a profit.

'It was the trap door under it.' He passed the bottle, from which he had poured the drams, to Ian. The small green bottle was labeled 'Glenavon Special Liquer Whisky'. 'The London auctioneers reckoned it came out of the cask over 100 years ago at the Banfifeshire distillery. Must have been put down by the first Earl and just forgotten after he died. Kept just three bottles, I sold the other thirty-three for a fortune, which reminds me, these are for you.' He handed Ian a set of car keys. 'I've arranged for it to be delivered to your office tomorrow.'

The *Chronicle*, awaiting him when he staggered into the office at lunchtime the following afternoon, solved the other mystery.

THE WRONG BOX COMES TO TOWN

Some of London's best known actors and comics descended on the Royal Crescent Hotel yesterday to reconnoitre the location of a major film production, soon to be filmed in Bath. Peter Cook and Dudley Moore of *Beyond the Fringe* fame, have returned from New York's Broadway for their first film role with Michael Caine in this adaptation of the novel by Robert Louis Stevenson, to be directed by Bryan Forbes and due for release in about two years. Victorian London crescents will be replaced by wild antics in the Royal Crescent, ending with a funeral coach and horses chase in St James Square. Other well known actors in the film, no doubt soon to be seen in Bath include Ralph Richardson, Peter Sellers and Tony Hancock.

CHAPTER SIXTY-NINE

Ten days later, two days before Christmas, a 'By Hand' letter arrived from McCloy, summoning, rather than inviting, Ian to a meeting with the Palmers at his office at two o'clock that afternoon.

McCloy's office was in a medieval street called The Shambles in Bradford on Avon. It was a little building, where he was shown into a small meeting room that appeared almost crowded with just three people seated around an oval Georgian table. One was a large stocky weather-beaten character of about sixty with thinning grey hair and bushy moustache. Next to him was a pale dapper young man, with almost identical looks, but half his age, blonde, clean shaven and noticeably taller. Their dress could not have been more different, father in a sports jacket with leather patches and open necked shirt; the son in a beautifully hand cut Brioni suit, presumably imported through Christopher Barry in Union Street.

The third man, in his late twenties, dressed in a three-piece suit with starched collar and dark tie, rose and proffered his hand.

'Welcome Mr Morris. I am Patrick McCloy and this is Mr Brian Palmer and his son, Mr Roger Palmer. Please have a seat.' His manner was deferential.

The younger Palmer wasted no time. 'So what can we do for you?'

'Hopefully, not just for me but for all of us.' Wrong reply, too smart he realised as soon as he had said it, but pressed on. 'I noticed that the lots you bought at the estate auction are the terraced properties originally built to house the thousands of workers who served the grand houses. An eighteenth century Georgian "new town", constructed to cope with demand around a tiny Roman and medieval monastic centre.'

Impatiently, the son interrupted. 'Thank you for the history lesson, but what has that to do with anything?'

'Well, unlike other cities, where poor workers were crammed into low quality cheap housing – slums just thrown up by their bosses – your houses are small replicas of the grand ones, beautifully designed and well constructed in identical Bath Stone, and good places to live. About a thousand are Grade III listed; their demolition and re-development will be very difficult, if not impossible to get past the Council.' He paused for effect, and looked straight at the younger Palmer. 'No doubt you know what I mean with regard to the cost of your involvement with the demolition and re-development of that tall block of flats on Snow Hill, and after that with the new bus station. Then there was the property in Kingsmead a year later, and last year, Abbey Green.'

'How the hell do you know about all this?' The younger Palmer glanced anxiously at his father.

Ian avoided the question, and changed the subject; the briefing from Malcolm Austwick had been thorough, but on the understanding he did not disclose his source. 'I believe I can expedite demolition with no come back on Zebrae. For example, regarding Lot Sixteen. Is it in your mind to knock all these houses down?'

There was a pause before the father looked at his son.

'You might as well tell him, we have nothing to lose.'

Roger Palmer slowly nodded and turned to Ian. 'Our architects have drawn up preliminary plans for a massive new block to be called Sovereign House, but it has got nowhere.'

'Here's my proposal,' Ian answered. 'Give me an exclusive deal on this site for six months.'

'Why on earth should we do that?'

'Because if I get you outline permission to demolish and redevelop, it is only reasonable that in return you appoint me sole agent.' He paused. 'And for every other lot you bought at the auction.'

Young Palmer exploded. 'That's outrageous. Why should we hand over the keys to our kingdom to an antiquated outfit such as Woods & Parker?'

'Who said anything about Woods & Parker? The deal would be with me personally, and I alone would deal with everything.'

'Wouldn't that be a breach of your contract of employment?' McCloy asked softly.

'Not if you word the appointment agreement in the right way. Make it personal to me. Then, if I ever leave Woods & Parker and set up on my own, your instructions move with me. The firm would no longer be involved.'

The solicitor looked at his clients. 'Mr Morris, do you mind leaving us for a few moments so that we can discuss this amongst ourselves?'

Fifteen minutes later he was called back into the room. McCloy began.   'My clients have instructed me to agree that you personally can have an exclusive deal to handle the Sovereign House site for three, not six months. If you obtain a demolition order and outline planning consent, again, you personally will have a sole agency, under which no one else but you can deal with it, and all the other properties purchased by my clients at the Lundy Estate auction. This will run for one year, at a performance fee, under which you get two per cent of any increase over what they paid at auction. Is that acceptable?'

'No,' Ian countered. 'I need a minimum of four months for Sovereign House, and a two year sole agency at five per cent.'

'Four months, OK, but one year and five per cent, or two years at three per cent. Take your pick,' bounced back Roger Palmer.

'Two years at four per cent.' Ian knew he had the deal within his grasp.

'Agreed.'

McCloy resumed. 'In the interests of all, the agreement will remain confidential and will be recorded by way of an exchange of letters, signed and sealed by each party, to be held by an agreed independent firm. These letters can only be opened and their contents revealed by agreement of both parties. The whole deal will be null and void if any action taken by you, Mr Morris, is shown, or later proves to be illegal.'

'Agreed,' Ian answered, and added, 'No need to agree another firm, Mr McCloy, I trust you to hold the letters.'

'Thank you, Mr Morris, that is much appreciated. I suggest we re-convene at nine o'clock tomorrow, by which time I will have the paperwork ready.'

'Until nine tomorrow then. Good to do business with you,' Ian said as he stood to shake hands with each of the men.

'Only time will tell if that is right,' Roger Palmer answered.

Ian was counting on Tanya. Little could he have guessed the consequences of her promotion at the Bath Town Planning Consultancy and how quickly things would happen.

CHAPTER SEVENTY

His office was in darkness, apart from the circle of light from the brass desk lamp with its smoked glass shade. It shone on the single sheet of paper smuggled out by Tanya after the shenanigans of the staff Christmas party.

'Tell me again how you got hold of this.' Ian had already read through the paper once, but couldn't believe his luck.

'Ex-lover boy couldn't keep his hands off my replacement. Obviously they had arranged to meet up after the party and lust couldn't wait. He asked if I could do him a big favour and hang around until the end and close the department. He handed me the keys and agreed I would hold them until we re-opened after Christmas. I chucked the last of the staff out an hour ago, and started to lock up. It was then that I noticed the small key on the ring. I had seen him use it to unlock the middle drawer of his desk so I went up to his office and opened it, and there this was.'

CONFIDENTIAL

DEVELOPMENT PROPOSALS

```
Our recommendation is that all of
'artisan' Bath's poor quality
housing be demolished within twenty
years, leaving only the
```

masterpieces like the Royal Crescent, the Circus, the Pump Room, Gay Street, Queen Square etc. Namely, all Grade I listed buildings.

Ruthlessness will be required if Bath is to be modernised. To placate conservationists, Bath Stone, or more cheaply re-constructed Bath Stone, should be specified for new buildings, which the council envisage should fill the sites created by the demolition as well as the remaining bomb sites. Of the 3,000 listed buildings, at least 1,000 under Grade III are not worth preserving as is the case for a large number of the Grade II properties.

Three aspects of this policy are paramount, before effective opposition is martialed: confidentiality, speed and ability to deliver. Therefore a short list should be prepared of appropriate construction companies. It is suggested that these be chosen from those that served the Council so effectively with the emergency repairs after the blitz of April 1942. Only one local builder should be recommended. This builder should be appointed by no later than 31st January 1963 in order to ease and speed implementation through the planning approval process.

If, as we understand is the case, this recommendation is accepted, its existence should remain confidential.

'Interesting?' Tanya asked.

'Unbelievable.' Ian took out the Minox miniature camera from his desk and adjusted the focus so that the wording was clearly readable before photographing it.

'I'll come with you to take this back,' he offered and put the paper in his jacket pocket. 'No time like the present, and you have the keys.'

Taking a torch from his desk, and as an afterthought the camera, Ian, Tanya on his arm, walked back to her office. Using the rear entrance, they entered the deserted building and made their way to her boss's office, and Tanya handed Ian the key. He opened the desk drawer, shone his torch in, and was about to replace the piece of paper when he noticed the top of another sheet at the back. He took it out and shone the torch over it.

'Gotcha,' he said. 'We have your revenge, Tanya.' He quickly took out his camera, handed her the torch and snapped the camera twice.

'How come?'

'I'll explain later, but you deserve a big kiss.'

'Well, what's stopping you?'

'Nothing,' he answered truthfully, now that he had got what he really wanted.

'In which case,' she said, sinking to her knees, and unzipping his trousers, 'I'm going first.'

CHAPTER SEVENTY-ONE

The next morning Ian rang his photographer in Winsley, who worked from a dark room in the basement of his home.

'Special rush job, and before you say anything, I know it's Christmas Eve, but I'll pay double rate if you can develop four prints from the Minox – six foolscap copies of each.'

Ian knew he could be trusted and was pushing on an open door as he had given the photographer all the work for the Lundy auction brochures.

'I'll bring them now and wait while you get them done.' He didn't want to let the negatives out of his sight, or contemplate the possibility of any spare prints.

The sleek dark blue convertible MGB from *Phillips* in Bradford had been a present from a grateful Lieberman after the Rowas Grange Estate resale. Andrew at *T & A* had super-tuned it to produce the throaty roar, and roof down despite the cold, Ian gunned the car up the drive of Widcombe House. Just the image he thought, stylish, with a lot of poke. Talking of 'poke' reminded him of the previous night's frantic sex with Tanya with none of Helénè's subtlety. He came to a halt, skidding slightly, displacing the gravel.

Marcus was outside the front door smoking his customary

cigar, and had watched the performance. 'A sign of prosperity or indebtedness?' he enquired, cocking an eyebrow as Ian approached the open front door.

Ian laughed. 'That depends on the second thing I have to show you.' Minutes later, they were in the study, and Ian brought Marcus up to date with the Palmer meetings.

'So, how do you propose to get them the demolition order, let alone the outline planning permission, when they've got nowhere with the Council?'

Ian took out the prints from his brown leather slip case, and slid the first across the table to Marcus.

'Exhibit one: The recommendations concerning the city's future, which I believe will be accepted.'

Marcus read it. 'How the hell did you get hold of this? I have heard rumblings about its attitude to old buildings, but this is incredible, it's setting out the wholesale destruction of much of Bath.'

'Let's just say, from "between the sheets".'

'Are you sure it's true, after all it's only a photographic print?'

'Absolutely, I snapped the original with the Minox you gave me as a birthday present last year.'

Ian handed Marcus the second print.

'Exhibit two: A job offer from the contractor who is being recommended to the person making the recommendation.'

'You have been busy. Other than your source, who else knows about these?'

'No one. The originals were borrowed and returned in a matter of two hours last night.'

Ian sank back into the leather armchair awaiting Marcus's reaction. He watched his mentor take a sip from his crystal whisky tumbler before leaning forward, puting his glass down and replacing the two photographs.

'Ian,' he said. 'You must take great care on two counts. Firstly your "borrowing" as you put it, is probably illegal and could land you and your source in serious trouble. The way round this is to never admit what you have done. Knowing is enough, not how you got to know. More importantly, letting the people concerned know that you know, you understand?' Ian nodded.

'The second issue is more difficult. The job offer. No crime has been committed. Notice how carefully it is worded. The position is being offered because of "the wide experience over many years with planning issues etc." Nor have you a shred of evidence that it has been solicited and will be accepted.'

Marcus sighed and lent back into his chair before continuing.

'Individually either photograph would be of relatively little value, but taken together and with the right person, these might be used to great effect.'

'I don't understand.'

There was a knock at the study door. It was Jennings.

'Madam says to remind you that the guests are due any minute,' the butler said.

'Tell her we will be right there,' Marcus replied before turning to Ian. 'Let's put them all away for now.' He walked over to the bookcase concealing the wall safe and Ian handed everything over.

'Now, let's find Susan and get ready to welcome some of Bath's finest, who may be useful to you in the years to come.'

'Just before we do,' Ian said as he reached into the inside pocket of his jacket for a letter. 'I thought you might like this – my Christmas present for Susan and you.' He gave it to Marcus.

The Royal Institution of Chartered Surveyors
12 Great George Street, London SW1

20th December 1963

I. Morris, Esq.
12 Great Pulteney Street
Bath

Intermediate Examination

It is with pleasure that I advise you that you have been successful and obtained the requisite pass marks for the above.

ROBERT IRONS FRICS (Secretary)

CHAPTER SEVENTY-TWO

'I had an interesting chat with the right person this morning, and I think a deal can be done,' Marcus said to Ian as they walked off the previous night's new year celebrations.

'Who's that?'

'Best you don't know, and anyway his name wouldn't mean anything to you. Just to say he is a modern day Beau Nash, John Wood and Ralph Allen all rolled into one. "Mr Bath" operates well away from the public gaze; I met him through the Freemasons.'

'Do you trust him?'

'Absolutely. He owed me a favour from way back, and I decided to call it in. So if you return the negatives, all prints, and you promise never to disclose their existence, Zebrae will get the planning consent for Sovereign House. If you get the application paperwork in on time, it can, and will be rubber stamped at the next planning meeting.'

'Can he really deliver that?'

Marcus nodded.

'There's more. The recommended contractor will sink without trace, leaving a clear field for you and the Palmers. But there will be nothing in writing, of course.'

The planning consent for Sovereign House arrived on Ian's desk on February 21st. Ian took it to McCloy's office and handed it over to the Palmers. They subsequently signed the sole agency agreement under which all of the other lots bought at the Lundy Estate auction came under Ian's personal control.

Ian was reading through the first Advanced Valuations paper for the Final Exam course, when the telephone rang; it was Henry Lieberman. They hadn't spoken since the present of the MGB.

'Hi Henry, this is a pleasant surprise? What can I do for you?'

'It's more what I can do for you Ian. Are you free for lunch tomorrow?'

'Business or social?'

'Strictly business, book a table at the Marlborough Tavern, you know it?'

Ian never ceased to wonder at his friend's knowledge of some of Bath's 'best kept secrets'.

'Yep, corner of Marlborough Buildings and Weston Road; one o'clock?'

'Fine, see you there.'

As always, Ian walked from his office to the meeting, noting any changes on his notepad, especially the six newly erected 'Letting' and 'For Sale' boards on his route. He would quiz the junior negotiator in his office for details when he got back. Good way of seeing if they were on the ball.

'Good to see you Ian.' Joe Cussens greeted him from behind the bar, while drawing a pint. Dark haired and handsome, the Tavern's suave proprietor was not your average publican. Dating back to George III, the Tavern had been a favourite watering hole for the sedan chairman carrying clients between the city and Royal Crescent. Joe, young and ambitious, had bought the shabby pub and in three years transformed the place, installing a modern kitchen, warmth and comfort. It was done cleverly, so as not to antagonise his long standing locals, who continued to drink at the Marlborough Buildings end and watch the comings and eating habits at the 'posh end', as they called the restaurant.

Henry was seated at an isolated corner table in the posh end, no doubt chosen because he could see everyone without their conversation being overheard, a large glass of tomato juice in front of him. Ian ordered tonic water; he too avoided drinking in the middle of the day. True to form, Lieberman dispensed with the usual civilities

'Ian, I am expanding my operation from country estate break-ups into other property fields, and I want you to head up the west country operation, starting with Bath.'

'Would that mean leaving Woods & Parker?'

'No, as a start up business, it could not justify the cost of your full-time employment, and anyway you would be of much more use staying where you are until we see how it goes. My eyes and ears in the south west. Any problems?'

Ian shook his head. He was relieved, given the recently signed Palmer deal.

'Good, all the usual terms, sole agency for Woods, with you, and only you, in sole control of all buying and selling, agreed?'

'Agreed.'

'Now, let's order lunch. As adviser to Beaconsfield Properties Limited, what do you recommend?'

Ian laughed. 'Great name.' He raised his tonic water. 'To the old school, the beatings, and lunch as it never was there!'

Afterwards they walked back through Royal Victoria Park to the office; Trish produced and they signed the appointment letter. Henry placed his copy in his Samsonite briefcase, and took out a white foolscap envelope and a brown parcel, both sealed and unaddressed. 'Now that everything is settled,' he handed both to Ian, 'take these home, and ring me with your thoughts. Now I must get back to London.' The two men shook hands.

Intrigued, Ian left the office early and went home. He opened the white envelope. It contained a single page legal document, signed by Henry Lieberman, granting Ian an option to purchase five per cent of Beaconsfield Properties Ltd for £5, exercisable on 1st January 1967.

The brown parcel contained a two-inch wad of poorly copied paperwork; attached was a compliment slip on which Lieberman had written 'Beaconsfield Properties Ltd's first deal?' Ian looked at the first sheet, an internal memorandum written eighteen months earlier.

CONFIDENTIAL

FROM: THE BRITISH TRANSPORT BOARD
DATE: 1st July 1962
TO: GREAT WESTERN OPERATIONS c.c. MOT
(Private Sec)
REF: BTB/30122012
Once the Transport Bill is enacted
(imminent), the new Act will, for
the first time in its history,
empower British Rail to close 30%
of its entire UK network, and
thereafter sell/develop any or all
of this surplus property.
Attached is:

1. The summary of Dr Richard Beech-
    ing's report, prepared following
    his appointment by the Rt Hon
    Ernest Marples as Chairman of the

British Railway Board in March
1961.

2. The detailed section dealing with
    the closures etc in your region.
    Could you please provide the Board
    with the following for its Septem-
    ber Board meeting:

    (i) Your comments on the feasibil-
    ity of the closures.

    (ii) A short list of possible
    purchasers for the surplus land and
    buildings under (i).

    The Railway Unions are totally
    opposed to any closures, so this
    information is extremely sensitive,
    and their members should be
    excluded from any discussions.

Ian turned to the summary, again a single page.

    To stem the present unsustainable
    losses of £11 million per year
    (£300,000+daily) it will be neces-
    sary within the next 24 months for
    the Board to:

        A. CLOSE 2,362 stations (55% of
            all stations)

        B. CLOSE 5,000 miles of track
            (30% of the total)

        C. MAKE 200,000 railway staff

394

redundant. (42% of the total
work force)

D. MAKE 235,000 further redun-
dancies over 10 years (50%
of remainder)

E. SELL 51,000 railway staff
houses. (100%)

The remaining pages were headed 'Part IV The South West'.
Instinctively he turned to the section relating to Bath.

CHAPTER SEVENTY-THREE

Ian telephoned Lieberman the following morning.

'Unbelievable Henry.'

'Go on.'

Ian wondered if Henry had read much beyond the summary of the report.

'What Beeching proposes nationally is mind-blowing. The biggest closures will be in the south west, with nearly 600 stations to shut and 70,000 jobs to go. It's massive and I'm only concentrating on the lines from Bath. They are going to close down the whole of the old Somerset and Dorset Railways. I can hardly believe it, starting with Green Park Station, Bath's second biggest, which has been operating since 1874. Every station. All the goods yards, railway houses and land for seventy miles along the line to Salisbury and on to Bournemouth. And the speed of it all, within a year.'

'So you think there's something in it for us?' Lieberman asked.

'Yes, if it ever happens. Do you really think that the National Union of Railwaymen will stand for it? Can you imagine the outcry from all the towns and villages who will lose their railway?'

'The government says it has no choice,' Lieberman replied. 'The railways are losing millions each year. Everyone can strike and protest as much as they want, it will go ahead. They've got the majority in the House of Commons, and nothing can stop it. I bet the Treasury are already calculating the extra cash they can get from selling all the property off. So can I confirm that Beaconsfield Properties is happy to be included on the board's shortlist of possible buyers?'

'You bet, the sooner the better. I'll start work on it today, and ring you when I have seen it all.'

'Good, it's all rather hush-hush; the board are closing the shortlist for interested parties tomorrow night.'

Ian put the phone down, picked up his camera and walked through to Trish's office.

'Get your coat.'

'Are we going somewhere nice?' She stood up.

'A train ride, in fact a lot of train rides – let the front desk know we will be gone for the rest of the week.'

'Will I need an overnight bag?'

'No, just a stack of shorthand notebooks and pencils.'

They walked down to Midland Bridge and stood looking out over the station and the vast expanse of railway lines in the goods yard enclosed by the river and James Street. He still found it hard to believe that all this was to go. He got out his camera to take photographs and started dictating to Trish.

'A site of over half an acre in a prime position in the centre of the city...'

They traveled up and down the line to Bournemouth, getting off at every one of the stations due to close: Frome, Wells, Castle Cary, Blandford Forum, Christchurch. Much to the bemusement of the few passengers, he photographed everything, stations, station master houses, signal boxes and land, all the time dictating descriptions, size and anything else he thought relevant. When asked by the railwaymen, he said he was a railway buff writing a history of the line and, oblivious of their fate, they were only too willing to provide the details which would not normally be obvious to a would-be buyer.

On the Friday evening, after all the hard work, Ian had invited Trish to one of his favourite restaurants, the Olive Tree in the Queensberry Hotel in Russel Street. The owners, Helen and Laurence Beere, a husband and wife team with natural flair, welcomed him into the Q bar, named after John Shotto, the eighth Marquis of Queensberry, who had lived in one of the five Georgian houses which formed part of the hotel in the 18th century. On the wall was the Spy Cartoon of him – the front cover of Vanity Fair in 1877 – entitled 'a good light weight', a reminder that the marquis invented the rules for boxing in England. An engraved mirror of a Georgian figure over the fireplace proclaimed: 'The sign of a true gentleman and lady is to know one's limits.'

'What will you drink, Ian?' Helen asked as they settled into the quirky purple furniture with the Union Jack cushions and carpets. Famed for its unlisted artisan produced whisky collection, Ian knew they kept numerous rare single cask malts, and chose his favourite, very peaty from Isla.

'Caol please.'

'Great choice.' Laurence approved. He was very active on the Bath tourist front, and Ian was always keen to hear his views.

'The mayor was quite right, it's about time the city woke up. Do you know we had over 300,000 visitors last year who spent £5 million plus? We must make up for lost time, all these derelict buildings, I feel so ashamed when the guests mention them and ask me when they are going to be rebuilt. Can't your lot do something?'

'We are doing our best, but it takes time, town planning, the preservation people, you know.'

'I don't suppose BAD will help?'

'I beg your pardon?' Ian wondered what Laurence meant.

'You know, Bath Against Development. The new bunch who don't want the city to change at all. Violently against re-building unless it's pastiche Georgian, and less than three storeys high. Held their inaugural lunch in my private dining room upstairs yesterday. The official launch won't be announced in the *Bath Chronicle* for a while, but I thought you would know about it, and I couldn't resist eavesdropping. A well-heeled bunch, headed by Alistair Lundy, a self-opinionated obnoxious young man in my opinion.'

'Earl Lundy?' Ian was amazed.

'Yes, that's him, do you know him?'

'Our paths have crossed.' He saw Trish walking towards them from the door.

'Well, mustn't keep you, here's your beautiful secretary.' The hotelier looked at the young woman approaching them. 'Hello Trish, as lovely as ever, which is more than I can say for your boss.'

'You cheeky so and so, what do you mean?' Ian feigned offence.

'Ask Trish, you are putting on weight.' Before Ian could respond, Laurence was showing them through to the dining room.

'Is it true?' he asked after Laurence had left them with the menus.

''Perhaps a little,' she nodded.

'I suppose that's what comes of having the benefits and none of the burdens of marriage,' Ian said. 'Even so, I'm still going to enjoy this meal.'

So the rumours in the office about the Tanya woman were

true, Trish thought, as she picked up the menu. A pity.

Trish did a wonderful job typing up Ian's notes on their railway excursion, and on the following Monday he spent much of the day putting values on everything they had seen. He thought he was ready to talk to Lieberman, and growing evermore excited over the numbers, he walked home in the early evening over Pulteney Bridge. Wearily he thought about the two hours of Landlord and Tenant Law awaiting him in Great Pulteney Street, but was pleased that he wouldn't be on his own and that Tanya would be waiting for him. She was no Rachel or Hélène, but she was useful for the time being, a live in cook and housekeeper with extra services. It suited him not to return to an empty echoing house, rather a warm welcome, a meal on the table and someone to share his bed.

Tanya looked across at Ian, brow furrowed, nose in a reference book and studying as he always did every night. She loved the way he stretched his fingers before running them back through his hair when he turned a page, and knew better than to disturb him. Instead, she went to the kitchen to check how his favourite, beef stroganoff, was coming along.

So much had happened in only three months following the late night visit to the Guildhall, when their relationship had finally been consummated. Afterwards, they had walked back to the wonderful house in Great Pulteney Street where she had spent Christmas and stayed.

Ian had warned her about the likely fallout and problems for her ex-lover and the planning department, when the leak was discovered. He hadn't asked her to leave her job but suggested it, and helped with her letter of resignation, 'because of a sudden close family bereavement' that was delivered by hand on Boxing Day.

In the same way, he hadn't asked her to move in with him and, officially, she hadn't, but he obviously liked the arrangement as much as she did.

Tanya avoided making any demands of him, and with no job to go to, dedicated her day making his life agreeable. She made sure that he was well fed in every way, with variety at the table as well as in bed. From her perspective, their life together was wonderful. They were very much in love and she assumed that it was only a question of time before Ian proposed and their relationship would become permanent.

Tonight, after dinner, she decided to move things along and would suggest that she finally give up her bedsit in Henrietta Street. Ian was very generous but would surely recognise that keeping it was simply a waste of money.

Unfortunately, her plans didn't work out because Ian was evidently tired even before he sat down to eat, and disappeared to bed immediately afterwards, with the excuse of an early train to London the next morning. Disappointed, Tanya cleared up and finished the wine before following him. Gone was the excitement of the sex in those first few weeks. Now he always seemed tired, his work and studying an obsession – it took priority over everything.

He had left her bedside lamp on. Quietly she undressed, slid into the large bed next to him, and turned out the light. He was lying on his back, naked, out to the world and snoring gently. The room was pitch black. She moved her body close to him but avoided touching so as not to wake him. Then very lightly she rested her hand on his chest; he didn't stir. Slowly she moved it downwards, through the thick hair, until it rested on top of his manhood, limp and warm. Her fingers stroked, and gradually her other hand moved underneath to encompass everything. The blood flowed and the erection began. Still asleep, his breathing changed, a sigh with a slight noise from the back of his throat, a pleasant sound. She smiled, an erotic dream about her? She arched her back up against the sheet, and careful not to put any weight on him, straddled him, her weight on her knees on either side of his waist. Using just her fingertips, she guided him into her, moist with anticipation; exquisite, it took all her self-control not to move, to just hover over him, barely touching. She did not want him to wake yet. Slowly, very slowly, she lowered herself onto him, he stirred.

'Rachel, Rachel, I love you so much.' Tanya felt him come inside her.

CHAPTER SEVENTY-FOUR

They were sitting in Lieberman's eighteenth century Mayfair house.

'Well Ian, no time to lose. The deadline for bids is a week tomorrow, the 1st of May. The Railways are boxing clever with a straight tender. It's a level playing field for everyone. Just state the price you are prepared to pay, with a ten per cent deposit. They have twenty-eight days to accept and bank the deposit, or refuse and return it uncashed. It's a binding contract, just like an auction, a month to complete the deal and pay the remaining ninety per cent.'

Ian interrupted. 'So Beaconsfield Properties will need all the money in advance when it actually bids?'

'Already done, for up to £1 million. The bank will put up three-quarters of Woods & Parker's formal valuation, I am good for the rest, up to £250,000. I'll use the profit from the Rowas Grange Estate break-up. I strolled across Berkeley Square yesterday afternoon for a cup of tea with your bosses, Jeremy Thring and John Mulholland. They have every faith in you, so let's get down to the details.'

'First there are the thirty-seven stations that they are closing,' Ian passed across the photographs, 'as you will see, most of these can be converted into houses, and will sell if cheap enough.'

Lieberman flicked through the photographs and paused

when he got to Limpley Stoke station. 'Why does this look familiar?'

'*The Titfield Thunderbolt*, the film was made there,' Ian explained before continuing.

'The thirty-five station master's houses are little gems and will make real money.' He handed Lieberman more photographs. 'Next there are the goods yards, often two for every station – these are mostly let to coal merchants or as builder's yards – no problem, the tenants will probably buy these. Then there must be 1,000 railway cottages, and great chunks of land, which could be used for new housing.'

And so they continued. After an hour they agreed they could bid half a million.

'Now we come to the joker in the pack,' Ian said. 'Green Park Station and goods yard in the centre of Bath. Frankly I don't know what it's worth, because I don't know what you could, or more importantly, would get permission to use it for. I spoke to the City Council, and as usual, the politicians are worried sick about the consequences of agreeing to anything.'

Lieberman put his hand up for Ian to stop worrying. 'Put your coat on, I want to show you something.'

At around the same time as Ian arrived at Lieberman's London home, Tanya awoke and lay in bed thinking. Ian had slipped away earlier without disturbing her but now she had questions. Who was Rachel? Was Ian two-timing her? Was this other woman the reason for their ever-diminishing sex life? Was their relationship secure? Had she imagined hearing another girl's name? One moment she feared that she might lose Ian and her comfortable life and the next she felt she was worrying about nothing. Finally she decided on a plan; Ian frequently worked late and she would pick her moment.

'Just here,' Lieberman said to his driver. They had come to Streatham, south of London. 'Take a look at the future of shopping, Ian.'

Ian had read about it in the *Estates Gazette*. They had been in America for years, but he didn't think that supermarkets would catch on in England. They were too big and impersonal for the British housewife. She wanted to shop where she was recognised by butcher, baker and greengrocer, not completely anonymous with everything under one enormous roof.

The Premier Supermarket stretched across the front of four shops. They went in and Ian marveled at the packed shelves and the wide aisles, under the bright fluorescent lights; it was packed with shoppers.

'Who owns this?' he asked.

'I'm not sure but I think it could be Jack Cohen of Tesco's.'

'But he was the one who first said that supermarkets would never work in this country.'

'That all changed when he bought the Irwin chain three years ago. Do you know that this shop is taking £1,000 a week? That's ten times more than normal and the key is car parking. I met Hyman Kreitman, Jack Cohen's son-in-law, who reckons all the main grocers are thinking about it. Word has it that Sainsbury's are looking for locations for megastores, ten times the size of this, 25,000 square feet.'

'But that's over half an acre,' Ian said. Lieberman nodded.

'So what do you think, a supermarket for Green Park, Ian?'

'It's certainly big enough, and an ideal location, but would our city councillors be brave enough to allow it, and more importantly, would the good citizens of Bath use it? There would be massive opposition from the existing small shopkeepers.'

'Like it, or not, it's the way forward, I bet that within the next twenty-five years every district in every city and every town in the country will have a supermarket.'

On that note, they went back to Mayfair to work some figures out. In the end it was a gamble and a guestimate. Lieberman gambled he could build a supermarket, and guessed the site would be worth £100,000 if he was right. They agreed that the bid to be submitted should be increased to £600,000.

God help them if they'd got it wrong, Ian thought, as he caught the last train out of Paddington back to Bath.

He got back to Great Pulteney Street just before one in the morning. To his surprise, Tanya was waiting up for him wearing a revealing red dress, and made up to the hilt. Bob Dylan's 'The Times They Are A-Changin'' was playing on the gramophone. He was ready only for sleep.

'I need to talk to you Ian.'

'It'll have to wait Tanya. I'm bushed.'

'It can't,' and then as he turned to go upstairs, she panicked and blurted out, 'I'm pregnant.'

Alistair, the fourth Earl Lundy, looked out over the Pump Room with satisfaction. Two years earlier he had sat at the back of the crowded auction room, and watched as all his family possessions were knocked down for a song to the dealers.

The first Bath Against Development conference had certainly hit a nerve. He looked down at the notices on the empty seats in the front row which he had reserved for: The Bath Preservation Trust, The Civic Trust, The Georgian Group, The Society for the Preservation of Rural England and The Society for the Preservation of Ancient Buildings. Hopefully, some would show.

He couldn't have asked for more. The room was packed, awash with people wearing the red BAD rosettes, being given out free at the entrance by Freddy Bradshaw. There was hardly a developer in sight. Just a handful, including the despicable housekeeper's son, sitting at the back, unbadged and trying to go unnoticed.

The idea for BAD had been born out of rage. His rage at what had been done to his family, especially to his proud mother, reduced to living with him in the tiny flat provided by one of his mother's family who were 'still in trade'.

The idea had been born over a drink at the County Club. Frequented by an ever aging and diminishing membership of past city worthies, bemoaning their loss of influence and power, the grumbles had turned to Bath Oliver biscuits. Invented in 1735, and said to be the first of it's kind, the recipe – a closely guarded secret – was, horror of horrors, now to be passed to Huntley & Palmer in Reading.

'Damn shame,' old Bradshaw had snapped. 'Everything is going to the dogs. No one seems to care any more. These barbarians from London intent on demolishing everything Georgian, and replacing it with raw bloody concrete.' The elderly colonel ranted on. 'Your great grandfather, the first Earl, must be turning in his grave. Bad, very bad. Why don't you youngsters do something about it?'

'No money,' Alistair answered.

'Not a problem. I know plenty of people who have, and care passionately. It just needs someone to put it together. If only I were twenty years younger, or Bradshaw junior had it in him. Don't know what's happened to young Freddy since leaving Pitt College. House Captain, Head Boy, so much promise, now just swans around, no job…'

Three pink gins later, with a pledge of £1,000, and young Freddy Bradshaw to assist him, the fourth Earl Lundy had found a role in life. The 'old guard' from before the war; their numbers swelled by the army and navy men, who had followed the Admiralty to Bath and now retired, were against all and any change. They deeply resented the recent 'incomers' and their antagonism to the London property 'spivs' using the city for profit could be harnessed.

The flash bulb exploded as the *Bath Chronicle*'s photographer got the shot.

'My name is Alistair Lundy, the founder of Bath Against Development, and it gives me great pleasure to welcome you all to its inaugural meeting.'

He waited for the applause to die down.

'Today our campaign begins, our proud city with its beautiful crescents and squares, must be protected from the Brutes and Brutalism.' He paused for effect and the applause. 'Brutalism, modernistic architecture, born in Hitler's Germany,' again he paused, and the applause was louder. 'I tell you what the German Luftwaffe could not do to this proud city in 1942, the enemy within, these Philistines, will flatten our beloved city.' Now they were not only clapping, but stamping their feet. 'It's time we kicked the money lenders out of the temple. The property developers, and their co-conspirators at the City Council, must be stopped. A new war has begun. The barbarians, interested only in profit, must be halted at the gates. Let us, who care and love Bath, take up arms.' He had to shout over the noise. 'Let's stop this rape. Let battle begin.'

He sat down to thunderous applause. Now the newspaper photographer was flashing away at the audience.

Ian grew more and more alarmed as the meeting progressed. Lundy certainly knew how to handle the crowd, and organised them, he thought as a host of motions were approved, setting up committee after committee for membership, subscriptions, constitution, architects, town planners, surveyors, each with a well-known city figure as chairman. Within an hour BAD had members, money and teeth, with the ability to monitor every would-be change, big or small, on the city skyline.

The dozens of ushers who had helped seat everyone at the beginning of the meeting, now reappeared at the end of each row and were handing out leaflets. Ian looked down at the single sheet that had been passed down to him. It was headed 'Bath Battlefield: No.1'.

Lundy was on his feet again.

'Read our inaugural edition of 'The Battlefield' on which are listed all BAD's primary targets, where we must stop the developers. No more monstrosities - no more concrete towers in Snow Hill, the slab of the Bath Technical College, or the horrendous Sovereign House. Call yourselves architects, not in my book; go back to where you came from, Gibberd, Snailum, Frost and Buchanan, you are not welcome in our beautiful city.'

More flashing light bulbs and thunderous applause.

Ian looked at the list and he counted, over twenty would-be development schemes, most of which he was involved in one way or another. To his horror, the closure of Green Park Station was included – he ringed it in pencil.

Ian didn't return to the office. Sick with apprehension, panic drove him home, back to Great Pulteney Street and Tanya's pregnancy. He didn't love her, nor had he ever told her that he did. She had been a pleasant accessory, undemanding, not essential to his life. Now, suddenly out of the blue, and through her own stupidity, she had become a threat, literally a fucking problem, and he was scared.

Earlier in the day, in desperation he had gone to the public library and looked up 'Abortion'.

Child destruction under Section (1)(1) of the Infant

Life (Preservation)Act 1929… and any person who, with intent to destroy the life of a child capable of being born alive, by any willful act causes a child to die before it has an existence independent of its mother… shall be liable on conviction, to penal servitude for life…

A note helpfully added that under the Criminal Justice Act 1948:

Penal servitude could be construed as a sentence of imprisonment for life…

On arriving home he had brushed aside Tanya's attempted embrace, refused the offer of coffee, and now sat glowering at her. Fury had replaced his shock of the previous night.

'How the hell can you be pregnant? Aren't you on the pill?'

'I forgot to take them with me that weekend we went up to stay with the Liebermans in London.'

'Are you sure? You don't look pregnant?' he spat out.

'I've just missed my third period. I'm sorry.' Her face crumpled and she started to whimper. This pathetic sound made him even angrier. He stood up and started to pace the room; now he was shouting at her.

'You stupid, stupid bitch. I'm not going to let you ruin my life, everything I've worked for.' He yanked her out of the chair and pushed her up the stairs to their bedroom and onto the bed. She sat there weeping as he grabbed a suitcase, pulled open the wardrobe, and threw her clothes and shoes into it. Next he cleared the bathroom of her make-up, perfumes, lotions and anything else he thought he was hers.

'But we love each other, Ian. What are you doing?' she cried.

'What does it look like? Throwing you out. We are finished, not that we ever got started, you were just a convenient fuck.'

'What about our baby?'

Now he was dragging her back downstairs.

'Your baby, your problem,' he shouted at her as he dragged her and suitcase through the front door. 'Just get out and stay out of my life.'

He slammed the door behind her.

CHAPTER SEVENTY-FIVE

He sat on the stairs, shaking and breathing heavily, before he slowly regained control. He had never lost his temper before and was shocked at how close he had come to actually hitting her. He walked up to the sitting room, and reason returned; he began thinking. How stupid had he been? What if she told the City Council, or worse still, the police about the leak from her employers? He should have handled it rationally, calmly, and pretended he cared. The enormity of his mistake reared up. He decided that he would have to go after her, apologise. The telephone rang.

'Ian.' It was Henry Lieberman. 'Good news, we won the tender.' Without pausing, he went on. 'In six weeks Beaconsfield Properties will be the proud owner of Green Park Station, and everything, railway stations, houses, and all the land from Bath to Weymouth. What do you think of that?'

Still distracted by the pending disaster of Tanya, Ian muttered, 'That's great Henry, I am very pleased.'

'You don't sound it, what's the matter?'

'A personal problem.'

'Serious?'

'Very.'

'How can I help?'

'I don't know if anyone can. It's the woman who I brought to your party,' Ian said gloomily.

'That all? I thought it was more serious; business.'

'It could be if she decides to open her mouth to the wrong people.'

'Ah, say no more on the telephone. I'm on my way – see you in about three hours.'

'Are you sure?'

'Cheer up, can't have anything upsetting my star performer. Remember, money usually solves everything. We need to meet anyway – all very exciting, now we are in the railway business.'

Despite the urge to do so, Ian had not gone round to Tanya's bedsit, but stayed at home, awaiting Henry's arrival. Now the two men sat opposite each other.

'Ian, tell me everything. We are partners now. If I'm to help, there can't be any secrets that jump out and bite my arse later.'

And so Ian did. When he had finished, Henry simply stood up, asked for Tanya's address, and said he was going to have a chat with her. He returned after a couple of hours.

'All done my boy. As usual, just a question of money and an irresistible relocation. A friend of mine is bringing the first Playboy Club to London, you know, Hugh Hefner of Playboy magazine and his bunny girls in Chicago. Tanya will make a perfect bunny and is off to New York to train.'

'What about the baby?'

'There isn't one – she made it up, she never was pregnant.' Ian was stunned. 'Don't worry, oldest trick in the world. I, rather than you, gave her the price she wanted. I've offered her a better opportunity and she knows it. She won't bother you anymore. Now to more important matters. Beaconsfield Properties and Green Park Station. When do we start work on the supermarket application?'

'We may have a problem.' He took out 'Bath Battlefield: No.1' from his pocket and handed it to Lieberman. 'I went to this meeting this morning,' Ian recounted what had happened.

'Tell me about Alistair Lundy, can he hurt us?'

'I don't know, he has certainly got the old vanguard of Bath fired up, and it won't help the cause if he knows I'm involved, he hates my guts and it's mutual. He won't be bothered about anything outside Bath, so I can continue to deal with everything except Green Park Station. Maybe you should bring someone else in, possibly from London.'

Lieberman nodded. 'I think I know just the person.'

CHAPTER SEVENTY-SIX

During the remainder of 1964, and into the early months of the following year, BAD managed to stall much of the development in Bath. However, Ian's quick footedness and knowledge, backed by Austwick's legal expertise meant that few of his schemes were delayed.

Cranes from different building sites added to central Bath's skyline as spring turned into summer in 1965. Still only twenty-three, when Ian arrived at Widcombe House in his beautiful blue MGB at the end of a working week in July he had the confidence and style of an affluent young businessman. He felt humbled by the continued support of Marcus and Susan, hugely valuing their Friday night sessions in preparation for his Final examination.

'Hello Ian.' Susan Rose greeted him warmly as Jennings showed him into the drawing room. She stood up and gave him an affectionate kiss on the cheek, before turning to an elderly, rather stout man, who was next to her.

'John, this is Ian, who I was telling you about. John Forrester, Ian Morris.' They shook hands. 'John has joined us for dinner, Ian, but Marcus has been delayed so we are to start without him.'

Marcus arrived halfway through the first course, by which time Ian was listening, fascinated as John explained how he had started at the bottom in his father's building firm in 1922, skivvying, and working as a labourer laying foundations.

'The business flourished until the Great Depression. Then suddenly in 1931 zilch, all the staff laid off. Tragic, some of the skilled craftsmen, carpenters, bricklayers, roofers – been with the firm for years – all went!' No work, just he and his father scraping by on odd repair work. Then, just as suddenly, in 1938 the demand for concrete sky-rocketed as war became inevitable. The firm won a massive order to supply hundreds of pill boxes and air raid shelters. Enter the Bath Concrete Company, a new firm split off from his father's company, with 'young' John as its head.

As German bombers loomed and invasion threatened, instead of building on site, John introduced prefabrication, using wooden shuttering, casting thousands of slabs, which could be transported and assembled a lot quicker. The insatiable demand for the sand and aggregates needed was solved by the use of the wartime Emergency Powers Act, under which quarries were requisitioned by the Coalition Government and put under John's control. By war end the company had become the largest producer of slab concrete, served by some twenty-three quarries, which John bought for an absolute song when they were de-requisitioned.

'After the war the company turned to emergency housing. Do you know we cast six hundred slabs for the prefabs here in Bath? When that work dried up, we turned our hand to the concrete kerbstones that were needed for the pavements. We simply adapted the same wooden shuttering that had been used for the war time pill boxes and shelters.'

Forrester chuckled. 'Lady Luck, one day in late 1949, we ran out of wood at the Bath works. With a delivery deadline looming, in desperation I had gone down to the Lower Bristol Road, found some old metal sheets and told the men to use these to cast the fifty or so kerbstones needed to complete the order. I didn't go back to see the finished job, just told them to put these fifty or so at the bottom of the load, hoping the Highways Department wouldn't notice the difference.

'The engineer rang me a week later – he was mad, not angry mad, excited mad. Demanded all future kerbstones to be as good as these last fifty. Puzzled, I went down to the yard, where there were a few over from the order. The kerbstones were silky smooth, not a bit like the rough old ones produced from the timber moulds. Overnight we switched from wood to metal. Demand was insatiable and has been ever since.

'We opened depots and yards in towns and cities all over the United Kingdom, most near to the quarries. Now the company provides the kerbstones, slabs and paving required by hundreds of town and city Councils.'

Widowed and elderly, he had acquired a new young wife, twenty-five years his junior. 'Not a marriage of love, but hate,' is how he put it. 'I hate loneliness, she hates poverty.'

Yes, others managed the business, but he wanted an end to the rough and tumble of the building trade. Now he yearned for a quiet life. The money had been made, the fire in the belly gone. The love of his life was a gin-palace of a motor cruiser of a boat, moored at a south coast yacht club. His wealth had bought him membership and, coupled with endless rounds of drinks deckside, got him elected as commodore of the club, even though he had never, nor could he think of anything worse than putting to sea.

Their usual session in the study, later that night, had gone well and Marcus seemed pleased. Ian changed the subject.

'I think I know how Mr Forrester can get out of his business,' he said, taking a sip from his whisky glass.

'Go on,' his mentor replied.

'I've been working with Berkeley Square on a similar situation. The firm has just solved the problem for an owner who has built up a chain of twenty greengrocer shops based in Bath and spread over the West Country. He's about the same age as Mr Forrester and wanted to quit and retire to the South of France. Basically, he had three options. Sell the lot to another greengrocery chain, or sell to a company who wanted to add greengrocery to its business.'

'And the third option?'

'Float on the London Stock Exchange.'

'Which did he choose?'

'We sold the business to a firm called Tesco's. It was really too small to float, but Mr Forrester's business is much bigger with all its depots and quarries.'

'Good idea, why don't you give him a call.'

'Yes, I will.'

'I wonder who he reminds me of?' Susan smiled as Marcus related the conversation to her as he joined her in bed that night.

'What do you mean?' Marcus said pretending indignation, 'I did my first deal at fourteen pushing that bloody cart of furniture up Oxford Street to Waring and Gillows every Friday night, just to pay the wages!' But then he became serious. 'He can achieve something I never had. Those letters after his name will buy respectability. Times are changing, the new rulers of the property world with the purse strings are the pension funds, and the insurance companies. They have woken up to how people like me made so much money out of them, and they won't let it happen again. Once Ian has fully qualified, he will become respectable, one of them. He won't be just another Jew Boy, and with flair…' the slim book on his bedside table had travelled with him for over forty years; read so often, he knew much of *The Prophet* by heart. This arrow *'will go swift and far'* he mused, as he turned the light out.

On Tuesday Ian rang Marcus to tell him that he had set up a

meeting for Forrester with John Mulholland. The Investment Department was instructed a week later.

Charged with having to value all of Bath Concrete's property assets, Ian set off to inspect the quarries without delay. The pre-war ordnance survey plan of the first quarry showed a massive hole in the ground with a gatehouse, which Ian presumed would be a small prefabricated shed. Instead, he found a substantial detached house and well-cultivated garden, let on a life tenancy to an attractive woman in her early forties.

And so it was at every one of the twenty or so quarries he visited. Over a cup of tea, or a meal, each woman would ask after John Forrester, reminiscing about his yearly quarry inspection and stay of two or three days; then there were the generous gifts he regularly sent, the last shortly before he remarried. Most nights, Ian accepted the life tenant's invitation to supper, and ended up staying the night and marvelling the next morning at the sheer stamina of the older man's annual 'royal progress'.

Back at the office John Mulholland chuckled but agreed that it was very difficult to add any 'vacant possession value' because each of John's 'caretakers' had a life tenancy. Even so, it would be a nice surprise for the shareholders in years to come.

Ian had to deliver the flotation document to John Forrester's home in Conkwell Village for final approval before it went to the London Stock Exchange.

The young woman who opened the door of the Queen Anne house was expecting him, and like the property, she was stunning. The top button on her white blouse was undone and his eyes were drawn down to an inviting cleavage, and below to where the shirt tails were tied at her slim waist above a biscuit-coloured tummy button.

419

'Oh, the clever young man, who Papa says is going to get us the new yacht, come in, come in.' The accent was Italian, the welcome warm, very familiar, as though she was greeting a close friend.

'Ian Morris,' he said, swallowing quickly to regain his composure and holding out his hand. She laughed and took it in both of hers, clasping it to her before responding.

'Cara.'

'I've come-' he withdrew his hand and she interrupted him.

'I know.' For some reason she made him feel gawkish, awkward, his normal self-assurance gone as she led him into the drawing room; a dazzling feminine affair of white carpets, curtains and even a white leather sofa.

'Have a seat. Coffee?'

Ian's gaze followed the retreating woman, and his mind strayed again from business to watch the rhythmic sway of her bottom tightly encased in faded blue jeans.

'Papa has been called away unexpectedly,' she said as she placed the tray on the white marble coffee table. He wondered how on earth Forrester had produced a daughter like Cara, but then he remembered the new Mrs Forrester, and realised she must be his step-daughter.

'When will your step-father be back?'

She looked puzzled. 'My step-father?'

'John. John Forrester.'

Again that magical laugh. 'John isn't my step-father, silly, he's my husband, Papa.'

'Papa?'

'Oh, it's my special name for him because he's so much older than me, the same age as my father back in Venice.' Ian remembered John's own description of his second marriage, the night they had first met at Widcombe House. 'Sugar Daddy' sprang to mind, and his thoughts again wandered to

420

the unthinkable before being reined in. Best to wait until after the flotation, no point in buggering up a good deal, not to mention the promised personal commission coming to him for introducing the business into the department.

He finished his coffee after Cara willingly parted with her ex-directory telephone number, Limpley Stoke 8331, and promptly left. His proffered hand was ignored for a kiss on each cheek.

Three months later the Bath Concrete Company Plc was successfully listed on the London Stock Exchange. John Forrester walked away with £1.5 million and he arranged for Ian to have 30,000 shares at a shilling each in the company.

One day, Ian thought, those quarry houses. But in the meantime he must thank the man for his generosity. He picked up the telephone and dialed the Limpley Stoke number. Instantly the beautiful Italian accent aroused him.

'*Pronto*.'

'Cara, it's Ian Morris.'

'Hello silly boy, how are you?'

'Great, is John around?'

'No. He's flying in from Nice in a couple of hours. He's been inspecting the new yacht. Can I help?'

'I just wanted to thank him for the shares.'

'Why don't you come round and thank him personally?'

'I can't I'm afraid, I'm due at Susan and Marcus's for dinner at eight o'clock.'

'No problem, come to us early and go on to them afterwards.'

'You sure he won't mind? Ok, thank you very much.'

'You are more than welcome, silly boy. *Ciao*.'

Cara opened the door, and he was taken aback by the short white tunic with large Chinese script and black stilettoes. Her long stockinged beautiful legs were visible to her thighs through the side slits. She ignored the proffered bottle of champagne, cradled his face in her hands and her mouth met his full on. Ian felt uncomfortable. Just as well her husband couldn't see into the hall, he thought, but maybe she was like this with everybody, and he was used to her young Italian exuberance.

Taking the wine from him, she put it down, guided him into the drawing room and onto the white leather sofa. She kicked off her shoes and sat down next to him. There was an ice bucket holding an open bottle, with two half-full champagne flutes on the glass coffee table. She lifted them and handed one to Ian. '*Saluté.*'

'Should we wait for John?'

'It will be a long wait, he is still in Nice, not due home until tomorrow.'

'But you said-'

'A little white lie.' She laughed. 'So that we can celebrate your cleverness.' She clinked and drained her glass. 'And I can thank you personally.'

She stood up and walked around the coffee table, and started to undress slowly, in time to an imaginary band, perfectly imitating a stripper. First the tunic, until finally she stood in front of him, naked, in just her high heeled shoes.

He laughed and clapped. 'Very good, Cara.' She had performed a superb parady of the classical seduction scene. But he suddenly realised she was not laughing. She looked at him, shocked by his rejection, picked up the discarded clothing to cover herself.

'*Bastardo – presuntuoso bastardo Inglese. Come ti permetti. No riglicotoute motti nomini. Vatlere – vatlere desta mia casa. Quando che dica a Papa quello che hai cercato disfasmi.'*

Ian fled, not understanding a word, only too grateful to escape this dangerous woman. Another bloody Tanya situation, he thought, but worse, she had a nice husband who had been very good to him. He hit the accelerator so hard, his MGB nearly ended up in one of the gardens off Winsley Hill.

CHAPTER SEVENTY-SEVEN

The whisky, wine, good food and the peace of the grand house had worked its usual magic. Ian became calm and now relaxed over the coffee; Marcus was talking about Jamaica.

'Well Ian, we finally got the planning consent. Susan and I are going to use it as an excuse for a trip out after Christmas. Nothing like a month of tropical sunshine, instead of the misery of January in the UK. Why don't you join us for a couple of weeks?'

'Wonderful idea, but I don't think they would give me the time off. Only the partners are allowed time off to ski in the early new year.'

'What if I offered to instruct them on Jamaica, like last time, you know, pay them a fee?'

'Won't work, I'm afraid, I have too much on. In reality I'm running the Bath office. Yes, Mulholland is in charge but he is spending more and more time setting up a new branch at Cirencester.'

'Why don't you ask for a partnership?' Susan said quietly.

'But I'm only twenty-three. They would never agree, you have to be at least thirty.'

'What do you think Woods & Parker will earn through you this year?' Marcus asked.

Ian had completed his personal commission calculation for the company's accountants a week earlier.

'With year end in a month, and assuming no further deals, there's £100,000 paid already, another quarter more for deals in solicitors' hands, say £125,000 for the Bath office in total.'

'How much of that has been through your personal introduction?'

He did the mental arithmetic, counting on his fingers the Palmer deal, Lieberman, Susan's trust, the floats, and a few bits and pieces.

'About half, £65,000 at least.'

'And how much do they pay you?'

'£2,500 a year plus 1% commission, I should earn £10,000 this year,' Ian said proudly. He didn't mention the shares in Beaconsfield Properties.

'Susan's right. Ask for a partnership,' Marcus snapped back, 'and when they refuse, which they are bound to do, leave. Set up on your own. We'll back you if you need some seedcorn money.'

'I agree, you're more than ready,' added Susan.

Over the next few days Ian went to see his two biggest clients. Roger Palmer was all in favour of him leaving, as he had always thought the firm antiquated, and Henry Lieberman was blunt.

'I wouldn't even bother asking about the partnership. Do you really think they will give one to a Jew?'

'But I don't practice the faith.'

'What's that got to do with anything? Anyway best of luck. You can let me know how it all went when I get back from holiday.'

'Where are you off to?'

'Madeira. An invitation from my father-in-law for the maiden voyage of the SS Salamis. He's on the board of its owners, the Greek shipping line who built it. Last word in luxury apparently. Sails in three days from Southampton.'

'Enjoy it, Henry. I'll have the Railway disposals programme ready for you when you get back.'

Ian envied his friend's trip and thought it yet another reason to be his own boss.

Ian rang Mulholland in Berkeley Square.

'I'm afraid I have got some good news and bad news, good for me, bad for Woods & Parker. I have just posted you my notice. I will be leaving in four weeks.' For a moment there was a shocked silence.

'Why, for God's sake, have you done that? It's all going so well. You only had to wait and you would have been a junior partner in ten years.'

'Better offer.'

'Who from? Can't we match it?'

Ian decided to come clean, Mulholland would find out soon enough.

'I am going out on my own.'

CHAPTER SEVENTY-EIGHT

Fifteen Queen Square, with its magnificent façade, was absolutely the right image, Ian thought for the umpteenth time. The firm's name had been a master stroke. The sole brass plate read:

FORSYTE MORRIS & COMPANY
SURVEYORS

Hopefully in a few months' time, with the Final Examination passed, he could change it to CHARTERED SURVEYORS.

Of course there was no Forsyte, it was the Gallsworthy invention of a solid Victorian dynasty to add the credibility of a very English name for the ring of long-established stability. Whilst the company occupied only the ground floor – he had insisted on only one name plate – so that many clients would come to the mistaken impression that the firm owned the whole building, giving it yet more substance.

As he guessed she would, Trish Traynor, being ambitious and seeing which way the wind was blowing, was more than happy to move with him.

He opened the street door, walked past the magnificent wooden staircase leading to the upper floors and into Trish's office overlooking the rear courtyard. Given real responsibility for the first time, Trish had grown into the job in a matter of weeks and fitted the efficient modern image that Ian wanted to portray.

'Morning, Trish.'

'Morning, Ian.'

'Do you need me for anything?'

'Just one. They are connecting the telex up today, they want a code of between six and ten letters. I thought FORSYTE.'

'No, one invention is enough. Give me a few minutes, I'll come back to you.'

He opened the door and walked into his office, the original reception room of the house, it was huge. Fifty foot long and some thirty foot wide. There had been no choice, as with many of the prime buildings of Bath, it was Grade I listed and any sub-division of the space was forbidden. Even the magnificent fireplace could not be tampered with.

Again, Trish and he had made it work with what they had bought from John Aldridge's auction house in Cheltenham Street, using the final personal commission money owed to him and paid grudgingly by Woods & Parker. With it had come notice recalling the interest-free loan of five thousand pounds on 12 Great Pulteney Street, and he had three months to work out a way to repay this.

The deep blue carpets matching the curtains to the two full length windows overlooking Queen Square were perfect. His desk was across the front corner and what Trish had playfully, and possibly hopefully, called the two large 'casting' blue sofas either side of the fireplace. The massive reproduction conference table, bought very cheaply because it was so long and of little use in modern houses, and ten chairs filled the rest of the cavernous space.

He sat down at the desk, took out the small black leather Mallory's notepad from his pocket, removed a page and started scribbling. Five minutes later Trish had followed him in bearing a tray with a bottle of champagne and two glasses which she placed on the mahogany coffee table between the two sofas.

'What's this, it's only eight in the morning?'

'I thought we ought to have an opening party, just the two of us, and don't worry, it's not real champagne, just fizzy wine made to look like it.'

'Well, damn the expense, let's do it.' He picked up the bottle, removed the wire around the cork which came out with a half-hearted pop. He filled the glasses and gave one to her.

'Mud in your eye,' he said raising his glass. 'Our first day, February 21st 1966.'

'Here's to Forsyte Morris & Co.' Trish paused and then added, 'and to us.'

Alarm bells rang in his head. Perhaps it wasn't such a good idea to have involved her so much. Next she will be asking for a share of the business. No going back on using first names, but he would have to tread carefully, complete involvement with the work, yes, after all she was a superb secretary, but none with him personally.

He handed her the slip of paper, she tried to pronounce the word 'TTLAKYBO'.

'What's this?'

'The telex code.'

'What does it stand for?'

'Trust the Lord and keep your bowels open. The secret of success in the property business, the gospel according to Brigadier Sale, the partner who interviewed me for my first job at Woods & Parker.'

'How long ago was that?' Ian looked at the calendar, and thought for a moment. My god, Marcus had got it right to the very day. 'Decades, metaphorically speaking.'

'My, hasn't the boy done well,' she said, laughing.

The telephone rang on his desk.

'Flattery will get you everywhere, but onward and upward, the rent has got to be earned,' he replied as he picked up the receiver.

It took a moment for him to recognise the voice; it was Susan Rose, but the usual calm was gone, she was choking, hardly able to talk. 'Ian, come quickly, it's Marcus.'

Without waiting to speak he slammed the receiver down and ran out of the office to the taxi rank outside the Francis Hotel.

Jennings opened the door. 'Dr Waldron is waiting for you in the library, Mr Morris.'

So it was medical. Ian nodded and went straight through. He had guessed as much in the cab ride, but feared the worst. John Waldron rose from his chair as Ian entered.

'It happened while Susan and he were having breakfast. He's had a heart attack,' the older man said.

'Shouldn't he be in hospital?' Ian asked.

'No, I think moving him would be too dangerous. I've given him morphine to reduce the strain on the heart and ease the pain.'

'How serious is it? Will he recover?'

'Impossible to say. First we have to stabalise him, then do all the tests.'

'Can I see him?'

'Of course. Susan is with him, and she asked that you go up as soon as you arrived. I will come with you.'

Outside the bedroom the doctor paused before opening the door. 'Have you ever seen someone immediately after a heart attack?'

Ian shook his head

'Prepare yourself, I'm afraid Marcus is as you have never seen him before.'

The room was darkened with curtains drawn. Ian looked at the bed. Susan rose from her bedside chair and opened her arms to hug him.

His idol, his God, his rock, the man to whom he could always turn and have his problems solved, lay so small in the king size bed, helpless and motionless. The eyes under the bushy black eyebrows were closed, his face ashen grey and mouth slackened. She guided him to her chair, pulled up another next to it, and sank slowly into it, placing her hand on Marcus's lying on top of the bedclothes.

John Waldron left, promising to be back later, after he had completed his morning clinic and surgery.

Jennings came and went with tea, coffee and sandwiches, which he laid out on the dressing table. They remained untouched.

John Waldron returned just after midday and examined the semi-conscious Marcus. 'Good, his blood pressure is slightly down and no further pain. I'll be back at tea time. In the meantime I am arranging for a private nurse for tonight. This is going to be a long haul, but at least he is starting to respond.'

He was not there at twenty to three in the afternoon, when the second and fatal heart-attack occurred.

CHAPTER SEVENTY-NINE

The letter was waiting when Ian got back from the funeral in London.

It had been his first brush with organised Jewry for years. He found it a deeply moving affair at the oldest Reform Synagogue in the country, a grand building in Upper Berkeley Street. A young American rabbi had officiated. The eulogy told of a remarkable life, unknown by Ian and heard by many in the packed synagogue; wartime comrades from the British Secret Service, heads of the property industry, British and Israeli political figures, and the elite of the Jewish community. Susan had insisted Ian stay close to her, grasping his arm tightly as they walked; like a son, he thought. The self-assured poised woman he knew looked vulnerable in her black attire.

Susan stayed with friends in London but Ian took the train back to Bath and thought about Marcus throughout the journey. He recognised how lucky he had been to know such a man. So important, yet wise and humble. He remembered Marcus's caution, all those years ago, about gods and clay feet. He walked from the station in the cold and darkness of the deserted streets.

He opened the letter.

The Royal Institution of Chartered Surveyors
12 Great George Street, London SW1

Mr Morris,

12 Great Pulteney Street

Bath

1st March 1966

Dear Mr Morris

<u>Final Examination</u>

It is with much pleasure that I tell you that you have been successful in the Final Examination.

I would also warmly congratulate you as the winner of the Pilkington Medal, which is awarded to the candidate who obtains the highest marks over 75% in the Advanced Property Valuation Papers of this Final Examination. The medal is accompanied by a cheque for £75.

Accordingly, I welcome you as an Associate Member of this Institution and ask you to attend here on April 24th to receive your Certificate of Admission, the Pilkington Medal and cheque from the hand of the President, Mr Frank Knowles PRICS.

My congratulations.

ROBERT IRONS FRICS (Secretary)

It had taken so long, and once again he thought of Marcus and remembered all those Friday night sessions after dinner, his criticism, encouragement, praise and shared anecdotes from an eventful life. He had given Ian his most treasured possession, his time and understanding, and Ian had missed giving him his gift in return by just nine days. Nine stupid days had been denied to this truly generous and kind man, the father he had never known. Ian didn't try to stem the tears as he started to weep, his sadness turning into sobs as he recognised how much he would miss Marcus and how great was his loss. Eventually he stilled, his grief turning to resolve. One day he would create something, something really worthy of his memory. He poured himself a drink, lit a cigarette and switched on the radio for the Home Service evening news.

'Reports are reaching the BBC of a catastrophic fire at sea, aboard the TSMS Salamis, which left Southampton on her maiden voyage just before Christmas, bound for Madeira. The Greek owners have confirmed that there are 1,050 people on board, and all but twenty of the passengers are British citizens, many elderly and retired.

'Four ships nearby have changed course and are heading for the area, and three United States Air Force planes from the Lajes Air Base in the Azores have dropped flares, life jackets and life rafts to the hundreds of people seen in the water. An RAF Avro Shackleton from Gibraltar, which is overhead, reports the ship to be ablaze from stem to stern. Many of the lifeboats are reported unlaunched and still in their davits, while the gangways have been lowered and people are walking down them in single file into the ocean.

'We have no news yet of casualties, but a heavy loss of life is feared, from passengers trapped in their cabins and unable to escape the fire, or from injuries jumping over-board, exposure or drowning...'

My God, the Salamis, that's the ship Lieberman is on.

'The shipping line have set up an emergency office and issued a special telephone number for anyone concerned about passengers. It is Southampton 26213, I repeat, Southampton 26213…'

Ian picked up the telephone, but before he could dial his thoughts were disturbed by heavy urgent knocking from below. Irritated, he went down and opened the front door. Facing him was a dapper man with unfashionably brylcreemed hair and dressed in a British Warm overcoat.

'Ian Morris?'

'Yes.'

'I have a present from Italy for you from Mr Forrester, a twenty-fourth birthday present is how he described it. Something to remind you of him and his wife,' he said pleasantly as he gestured to the thickset young hulk who stepped forward out of the dark.

'I don't understand?'

He heard the words, 'Not so sexy now, pretty boy,' as the knuckle-duster smashed into his face, and he fell to the ground unconscious. He knew nothing of the well aimed kick to the side of his head, gratuitously struck by the older man before the two assailants strolled through the deserted street to their car parked in the shadows of Henrietta Park.

Susan Rose had left, and Trish Traynor sat quietly by Ian's bed in the Isaac Abrahams Intensive Care Unit of St Peter's Hospital. His head had been shaved and partially bandaged; his face was unrecognisable. Pink swollen eyelids were closed above the heavy black stitching quilted into puffed cheeks where the knuckle-duster had done its damage. On a ventilator, he remained unconscious, despite the deep pain stimulation applied an hour earlier. David Medlock, the Consultant Surgeon of the hospital entered, holding some paperwork.

'What are his chances?' Trish asked.

'Impossible to say, there is nothing more we can do, other

than wait. It's in the lap of the gods. By the way, his registration form has a couple of blanks, "Next of Kin?" and "Religion".'

'None in each case,' answered Trish.

Get in touch

**To find more details about the author, the novel
and the next book visit www.douglaswestcott.com**

Please contact
Valley Spring Press
PO Box 2765,
Bath
BA2 7XS

or goswiftandfar@outlook.com

- To re-order, become a stockist or for any other queries.

- If you run or are involved in a reading group, multiple copies of the novel are available at preferential prices.

- To contact the author or for freely available talks and readings.

- Full and half – day walking tours with your own personal guide are available based on the novel and both the highlights and lesser known parts of beautiful Georgian Bath.

READING GROUP
NOTES

Topics For Discussion from the novel

- How does 'The Prophet' set up the novel?

- Can one glean what Yann feels as he grows up at Cassofiori House?

- Was Ruth right to agree to Yann going to Beaconsfield?

- Why did Isaac join the William Pitt Club and become involved with Bath Estates?

- Could the change in Yann's relationship with his mother after he went away to school been prevented?

- Was Ian's obsession with wealth and success inevitable?

- Describe Ian's relationship with Sue and Marcus Rose, and vice-versa.

- What did Ian feel for every one of the women, who figured in his life?

- How have social attitudes changed since the period of the book?

The Author in conversation with Kate Authers

Q. Property magnate, philanthropist and now author, what prompted the move into writing?

A. I've always wanted to write a story, I've always been a storyteller, but like everything I didn't have the time to do it until I retired.

Q. How would you describe the new book, Go Swift and Far...

A. It's a coming-of-age story set in Bath of a young man born in April 1942 and it's part of a trilogy – this one runs from 1942 – 1967. Much of it is autobiographical, beefed up, because it would be very boring if it was just my story. I think Bath is a fascinating place because it's a goldfish bowl. What's so unique is that it's so small and so familiar; there are 40 real people in this book who have wonderful walk-on parts. You could never do something like that in London and you certainly couldn't do it in Bristol. It's an ideal setting really, if you know the city well, and I've lived here for nearly 35 years.

Q. Why did you write this book and what do you want people to take from it?

A. I want people to know my story and I want recognition for what it's taken to tell it. I want people to love the book for what it is and for people to say 'this was a good read, a good page-turner, and I'm looking forward to reading the second and the third books'.

Q. Were there specific criteria to make up your 'cast' of 40?

A. No. They were just mates. For example, Chris Johnson, who is the manager of Handelsbanken in Bath, plays a bank manager of a mythical bank in the 1960s in the book – actually he's just bought the first copy; that was the condition of it! All those people got copies of the draft book two years ago and were asked for their comments, and so it was an incredibly helpful process.

Q. Why the pseudonym?

A. I spent 10 years writing this and I wasn't prepared to alter anything inside the covers and if the publishers didn't like that I wasn't going to stay with them. They accepted that and promptly changed the title – it was originally called Bath 42 – and said they would want me to write under a pseudonym because my own name wasn't sexy enough. Now they've made me feel like a retired RAF Battle of Britain pilot with a name like Douglas Westcott! But the title change was a brilliant one.

Q. Where's home in Bath?

A. Combe Down. I love the countryside around Bath. We've got an ultra-modern extraordinary house – 50 per cent of the walls are glass. We moved there two years ago and it's like being in a chalet on the top of a mountain. I absolutely adore the light and the space.

Q. What are the pros and cons of living in Bath?

A. It's the most beautiful city imaginable, I've always felt that from the day I first came here. Because of the tourist industry it has the most amazing range of restaurants, museums, and the theatre. So you couldn't get better than what you've got for such a small population, it's an extraordinary thing. There are only two antis; there's the traffic problem and I think living in Georgian houses is a wonderful experience but quite restrictive.

Q. Share a favourite spot in the city?

A. Outside, Bath Rec on a rugby day. Inside, I like places like the Little Theatre because it's a very civilised way of watching a film without noise and mobile telephones and all the rest of it.

Q. Where do you enjoy eating out and/or drinking in Bath?

A. My favourite restaurants are Joya, Raphael, Firehouse Rotisserie, The Circus and Hudsons. If I'm taking the children out, they love Wagamama. My local is the Hope and Anchor at Midford– it's fabulous.

Q. How do you relax?

A. I do a lot of reading, I go to the theatre a lot and I love the small theatres in London. Funnily enough I find writing relaxing, writing started as and still is my main hobby.

Q. What's been your finest hour (so far)?

A. Being at the birth of my first child, which was the most amazing experience. It's a magical moment.

Q. Surprise us…

A. My wife's father, who was president of the Royal Institute of Chartered Surveyors, gave me my degree, 30 years before I met her.

Permissions from Bath Life Magazine

Notes

Notes

Notes

Notes

Notes

MORE PRAISE FOR *GO SWIFT AND FAR*

'A great read for everyone.
And a must read for all Bathonians'
Michael Godwin

'Grande narratore. Un debuto di successo'
Lidia Crestani

'Packed with sharp dialogue, an appealing cast and
vivid cameos of the more sinister faces of Bath after
the Second World War'
Stan Frith

'Notable fiction and historically accurate –
an excellent story'
Martin Kohn

'The story has real momentum and the characters are
vividly drawn. So much so that I felt I knew them!'
Nigel Thomas

'Oh boy is this readable – bring on the sequel'
Christine Barnes

'A story of what really went on in
post-war Bath – a great read'
Sue Rose

'Could not put it down'
Howard Edgington

'An unusual and informative period of Bath history
interwoven with colourful characters'
Julie & Peter Knee

'This incredible story is a must-read page-turner
for all Bathonians'
Greg Ingham

'Engrossing from the very beginning.
An informative and absorbing read!'
Donna Lodge, Bath Tourism Plus

'An intriguing read: What is fact, what is faction'
Ruth Morris

'Intriguing personal insight of the recovery of a
post war wounded city'
Trevor Jones, Professional Bath Guide

'Terrific read. Looking forward to the next book'
Jack Jenkins

'I was moved the story had such an authentic feel!!'
Amanda Kendrick

'It's a page-turner'
Mike Gordon

'History and location make a great story and a
thoroughly enjoyable read'
Phillip A. Cameron

'First class read, recognised people, business and places,
when is the next instalment in print?'
John Ricketts

'A great book – looking forward to the next one'
Cath & Alistair Colston

'A mischievous insight into the shenanigans of
the post-war property market'
Stephen Green

'A fascinating book'
Peter Green